DARK SEDUCTIONS

Submit to his pleasure...

**Together for the first time, read three
sensationally seductive stories giving you
everything your heart – and body –
could desire.**

Raw Silk by Anne Mather
'...adept at taking on...the sensual
beast within...'
—*Romantic Times*

Dark Apollo by Sara Craven
'...sizzles with sensual tension...'
—*Romantic Times*

Dark Fire by Robyn Donald
'Robyn Donald captures passion in its
rawest form...'
—*Romantic Times*

New York Times bestselling author **Anne Mather** has written since she was seven, but it was only when her first child was born that she fulfilled her dream of becoming a writer. Anne has now written more than 150 novels, reaching a readership which spans the world. Born and raised in the north of England, Anne still makes her home there with her husband, two children and, now, grandchildren. Asked if she finds writing a lonely occupation, she replies that her characters always keep her company. In fact, she is so busy sorting out their lives that she often doesn't have time for her own! An avid reader herself, she devours everything from sagas and romances to mainstream fiction and suspense.

Sara Craven was born in South Devon, and grew up surrounded by books in a house by the sea. After leaving grammar school she worked as a local journalist, covering everything from flower shows to murders. She started writing for Mills & Boon in 1975. Apart from writing, her passions include films, music, cooking and eating in good restaurants. She now lives in Somerset. Sara Craven has appeared as a contestant on the Channel Four game show *Fifteen to One* and is also the latest (and last ever) winner of the *Mastermind of Great Britain* Championship.

Robyn Donald has always lived in New Zealand, initially on her father's stud dairy farm at Warkworth, then in the Bay of Islands, an area of great natural beauty, where she lives today with her husband and an ebullient and mostly Labrador dog. She resigned her teaching position when she found she enjoyed writing romances more, and now spends any time not writing by reading, gardening, travelling and writing letters to keep up with her two adult children and her friends.

DARK
SEDUCTIONS

ANNE MATHER

SARA CRAVEN

ROBYN DONALD

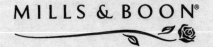

MILLS & BOON®

First published in Great Britain 2005
Harlequin Mills & Boon Limited,
Eton House, 18-24 Paradise Road, Richmond, Surrey, TW9 1SR

DARK SEDUCTIONS © Harlequin Enterprises II B.V., 2005

Raw Silk, Dark Apollo and *Dark Fire*
were first published in Great Britain by
Harlequin Mills & Boon Limited in separate, single volumes.

Raw Silk © Anne Mather 1994
Dark Apollo © Sara Craven 1994
Dark Fire © Robyn Donald 1994

ISBN 0 263 84577 X

109-0905

Printed and bound in Spain
by Litografia Rosés S.A., Barcelona

RAW SILK

by

Anne Mather

CHAPTER ONE

THE sunset was spectacular, spilling its crimson light over clouds that already had a tinge of purple about them. It wasn't gentle, and it wasn't peaceful, but its sombre, brooding presence mirrored Oliver's mood.

He stood at the apartment window, long legs braced, shoulders set, hands thrust deep into his trouser pockets, gazing out at the view that encompassed half the Tsim Sha Tsui peninsula. It should have soothed him, but it didn't. By anyone's reckoning it was impressive, with the hillside falling away to give an uninterrupted view of the harbour. And there was the Hong Kong skyline rising across the water, acres of solid real estate in concrete, steel and glass. But Oliver was not impressed; he scarcely even saw it.

'But, darling, you have to come with me!'

Behind him, Rose Chen's voice persisted in its persuasive refrain. For over an hour the delicate Chinese girl had been trying to convince him that she couldn't go to England without him, and for equally that long Oliver had been insisting that she must.

'Why?' he asked again, for at least the tenth time. 'You're not a child, Rose. You don't need me to hold your hand.'

'Oh, but I do!' With a little cry, Rose Chen abandoned the provocative position she had been sustaining on the wide, oriental-quilted bed, and came to drape herself about him. With the sole of one foot sensuously caressing his calf, and her arms wound around his waist, her soft cheek pressed against his spine, she repeated her assertion. 'Darling, I've never been to London. You have. I need you to come with

5

me. They're going to hate me, aren't they? I need your support.'

Oliver withstood her concerted attempts to arouse him with admirable restraint. It would be so easy to succumb to her allure, so easy to relax and give in to everything she asked of him. Rose Chen was nothing if not dedicated in everything she did, and the sinuous little body, clad only in a silk robe, arched against his back, was undeniably tempting. Even though he was dressed, he could feel her pointed little breasts through the thin silk of his shirt.

But unfortunately for Rose Chen Oliver had a strength of will that equalled her own. And he also knew that the Chinese girl wasn't half as helpless as she liked him to think. Rose Chen could be quite ruthless when it came to business, and he had no doubt at all that she could handle her London relations without any assistance from him.

And that reminded him that he had to stop thinking of her as being wholly Chinese. She wasn't. She was half English. Amazingly, she had been James Hastings' daughter. Not his mistress, as his own government had believed, but the illegitimate offspring of a liaison Hastings had had before Oliver had thought of crawling through the stinking jungles of South-east Asia. Which had altered the situation considerably...

'You'll make it,' he assured her now, removing the slim hand which had been attempting to unzip his fly, aware as he did so of the half-hearted arousal she had achieved. Obviously, his body was not as easy to control as his mind, which was some justification for the frustrated cry his action solicited.

'Don't you want me?' she exclaimed, her oval eyes narrowed and appealing, and Oliver wondered, somewhat ruefully, why he'd let it get this far.

But when he'd been recruited by a United States government agency to carry out a surveillance operation on James

Hastings he had found a small irony in attracting and seducing the woman he had believed to be the Englishman's
mistress.

Rose Chen had worked with James Hastings. She knew
him well. When he had visited the Colony, he had stayed in
the same apartment building she did. Not in the same apartment, as Oliver now knew, but that was splitting hairs. The
fact remained that James Hastings had treated her rather
well, and Rose Chen lived in vastly superior surroundings
to those her salary at the import and export company
Hastings had run would warrant.

Besides, it had seemed such a satisfactory solution to the
problem of getting close enough to James Hastings to find
out his comings and goings. No one, least of all the arrogant
Englishman, had suspected Oliver of being anything more
than the war-weary veteran he appeared. Hong Kong was
full of drop-outs from one part of the world or another, and
it was true that when Oliver had arrived in the territories he
had been nothing more nor less than any of his fellow exiles.

In the beginning he hadn't much cared about anything or
anybody. He was still escaping the horrors of a war that had
gone so dreadfully wrong. He didn't care about the future.
He tried not to think about the past. He lived his life from
day to day, seeking oblivion with any kind of anaesthetic
available.

Of course, his family had expected him to return to the
United States when his term of duty was over, but Oliver
hadn't done that. Not then. He couldn't bear the thought of
returning home to Maple Falls, where life was so clean and
simple. His mind was still trapped in the jungle, with the
poor, pathetic victims of someone else's conflict.

Ironically enough, it was the army that had eventually
rescued him, and restored his self-respect. Or his retired
commanding officer, to be precise. Colonel Archibald
Lightfoot had swept him off the streets—where he had been

living since his severance pay ran out—and installed him in a rehabilitation clinic. And by the time his system had been laundered his mind was clear as well. That was when he had returned to the States—but only for a visit. The colonel had persuaded him he could be some use to him in the territories, and instead of becoming the youngest district attorney in his home state of Virginia he had returned to Hong Kong.

Naturally, his family had been disappointed. His father, once an attorney himself, but now a Supreme Court judge, had expected his eldest son to follow in his footsteps. His younger brothers and sisters were all employed in one aspect of the law or another, all safely married and settled, and a credit to the family. Only Oliver had refused to conform; only Oliver had let them down: first, by volunteering for Vietnam, and then by returning to live in South-east Asia.

These days his family knew better than to criticise his motives. His work for the Hong Kong government, and for the United States agency involved in the control of narcotic substances, had enabled him to amass a fairly substantial bank account, and although his job required him to live in fairly modest surroundings he owned an apartment in Kowloon just as comfortable as Rose Chen's. He was a valued member of Colonel Lightfoot's staff, and when he eventually chose to return to the United States he had the necessary contacts to find suitable employment there.

Of course, Rose Chen knew nothing of his involvement with the agency. So far as she was concerned, Oliver lived by his wits, making enough money from so-called 'deals' the agency sent his way to enable him to support the lifestyle he maintained. The fact that he seldom discussed his own affairs had convinced her that what he was doing wasn't exactly legal, a belief he nurtured on every possible occasion. He had wanted Rose, and James Hastings, to think he was corruptible. It suited his purposes very well.

Not that Oliver was thinking of this now as he watched

the glittering display of neon that was emerging as the lights were turned on in the tall buildings lower down the hillside and across the water. Darkness gave the city a different kind of energy, an energy that masked the abject poverty found on the streets below.

'I'm not coming to London,' he stated flatly, moving out of her embrace. 'I'll take you to the airport, but that's as far as I go.'

Rose Chen's rose-tinted lips took on a sulky curve. 'Suntong will take me to the airport,' she declared shortly, and Oliver inclined his dark head.

'Of course he will,' he agreed, acknowledging her new authority over her father's massively fat chauffeur. 'So...' He spread his hands. 'When are you planning on leaving?'

'Soon.'

Rose Chen regarded him with dark hostile eyes. The evidence of her frustration was there in every line of her slim, provocative body. Rose Chen generally got what she wanted, and right now she wanted him. Wanted him so badly, in fact, that she had even risked the wrath of her employer.

No, not her employer, Oliver reminded himself yet again. Her *father*! The father she hadn't known she'd had until his death in England had necessitated the news to be conveyed to her. It had been there, in his will, all along. As well as the son, who had expected to inherit his father's company, James Hastings had at last acknowledged the existence of his daughter. Rose Chen was to share everything he had left, including half his assets in London.

'Please, Lee,' she begged now, and Oliver realised that, while he had been considering what this new development might mean to his investigation, Rose Chen's face had undergone another change of expression. 'Please,' she said again, 'change your mind. This is all so new to me. Jay-Jay never even hinted that he might be—that he was my—' She broke off and wrung her slender hands together. 'You can't know what this means to me. If only I'd known...'

Oliver's sympathies were stirred. He knew, better than anyone, how persuasive Rose Chen could be if she set her mind to it. Images of her naked body entwined with his were all too vivid a memory when she looked at him that way, and in the pearly evening twilight her sexuality was almost irresistible.

'And what am I supposed to do while you deal with these new relatives of yours?' he enquired softly, as the obvious reaction Colonel Lightfoot would have to her sudden change of status forced him to reconsider. It was almost certain that the colonel would consider the opportunity for a closer look at the London end of Hastings' operation too important to miss, and, while Oliver had no real desire to accompany her, the prospect of an expenses-paid trip to England was not unappealing.

Rose Chen's oval eyes widened. 'You'll come?' She caught her breath and started towards him. 'Oh, Lee—'

'I didn't say that,' he stalled her, holding up a warning hand. 'I was just curious to know how you would introduce me. I don't think your brother will welcome an intruder.'

'You mean *another* intruder,' said Rose Chen shrewdly, and then snapped her fingers. 'What do I care what—Robert,' she said the name experimentally, 'thinks? He hasn't even responded to the fax I sent him when I was first informed of Jay-Jay's death. Before I even knew Jay-Jay was my father.' Her lips twisted. 'It was a shock even then.'

Oliver shrugged. 'I doubt it's been easy for Robert either,' he remarked drily, but Rose Chen's expression showed no compassion.

'No,' she answered, her tone mirroring little concern for her half-brother's feelings. She looked pensive for a moment, and then, as if dismissing what she had been thinking, she looked at him again. 'So—will you come with me? It would mean so much to me if you would. You're the only person I care two figs about.'

Oliver's mouth thinned. 'What about your mother?'

'Her?' Rose Chen looked contemptuous. 'She's never cared about me, so why should I care about her? Besides, she doesn't approve of me. She never wanted me to work for Jay-Jay in the first place. Now, I know why.'

Oliver frowned. 'Does she know about—?' He paused and arched his brows with obvious intent. 'Have you seen her since the lawyer contacted you?'

'No.' Rose Chen pushed her hands inside the wide sleeves of her robe and hugged them to her. 'It's nothing to do with her. Jay-Jay didn't care about her. He cared about me. If only he'd told me. If only I'd known.'

Privately, Oliver doubted James Hastings had cared about anyone but himself. Why else had he kept Rose Chen's identity a secret from her all these years? Her mother, a frail old woman whom Oliver had only seen once, and then only by chance, probably had more feelings for her estranged daughter than James Hastings had ever had. And his reasons for acknowledging his daughter now might have more to do with safeguarding his reputation than any sense of justice.

As for his wife and son in England...

Oliver could well imagine this turn of events had been a salutary blow to them. They couldn't have known of Rose Chen's existence either. But what did they know of James Hastings' dealings? That was the question. What did Rose Chen know, for that matter? How closely had she been trusted?

'You'll go with her, of course.'

Colonel Lightfoot's reaction was predictably positive. The burly professional soldier looked positively delighted at the prospect, his brows jerking excitedly, his bushy moustache quivering as he licked his fleshy lips.

'Will I?' Oliver leaned back in the chair across the desk, and propped one booted ankle across his knee. 'What if I don't want to go to England? What if I have other commitments here in the Colony?'

'Your only commitment is to me, Lynch,' began the colonel brusquely, and then, as if remembering that coercion had never worked with this particular operative, he allowed a cajoling note to enter his voice. 'Come on, Oliver,' he urged. 'We can't let the bastard get away with it. And until we know for certain how they're dealing with the stuff in England, we don't stand a rat's ass of making a conviction stick.'

Oliver considered the older man's words for a few moments, and then said, 'You believe Rose is involved, don't you?'

The colonel looked grim. 'Don't you?'

Oliver swung his leg to the floor and got up from his seat. Then, scowling, he paced across the floor. 'I suppose so.'

The colonel regarded him dourly. 'It doesn't bother you, does it?' He paused. 'You're not—' his mouth compressed as if he disliked having to ask the question '—in love with the girl, are you?'

Oliver's expression was sardonic now. 'No,' he said flatly. 'No, I'm not in love with her, Colonel. But—I suppose I care about what's going to happen to her. You can't sleep with a woman for almost six months without feeling some responsibility.'

The colonel's brows lowered above broad cheekbones, and he tapped an impatient finger on his desk. 'Might I remind you that Rose Chen probably knew exactly what she was doing? You may feel that you seduced her, but our sweet little dragon lady was desperate for your body.'

Oliver's lips twisted. 'You know that, of course.'

'I know that Hastings didn't trust you. I know he'd have separated you if he could.'

Oliver frowned. 'He knew about us?'

The colonel sighed. 'Yes. Didn't I tell you?' But Oliver could tell from his manner that he'd made a mistake.

He came to rest his hands on the colonel's desk, pushing his face close to that of his superior. 'No, you bloody well didn't,' he retorted, his stomach tightening at the risks he had been taking. 'God, Colonel, if Rose had been his mistress, Hastings could have had me killed!'

'Oh, I think you're exaggerating,' muttered the colonel, but they both knew life was cheap among the criminal fraternity of Hong Kong. And if Hastings had been the man they'd thought him, disposing of a possible rival wouldn't have proved at all difficult.

Oliver swore, loudly and succinctly, before withdrawing his hands from the desk. Then, pushing them into the pockets of his trousers, he gazed long and hostilely at his employer. 'I'm dispensable, is that it?' he asked at last, and Colonel Lightfoot uttered a frustrated oath before getting up from his desk.

'No,' he said wearily, coming round the desk. 'For God's sake, man, if I'd thought there was the slightest danger—'

'Did you know Rose Chen was Hastings' daughter? I mean—before his will was read?'

'I—suspected it.' The colonel sighed. 'Oliver, I'm sorry if you think I should have been more honest with you. But I couldn't risk your saying something that might have jeopardised the operation.'

Oliver's mouth curled. 'Really?'

'Yes, really.' Colonel Lightfoot gazed at him unhappily, and then, when it became obvious that Oliver wasn't going to buy that, he added heavily, 'We wanted Hastings to show his hand.'

'By killing me?' Oliver found he was amazingly indifferent to the suggestion.

'No, not by killing you.' Colonel Lightfoot conversely

was growing increasingly desperate. 'Oliver—there was always a chance, a hope, that Hastings might attempt to recruit you.'

'To recruit me?'

'Of course.' The colonel nodded. 'If Rose Chen is involved, and, as I've told you, we think she is, isn't it a natural progression? She wanted you; she *wants* you. If, as we surmise, she refused to give you up, Hastings must have realised it was the only way to guarantee your silence.'

Oliver was silent for a moment. Then, he said, 'You hoped he would, didn't you?' He expelled his breath disbelievingly. 'You gave me this assignment because you thought I'd be the fall guy. Hey,' his voice harshened as he imitated the colonel's voice, 'why not give this one to Lynch? He's an ex-junkie, isn't he? He came out of Vietnam so screwed up, he didn't know what day it is. So what if Hastings grinds him down? Once a junkie, always a junkie, that's what I say!'

'That's not how it was,' insisted the colonel heavily. 'Dammit, Oliver, you know what I think of you; what I've always thought of you. You're a fine man, and a damn fine soldier. I gave you this assignment because you were the best man for the job. And if Hastings hadn't bought the farm we wouldn't be having this conversation.'

'No, we wouldn't.' Oliver flinched away from the reassuring hand the colonel attempted to lay on his shoulder. Then, with a shrug of his shoulders, he added, 'OK, Colonel, I'll go to London. I'll do what you want this time, but don't fix any more assignments for me, right? Suddenly I've got a yen to see Maple Falls again. And, you know what? Even the idea of taking that job as an assistant district attorney doesn't sound so bad after all. I guess I'm getting old. Too old to be—jerked off—by someone like you!'

CHAPTER TWO

'DEUCE.'

'It's game. The ball was out. I saw it.'

'Well, you would say that, wouldn't you?'

'The ball was out.'

'No, it wasn't.'

The twins' voices echoed intrusively from the tennis court, and Fliss, seated rather uncomfortably on the rim of the goldfish pond, thought how indifferent they seemed to their father's demise. But then they were only fifteen and, as far as she could gather, none of the Hastingses seemed particularly distraught about Mr Hastings' death. Bitter, yes; angry, certainly. But heart-broken, distressed, grief-stricken—no.

'Isn't it absolutely bloody sickening?'

Her fiancé, Robert, rocking rather more comfortably on the swing-set, set the cushioned seat moving at a nauseating pace. Fliss, who had been envying him his position only moments before, was glad she wasn't sitting beside him now. She was sure she would have been sick.

'I feel sorry for your mother,' she said, after a moment, not quite knowing how to answer him. The discovery that Mr Hastings had been leading a double life was embarrassing, no doubt, and Mrs Hastings couldn't avoid being the brunt of some gossip in the cloistered environs of Sutton Magna.

Robert was unsympathetic. 'Why feel sorry for her?' he demanded unfeelingly, revealing a side of his character Fliss had been totally unaware of until recently. 'If it weren't for her, the old man wouldn't have looked elsewhere for his pleasures. She's a cold fish, my mother. Or hadn't you noticed?'

In actual fact, Fliss had noticed. Her own dealings with Robert's mother had never been exactly friendly. Amanda Hastings didn't encourage any kind of closeness between the girl her only son was going to marry and herself, and although Fliss was a frequent visitor to the house she didn't feel at home there.

Nevertheless...

'Imagine,' Robert went on in the same bitter vein, 'having a Chinese mistress! God, do you suppose she'll bring a whole gaggle of orientals with her? The Chinese are big on family ties, aren't they? Dammit, Fliss, how could the old bastard do this to us?'

Fliss tried to be practical. 'Mr Davis didn't say anything about the girl's having a family,' she pointed out, but Robert wasn't convinced.

'Huh, Davis,' he grunted. 'What does he know? Where's the girl's mother? That's what I'd like to know. Is she expecting a share of this, as well as her daughter?'

'So far as we know there only is—Rose Chen? Is that right?' replied Fliss, more calmly than she felt. 'The girl's probably an orphan. That's why your father felt some responsibility for her.'

'But what about us?' protested Robert. 'Liz and Dody and me? You don't seem to realise, Fliss, my father has left her half of everything. The trading company; the shops; even this house! What if she wants to sell it? Where are we going to live?'

Fliss could see it was a problem, though for herself she wouldn't be sorry if she and Robert didn't have to live at the house after they were married. Sutton Grange, as it was rather pretentiously called, was not an attractive example of Victorian architecture, and she much preferred the old vicarage, where she and her father lived.

Not that she and Robert could move in there, she conceded, in a momentary digression. Although Robert and the Reverend Matthew Hayton tolerated one another's company, she couldn't deny they had little in common. Since her mother had died some years ago her father had developed an interest in local history, and every moment he had free from his duties as the village clergyman he spent researching the parish records. He had no interest in sailing, or horse-racing, or playing golf. Or in fine arts either, Fliss conceded.

As far as Fliss was concerned, her mother's death, while she was still at university actually, had left a void in both their lives no one else could fill. And because her father obviously needed someone, not just to take over his wife's role in the community, but also to act as his secretary, she had found herself accepting that position, and abandoning any ambitions she had had to have a career of her own.

She had never really regretted it, even though the life she led in this Buckinghamshire backwater was vastly different from the life led by most young women of her age. At twenty-six she enjoyed an almost bucolic existence, and only since her engagement to Robert Hastings had she had the kind of social life he had always taken for granted.

Which was why, she supposed, Mrs Hastings had not been exactly enthusiastic about the match. Robert's mother had no doubt expected him to marry someone from a similar background to their own; someone whose father was fairly wealthy, or whose family had a title. A daughter-in-law she could present to the world, a daughter-in-law she could be proud of.

Fliss knew she was none of those things. Vicars' daughters were not titled, and they were not wealthy, and as for Mrs Hastings being proud of her, well… She shrugged her slim shoulders. She had often wondered what Robert saw in her, what had possibly persuaded him to ask her out?

They had met at the village fair last autumn. Fliss had been in charge of the book stall as usual, spending at least part of the time examining the merchandise, indulging herself shamelessly in any and every volume. Books were Fliss's one weakness, and she invariably bought the books herself if no one else was interested.

Why Robert had been there at all, she couldn't imagine. The noise and bustle of a village fair didn't seem his scene at all. Though he had been interested in the bric-a-brac stall, she remembered. Probably in the hope of snaring a bargain. Mr Hastings owned several fine art shops, and, although no one could confuse Mrs Darcy's pot dogs and stuffed owls with fine art, just occasionally a piece of crystal or a chipped Crown Derby plate found its way on to the stall.

She had been admiring an old copy of poems by Lord Tennyson when Robert had stopped at her stall. His appearance had surprised her, but Fliss seldom got flustered. Indeed, she was of the opinion that she was one of those people who didn't have it in them to feel any uncontrollable surge of excitement, and although her golden eyes widened she was perfectly composed.

And, unaware as she was of it, it was that air of cool untouchability that caught and held Robert Hastings' interest. That, and the fact that she was tall—taller than average—and unfashionably curvaceous, with full, rounded breasts, and long, shapely legs. She also had a mass of sun-streaked brown hair, that hung quite untidily about her shoulders. In short, she was an extremely feminine example of her breed, and if her nose was too long, and her mouth too wide, the overall impression was delightful.

So much so that Robert, a fairly discerning connoisseur of her sex, was instantly attracted, and showed it. Much to her father's dismay, she was sure, he had spent the remainder of the afternoon hanging round her stall, and when the fair was over he'd spirited her off to the pub for a drink.

Fliss, who seldom drank anything stronger than the communion wine, found herself with a cocktail glass on one hand and an ardent suitor on the other, and for once she was glad she wasn't easily excited. Another girl might have been bowled over by the fact that probably the most eligible bachelor for miles around was giving her his undivided attention. As it was, Fliss found it all rather amusing, and not at all worrying as her father seemed to think.

And, although Robert might have expected a different response from a young woman without any obvious advantages, he had soon had to accept that, if he wanted to get anywhere with Fliss, he would have to be a lot less arrogant, and a lot more patient. And he had been. To her immense surprise and amazement, he admitted to having fallen in love with her, and, as an abortive affair when she was in college was all Fliss had to compare her own affection for him with, she had come to the eventual conclusion that she must love him too. Certainly she liked being with him. He was warm and affectionate, and he made her feel good.

And, after a winter in which Robert had sustained his assault on her emotions, she had finally agreed to his announcing their engagement. The only disadvantage she had found since that event was Robert was now twice as eager to consummate—as he put it—their relationship; only consummation, as a vicar's daughter, meant something rather different to Fliss...

'I should think,' she said carefully now, desperate to escape the implications of that particular thought for the present, and returning to the subject of the house, 'that your mother might welcome the opportunity to find somewhere smaller.' Knowing Mrs Hastings as she did, she doubted this was really true, but she pressed on anyway. 'I mean, now that your father's—dead—' she licked her upper lip

delicately '—she won't have to host all those country week-
ends and dinner parties that Mr Hastings wished upon her.'

Robert stared at her impatiently. 'You're not serious.'

Fliss smoothed slender fingers over a bare shoulder, exposed by the bootlace straps of her sundress, and gave a
little shrug. 'Why not?'

'Why not?' Robert was briefly diverted by the un-
knowing sensuality of her action, but he eventually shook
his head as if to clear it, and exclaimed irritably, 'As I shall
be running the company from now on, this should have
been my house, not my mother's. And as for entertaining,
I should have been hosting all social occasions from now
on.'

'Yes, I know, but—'

'This was going to be our home, yours and mine,' he
added grimly. 'We would have carried on the family tra-
dition.'

Fliss had been afraid of that, and she wondered if it
would be too disloyal of her to feel some relief that the
prospect had been put in jeopardy. Was Robert suggesting
they would have lived here with his mother and his twin
sisters? Dear God, she couldn't have done that. It simply
wasn't on.

She also forbore from pointing out that the 'family tra-
dition' he spoke about was barely twenty years old. As far
as the villagers were concerned, they were still newcomers.
Besides, James Hastings' indiscretions were bound to put
a halt to any delusions of grandeur.

'Well,' she said evenly, 'whatever happens, I think we
should start married life in a home of our own. Not here.
We should choose our own place. Somewhere we can dec-
orate and furnish as we like.'

Robert brought the swing to a sudden halt. 'What's
wrong with the Grange?'

'Nothing.' Fliss realised she had to be tactful here. 'But

this is your mother's home—at least, for the present. And—
and it's Liz and Dody's home, too. Haven't you just said
so?'

Robert frowned, the deepening cleft between his blonde
brows drawing attention to the fairness of his skin. Even in
the height of summer, Robert's flesh never changed colour.
The sun might burn it sometimes, but he never got a tan.

Conversely, Fliss's skin was of that creamy variety that
browned easily. Unlike her hair, which was bleached by
the sun's rays, her arms and legs took on the healthy glow
of honey. A fact that dismayed Mrs Hastings, who protected her own skin with almost fanatical zeal.

'I don't want to move,' Robert declared now, his gaze
moving over the acres of formal garden to where his sisters
still squabbled on the tennis court. And it was true, the
neatly trimmed hedges and rose gardens were a delight,
particularly at this time of year.

'Maybe you won't have to,' Fliss offered, stifling for the
moment her own misgivings about living at Sutton Grange.
'You're endowing this woman—Rose Chen—with characteristics you can't possibly know she possesses. She may
be just as upset by the situation as you are. Didn't you say
Mr Davis was of the opinion that she hadn't known the
truth before your father's will was read?'

Robert shrugged his shoulders. He was a tall man, inclined to sturdiness, and he had played rugby in his youth.
In fact he was still a formidable opponent on the field. Yet,
for all that, there was a certain weakness about his chin that
had nothing to do with his good looks, and a sulkiness
about his mouth that was presently all too apparent.

'You don't really believe that, Fliss, do you?' he asked,
and although his expression hadn't changed his voice was
softer. 'Oh, hell, and this was supposed to be the happiest
year of our lives. We were getting married at Christmas. I
don't know what's going to happen now.'

He held out his hand towards her, and, not sorry to leave the concrete rim of the pond, Fliss allowed him to pull her on to his lap. The swing rocked gently now as he nuzzled his face against her shoulder, and she wished there were something she could say to ease his troubled thoughts.

'There's plenty of time,' she comforted, putting her arm about his neck and cradling his head against her breast. Really, she thought, there had been occasions lately when she'd felt more like Robert's mother than his girlfriend. He could appear totally helpless at times.

Well, perhaps that was an exaggeration, she conceded quickly, feeling his hand invading the camisole neckline of her dress. She shouldn't mistake petulance for vulnerability. Robert was usually fairly adept at getting what he wanted, and who knew that he wouldn't soon have the Chinese girl, his half-sister, Rose Chen, eating out of his hand?

She was about to put his hand away when one of the twins, Fliss thought it was Dody, came tearing across the lawn, and achieved her objective for her. 'Rob! Rob!' Dody was calling, her plump adolescent legs pumping urgently inside her biker's shorts. 'Rob, Mummy says you've got to come up to the terrace immediately. That woman's arrived! Our—*sister*! And she's brought ever such a gorgeous hunk with her!'

Even allowing for Dody's tendency towards exaggeration, Fliss had to admit that Oliver Lynch was one of the most disturbing men she had ever laid eyes on. *The* most disturbing, she suspected, although that seemed a little disloyal towards Robert.

Nevertheless, Oliver Lynch did present a most imposing presence, and even Robert, at six feet exactly, had to look up at the older man. And he was much older, Fliss decided, using that acknowledgement as a means of reparation. He might not look it, but he had to be forty-one or -two, at least. To a polite question from Mrs Hastings, he had admitted to spending some time in Vietnam, and that war had been over for twenty years or more.

But the fact remained, he was disturbing, and attractive. He wasn't handsome, as Robert was handsome. His features were too strongly moulded for that. But there was something very masculine—very sexual—about deep-set eyes, hollow cheekbones and a thin-lipped mouth. In some ways it was a cruel face, enhanced by the unconventional length of his hair. Long and black, he pushed it back with a careless hand, the rolled-back sleeves of his shirt exposing a long white scar that marked the flesh from elbow to wrist.

He not only looked disturbing, he disturbed her, thought Fliss uneasily, not really understanding why this should be so. She tried to tell herself it was because of Robert, that his association with the woman, Rose Chen, made him as much of a threat as she was, but that wasn't it. If she was honest she would admit he disturbed her in a much more personal, purely visceral way. Just looking at him caused a curious pain to stir, down deep in her stomach. And when Rose Chen touched his arm, or his hand, as she did frequently—as if she needed to display her possession—Fliss looked away, as if the image offended her.

Of course it was all quite silly, she reproved herself half mockingly. She didn't even know why she was giving him a second thought. It wasn't as if she had any desire to change her comfortable existence. However petulant Robert might be, he was also tender and kind, and incredibly patient. Not characteristics she could apply to Oliver Lynch, she was sure.

From her position, curled up on one of the cushioned lounges at the far end of the terrace, she was able to observe the behaviour of the other people present without drawing attention to herself. They were all being amazingly civil,

she thought, remembering how bitter Robert had been before their arrival. But then his mother hadn't met Oliver
Lynch then, nor been seduced by his southern courtesy and
charm.

Forcing her attention away from Oliver Lynch, she wondered what her fiancé was really thinking. Tea had been
served, and presently he was exchanging pleasantries about
their journey with the woman, Rose Chen. No one could
be more polite, or more facile, than an Englishman, Fliss
reflected drily. Unless it was an American. There was no
denying that Oliver Lynch was displaying his share of di-
plomacy.

She forced her mind back to the Chinese woman. Rose
Chen—was that really her name?—was older, too, than
they had expected. Was that why they were all being so
civil to her? Had the realisation that she was not a young
girl reassured Amanda Hastings of her own credibility?

Whatever, it was obvious that Mr Hastings' affair with
Rose Chen's mother must have happened at least thirty
years ago. Maybe thirty-five. Fliss couldn't be absolutely
certain. And if that was the case, Robert hadn't even been
born when his father took a mistress.

'Do you think she's his mistress?'

The whispered words so closely following Fliss's
thoughts, caused her to gaze at one of Robert's sisters
blankly.

'Who?' she answered, in an undertone, hoping no one
else was listening to their exchange, and the twin—Liz, she
thought—rolled her eyes impatiently.

'Oliver Lynch, of course,' she hissed, glancing surreptitiously over her shoulder. 'Don't tell me you haven't
thought about it, too. I saw you looking at him earlier.'

Fliss was glad the vine-clad roof that overhung the terrace cast her face into shadow. Liz's words had caused a
faint tinge of hot colour to enter her cheeks, and she

wouldn't have liked to have to explain it to anyone else. 'Contrary to what people of your age believe, older women do not speculate about other people's sexual habits as soon as they've been introduced,' she replied quellingly. 'He could be her husband, as far as we know.' Though that caused another discomforting flutter in her stomach. 'It's nothing to do with us.'

'Older women!' said Liz disparagingly, picking up on the one topic she could argue with. 'You're not old, Fliss, and you know it.'

'I'm twenty-six, and sometimes I feel old enough to be your mother,' retorted Fliss drily. 'In any case, that has nothing to do with it, I'm not interested in Mr Lynch.'

'Mummy is.' Liz tipped her head defiantly. 'She hasn't taken her eyes off him since he and—Rose Chen—got out of the car. Did you see the car he was driving, by the way? I think it's a Ferrari. It's long and low and really mean. Dody was nearly drooling!'

Fliss shook her head. 'Liz! Your father's only been dead just over three weeks. Show a little respect.'

Liz grimaced. 'I'm not being disrespectful,' she argued. 'Haven't you noticed the way Mummy's stationed herself at his elbow? How old do you think he is, anyway? Eight— ten years younger than she is?'

'Liz!' Fliss was getting very impatient with this conversation. 'Go and find someone else to pester, will you? You're giving me a headache.'

'That's because you're frustrated,' Liz retaliated, in parting, and Fliss was so glad to see her go that she didn't dispute it.

Instead, she uncoiled her legs from under her and reached for the cooling cup of tea resting on a nearby end table. She wished she could go, she thought. Robert didn't need her at the moment, and she had no doubt she would hear all about his conversation with Rose Chen. To dis-

traction, probably, she mused ruefully, recalling that since
his father's will had been read it had become almost the
sole topic of conversation. She sympathised with him; or
course she did. But surely half the company was enough to
satisfy even the most prodigal of heirs. She appreciated the
things that money could buy, but she couldn't understand
why some men were prepared to sacrifice everything, even
their self-respect, in the pursuit of great wealth. Her father
said it had to do with power, with the power that money
brought. But Fliss—probably due to her father's influence—had little use for either.

'Are you?'

The lazily spoken enquiry was so unexpected that Fliss
almost spilled her tea. She had been so absorbed with her
thoughts that she had been unaware of anyone's approach,
least of all that of the man who had eased his long length
into the chair beside hers.

'I beg your pardon?' she said, glad to find that for all
her trepidation she sounded pleasantly composed. She
crossed her legs, swiftly gathering together the skirt of her
dress when its wraparound folds threatened to part. 'Did
you say something?'

'I said—are you?' Oliver Lynch repeated levelly, though
she could tell from his expression that he didn't believe she
hadn't heard him the first time. With an errant breeze lifting
the ends of his dark hair, and his muscled forearms resting
along his thighs, thighs that had parted to accommodate the
booted feet set squarely on the floor of the terrace, he was
too close for comfort. The neckline of his navy silk shirt
was open to display a disturbing glimpse of body hair as
well, and Fliss thought he looked like a predator, his casual
air of relaxation as spurious as his smile.

'Am I what?' she asked politely, returning her fragile
cup to its saucer. She gave him an enquiring look. 'I fear
you have me at a disadvantage, Mr—er—Lynch.'

Oliver Lynch's thin lips parted. 'I doubt that, ma'am,' he countered, with equal formality. 'The kid accused you of being frustrated. I wondered if you agreed.'

'Did you?' Fliss's breath escaped with a rush. She didn't believe it for a moment. 'I don't really think you expect me to answer that question.' She glanced along the terrace and saw Robert's mother watching them with undisguised hostility, and inwardly groaned. 'Um—is this your first visit to England?'

'No.'

He was non-committal, curiously pale eyes—wolf's eyes, she decided imaginatively—assessing her appearance intently. Was he only trying to embarrass her? Or was he bored by their company, and eager for diversion? Whatever the prognosis, she wished he'd chosen someone else to practise on.

'You're an American,' she observed now, striving for a neutral topic. 'But you live in Hong Kong. Do you have business interests there, too?'

'You could say that,' he responded carelessly, and she immediately felt as if she was being unpardonably inquisitive. But, heavens, what was she supposed to say to a man who was so obviously out of her realm of experience? She had never considered herself particularly good at small talk, and his kind of verbal baiting left her feeling gauche.

'Do you live in Sutton Magna, Miss Hayton?' he asked after a moment, and Fliss was relieved he hadn't made some other mocking comment. 'Mandy says you're going to marry Robert,' he added, with a slight edge to his voice. 'Is that right?'

Mandy?

It took Fliss a second to realise he was talking about Mrs Hastings. She had never heard Amanda Hastings referred to as 'Mandy' before. 'Um—yes,' she answered hurriedly. 'To both your questions. My father is the local clergyman.

Maybe you and—your friend would like to visit the church
while you're here. It's a Norman church, and parts of it
date back to the twelfth century.'

'I'm not a tourist, Miss Hayton.' Oliver Lynch's tone
was vaguely hostile now, and Fliss wondered what she had
said to annoy him. She had only been trying to make conversation. There was no need for him to be rude.

But her innate good manners wouldn't allow her to put
him in his place as she should, so 'I'm sorry,' she said
courteously. 'I didn't mean to imply you were.'

Oliver Lynch's eyes darkened, a curious phenomenon
that caused the pupils to dilate and almost obscure the pale
irises. 'Forget it,' he said, his low voice harsh and impatient. 'I'm an ignorant bastard. I guess I'm not used to
mixing in polite company.'

Now what was she supposed to make of that? Fliss's
tongue moved rather nervously over her upper lip. She
wasn't sure how to answer him, and she wished Robert's
mother would stop scowling at her and come to her rescue.

'Er—let me get you some more tea, Mr Lynch,' she ventured, relieved at the inspiration. 'It really is a hot afternoon, and I'm sure you must be thirsty.'

'I am,' he agreed, his pupils resuming their normal size,
and a humorous grin lifting the corners of his mouth.
'But—' he laid a hand on her bare arm as she would have
got to her feet '—not for tea! If there's a beer lying around
here, I'll take it. But not more of the lukewarm—stuff—I
was offered earlier.'

Fliss jerked her arm back as if he'd burned her. And
indeed, the sensation his hand had induced on her flesh was
not unlike that description. His fingers, lean and hard and
cool, had left an indelible imprint. So much so that, for a
moment, she had hardly been aware of what he was saying.

Instead, she found herself wondering how it would feel
to have his hands on her body; and not just her limbs, which

were already melting at the thought. But on her waist; her hips; her breasts. She caught her breath. The idea that he might also touch her intimately was a fascinating prospect, and it took Robert's voice to arouse her from the dangerous spiral of her thoughts.

'I see you've introduced yourself to my fiancée, Lynch. What have you been saying to make her look so guilty?'

The American rose in one lithe easy movement, in no way daunted by the faint edge of animosity in the Englishman's tone. 'Oh—we were discussing the relative merits of tea, among other things,' he replied, not altogether untruthfully. 'As a stranger in your country, I'm not accustomed to the—customs.'

Robert seemed to realise there was something rather ambiguous about this statement, but short of asking what he meant outright there was little he could say. 'Well, I hope Fliss has satisfied your curiosity,' he remarked tightly. 'Naturally, we'll all do what we can to make your stay as pleasant as possible.'

Oliver Lynch's smile didn't reach his eyes, but there was genuine warmth in his voice as he replied, 'Your fiancée has been most charming. I hope you appreciate her.'

'Oh, I do.' Even if Fliss had not been thinking of getting to her feet at that moment, she felt sure the possessive hand Robert placed about her arm would have achieved it. There was anger now, as well as proprietorial ownership, in the way he drew her up beside him, sliding his arm about her waist, as if to underline his claim. 'Fliss is my one weakness,' he said, though there was little leniency in his voice. 'She can wrap me round her finger any time she likes.' And, bending his head towards her, he bestowed a prolonged kiss on her startled mouth.

If Fliss hadn't been embarrassed before, she was now, with Oliver Lynch's pale eyes observing their every move. If it weren't so fanciful she'd have said he knew what she was thinking. Though not what she'd thought before, please God, she prayed with some conviction.

'You're a very lucky man,' Lynch remarked now, into the vacuum that Fliss felt was as visible as it was heard. If Robert had intended to disconcert the other man, he was going to be sadly disappointed. Oliver Lynch was only amused by her fiancé's behaviour. Amused at, and slightly contemptuous of, his attempt to display possession.

CHAPTER THREE

'BUT why do we have to have separate rooms?' asked Rose Chen impatiently. 'It's not as if we have to keep our relationship a secret or anything. I know you've always insisted on keeping your own apartment in Hong Kong, but surely this is different? We are travelling together.'

'I've told you: I need my own space,' said Oliver shortly, growing tired of the argument they had been having since they booked into the hotel.

They were staying at the Moathouse in Market Risborough, which was the nearest town to Sutton Magna. The night before, Rose had stayed with her father's agent in Fulham, and Oliver had occupied a room in a small hotel off Piccadilly.

Rose heaved a deep breath now. 'Have I done something wrong?' she demanded. 'I thought our first meeting with the Hastingses went off rather well. At least they aren't openly hostile. It was a brilliant idea of yours to make the first move so informal. They could hardly throw us out without creating quite a fuss.' She paused. 'Though I did detect some undercurrents, didn't you?'

'Maybe.'

Oliver was non-committal. In truth, he hadn't devoted as much attention to the reasons why they had gone to Sutton Grange as he should. From the moment he'd laid eyes on Felicity Hayton he'd been hard pressed to keep his mind on anything else. Her cool, honey-blonde beauty had done forgotten things to his nervous system. Just thinking about how her skin felt—smooth and soft beneath his fingers—still caused a definite tightening in his groin.

31

Which was fairly pathetic, and he knew it. Ever since the youthful marriage he had contracted in college had ended with a 'Dear John' letter while he was in Vietnam, he had had no use for emotional relationships. There had been women, of course—plenty of them, he acknowledged without conceit—but they had served their purpose and been forgotten. He supposed his association with Rose Chen was the closest thing to a permanent relationship he had had since his teenage years.

But it was just a job, and one which he sometimes despised himself for. He liked Rose, he admired her spirit, and sometimes he'd even felt some affection towards her. But he didn't love her. He doubted he had ever really loved anyone.

'Something is wrong, isn't it?' Rose was nothing if not persistent. 'What did Robert say to you? He wasn't awkward or anything, was he? I know his mother was a real pain, but I thought he kept his cool.'

Except where his fiancée was concerned, thought Oliver drily, remembering the way the other man had dragged Felicity—*Fliss*—up from her chair and practically savaged her. Oliver could still feel the fury he had felt when Hastings had put his hands upon her. He hadn't cared at that moment whether the younger man had known of his father's dealings or not. All he'd wanted to do was put his hands about the other man's thick neck and squeeze, and squeeze, and squeeze…

'He's a runt,' declared Oliver succinctly, his own feelings briefly getting the better of him. He knew it wouldn't do to alert Rose Chen to the dislike he felt for her half-brother, but it felt good to voice his contempt just the same.

'You think so?'

Naturally, Rose Chen was interested in his opinion, and Oliver had to quickly fabricate a reason for his remark. 'I gathered from his mother that he doesn't like work,' he said dismissively. 'If even half what she says is true, he seems to spend most of his time either at the race-track or on the golfcourse.'

'I see.' Rose Chen caught her lower lip between her teeth. 'That could be useful, couldn't it? If Robert isn't too familiar with running the business, he may not be so opposed to my taking charge.'

'In a pig's eye,' said Oliver, wondering if Rose could really be as gullible as she liked to appear. Personally he didn't believe it for a moment. She was James Hastings' daughter; she must know what there was at stake.

Rose Chen lifted her slim shoulders now. She'd worn a cream silk suit to go to Sutton Magna, but she'd shed the jacket since she got back, and her arms were bare. Her hair was short, moulding her shapely head like a black cap. Her small breasts were taut against her silk vest, and the short skirt of the suit showed her legs to advantage. She was small and exotic and sexy, but Oliver felt no attraction as she preened before his gaze.

The trouble was, he was comparing her dainty appearance to the long-legged Englishwoman he had met on the Hastingses' terrace. And, although Fliss didn't possess Rose Chen's sophistication, she was infinitely more feminine. Tall, easily five feet eight, he guessed, and not thin in the way most women these days were thin, but supple, and shapely, with breasts a man could die for. She was elegant and classy, with legs that went on forever. Not at all like the women he was used to, with her golden skin and hair...

'Whatever,' Rose Chen murmured carelessly, lifting her arms and cupping the back of her neck. Her oval eyes sought Oliver's as he lounged against the writing table. 'I think I'll take a shower. D'you want to join me?'

Oliver straightened. 'No, thanks,' he said swiftly, and then tempered his refusal with a brief smile. 'I've got some unpacking to do, and I thought I might call home.' He grimaced. 'It's cheaper ringing from London than it is from the Far East.'

Rose Chen hid her impatience badly. 'We will dine together, I assume? You won't be too tired? Or suffering from jet-lag?'

Oliver strolled towards the door. 'I'll try to keep awake,' he responded over his shoulder. 'Shall we say seven-thirty? We'd better not make it too late. Hastings is picking you up at eight o'clock tomorrow morning, isn't he?'

'He's picking *us* up,' amended Rose Chen tersely. 'I want you to come with me, Lee. You're so much better at reading people's faces than I am.'

Oliver acknowledged her remark with lazy indulgence, but as soon as the door had closed behind him he frowned. He knew that as far as the colonel was concerned things could not be going better. The old man had actually asked Oliver to try and get inside the Hastings offices and find out as much as he could about distribution and so on. And, while accompanying Rose Chen was not quite what he had had in mind, it might be possible to use the visit to his own advantage.

He called Hong Kong while he was waiting for room service to deliver the bottle of Scotch he'd ordered. It was already the early hours of the following morning there, but he guessed Colonel Lightfoot would be waiting for his call. Rose Chen had no idea that 'calling home' were his own code words for keeping in touch with the agency. So far as she was concerned, he was keeping in touch with his family. And, doubtless he'd do that, too, if only to cover himself. Besides, his mother would appreciate it.

Colonel Lightfoot's voice was barely drowsy. If he had been asleep, he was one of those people who was instantly awake. Oliver guessed he'd half expected him to call the

previous evening. But until he'd encountered Robert
Hastings he'd really had nothing to report.

'The family,' said the colonel, after Oliver's initial im-
pressions had been aired. 'Do you think his wife is aware
of what's been going on?'

'Difficult to say.' Oliver wasn't sure what he thought
about Amanda Hastings. The woman had come on to him,
but that might have been her way of sounding him out. She
had certainly been curious about his relationship with Rose
Chen, but once again she might have had her own reasons
for asking so many questions.

'You say you're going to the company's offices tomorrow?' The colonel didn't waste time on speculation. 'I
don't think anyone will make any mistakes while you're
around, but you may be able to assess whether Rose Chen
has any authority.'

Oliver absorbed this without comment. Unless the up-
heaval of learning she was Robert Hastings' daughter had
made Rose Chen more vulnerable, he doubted he would
learn anything from her behaviour. As far as business was
concerned, Rose Chen had been the ideal employee: she
had respected her employer's confidence, and never betrayed any of his secrets, even in the heat of passion.

'Of course, it's her reaction to Robert Hastings we're
interested in,' the colonel went on doggedly. 'The apparent
animosity between them may be just a front. We can't be
absolutely sure that neither of them knew of the other's
existence before Hastings cashed his chips.'

Oliver didn't argue, but personally he was fairly sure
they hadn't. Even without Rose Chen's response he had
sensed that, for all his apparent affability towards his half-
sister, Robert Hastings was inwardly seething.

There had been that moment with his fiancée, for example. He hadn't just been reacting to the fact that another
man was showing her some attention—though if he'd

known Oliver's thoughts he might have been; there had
been anger and barely suppressed violence in his actions.
And it hadn't been just because he was a man. It was who
he was that mattered. As far as Hastings was concerned,
he—Oliver—was irrevocably linked with Rose Chen.

'You're not saying a lot,' Colonel Lightfoot commented
at last, and Oliver gathered his drifting thoughts.

'There's not a lot to say,' he responded evenly. 'I'll be
in touch again when I've got something to report.'

'Right.' The colonel hesitated. 'You wouldn't go soft on
me, would you, Lynch? I'd hate to see that solid gold reputation sullied because you've let your—sexual urges—rule
your head. I know you care about the woman. But don't
think that warning her will do her any good.'

The short laugh Oliver uttered then was ironic. If only
Archie knew, he thought wryly. It wasn't his Chinese nem-
esis the colonel had to worry about. It was a cool, innocent
Englishwoman, Oliver was remembering. With skin as
sweet as honey, and hair as fine as silk...

'And you say Robert isn't coming to terms with the situation?' Matthew Hayton remarked thoughtfully, looking at
his daughter over the rims of his spectacles. 'Well, I don't
really see what choice he's got.'

'Nor do I,' averred Fliss energetically. 'The woman's
identity's been verified and, if that wasn't enough, she's
shown a remarkable aptitude for filling the void left by Mr
Hastings' death. Honestly, Rose Chen knows more about
the business than Robert ever has. She's a natural organiser,
and she certainly gets things done.'

'Which is probably another reason why Robert objects
to her presence,' declared the Reverend Matthew Hayton
drily. 'I mean, you can't deny that Robert seldom showed
a great deal of interest in the company when his father was

alive. He spent more time playing golf and sailing his yacht than he ever did in the office.'

'Robert's always maintained that his father never gave him any responsibility,' Fliss exclaimed loyally. 'And after all, Mr Hastings was only in his fifties. Who'd have thought he'd die so young? He never seemed to have much stress in his life. Though I suppose if he was leading a double life there must have been some strain.'

'Hardly a double life, Felicity.' Her father was the only person who ever called her by her given name, and now he viewed his daughter with some misgivings. 'We can't really speculate about Hastings' life in Hong Kong. And if neither Robert nor—'

'Rose Chen?'

'—nor Rose Chen knew of each other's existence, the affair—if that was what it was—must have been over some time ago.'

Fliss nodded. 'I suppose so.'

'In any event, it's not our concern, Felicity, and I hope you don't encourage Robert to criticise his father's behaviour.' He pushed his spectacles back up his nose, and returned his attention to the sermon he was trying to compose. 'People who live in glass houses, Felicity. Need I say more?'

Fliss snorted. 'I don't encourage Robert to talk about his father, Dad, but he does it anyway.' She grimaced. 'He talks about little else. Oh, and he moans about Oliver Lynch's influence on Rose Chen, as well. Apparently, she's insisted he sits in on their meetings—like a skeleton at the feast, according to Rob.'

Matthew Hayton looked up again. 'Oliver Lynch?' he frowned. 'Oh, that American you said had accompanied her. What is he? Her accountant? Her solicitor?'

Fliss shuffled the pile of reference books she had been tidying, and gave a careless shrug of her shoulders. 'Her—

partner, I think,' she said, bending her head so her father shouldn't see the colour that had stained her cheeks at his words.

'Her partner?' Matthew Hayton frowned. 'You mean, he has a share in the business, too?'

'No.' Fliss wished she hadn't mentioned Oliver Lynch at all. 'He's her—boyfriend, I believe. At least, Robert says she can't keep her hands off him.'

'I see.' Her father arched his brows that were several shades lighter than his daughter's. 'And Robert thinks this man exercises some undue influence on his—sister, is that right?'

'Well—something like that,' agreed Fliss uncomfortably. 'No one seems to know what he does exactly. He doesn't appear to have a job, and—well, Robert thinks he must be living off Rose Chen.' She hesitated and then added reluctantly, 'He certainly wears expensive clothes for someone without any obvious means of support.'

Matthew Hayton took off his spectacles now, and gave his daughter a reproving look. 'Felicity, this is all hearsay, isn't it? I doubt very much whether Robert has actually asked Rose Chen what this man—Lynch, did you say?—does.'

'No, but—'

'He may be a man of substance. He may have independent means. I don't think you should immediately assume he's some kind of—what's the word?—pimp? Just because Robert's feeling betrayed by his father's deception.'

'No,' said Fliss again, but with rather less emphasis. And, after all, her father had a point. Robert really did know nothing about Oliver Lynch. If she was perfectly honest, she'd have to admit that she'd only sympathised with him because she'd been intimidated by Oliver Lynch's tall, dark presence.

'So, what did you think of the man?' Reverend Hayton

prompted now, and Fliss realised that her careless words had got her into even deeper water. The last thing she wanted to do was discuss Oliver Lynch with her father. Particularly as her reaction to him had been so disturbingly confused.

'He seemed—very nice,' she said carefully, avoiding making any statement that might initiate a follow-up. 'Um—I think I'll go over to the church. I promised Mrs Rennie I'd help her with the flowers.'

Her father looked as if he might have some further comment to make, and she balled her fists in the pockets of the linen trousers she was wearing as she waited for the verbal axe to fall. But all Matthew Hayton said was, 'Ask Mr Brewitt to check on the communion wine, if you see him,' before pushing his spectacles back in place and returning to his sermon.

Outside the pleasantly cool environs of her father's study, the air was hot and decidedly humid. At this time of year, any long spell of hot weather was usually followed by a bout of thunderstorms, and the sky had that ominous overcast sheen that often heralded bad weather.

Other than that, the village looked rather pretty at the moment. The cottage gardens were filled with every kind of flower imaginable, and sunflowers and hollyhocks rose thickly above the rest. There were geraniums, too, in great numbers, spilling from every hedge and border, and tumbling riotously from stone urns and planters. Only the lawns looked rather parched, because sprinklers had been forbidden.

The vicarage garden was no different from the rest, and Fliss, who invariably ended up having to do the weeding herself, viewed its dried beds with some misgivings. The church did employ a caretaker, part of whose duties was to keep the grass neat in the churchyard, and to look after the rather large gardens of the vicarage. Church fêtes were always held on the back lawn, and it was important to keep the weeds at bay. But Mr Hood was really too old now to do all that was needed. Even with a tractor mower, he found it hard to pull his weight. Not that the Reverend would ever force him to retire, thought Fliss affectionately. Not as long as Mr Hood wanted to work. Until he chose to retire, the job was his.

Walking up the gravel path to the vestry door, Fliss lifted the weight of her hair from her neck with a slightly weary hand. She really ought to have her hair cut, she thought ruefully. Or confine it permanently in a braid. Having long hair might look nice, but it certainly wasn't easy to handle. And it could be rather tiresome at this time of year.

Still, it wasn't really her hair that was making her feel so tired all of a sudden. The truth was, she wasn't sleeping well. These warm, humid nights left her feeling limp, not rested, and the problems Robert was having were creating troubles for her, too.

Ever since their engagement, Robert's attitude towards her had become more and more possessive, and she wondered if it was because she had so far evaded giving in to his demands that he was so aggressive. Since Rose Chen came on the scene he had become increasingly persistent, and he was no longer willing to make compromises. He wanted her, he said. Not at some nebulous date in the future, but now. Nothing in his life was certain any more, and he needed her with him to keep him sane.

Her protestations that she was *with* him, that possession was nine-tenths in the mind anyway, didn't persuade him. How could he feel she was really his when she drew the line at the bedroom door? he asked. When two people loved one another, there should be no lines, no barriers.

Of course, there were other arguments: that she was prudish and old-fashioned—arguments she couldn't really defend. Perhaps she was both those things, but there wasn't much she could do about it. Sex had never figured highly in her thoughts.

And the truth was, although she liked Robert, and cared about him, after her experience at college she didn't know if she had it in her to feel any more deeply than that. There were women—she had read about them in magazines—who were happily married, with a handful of children, who'd never known what real passion was. The importance of feeling loved, of feeling wanted, was what they cared about. Orgasm—a word which was freely bandied about today, and which her father abhorred—was not something she was eager to experience. She was sure it was vastly over-rated; something men had introduced to try and get their way.

She sighed. Not that that conclusion in any way solved her problem. She still had to deal with Robert's plans for their future. If only she were a more emotional person, she thought wistfully. It wouldn't seem so cold-blooded then, discussing the terms of her surrender.

When she reached the porch, she noticed a car parked at the kerb, just beyond the lych-gate. It was a black saloon, long and sleek, but nothing like the racy sports car Rose Chen and her escort had arrived in a week ago. She expelled her breath rather relievedly, not really appreciating, until that moment, that she'd experienced a moment's unease. It wasn't that the sight of a strange car alarmed her, she assured herself. Because of its history, the old church occasionally attracted visitors in the summer months. It was the association with that other strange car that had startled her. And the realisation that she was not looking forward to meeting Oliver Lynch again.

Entering the church, she immediately felt the sense of peace that always invaded her consciousness whenever she did so. Perhaps she wasn't meant to be a wife at all, she reflected thoughtfully. She got so much pleasure from spiritual things; perhaps she ought to consider becoming a nun.

She was smiling to herself, thinking how horrified her father would feel at this suggestion, as she pushed open the door into the choir. It was quite dark in the church, the overcast sky leaving the pulpit in shadow. Mrs Rennie hadn't put on any of the lights; indeed, there was no sign of Mrs Rennie at all. Instead, a man was standing at the foot of the nave, gazing silently up at the altar.

Fliss's heart skipped a beat, and, although she endeavoured to calm herself, the realisation that she wasn't alone had given her quite a shock. But it wasn't just the presence of a solitary man that had startled her. It was the awareness of who that man was that had her wishing she were any place but here...

CHAPTER FOUR

IT WAS Oliver Lynch. Even without the evidence of his superior height, she would have known it was him immediately. It was something she didn't understand; something she certainly didn't wish to consider. A kind of recognition in her bones that left her feeling weak.

Why he should have this effect on her, she had no idea. It wasn't as if she even liked the man. Their conversation on the terrace at Sutton Grange had left her with the uneasy impression that he could be totally ruthless if the occasion warranted it. And he'd had only contempt for Robert, of that she was very sure.

And now, here he was, invading the only place of sanctuary she had ever found. In a black shirt and black jeans, low-heeled black boots echoing solidly on the stone flags, he approached her, his expression mildly amused at her obvious disconcertment.

He appeared to be alone. A quick glance round the church assured her that the Chinese woman was not with him. So where was she? At the Grange? And why wasn't he driving the Ferrari today, if the car outside was his?

But all these thoughts were secondary to her own unwelcome reaction to the man himself. Everything about him—from the perverse length of his hair to the lazy sensuality of his mouth—assaulted her senses. Even the way he moved was almost sinful in its grace and sexuality, and when he tucked his thumbs into the back of his belt his appeal was frankly carnal.

'Hi,' he said, and she wondered if he had recognised her as instantly as she had recognised him. Probably not, she decided tensely. He had to be aware of the effect he had on women.

'Um—hello,' she responded, rather offhandedly, wishing she had something in her hands—a vase or a bunch of flowers, for example—to give her a reason for being there. She'd hate him to think she'd followed him.

'You're right,' he said, reaching the step that led up to the choir stalls, and resting one powerful hand on the rail. 'It is a beautiful little church. I'm glad you told me about it.'

Fliss wished she hadn't, but she took a steadying breath and moved out into the aisle. 'We like it,' she said, and for all her efforts to appear casual, she knew her voice sounded clipped. She swallowed. 'Is—Miss Chen with you? I didn't notice her car.'

'*My* car—or at least the car I've hired—is outside,' said Oliver, hopefully getting the message Fliss had been trying to convey. 'And no: Rose isn't with me. I drove down from London on my own.'

'Oh.'

Fliss absorbed this with mixed feelings. She'd heard that Robert's half-sister had found an apartment in London, that she intended to lease while she was in England. It obviously wasn't practical for her to stay in an hotel, and although they'd stayed at the Moathouse in Market Risborough for a couple of nights they'd soon left the district. Besides, Robert said staying there had just been a ploy to get them into Sutton Grange. A successful ploy, as it had turned out. People were naturally less guarded in their own home.

And now, hearing Oliver say that he'd driven down from London confirmed that they were obviously still together. And why not? She was probably his meal ticket, for heaven's sake. Whatever her father said, she believed Oliver Lynch was not just along for the ride.

'That's the house where you live, next door,' he remarked, and Fliss was so relieved he hadn't said anything controversial that she nodded.

'The vicarage,' she agreed, smoothing her damp palms over the seams of her trousers. 'It's old, too; though not as old as the church,' she conceded.

'And your father's the vicar of Sutton Magna?'

'Of Sutton Magna, Sherborne and Eryholme, actually,' Fliss said, with an involuntary smile. 'It sounds grand, but it isn't really. Sutton Magna has the largest population.'

Oliver smiled, too, his thin lips parting over teeth as attractive as the rest of him. The smile—a genuine one this time—gave his lean features an irresistible charm and personality, and Fliss's stomach quivered in involuntary response.

'I suppose you spend a lot of time here,' he said, and for a moment she was too dazed to understand what he meant. 'In the church,' he prompted, by way of an explanation. 'I gather you act as your father's deputy, as well as his secretary.'

Fliss wondered where he'd *gathered* that. Not from Robert, she was sure. Her fiancé hadn't exchanged a civil word with the American, and she doubted she was a topic of conversation when Oliver and his mistress spoke together. If they did any speaking, she appended cattily...

'Well, my mother's dead,' she told him reluctantly, bending to pluck a wilting bloom from the display of chrysanthemums that stood at the foot of the pulpit steps. 'She died while I was at university.'

'So you came home to look after your father,' said Oliver, making no attempt to get out of her way. If she wanted to move into the body of the church, she would have to get past him. And with one foot propped on the step he was a formidable obstruction.

'Er—well, he took my mother's death rather badly,' Fliss continued now, as much to keep their conversation on a

fairly impersonal footing as to satisfy his curiosity. 'She—
she was quite young, you see, and a clergyman needs a
wife.'

Oliver frowned, his dark brows drawing together above
those pale, penetrating eyes. 'So what will he do when you
marry Hastings?' he asked, and Fliss's hopes of avoiding
talking about her fiancé died a sudden death.

'As Robert and I will be living in the village after we're
married, it shouldn't be a problem,' she declared, refusing
to be any more specific than that. The fact that the
Reverend Matthew Hayton had any number of village
women all eager to assist him was not Oliver Lynch's business. Nor that a certain widow from Eryholme was only
waiting to be asked.

Oliver's eyes narrowed. 'I got the feeling Hastings isn't
too generous with your time,' he remarked casually, tipping
his boot forward on to the toe, and then backward on to
the heel. 'Or is that only with other men? Men who might
create a problem?'

Fliss sucked in a breath. 'I don't know what you mean,'
she said quickly, deciding this uneasy conversation had
gone on long enough. She stepped forward. 'If you'll excuse me, I'll go and see if Mrs Rennie is in the baptistry.'

Oliver didn't move. 'She's not.'

Fliss swallowed again. 'How do you know?'

His mouth turned down, and he glanced about him. 'Because there's no one else here,' he said levelly. 'I guess
she's forgotten your appointment—if you had one.'

Fliss's nostrils flared. 'Mrs Rennie asked me to help her
with the flowers,' she declared, not altogether truthfully. In
actual fact, she had offered to help Mrs Rennie. But, judging by the vases that were decorating every niche and table,
she'd arrived a little too late.

Oliver withdrew his foot from the step and straightened.
'Well, it looks as if the old lady's been and gone,' he re-

marked drily, and, although Fliss had been thinking much
the same thing, she bridled.

'How do you know Mrs Rennie is an old lady?' she
argued, using her position on the step above him to give
her some advantage. But Oliver only grinned.

'Because it was a safe bet that you wouldn't offer to help
someone of your own age,' he responded. He held out his
hand. 'Come on. Why don't you give me a conducted
tour?'

'I—I don't have time—' Fliss ignored his hand, and
edged awkwardly past him.

'No?' Oliver regarded her cynically. 'Not even the time
you expected to spend with—what was that name? Mrs
Rennie? Oh, Fliss, what would your father say if he could
hear you tell such lies?'

Fliss halted, realising she had to put a stop to this here
and now. It was obvious he enjoyed baiting her, but she
didn't enjoy it. And nor did she like being made fun of just
because his girlfriend wasn't around to entertain him.

'I'm sure you're perfectly capable of looking round the
church on your own,' she said tersely, tilting her head. 'And
just because the woman you live with has some tenuous
connection with my fiancé's family, don't imagine that
gives you an automatic right to the same privileges. I don't
know what you're doing here, Mr Lynch, and I don't want
to know. We—we've got nothing in common, and I'd prefer it if you understood that at the start.'

'Whoa!' Oliver held up a hand in mock defence. 'Did I
say I expected any privileges?'

'No.' Fliss licked her lips, uneasily aware that her attempt at being condescending hadn't quite come off. 'But
you can't deny that you're here, and that you expect me to
be civil to you.'

'Civil!' Oliver's lips twitched, and she had the distinct
impression he was laughing at her. And why not, she

thought dourly. She was behaving like the irate heroine of some Victorian novel.

Sighing, she made a dismissive gesture. 'I—well, I don't know how people do things where you come from, but here we're more—' she groped for a suitable adjective '—conservative.'

'I guess.' He inclined his head. 'But I wonder where you think I do come from. You're acting as if I've got horns and a tail. What's wrong with being friendly? I'm not suggesting we have sex on the altar!'

Fliss gasped, and, as if realising he had gone too far, he uttered an impatient oath. 'I'm sorry,' he said roughly and, curiously, she knew he meant it. 'I'm not usually so graceless. You must bring out the worst in me.'

'Must I?'

Fliss's response was barely audible. She knew her chest was rising and falling, so she must be breathing, yet there didn't seem to be any air in her lungs suddenly. As he spoke, he had stepped in front of her, and now his shadow cast her into shade. But his eyes were still as vivid, grey and arresting in the pale fluted light.

He took a breath and the air he expelled stirred the tendrils of hair that clung to her damp forehead. 'Are you afraid of me, Fliss?' he asked suddenly, and her throat constricted. She knew she had never been aware of anyone as she was aware of him at that moment, and the fact that he had so accurately diagnosed her reaction was frightening.

But, 'No,' she managed swiftly, even though it hurt to say anything. Her saliva glands appeared to have stopped working, and her tongue felt swollen as it clung to the roof of her mouth.

'No?' he countered, and his mouth compressed. 'But you're not happy with me, are you?'

'I hardly know you, Mr Lynch,' she protested, wishing Mrs Rennie would appear and end this unnerving encounter. 'Um—if you don't mind, I've got to be getting back. My father will be waiting for his tea.'

'Oliver,' he said, not moving, and she frowned. 'My name's Oliver,' he repeated, as if she didn't already know it. 'The least you can do is use it, if I'm going to call you Fliss.'

'I didn't ask you to call me Fliss,' she exclaimed, and his brows arched in rueful acknowledgement.

'No,' he conceded. 'But, where I come from,' and he used the qualification deliberately, she was sure, 'we're not so formal. We even show kindness to strangers, believe it or not. We don't accuse them of—presumption, or pitch them out of our churches.'

'I never—'

Fliss broke off as the hot colour invaded her cheeks, and she wished the floor would just open up and swallow her. Everything he'd said was justified, and, while it was true that Robert wouldn't approve of this meeting, she had no good reason for behaving so churlishly.

Except her unwelcome reaction to him...

'OK.'

With a resigned gesture he stepped away from her, clearly taking her involuntary protest as her final word. She was free to go now, in whatever direction she liked, while he just stood there watching her with impassive guarded features.

'I—' Now it was Fliss's turn to feel rejected. 'I'm—sorry if you think we're rude.'

'We?' One dark brow arched. 'From where I'm standing there is no "we". Just you—*Miss* Hayton. There is no one else.'

Fliss hesitated. 'I've said I'm sorry.'

'Yes, so you have.' But his tone was sardonic. 'Forgive me if I don't believe you mean it.'

She pressed her lips together. 'Why did you come here, Mr Lynch?'

'Because I felt like it.' He moved his broad shoulders indifferently. 'Is that good enough for you?'

Fliss sighed, uneasily aware that their positions had been reversed. 'Because you felt like it?' she echoed.

'Right.' He ran a hand into the open collar of his shirt and massaged the muscles of his neck. 'I was at a loose end, and I felt like getting out of town. As simple as that.'

She shook her head. 'And—what will you do when you leave here? Drive back to town again?'

'Could be.'

'You're not going to the Grange?'

'No.'

She caught her lower lip between her teeth, realising that what she was about to say could be misconstrued, but saying it anyway. 'Then would you like to come and have tea with—with my father and me. It's nothing special, you understand,' she hurried on awkwardly. 'Just sandwiches and some cakes, and Mrs Neil—my father's housekeeper, that is—may have baked some scones.'

There was complete silence after she had issued her invitation. Oliver's eyes had narrowed, but his thick lashes already veiled what little expression she could read there.

Then, 'Tea?' he said harshly. 'Are you serious?'

Fliss nodded. 'Why not?'

'Why not?' Oliver's jaw sagged. 'Hell—five minutes ago you were treating me like—' He bit back the word he had been going to use and amended it to, 'dirt.' He paused. 'What changed your mind?'

Fliss shrugged, half wishing she had not been so reckless. 'Er—you did,' she admitted, after a moment. 'I think perhaps I was a little hasty. I'm sure—Rob—wouldn't want me to be inhospitable.' She lifted her head. 'Well? Would you like to join us?'

Oliver regarded her wryly. 'Let's get one thing straight, shall we?' he said. 'I don't think—Rob—would care if you spat in my eye!' He tucked his hands beneath his arms and his eyes gleamed devilishly. 'But on that understanding, I'd be happy to accept.'

Fliss glanced back towards the vestry, trying not to think how Robert would react when he found out what she'd done. 'We'll go this way,' she said, forcing herself to go ahead of him. But she was intensely aware of his eyes on her back as she hurriedly led the way out of the church.

The air outside was still muggy, but to Fliss it felt infinitely less charged than the atmosphere inside had done. But that was just her overloaded imagination, she thought impatiently. And the fact that in the churchyard Oliver didn't seem so threatening.

'These graves look pretty old,' he remarked, gesturing towards the gnarled stones whose engraved inscriptions were barely readable, and Fliss was relieved to have something positive to say.

'They are,' she said. 'Not so many people are buried these days, and the few new graves there are are over at the other side of the church. Some of these stones date back to the seventeenth century. There are even a few of the plague victims, though most of them were buried in a mass grave under the village green.'

Oliver shook his head. 'Plague victims,' he said ruefully. 'I guess we didn't have so many of them back home. The epidemic—that was in the seventeenth century, wasn't it? Just before the Great Fire that wiped out half of London.'

Fliss was surprised. 'Are you interested in English history?'

'I was.' Oliver shrugged. 'When I was studying law, we covered various aspects of the British legal system, and I guess I got hooked. Some of our laws were founded here, and it helped to understand why they were made.'

Fliss gazed at him. 'You're a lawyer?'

Oliver's mouth turned down. 'Not any more.'

'What does that mean?'

'It means I dropped out,' he said flatly, going ahead to open the gate that led into the vicarage garden. 'I guess we have something in common after all.'

Fliss's father met them on the flagged terrace that ran along the back of the house. Evidently he had abandoned his sermon for the time being, and was presently seated in a canvas chair, examining the manuscript of the article he was writing for an historical journal. He looked up in surprise when he saw his daughter crossing the lawn towards him accompanied by a strange man. Putting his papers aside, he rose to his feet, with a look of not unpleased speculation on his face.

Fliss, who was still smarting from Oliver's latest mocking comment, had some difficulty in keeping the rancour out of her voice. 'Um—this is—Mr Lynch, Dad,' she said offhandedly. 'You remember, he accompanied Robert's half-sister from Hong Kong. He was—visiting—the church, so I've invited him to tea. I—Mr Lynch, this is my father, Reverend Matthew Hayton.'

'How do you do, sir?' said Oliver politely, as the older man held out his hand. 'I hope I'm not intruding.'

'Not at all.' Fliss's father was clearly impressed by the American's courtesy. 'We don't get a lot of strangers in Sutton Magna. It's a bit of a backwater, Mr Lynch, but I must confess, I like it.'

'So do I,' answered Oliver at once, as Fliss started across the terrace, to tell Mrs Neil they had a visitor. 'You're very lucky to live in such beautiful surroundings.'

'I think so,' agreed the Reverend, gesturing the other man to a seat. 'Did I understand Felicity to say you live in Hong Kong, Mr Lynch? That must be very different from here.'

'It is. And I wish you'd call me Oliver,' he replied disarmingly. 'Fliss—Felicity—was just showing me the graves in the churchyard. I guess the age of the headstones is some indication of the village's permanence.'

Fliss's jaw clenched as she went through the french windows. Had she told Oliver Lynch that her father was an amateur historian, he couldn't have said anything more likely to attract the Reverend's interest. And obviously her father was prepared to accept their guest at face value. She scowled. The trouble was, her father always saw the best in everyone. She wondered irritably why she couldn't do the same.

By the time she came back carrying the tray herself, with Mrs Neil coming along behind with the teapot, the two men were comfortably absorbed in a discussion of the relative merits of land rights, and what evidence there was that large estates benefited from continual ownership.

'I realise that we're talking about vastly different areas of tenure,' her father was saying earnestly. 'Naturally, untended open spaces need good land management, or the kind of erosion you spoke of can take place.' He cast an absent glance up at Fliss, as she set the tray on the wicker table beside him, and then continued, undeterred, 'But is it fair that one family or one concern should own thousands of acres of our countryside, when, if it was split into smaller holdings or farms, we might not get the drift of young people into the cities in search of employment?'

'I'm not sure the two things are mutually compatible,' said Oliver, getting to his feet and waiting for Fliss to sit down before resuming his own seat. 'Back home, kids seek the city life regardless. They're not interested in working fourteen-hour days just so they can say a place is their own. Hell, small towns bore them!' He grimaced. 'Excuse me. But I've seen too many kids in the courtroom who thought living in the city was the American dream!'

'In the courtroom?' exclaimed Fliss's father with interest, and then, realising he was ignoring his daughter, he made an apologetic gesture. 'You must forgive me, my dear, but it's so rarely that I find someone with whom I can share my views. Did you know Oliver studied law at Harvard? And he knows all about our feudal system and the outdated laws it established.'

'Not all,' said Oliver modestly, but Fliss couldn't help resenting the way he had beguiled her father. It was years since she had seen the older man look so animated about anyone, and it took a great deal of self-control not to demonstrate her feelings.

Mrs Neil set the teapot on the table, and stood back to admire her handiwork. Sandwiches, which were slightly more substantial than they should be; a sponge cake Fliss had made, which she was sure would be heavy as lead; and the famous fruit scones, a favourite at village fêtes—whose presence could usually ensure a complimentary response from their guests.

'It all looks most delicious, Mrs Neil,' Matthew Hayton declared, as he always did, and the elderly housekeeper beamed.

'There's more tea, if you want it, Vicar,' she said, giving Oliver an inquisitive stare. 'You'll come and get it, won't you, Fliss? It'll save my old legs a journey.'

'Of course.'

Fliss spoke quietly enough, but Mrs Neil had drawn attention to her once again. Not that she thought Oliver had ever quite forgotten her, but the housekeeper's words had given him the excuse to taunt her with his smile.

Mrs Neil withdrew, and Fliss realised it was up to her to pour the tea. It was what she did every afternoon, after all, but today she could have done without the responsibility. She was sure her hands were shaking; sure Oliver Lynch knew exactly how she felt. It was infuriating that he should look so at home here. But, like a chameleon, he adapted himself to any situation.

'You said—back home?' her father remarked, and she was so relieved that he had spoken she could have hugged him. She actually sensed the moment when Oliver's clear, penetrating eyes were removed from the downward curve of her cheek, and she hurried to attend to the cups while his interest was elsewhere.

'I assume you mean back home in the United States,' the older man prompted, and although Fliss told herself she wasn't interested, she couldn't help listening for his answer.

'Yes. Virginia,' replied Oliver at once, relaxed and disturbingly familiar in the chair beside hers. With one ankle propped across his knee, and one lean, brown-fingered hand resting on it, he should have presented no problem to her at all. But the rolled-back cuffs of his shirt meant his muscled forearm was close to her sleeve, and one powerful thigh was uncomfortably near her leg.

It was a hairy forearm, she noticed uneasily, as she splashed hot tea into the cups. A slim watch, on a leather strap made a distinctive band across his wrist, and there was that scar that started below his elbow and disappeared under his sleeve. She wondered when he had acquired that, and whether she'd really like to know.

'Virginia,' echoed her father, as Fliss forced herself to concentrate on what she was doing and nothing else. 'Of course, you'll know it was named after our first Queen Elizabeth, the "virgin" queen, as she was known. What part of the state do you come from?'

'The south-west,' replied Oliver easily, apparently willing to satisfy her father's curiosity. 'A small town called Maple Falls. Do you know it?'

'I'm afraid not.' Matthew Hayton turned to take the tea his daughter offered him. 'Apart from the capital—Richmond, isn't it?—and Chesapeake Bay, I know very little about the area. I've never been to the United States, you see. I'm just an armchair traveller.'

'You must try it some time,' said Oliver, and, although Fliss had managed to avoid his eyes up till now, the necessity of asking how he liked his tea brought his gaze into conflict with hers again. 'You too—Felicity,' he added, after accepting milk but no sugar. Then, knowing it would annoy her, 'Perhaps you could persuade Robert to take you to the States for your honeymoon.'

'I think not,' said Fliss stiffly, aware that her father was watching them now, and compelled to be polite.

'No, I think Rob's more likely to choose Bermuda,' put in the Reverend with a smile. 'I understand it has some good golfcourses, and my future son-in-law is quite a fanatic.'

'Dad!'

Fliss was flushed, but Oliver only said, 'Really?' and let the older man expand.

'My goodness, yes,' exclaimed her father cheerfully. 'I've often said Rob's infinitely more at home on the golf-course than he is in the boardroom. I don't know what will happen to Hastings' if he's in the chair. Without his father's brilliance, I fear the company may fold.'

'Do you?'

Oliver sounded intrigued, and Fliss hurriedly pushed the sandwiches in her father's direction, hoping his interest in the food might distract him from discussing Robert's business. But Matthew Hayton was so used to speaking to people who had no ulterior motives that it didn't occur to him to think Oliver Lynch might have motives of his own.

'I'm afraid so.' The older man nodded now, accepting a sandwich, but studying it before he took a bite. 'I dare say your—fiancée—knows all about the problems they're facing.'

'Rose Chen is not my fiancée,' said Oliver flatly, as Fliss

cast an unwary glance towards him. 'But, you're right, the company is facing certain—difficulties. I don't suppose—Rob—has mentioned anything about it to you.'

'Good heavens, no.' The Reverend laughed. 'I doubt Rob knows one end of a balance sheet from the other.' He frowned. 'It may be that your—that *Miss Chen's* intervention could be a blessing in disguise. I understand she has been involved in the Hong Kong end of the business for some time.'

'Yes.' Oliver sounded thoughtful. 'So you don't think your daughter's fiancé enjoyed his father's confidence?'

'Well, if he did, he hid it very well,' declared her father ruefully, and Fliss, who had been making a concerted effort to enjoy her tea, banged the cup into the saucer with unnecessary force.

'If you'll excuse me,' she said, bestowing a less than approving look on both of them, and, snatching up the teapot, she marched into the house.

CHAPTER FIVE

MRS NEIL had gone, she saw at once, leaving the casserole she had prepared for supper waiting to be put in the oven. Another pot of tea was sheltering under a padded cosy, just in case it was needed. But Fliss didn't bother to uncover it. Instead, she carried the empty pot over to the sink and dropped the used teabags into the waste bin. She needed a few minutes to herself, she thought wryly. It wasn't just the humidity that was making her feel so limp.

She was letting water from the cold tap cool her wrists when she sensed she was no longer alone. She didn't quite know how she knew, but she felt as if the air in the room had quickened. When she glanced round and saw him, she couldn't say she was altogether surprised. But that didn't make his appearance any more welcome, and her heart raced accordingly.

Moistening her lips, keeping her hands under the cool water, she looked at him over her shoulder. 'Yes?'

'I've brought the tray,' Oliver said, and she realised her eyes had never left his face.

'Oh—thanks,' she offered lamely, forcing her attention back to the sink. 'Just put it on the table, would you?'

She heard the thunk as the tray was set on the scrubbed pine of the kitchen table, and then strained her ears to hear the sound of his departure. He wouldn't stay, she assured herself. Not when her father knew where she was. And what excuse could he give for talking to her, when Matthew Hayton was so much enjoying their conversation?

'I like your father,' he said suddenly, and she realised his deck shoes had made no sound on the tiled floor. He

58

was standing beside her now, to one side of the porcelain
sink. She'd been so intent on wishing him gone, she'd
missed the sound of his approach.

'So do I,' she managed awkwardly now, turning off the
tap, and reaching for a paper towel to dry her hands. Then,
reluctantly, 'I—er—I hope you won't take what he says
too—too literally. Robert isn't really as useless as my father
likes to make out.'

Oliver's mouth twisted. 'I'm not into telling tales,' he
remarked, lodging his hips against the drainer and regarding
her with steady eyes. 'Besides, I'd like to come here again.
I wouldn't want to screw up my welcome.'

Fliss stared at him. 'Why would you want to come here
again?' she protested, not a little disturbed by his answer.

Oliver's eyes dropped to her mouth. 'Why do you think?'
he asked, that blatant gaze searing her lips like a fire. Dear
God, she thought, it was as if he'd touched her. His silvery
eyes were as sensual as the disturbing curve of his mouth.

'I think—' Her own mouth dried, and with a concerted
effort she started again. 'I think you ought to go, Mr Lynch.
I don't know what you want with us, but I know you're
wasting your time.'

'Am I?' He moved then, fluidly and sensuously, stretch-
ing out his hand and linking his fingers loosely about her
wrist. It seemed to happen in slow motion, and she should
have had the chance to avoid him. But this whole affair
had an unreal quality that left her feeling weak. 'What if I
say I don't think so?'

A *frisson* of alarm slid down Fliss's spine. 'You're—
impertinent, Mr Lynch,' she said, forcing herself not to
panic. 'I suggest you let me go before my father comes to
find us.'

'Oh, I don't think he'll do that.' Oliver sounded absurdly
confident, lifting her wrist to his mouth and tracing the
network of veins on the inner side with his tongue. He

licked his lips then, as if the taste of her met with his approval. 'When I left him, he was dozing. If I didn't know better I'd have suspected you'd spiked his tea.'

Fliss gasped. 'You didn't—'

'No, I didn't.' Oliver sounded mildly put out. 'For God's sake, what do you take me for? I'm not your enemy, Fliss. Though I suspect you wish I were.'

'I don't know what you mean.' Fliss made a not very dignified effort to free herself, which met with no success. Panting, she exclaimed, 'You're not my friend, Mr Lynch. I don't even like you. And I don't think you care about anyone but yourself.'

Oliver's expression didn't change, but his response was vaguely wounded. 'So, what have I done to deserve an attack like that? I thought we were making some progress earlier on.'

Fliss blinked. 'Progress?' She shook her head. 'Progress towards what?'

'Towards being friends, of course,' he answered softly, his gaze straying from the downy sweep of her cheek to the unbuttoned neckline of her shirt. 'I want us to be friends, Fliss.' His mouth curled. 'I want us to be more than that, but it will do for a start.'

Fliss felt as if she was choking. And, although she was sure he couldn't see anything beyond the sun-tinted column of her throat, the skin in the V darkened anyway. Between her breasts, a tiny trickle of perspiration dampened her bra, and deep down in her stomach that uneasy torment stirred.

'I don't want to be your friend,' she said unsteadily, wishing, for the first time, that Robert would come and interrupt this illicit confrontation. Oliver Lynch was frightening her—or was she frightening herself?

'What do you want?' he asked, and now his free hand came to stroke along the curve of her cheek. His thumb brushed the slightly parted corner of her mouth, and although she snapped her lips together instantly she could still taste the saltiness of his skin.

'Nothing,' she gulped, but she knew he was hardly paying attention to her words. His fingertips had invaded the silky curtain of her hair, drawing it forward against her cheek, and rubbing it against her skin.

'You're beautiful,' he said, his hand finding the nape of her neck now and drawing her insistently towards him. 'Don't tell me you don't want to know that. Because you know what?' He tilted her face up to his. 'I'm not going to believe that either.'

Fliss knew she should be struggling, knew she should be using any means within her power to get away from him. If she didn't do something soon he was going to kiss her, and then how disgusted with herself she would feel, knowing she could have stopped him. Not to mention the fact that she was betraying Robert by just standing here. Just letting Oliver Lynch touch her wrist and her lips and her hair. Dear God, she was practically condoning his behaviour. Why didn't she slap his arrogant face or bury her fist in his flat stomach? She had the feeling he wouldn't stop her. So what was she waiting for?

'Please,' she said, and hearing the pleading note in her voice she despised herself anew, 'if I've given you the wrong impression, if you think I'm—well, I'm sorry. But—I am—engaged to Robert.'

'I know.' He conceded her words without concession, his breath warm against her flushed cheeks. 'So why do you look so—innocent? If you are Hastings'—lover—why do you act as if you're untouched?'

'I don't. I'm not—' Fliss was panicking, and she knew it. But she could feel his legs against hers now, and the caressing fingers at her nape were forcing her upper body into intimate contact with his. Already her breasts, taut and knotted with emotions she didn't even want to recognise, were nudging the dark fabric of his shirt. Did he know? Could he feel their raw excitement? Did he realise what he was doing to her? Oh, God, of course he did. He knew exactly what he was doing.

'Let's find out,' he murmured huskily, releasing her wrist to slide both hands into the sun-streaked tumble of her hair. With infinite patience, he positioned her face, and then, with equal deliberation, he lowered his mouth to hers.

Fliss's head swam at the first touch of his lips. His kiss was so different from Robert's, light, and not at all intrusive, tasting her gently, yet inciting her response. He didn't constrain her, or force her, but she was intensely conscious of his power. He held her very loosely, yet very purposefully, brushing her mouth insistently and biting softly at her lips.

Fliss's legs turned to jelly. Her bones felt soft, malleable, barely capable of supporting her weight. She couldn't have moved away to save her life, and instead she found herself swaying against him, inviting him to touch her, luxuriating in the way her breasts flattened against his chest. She leant into him shamelessly, allowing the sinful embrace to continue, almost mindless with delight.

He parted his legs so that when his hands moved down her back to her hips she was automatically drawn between them. His strong fingers caressed her spine and the rounded curve of her bottom, moulding her against him, so that she could feel every intimate angle of his body. Allowing her to feel his hard arousal, letting her sense the awareness of danger that was so barely leashed.

But before her dazed mind could absorb that thought and act on it, Oliver deepened the kiss, his mouth settling ever more surely over hers. And because she was hot and breathless, and desperate for air, her lips parted automatically, and his tongue found no opposition to its entry. On the contrary, she welcomed its muscled invasion with an eager urgency, and a low moan rose in her throat as he ravaged her yielding mouth.

Heat spread like a raging fire along her veins. Its core was in the passionate melding of their lips. Oliver's kiss seduced her and drugged her, made her a willing prisoner to his demands. She couldn't think, she couldn't act, she could only feel. And, in that feeling, react to the wildly erotic madness he was inspiring.

She clutched at him urgently, finding the opened collar of his shirt and the hair-roughened skin beneath. Skin that was hot and male, and responsive to her desires. But— unfamiliar. This was not Robert—had she ever thought it was? This man was a stranger to her. And she was giving him freedoms she had never allowed her fiancé.

And, as this thought brought her brain into reluctant action, horror began to take the place of bemusement. What was she doing? she asked herself, appalled at the shameless way she had been responding to his touch. What was she thinking of, allowing the man to *use* her? The swollen thrust of Oliver's sex against her stomach was not exciting any more, it was disgusting. How could she have permitted such unbridled lust to possess her? It wasn't possible; it wasn't like her. She wasn't a wanton; she was a lady. And ladies didn't pant and moan like a cross-bred bitch in heat.

Tearing her mouth from his, she spread her palms against his chest and pushed. And, perhaps because Oliver had been as dazed by his emotions as she had until that moment, his hands dropped unresistingly to his thighs. She was free, and with a jerky backward movement she put some space between them, grasping the table behind her for some badly needed support.

'I—think you'd better go,' she said tensely, realising how inadequate words were at a time like this. Watching him, *hating* him, despising him for what he had done to her, she just wanted him to leave. She wanted him out of her sight, before she gave in to the temptation to attack him physically. She wanted to scratch his eyes out, for making her feel so cheap.

'If that's what you want,' he said at last, his lids drooping, his eyes still heavy with the aftermath of their lovemaking. If she hadn't known better she'd have said he looked as shocked as she was, his harsh features hollowed, deep lines engraved beside his mouth.

'Of course it's what I want,' she told him fiercely, holding on to her composure with some difficulty. 'If you remember, it's what I asked you to do before—before—'

'Before I kissed you?' he prompted, brows arching in a strangely self-deprecatory gesture, and Fliss's mouth compressed.

'Before you ruined a perfectly good afternoon,' she retorted, ignoring the taunting voice inside her that hinted at another interpretation. 'What do you expect me to say, Mr Lynch? I think you're absolutely despicable. I invited you here in good faith, and this is how you've repaid me.' She hesitated a moment, and then added bitterly, 'Aren't you ashamed?'

Oliver smoothed his palms along his thighs before straightening, and although Fliss's instinctive reaction was to recoil from him, she stood her ground. Nevertheless, she couldn't meet his eyes, and she had to forcibly restrain herself from looking at his trousers.

'Do you want to tell me what I'm supposed to be ashamed of?' he suggested at last, and although his tone was mild there was an underlying note of warning. Evidently, like her, his brain was functioning again, and, contrary to her hopes, he didn't regret a thing.

'For—for abusing my father's hospitality,' she declared primly, finding it difficult to put her own outrage into words. Would she have felt as outraged if he hadn't threatened the image she had always kept of herself? Was it because he had breached her defences that she felt so resentful now?

But no. She calmed her rising panic with a fervent effort. It wasn't just resentment she was feeling, but indignation too. On Robert's behalf. What could you say to a man who thought nothing of making love to another man's fiancée? How could you get him to feel shame, when it wasn't in his vocabulary?

And, as he had still made no response, she went on doggedly, 'How do you think he—my father—would feel if he knew what you'd been doing? In spite of his doubts about Robert's competence in the boardroom, he does respect him, you know.'

'Does he?'

Oliver was laconic, and Fliss felt even more aggrieved. If only she didn't feel so guilty herself, she thought frustratedly. If only she'd repulsed him before things had gone so far.

But, 'Yes, he does,' she averred now, lifting a hand and pushing back the heavy weight of her hair. It was damp close to her scalp, the tendrils moist and clinging. He had done that to her, she thought. She'd never got so hot and bothered with Robert.

'Well, good for him,' drawled Oliver, his eyes following her every move. 'Forgive me, but I got a different impression.'

'Well, you would,' said Fliss, feeling suddenly weary. 'Anyway—that doesn't alter the fact that I want you to go. Now.'

'OK.' Oliver inclined his head. 'Never let it be said that I refused a lady.' He paused, his eyes mocking her. 'Anything.'

*   *   *

'But why would you go there, of all places?' demanded
Rose Chen angrily. 'For God's sake, Lee, are you trying to
make a fool of me?'

Oliver's grey eyes narrowed. 'Why would my going to
Sutton Magna have any effect on you?' he inquired evenly.
'My life is my own, Rose. I may have agreed to come to
England, but I never agreed that you should have some
divine right to organise my movements. I wanted out of the
city, and Sutton Magna seemed as good a place as any.'
His brows arched. 'Besides, I'd have thought you'd be interested to hear what other people have to say about your
brother.'

'My *half*-brother,' corrected Rose Chen tersely, flinging
herself into one of the comfortable armchairs in the living-
room of the penthouse apartment she had leased in Knights-
bridge. 'And why should I be interested in what some old
priest thinks of Robert? I know what he is. He's an ass. He
doesn't know the first thing about the company.'

'Doesn't he?' Oliver adjusted his position against the
mantel, endeavouring not to sound too interested. 'What
makes you say that?'

'Oh—you know!' Rose Chen sounded exasperated.
'You've sat in on the meetings. As far as he's concerned,
Jay-Jay was running a small but fairly profitable business
in fine arts. He specialised in jade and precious metals, with
a fairly lucrative sideline in oriental porcelain. He used the
handful of shops he owned to distribute the merchandise,
and everyone thought he was a respectable entrepreneur.'

Oliver tensed. 'And he wasn't?'

Rose Chen looked up at him critically. 'Oh, yes. He
was,' she said, lifting one hand and examining her finger
nails. 'Very respectable, as it happens.' Her eyes narrowed
now. 'Didn't you think so?'

Oliver let his breath out on a careful sigh. 'I don't think
I have an opinion, one way or the other,' he replied, aware
that he had been in danger of appearing too interested. 'It's

nothing to do with me, is it?' He sauntered across the room to the tray of drinks residing on a side table. Then, indicating the various bottles and glasses, 'D'you want something?'

Rose Chen hesitated. 'Do you think I'm a fool, Lee?' she asked, crossing one slender leg over the other, and for a moment Oliver felt the cold draught of exposure invading his spine.

'A fool?' he echoed, playing for time, and to his relief Rose Chen transferred her gaze to her fingernails again.

'Yes, a fool,' she said, but there was no rancour in her voice now. 'I'm sure Robert Hastings does. But that's because he doesn't know me.' She snorted. 'God help him, he didn't even know his own father!' She shook her head. 'Can you believe that? Jay-Jay didn't even tell his son what he was doing.'

Oliver raised the glass of Scotch he had poured himself to his lips. 'Didn't he?' he asked casually. 'Well, I've heard that's not uncommon in a society that sends its kids to private school as soon as they're old enough to tie their own bootlaces.'

'Public school,' amended Rose Chen automatically. 'Robert went to public school, Lee. That's what they call it here. A pretty famous one, I believe. Jay-Jay used to talk about the education he'd given his son.' She grimaced. 'Of course, I didn't know he was talking about my own half-brother at that time.'

Oliver hesitated. 'And how does that make you feel? Now, I mean? Do you resent the fact that—that your father didn't treat you as he treated his son?'

Rose Chen sighed. 'Sometimes.'

Oliver inclined his head. 'But it seems he did trust you more than he did Robert,' he ventured, and Rose Chen gave him another speculative look.

'What do you mean by that?'

Oliver gave an inward groan. 'You've just said that Robert didn't know his father,' he defended himself tersely, and expelled a relieved breath when Rose Chen's shoulders sagged.

'Oh, yes,' she said ruefully. 'I'm sorry. I know I must sound paranoid to you, but honestly, it's hell when you don't even know who your friends are.'

'Well…' Oliver chose his words with care. 'I'd have thought you could confide in the Hastingses. After all, it's in their best interests to co-operate, isn't it?'

Rose Chen's expression was unreadable, and Oliver reflected that the term 'inscrutable oriental' was not as dramatic as some people might think.

'You don't understand,' she said finally.

'Then explain it to me.'

'I can't.'

Oliver shrugged. 'OK.' Hiding his own disappointment under a veil of indifference, he indicated the drinks again. 'Are you sure I can't offer you something? A glass of wine? Sherry?'

Rose Chen shook her head. 'Nothing,' she said, tipping her head back against the dark upholstery. Then, tilting her gaze towards him again, she said softly, 'Can I trust you, Lee? Can I really trust you?'

'Do you doubt it?' responded Oliver obliquely, not liking the brief surge of contempt he felt for his own position. But then, common sense, and the bleak knowledge of what James Hastings—and perhaps Rose Chen too—had really been doing overrode any finer feelings he might have entertained. 'Have I ever given you a reason not to?'

'N—o.' Rose Chen conceded the word slowly. 'Except I don't like you speaking to anyone behind my back, in my best interests or otherwise.'

'The Haytons,' said Oliver flatly. 'Rose—'

'You saw Felicity Hayton, too?' Rose Chen abandoned

her reclining position and came upright in her seat. 'You didn't tell me that.'

Oliver expelled his breath wearily. 'Yes, I did—'

'No, you didn't.' Rose was very certain about that. 'You gave me to understand that you met Father Hayton in the churchyard. You didn't say a thing about his daughter.'

'He's a *Reverend*,' Oliver corrected her now, using the ploy to give him time to think. 'And I don't believe I said how I met him. As a matter of fact, it was Fli—Felicity— I met while I was looking round the church. She recognised me—'

'Of course.' Scornfully.

'—and she invited me to tea with herself and her father. End of explanation.'

'As simple as that.'

'As simple as that,' agreed Oliver shortly, cursing himself for creating the distraction. He wasn't certain, of course, but it had seemed that Rose Chen had been on the verge of confiding in him. Now she was more concerned with his relationship with Fliss. And although Oliver knew she had some reason for her suspicions, she didn't know that.

She *mustn't* know that, he reminded himself grimly. Whatever kind of fool he had made of himself with Fliss Hayton, Rose Chen must never find out. Not if he hoped to continue with his investigation. And, after all, that was the only reason he was here...

'So...' Rose Chen regarded him with vaguely hostile eyes now. 'What do you think of her? The Hayton woman, I mean. I noticed you made a beeline for her that first day we went to Sutton Grange.' She uttered a short laugh. 'Funny, I didn't think she was your type.'

'She's not.' Oliver's response was harsher than he'd intended, but frustration was a hard task-master. 'Dammit,

Rose, can't I speak to another woman without you accusing me of God knows what?'

Amazingly, his bitterness achieved what logic hadn't. Now it was Rose Chen's turn to look a little shamefaced, and she pushed herself up out of the chair and came towards him with little-girl ruefulness.

'I'm sorry,' she said, tucking her arm through his, and resting her head against his shoulder. 'I'm a bitch, and I know it. But, you don't know what it's like, Lee. You're the only person I can be myself with. The Hastingses—Jay-Jay's employees—they're all strangers to me. I don't even know if they trust me. But, you're different. You're my friend; my lover; my man! I don't like it when you show interest in other women. Any other women. But particularly not the woman Robert's going to marry.'

Oliver contained his impatience. 'I wasn't showing interest in her,' he lied tautly. 'For Pete's sake, Rose, we had tea with her father. How was I supposed to come on to the woman with her father breathing down my neck?'

How indeed? he chided himself mockingly, remembering that interlude in the Haytons' kitchen with a feeling akin to disbelief. Dear God, he had nearly seduced the woman in her own kitchen. Would have seduced her, too, if she hadn't belatedly come to her senses. His body still ached with the aftermath of aborted passion, and, crazy as it seemed, he could still feel the imprint of her breasts against his chest, still rise to the pressure of her thighs against his pelvis, still smell the light fragrance of her perfume mingling with the clean scent of her body...

'I know, I know,' Rose Chen was assuring him now, as he revelled in the treacherous memories of another embrace. 'I'm just a jealous cow, and I don't deserve you. But be patient with me, Lee. This isn't an easy time for me, and I guess I'm looking for trouble in the most unlikely places.'

'Trouble?' Oliver managed to sound only marginally interested. 'What trouble?'

'You don't want to know,' said Rose Chen, drawing away to run one scarlet-tipped nail down his roughening cheek. 'You need a shave, darling. But don't worry. I like you rough or smooth.' Her voice grew husky. 'Come with me and I'll show you.'

CHAPTER SIX

FLISS viewed her appearance in the long cheval glass in her bedroom with a critical eye. Dinner parties were not her ideal form of entertainment, and this particular dinner party promised to have more than its share of problems. Oliver Lynch was going to be there, for one thing, and, apart from the obvious pitfalls that portended, Robert was in no mood to be amenable.

Ever since he had learned that Oliver Lynch had had tea with his fiancée and his prospective father-in-law, he had been less than conciliatory. It was his opinion that Fliss had been far too friendly towards someone whose involvement with his family was decidedly dubious. It was bad enough, he said, having to be civil to his father's bastard. Fliss had had no right to treat the American like any ordinary guest in their house. So far as Robert was concerned, Oliver Lynch was a freeloader and a parasite, using his association with the Chinese woman to gain entry to polite society.

Polite society? Fliss chided herself now, recalling the less than polite way Oliver had taken advantage of her. And he *had* taken advantage of her, she assured herself firmly. Just because she hadn't prevented him from holding her and touching her, and treating her in a way she had never allowed any man to treat her before, was no excuse for his behaviour. He had abused her father's hospitality, as she had said, and his mockery of her accusations didn't make them any the less appropriate.

All the same, she had had a few bad moments since that encounter in the kitchen. Even before she had had to confess to Oliver's visit, she had found it incredibly difficult to put what had happened between them to the back of her mind. Not least when she was with her fiancé, she admitted unwillingly. It was virtually impossible not to feel some sense of guilt when Robert took her in his arms, and the fact that she was still holding him at arm's length was another source of shame to her.

She was confused, that was all, she told herself now. Instead of making her relationship with Robert easier, it had merely complicated the situation, making her twice as sensitive to feelings of doubt and uncertainty. She still loved Robert—of course she did—but so long as Oliver Lynch was around she was going to find it hard to dissociate herself from his treachery.

And now, there was this dinner party to contend with. After her husband's betrayal, Fliss didn't see why Mrs Hastings should want to give a dinner party for the woman who was threatening to destroy the life she had striven for all these years. If everything Robert said was to be believed, Rose Chen had quickly installed herself in the position of greatest authority in the company, and he was already complaining that she, as much as his father, was denying him the birthright he deserved.

If only she didn't have to be involved, Fliss thought wearily. She agreed with Robert: there should have been no question of who inherited the business, and his father had treated him abominably by not warning him of what he planned to do. But then, that would have meant revealing his relationship to Rose Chen sooner, and who knew what a clever lawyer might have made of James Hastings' intentions of acknowledging his illegitimate daughter. Certainly, Robert and his mother and the twins would have had a good case for compensation, without the obvious advantages that Hastings' indiscretion would have given them.

But James Hastings had been nothing if not cunning, and Fliss, who had always found him rather too smooth, was not at all surprised that he had chosen to deceive all of them. She even believed Rose Chen had been as ignorant of her real identity as the rest of them, and although she didn't like the woman she had some sympathy for her position, at least.

Which still didn't make the reasons for this dinner party any easier to understand, Fliss reflected now, giving her appearance a critical appraisal. It simply wasn't like Amanda Hastings to be so accommodating, and she was not looking forward to having to make small talk with the woman whose arrival had made such a significant dent in her own normally placid existence.

Now, thrusting the connotations of that particular thought aside, Fliss turned from side to side, viewing her appearance from every angle possible. Was the dress suitable? she wondered, for the umpteenth time. In the shop in Market Risborough it had looked a lot better than it did now, and she had the unpleasant feeling that it was not the sort of thing to wear to a social gathering at your future in-laws'. It was far too clinging, for one thing, and the V neckline which had appeared almost conservative in the boutique now seemed to expose an inordinate amount of cleavage. Who would have thought that dusky pink satin could look so—so revealing? It had loose, elbow-length sleeves, for heaven's sake, and the hem fell to well below mid-calf. It should have looked modest. Instead, it accentuated her bosom, and drew attention to the narrow waist above far too generous hips.

But time was getting on, and, deciding there was nothing she could do about it now, Fliss transferred her attention to her hair. The silky fall of sun-bleached hair had been secured in a loose knot on top of her head, and she hoped the fact that it was newly washed wouldn't cause any other mishap. Already, several golden tendrils were curling beside the gold hoops that dangled from her ears, and she

could only hope that people would think they were a deliberate affectation.

She sighed as she smoothed a dusky coral gloss over her
lips. She didn't really know why she was making such a
fuss. It was just a dinner party, for heaven's sake. The way
she was acting, anyone would think her life depended on
it.

Well, perhaps it did, she conceded unsteadily as she went
downstairs to greet her fiancé. This might be her last chance
to convince Oliver Lynch that whatever he cared to think,
she shared her fiancé's opinion of him.

All the same, she hoped Robert wouldn't cause a scene.
In spite of her convictions, she had the unhappy feeling
that in an exchange of words or actions the American was
unlikely to flinch from using any weapons at his disposal.
And, unfortunately, she herself had provided him with the
perfect ammunition.

Robert was waiting in the sitting-room, enjoying a glass
of sherry with her father. The two men were obviously
having difficulty in finding any mutual source of discussion,
and in consequence they both turned towards Fliss with
evident relief.

'Hey!'

'My, my!'

The two men's reactions were reassuringly positive, but
Fliss wasn't altogether happy with the look in Robert's
eyes. There was a distinctly proprietorial gleam there, and
she wished now she had had the guts to tell him what
Oliver Lynch had done. Not that it would have made their
relationship any easier, but at least it would have denied
the American any chance of making a fool of him. As it
was, she felt she was going out to dinner under false pretences, and accepting Robert's compliments in much the
same spirit.

'You look very pretty, my dear.'

It was her father who made the first motion towards her, taking her hands in his, and surveying her as he used to do years ago when she was on her way to a friend's birthday party.

'Doesn't she, though?'

Robert's response was more personal, and when her father released her hands he drew her into an uncomfortably close embrace. Really, Fliss thought, with a faintly hysterical sense of *déjà vu*, Robert was getting decidedly possessive. Was it just his reaction to their engagement, or was he simply staking his claim? Either way, she dreaded Oliver Lynch's response if her fiancé chose to make an issue of it.

'Well—enjoy yourselves, won't you?' the Reverend adjured them now, and Fliss could tell he wasn't happy with such a blatant display of possession.

'I will,' Robert replied, apparently immune to any feelings of disapproval. 'How could I do anything else when I'm going to be with the most beautiful woman there?'

Robert's Jaguar was waiting outside, and he helped Fliss inside with evident delight. 'You do look stunning,' he added, as he came round the bonnet and got in beside her. He leaned over to find her mouth, but Fliss turned her head away.

'Lipstick,' she said hurriedly, as his kiss landed on her cheek. Then, rather breathily, 'Isn't it warm?'

'Well, I'm warm, certainly,' agreed Robert, though as his eyes moved over her again his meaning was obvious. 'Just let Lynch make any move towards you this evening. I'm just in the mood to tell him exactly where to get off.'

Fliss swallowed. 'Oh, Rob—'

'Oh, don't worry. I won't start anything,' Robert assured her impatiently, as he started the car. 'I've already promised my mother I won't cause any trouble. She knows how I feel about this dinner party, but she has some crazy idea that if we antagonise Rose Chen she might do something to upset the apple-cart.'

Fliss frowned. 'I don't understand. What could she do?'

'Well, you know she's virtually taken over the running of the company?'

'Hardly that, surely.'

'Oh, yes.' Robert was bitter. 'Just because I was never pally with the employees, she's used that to insinuate herself into everybody's good books. They all think she's the only one who knows what's going on, and no matter how I try to get a handle on things she's always there first.'

Fliss sighed. 'Are you sure you're not exaggerating, Rob? I mean, Rose Chen was a stranger to these people—'

'Don't I know it?' Robert snorted. 'Sometimes I think if Father wasn't dead I'd feel like killing him myself! He's ruined my life, do you know that, Fliss? I'm never going to amount to anything, and I've only got him to blame.'

Fliss hesitated. 'But—well, you do have other options, Rob.'

'What? What options?'

'Well, you have a fairly good degree in business studies.'

'So?'

'So—why not let—Rose Chen buy you out, if she's willing to? You could use the money to start your own business—'

'What kind of business?'

'I don't know.' Fliss was beginning to wish she'd never got involved in this. 'What do you know about?' She waited, and when he said nothing, she added awkwardly, 'You could always start your own import and export company. Maybe you could keep a couple of the shops—'

'I'm not a shop-keeper, Fliss.' Robert sounded insulted now. 'For God's sake, surely you can see I'm going to have to deal with Rose Chen, whether I like it or not?'

'And—and that's what this dinner party is all about?'

'I guess so.' Robert was sullen. He scowled. 'And it would be a damn sight easier if she didn't drag Lynch to every bloody meeting we have.'

Fliss took a steadying breath. 'You don't like him much, do you?'

'No.'

She moistened her lips, aware that she was treading on dangerous ground, but compelled to ask the question just the same. 'Um—why?'

'You ask me that?' Robert was indignant, and for a moment Fliss was afraid she had said too much. But his next words relieved her of that particular fear while imbuing her with an impending sense of dread. 'The man's a leech, and you know it. Not content with making a fool of my mother, he's made a nuisance of himself with you and your father. Not to mention looking at you as if he can't wait to get your clothes off. He's a crook, Fliss. I knew it as soon as I saw him. God knows what hold he's got over Rose Chen, but if I have anything to do with it he won't get a penny out of us!'

'And what exactly do you do, um—Fliss?' inquired Rose Chen lightly, and Fliss immediately felt totally useless.

'I—help my father,' she replied at last, aware that the Chinese woman's question had been inspired more by a desire to embarrass her than by any real interest in her activities. Tonight, there was an edge of hardness about Rose Chen that boded ill for anyone who crossed her, and the fact that her purple cheongsam clashed outrageously with Fliss's dress could not have slipped her notice.

'You help your father?' she echoed scornfully. 'You mean, you don't have a career of your own?'

'No.' Fliss refused to be provoked by the other woman's rudeness. 'My mother died when I was at college, and my father took it rather badly.'

Rose Chen grimaced. 'You English,' she said, as if those two words explained everything, and despite her determination to remain immune to anything that was said Fliss had to respond.

'I know,' she said ruefully, as if Rose Chen hadn't just insulted her. 'It must be hard for you to understand. I can hardly believe you're half-English yourself.'

The barb found its mark, and Rose Chen's lips thinned. 'Oh, but I am,' she said. 'Believe it. Your boyfriend does. Hasn't he told you I'm more like our father than any of his English offspring?'

'I believe he has said that you're a fairly tough customer,' agreed Fliss, drawn into the fray in spite of herself. 'Tell me, is that a Chinese characteristic? Toughness? A lack of femininity?'

'Why, you—'

Heaven knew what Rose Chen might have said then, and Fliss, who already knew she had gone too far, was girding herself for a full-frontal attack, when another voice intervened.

'Making friends?'

Oliver Lynch's mocking tones might have been the last ones Fliss wanted to hear, but in the present circumstances she would have welcomed any interruption, and Rose Chen's features underwent a remarkable, and instantaneous, change.

'Sort of,' she said, the edge in her voice giving way to a silky purr. 'Where've you been, baby? I missed you.'

Fliss looked away in some distaste as Rose Chen slid her arm through Oliver's dark-clad sleeve and rubbed herself against him. Oh, God, she thought desperately, where was Robert, never mind anyone else? Since their arrival some fifteen minutes ago he had deserted her to attend to some request of his mother's, and she had been left in the doubtful company of his half-sister.

'I was finding some place to park the car,' she heard
Oliver say carelessly, his lazily attractive baritone reminding her of how a certain hoarseness had entered his voice
when he was making love. She shuddered. Dear God, how
could he stand there and let Rose Chen crawl all over him
when he must know how it made her feel? Did he get some
perverse thrill out of seeing her squirm? 'Is there anything
to drink around here?'

'Of course.'

Rose Chen detached herself long enough to bring him a
scotch over ice, and Fliss pretended to be looking for something in her clutch bag until the other woman came back.

But she couldn't ignore him, not without attracting some
curiosity. And she couldn't walk away from them without
the other woman thinking she had frightened her. So, as
there was still no sign of Robert, and his mother's other
guests hadn't yet arrived, she felt obliged to offer some
remark, however trivial.

But, she unfortunately chose a moment when Rose Chen
was using the excuse of straightening his tie to stroke
blood-red nails along his jawline, and Fliss's unwary gaze
met only Oliver's pale wolf's eyes. Met—and was held by
the compelling awareness of a sensuality only lightly
veiled. His eyes drifted deliberately downwards. Over the
dusky V of her cleavage, pausing for a moment to enjoy
the sudden palpitation his appraisal had evoked. Then, reluctantly onwards, over the hands she had clasped tightly,
and revealingly, at her waist, before seeking the unknow-
ingly voluptuous curve of her hips.

Fliss's breath came in short, shallow gulps, the words
she might have spoken stifled by her emotions. How could
he look at her like that? How *dared* he look at her like
that, with Rose Chen's face only inches from his? He had
only to turn his head for Rose Chen to fasten her mouth to
his, a fact he must be as aware of as Fliss was.

'All alone?' he queried, in a voice that would have melted ice-caps, and although it clearly wasn't to her liking the Chinese woman was forced to turn around, too.

'I—no,' Fliss was beginning, when Rose Chen intervened.

'Robert's opening the wine for his mother, so Fliss and I were keeping each other company, weren't we?' she asked silkily, daring the other woman to contradict her. 'I was just asking her what people do for entertainment in this rustic backwater. But apparently Fliss likes it. She doesn't even go out to work.'

Fliss's cheeks coloured. 'I was just explaining that I work for my father,' she declared, hating the way she felt obliged to defend her position, but to her dismay Oliver chose to support her.

'Yes,' he said, addressing his remarks to Rose Chen, 'the Reverend's something of an historian. Fliss is helping him write a book about the history of the village. He was telling me about it, when we had tea together. Isn't that right—Fliss?'

'Well—OK.' To her relief, Rose Chen chose to put an end to that particular topic, though the look she cast in Fliss's direction was in no way conciliatory. 'Who cares, anyway? As far as I'm concerned, I prefer a little more action in my life.' Her lips took on a sensuous slant. 'And in my men,' she appended, fingerwalking up Oliver's chest. 'Well, one man, at least.'

Fliss turned away again, and to her relief she saw her fiancé coming towards them. He didn't look pleased to see her with Rose Chen and Oliver Lynch, but in Fliss's opinion even looking at his dour countenance was preferable to being an unwilling voyeur to the other couple's flirtation.

'Well, here you are again, Lynch,' Robert greeted the older man coldly. 'I'd have thought you'd be heading back to Hong Kong by now. Isn't that where the action is?

According to my sister, you find us a pretty boring substitute.'

Fliss felt her own nerves tighten then, half in resentment, half in apprehension, but Oliver only shrugged his broad shoulders. Unlike Robert, who was wearing a dinner-jacket, he was dressed in a charcoal lounge suit this evening, the sombre colour only adding to his dark attraction.

'Did Rose say that?' he responded, without rancour, as the woman in question gave Robert a killing look. 'No, I'm not bored. How could I be, in such delightful company?'

Robert's brows lowered. 'What's that supposed to mean?' he demanded suspiciously, and Oliver gave him an innocent smile.

'It doesn't—mean—anything more than it says,' he essayed easily. 'Your fiancée was kind enough to introduce me to her father the other day, and one way and another I'm beginning to feel really at home.'

'Yes—well, I wanted to talk to you about that,' said Robert aggressively, and, realising she couldn't allow this to deteriorate into a slanging match, Fliss intervened.

'Did I tell you Mr Lynch shares Daddy's interest in history?' she exclaimed, addressing her remarks to Rose Chen, even though she was sure the Chinese woman had no interest in her conversation. She moistened her lips. 'When he was studying law at Harvard, he—'

'Hold it!' Before she could go any further, Rose Chen turned to the man beside her. 'You studied *law* at Harvard?' she exclaimed disbelievingly. 'You didn't tell me that, Lee.'

'Didn't I?' Fliss had the sudden impression that Oliver was disconcerted now. But he quickly recovered himself, spreading his hands in a careless gesture. 'Hey, I told you I dropped out. Where the hell d'you think I dropped out from? High school?'

'I don't know.' Clearly Rose Chen was having some dif-

ficulty dealing with this revelation. 'I guess I thought—'
She broke off and shook her head. 'But—Harvard! It costs
a lot of money to go there, doesn't it?'

'Why do you think I dropped out?' exclaimed Oliver,
rolling his eyes, but Fliss wasn't deceived by his bland
dismissal of his past. She was fairly sure he hadn't wanted
Rose Chen to know that particular piece of his history,
though why that should be so she couldn't imagine.

CHAPTER SEVEN

BUT, before Robert could take him up on it too, the doorbell rang, heralding the arrival of Mrs Hastings' other
guests. The local doctor and his wife, plus the owner of a
nearby stud farm and his live-in girlfriend, put an end to
any intimate conversation, and Fliss found herself accepting
another glass of white wine and assuring Dr Carpenter that
her father was in the best of health.

All the same, she found her eyes following Oliver as he
accompanied Rose Chen around the room. Whatever her
personal feelings, Robert's mother was making a concerted
effort to behave as if she had accepted the situation, and
her acknowledgement of Rose Chen was obviously going
a long way to legitimising her position. In consequence,
her introductions were, if not warm, then at least cordial.
And, although Rose Chen had expressed contempt for village life, she evidently saw the sense in not antagonising
anybody.

The final guest to arrive was Ralph Williams, the owner
of a large estate that bordered on Sutton Magna, and a local
magistrate. A widower for several years, he considered
himself the most eligible bachelor hereabouts, and although
Fliss knew he had only been invited to even the numbers
he was blind to any indignity.

'Smug devil,' Robert exhorted, glowering as the new arrival hung on to Rose Chen's hand rather longer than was
necessary. 'Can't he see what a fool he's making of himself? She's not going to look at him with Lynch breathing
down her neck.'

Fliss endeavoured to speak casually. 'Is—Mr Lynch

breathing down her neck?' She hesitated. 'He appears to be talking to your mother.'

'Mmm.' Robert grunted. 'He's a regular charmer, isn't he? They both are. Like snakes!'

'Oh, Rob—'

'Well.' He swallowed the remainder of the scotch in his glass, and Fliss wondered how many he had had. 'Just because I have to go along with this, it doesn't mean I like it. And if that—that—creep—speaks to you one more time—'

'Rob, please.' She sighed. 'Why can't we just forget Oliver Lynch for the rest of the evening? He's not important. Can't you see that?'

Robert scowled. 'I don't like him. I don't like his attitude. And I particularly don't like your father telling me what an interesting fellow he is.'

Fliss swallowed. 'Did Daddy say that?'

'Yes.' Robert hunched his shoulders in an aggressive gesture. 'He spoke as if Lynch was making some useful contribution to the world, while I was just one of life's hangers-on!'

'Oh, Rob, I'm sure he didn't say that.'

'No, he didn't say it. It's just implicit in what he does say. I wonder sometimes if he even likes me. He's never referred to me as an "interesting fellow". Not in my hearing, anyway.'

Fliss was relieved when the Hastingses' housekeeper came to announce that dinner was served, and she could abandon any attempt to restore Robert's good humour and concentrate on the food. The meal would be over soon, she consoled herself. And if Amanda Hastings had anything to do with it there was no chance that Oliver Lynch would be sitting anywhere near her.

He wasn't. With Mrs Hastings occupying one end of the table, and Robert taking his father's place at the other, they were at least two places diagonally across from one another. Although Amanda had been forced to place Rose Chen at her right hand, she had positioned Oliver on her left, with the undemanding presence of Mrs Carpenter on his other side. Fliss, meanwhile, was next to Robert, with Dr Carpenter opposite and Brian Vasey, the stud owner, and his girlfriend, Lucy Wales, occupying the middle ground. Ralph Williams, who might have expected to sit next to his hostess, was on Rose Chen's other side, and no doubt Robert's mother hoped he would take care of her so that she had Oliver all to herself.

Thinking this, Fliss realised how ridiculous it was that she should even be making such a deduction. It was nothing to do with her how Amanda Hastings conducted herself, even if monopolising her escort was no way to win Rose Chen's confidence.

A creamy asparagus mousse, wrapped in smoked salmon, preceded a crisp rack of lamb, and Fliss made a concerted effort to enjoy it. Mrs Hughes, the Hastings' housekeeper, always prepared such delicious meals, and this evening she had the help of her niece to serve the food.

Alison Hughes was a pretty girl in her teens, who was evidently just as susceptible to Oliver's charm as her employer. She coloured becomingly when he made some comment as she removed his plate, and her smile only disappeared when she caught Amanda Hastings' eye. The fact that Fliss was aware of this, and of Rose Chen's less than friendly reaction to the exchange, only added to her own feelings of frustration. She couldn't wait for the meal to be over so that she could escape her treacherous observations.

'I haven't seen you at the stables recently, Fliss,' Brian Vasey remarked, as he carved the pink flesh on his plate. As well as breeding horses he also ran a fairly successful riding stables, and from time to time Fliss hired a mount and went hacking.

'No.' Fliss was glad of the diversion. 'It's been so hot, and what with one thing and another...'

'You mean this business over James's will, don't you?' Brain murmured, his tone low enough not to attract attention. 'Must have been quite a shock when—she—turned up.'

'Mmm.'

Fliss didn't want to get into a discussion about that, but she couldn't prevent the involuntary glance she cast towards the other end of the table. And, although Oliver had his head bent towards his hostess, evidently listening to something she was saying, and couldn't possibly have overheard Brian's remark, he looked up at that moment and intercepted her gaze.

She looked away at once, one hand going nervously to the gold ring suspended from her ear, but not before Oliver's eyes had narrowed perceptively. And, even though she consoled herself with the thought that she had done nothing wrong, she hoped no one else had noticed the exchange.

'I like your dress,' Lucy Wales complimented her from across the table. An attractive blonde in her late thirties, Lucy had been with Brian for more than fifteen years, and although their relationship had raised a few eyebrows when they first came to live in the village, these days it was accepted that they were as much of a pair as any married couple. They had no children, and as far as Fliss knew they had no intention of having any. Which, in her view, constituted the main reason why people should seek the endorsement of the church. 'That colour really suits you,' Lucy added, guilelessly. 'You've got such gorgeous skin!'

Fliss felt the hot colour invade her cheeks. She was aware that Lucy's voice had carried clearly round the room. Everyone, including Oliver Lynch, she saw unhappily, was looking in her direction now, and she offered a muttered disclaimer before resuming her efforts to eat the food on her plate. But she knew that at least two of the women present resented her unsought notoriety. Rose Chen looked as if she didn't appreciate any bid to divert attention from herself as the guest of honour, and Mrs Hastings obviously considered it an unnecessary intrusion. But then, Lucy was not one of her favourite people, and she only tolerated her because Brian was such a useful addition to her dinner parties.

'I've got good taste, haven't I?' Robert remarked smugly, prolonging Fliss's embarrassment. 'Unlike—'

Whether he had been about to say his father, Fliss didn't wait to find out. She knew Robert had been drinking fairly steadily since they arrived, and his wine glass had been refilled several times as well. Judging by the hectic colour in his cheeks, he was well on his way to reaching his limit, and when Robert was drunk, he didn't care what he said.

'Unlike me, do you mean?' she interrupted him lightly, deliberately softening her remark with an intimate squeezing of his hand. 'Why don't you pay me compliments like that, darling? Don't I deserve them?'

Robert stared at her with blank eyes for a moment. Her behaviour was so unlike the Fliss he was used to, that his muddled brain couldn't immediately cope with the change. But when she tried to withdraw her hand again, he seemed to come to his senses. Turning his hand over, he grasped her fingers, holding on to them forcefully, causing her to wince.

'Is that what you want?' he demanded in a low voice, and Fliss, who only wanted to escape now, gave him a nervous smile.

'All I want at the moment is my hand back, please,' she exclaimed, forcing herself to sustain her girlish character. 'Rob, you're hurting me. Let me go. I want to finish my dinner.'

Robert looked as if he might resist, and she was wishing Lucy had never said anything when he let her go. And, as she thrust her numb fingers below the level of the table-cloth, she was aware that Oliver Lynch had observed the whole incident. His pale eyes mirrored an expression of anger or contempt or both, and she guessed he despised her for making such an exhibition of herself.

The fact that it hadn't been her fault, and that she had only been trying to prevent any further unpleasantness, wouldn't occur to him. As far as he was concerned, she had proved her weakness by the fact that Robert obviously knew nothing about what had occurred in the kitchen at the vicarage.

The meal dragged to its inevitable close, and when Mrs Hastings suggested they all adjourn to the drawing-room for coffee Fliss couldn't wait to find a quiet corner, where she could regain a little of her anonymity. She wasn't used to being the centre of attraction, and she hoped Robert wouldn't do anything else to embarrass her.

To her relief, his mother must have realised her son had been in danger of embarrassing her, too, not to mention antagonising the one person they could least afford to an-tagonise, if they hoped to retain any measure of credibility here. While Fliss accompanied the other guests into the lamplit drawing-room, Amanda Hastings carried her son off to the kitchen, ostensibly to get the coffee. But, privately, Fliss suspected his mother's intentions had more to do with sobering him up than a desire for his assistance.

In consequence, Fliss was free to seek the window seat, installing herself on its padded bench in such a way as to discourage anyone else from joining her. Outside it was just beginning to get dark, enabling her to see her reflection in the shadowed pane. Was that wild-eyed stranger really her? she wondered unhappily. Where was the languid-lidded woman she used to be? When had she changed from cool indifference to feverish panic?

She saw his reflection in the darkened window before she was obliged to turn her head and feign surprise. His tall, broad-shouldered frame was unmistakable—at least, to someone who had thought about little else but him all evening.

'Slipped the leash?' Oliver enquired, with scarcely veiled insolence. 'After that little display at the dinner table, I'm surprised he isn't dragging you up the stairs to his bedroom?'

Fliss cast a horrified glance about her, but to her relief there was no one else within earshot. 'What do you want?' she asked, in a low incensed tone. 'Do you make an effort to be rude, or does it just come naturally to you?'

'I'm working on it,' replied Oliver shortly. 'So where is he? Sleeping off the effects of the two bottles of Chablis he consumed at dinner?'

'He's helping his mother get the coffee, as a matter of fact,' retorted Fliss, biting her tongue when Mrs Hughes and her niece appeared with two trays. As there was still no sign of her fiancé, that was patently not his mission, and Oliver's lips twisted as he recognised her plight.

'OK,' he said, turning with the obvious intention of seating himself beside her, and Fliss was obliged to shuffle along the bench to make room for him, 'so do you want to tell me how you came to be involved with that p—idiot?'

Fliss closed her eyes for a moment, realising there was no point in trying to reason with him. In fact, there was no talking to him at all, and instead of answering she looked pointedly across the room.

'The silent treatment, hmm?' he said softly, putting his hand down and covering the hand she had used to edge herself out of his way. She was still gripping the edge of the cushion, half prepared to find somewhere else to sit.

But as she'd had no wish to draw any more attention to herself, she'd hesitated. She'd been unaware of her vulnerability until he'd touched her.

'Don't!' she exclaimed instantly, snatching her hand away and imprisoning both hands between her knees. 'Why don't you go and torment your girlfriend?'

'You didn't like it when I did,' he declared softly, and although he wasn't touching her now, Fliss felt as if he was. Her palms grew so sticky, they felt as if they were glued together, and their reaction spread along her legs and centred in the moist heat between her thighs.

'I couldn't care less what you do,' she told him, not altogether truthfully, aware that Rose Chen had noticed Oliver's whereabouts and was watching them with a gimlet gaze. But unfortunately Brian Vasey had engaged her in conversation, and she was apparently unwilling to be rude to the handsome horse trainer. Fliss took a steadying breath. 'Aren't you afraid she'll—object to your neglecting her?'

'Oh, I don't neglect Rose,' he assured her, with infuriating candour. 'I admit, she can be a little—possessive. But nothing I can't handle.'

Fliss sucked in her stomach. 'You're disgusting!' she exclaimed, forcing herself not to look at him and betray her real feelings to anyone else in the room. 'I can't think what she sees in you.'

'Can't you?' His voice was gently mocking now. 'Come on, Fliss. Who do you think you're fooling? Me? Or yourself?'

Fliss gasped. 'How dare you?'

'How dare I what? Remind you that you're not as composed—*controlled*—as you'd like to think? You may look as if you've got a mouthful of ice-cubes, but we both know better than that. That's why I find you so irresistible. You're such a delicious mix of virgin and wanton!'

Fliss couldn't listen to any more of this. With a feeling

akin to panic she made to get up, only to find her progress impeded by his fingers clutching a handful of her skirt.

'Where are you going?' he protested, when she was compelled to turn desperate eyes in his direction. 'Don't look at me like that. Do you want Rose to think there's something going on between us? She's already suspicious. I'd hate her to feel she had a need to get her claws into you. Literally, I mean.'

Fliss stared at him. 'You don't give up, do you?' She forced herself to stay calm. 'And don't transfer your own fears on to me. It's your eyes she'd scratch out, not mine.'

'Think so?' Oliver was unrepentant. 'What an innocent world you live in, Fliss. My punishment would be much less respectable. There are other parts of my anatomy Rose would aim for. Believe me, she takes no prisoners.'

'Takes no prisoners?' Fliss looked blank for a moment, and then the realisation that he was mocking her brought the hot colour into her neck again. 'Oh—go away' she hissed, intensely aware that the hand tangled in her skirt was also uncomfortably close to her thigh. 'I really don't want to discuss it.'

'Nor do I,' he declared mildly, confounding her resistance. 'Now, here comes Alison with our coffee. You're not going to walk out on me, are you?'

Fliss was torn between the need to put some space between them so that she could get things into perspective again, and the awareness that any move on her part now would look strange. As far as the other guests were concerned, they appeared to be having a perfectly innocent conversation, and it seemed the lesser of two evils to stay where she was.

'Just sugar, thanks,' Oliver said, when the young waitress served his coffee. 'That's great. You're doing a good job.'

'Thanks, Mr Lynch.'

Alison was clearly fascinated by the dark stranger, and

Fliss had to bite her tongue again to prevent herself from commenting on it after she had gone. She had no wish for Oliver to think she cared one way or the other. All the same, deep down, a tiny spark of irritation flamed, and she had to tamp it down firmly before it ignited.

'Why didn't you tell Robert I—touched you?' he asked suddenly, his soft voice startling her. And Fliss, who had been congratulating herself on her restraint, returned her coffee-cup to its saucer with rather more force than she'd intended.

'Can we just forget all about that, please?' she said, through her teeth. 'I think we've agreed that it should never have happened, and I see no reason in upsetting Rob over something so trivial.'

'Was it?' he persisted huskily. 'Trivial, I mean? I don't believe that.'

'I don't care what you believe.' Fliss could hear her voice rising in concert with the shallowness of her breathing. She struggled to control herself, and then went on unevenly, 'I don't want you to mention this ever—ever again, do you hear me? You have your life, and I have mine. I'd be grateful if you'd respect that.'

'So prim,' mocked Oliver, setting his cup aside. 'No wonder Robert guards you like the crown jewels. He must think you've never—'

'Now, isn't this cosy?'

Rose Chen came sauntering towards them on spiky heels. With a complete disregard for Fliss's feelings, she manoeuvred herself between them, perching on Oliver's knee, and draping her arm around his neck. Then, with her possession clearly staked, she permitted Fliss a triumphant smile.

'Don't believe a word he says,' she added, scraping her nail over Oliver's roughening jawline. 'He's a real bastard. And I can vouch for it.'

Well, you'd know, Fliss wanted to say cattily, and was appalled at the instinct she had to play the other woman at her own game. Apart from anything else, she wasn't like that. She had never been like that. Jealousy simply wasn't part of her make-up, and it was infuriating to think that she was even entertaining such emotions about Oliver Lynch.

'Um—Mr Lynch and I were just talking about—indoor sports,' she offered, and then wished she'd chosen to say anything but that when both Rose Chen and Oliver gave her an amused look.

'Oh, we know all about them, don't we, Lee?' the Chinese woman declared mockingly. 'What particular indoor sport did you have in mind? Is it a ball game.'

'It was cards, actually,' lied Fliss, refusing to let them make a fool of her yet again. 'Excuse me. I must go and find Robert.'

'Try the john,' called Rose Chen, as she walked away, and Fliss's skin crawled at the burst of laughter that followed her. It was all she could do not to head for the door and freedom, and she was inestimably relieved when Robert himself appeared, looking pale but composed.

'Are you all right?' Fliss asked, going up to him, and Robert gave her an aggrieved look.

'Why shouldn't I be?' he demanded. 'Just because I needed a bit of fresh air, don't you get on my back as well.'

'As well?' Fliss frowned.

'As my mother,' retorted Robert, glancing half apprehensively over his shoulder. 'The old girl seemed to think I was in danger of insulting the old man. Though why she should worry, I don't know.'

Fliss doubted Amanda Hastings would appreciate her son's description of her, but she was too eager to leave to waste time taking him up on it.

'Can we go now?' she asked. 'I—actually, I've got a bit of a headache myself.'

'Leave?' echoed Robert, looking round the room. 'I've only just got here. Where's the coffee? I could surely use a cup.'

Fliss sighed. 'Over there,' she said wearily, gesturing to where Mrs Hughes and her niece had left the trays. 'Rob—'

But Robert was already threading his way across the room, exchanging a word here and there as he headed for his objective. For the moment she was on her own, and with a determined stiffening of her spine she walked out of the room.

She met Mrs Hastings in the hall outside. Robert's mother was checking her hair in the mirror above a small occasional table, and she looked rather irritably at Fliss when she appeared.

'Couldn't you have stopped Rob from making such a fool of himself?' she demanded, launching immediately into an attack, and Fliss stepped back in surprise.

'Making a fool—'

'Drinking too much,' snapped Amanda Hastings impatiently. 'You know what Rob's like when he drinks too much.'

'No. I—'

'He's indiscreet,' the older woman stated grimly. 'I almost died when *he* said he had good taste. You must have noticed.'

'Well, yes—'

'Very well, then. We'll have to make sure it doesn't happen again. Not when Rose Chen is here anyway.' She took a breath, as if mentally shifting into another gear. 'Now— where are you going?'

Fliss swallowed. 'The—the bathroom?'

'Mmm.' Mrs Hastings nodded. 'All right.'

'Then I thought we might—go,' Fliss ventured carefully. 'We?'

'Robert and me.'

Mrs Hastings snorted. 'You don't expect him to drive you home? Not in his condition!'

'No.' In truth, Fliss had been so intent on getting away, she hadn't considered the mechanics of it. 'Well—I can wait—'

'Nonsense. Brian Vasey can take you. It's hardly out of their way.'

'Oh—really—'

'No. That's settled.' Mrs Hastings sniffed and regarded Fliss with some irritation. 'Well? What are you waiting for? I thought you wanted to go to the bathroom.'

'Oh, yes.' Fliss nodded, and went obediently up the stairs.

But, in the bathroom, common sense reasserted itself, and she gazed at her reflection in the mirror with some amazement. Honestly, she had let Robert's mother speak to her as if she was about five years old. Was that really how Mrs Hastings saw her? As an ineffectual female, incapable of speaking up for herself, or fighting back?

She sighed. The fact that the conversation she had had with Oliver Lynch had left her in a state of some confusion had to bear some of the burden, of course. But she was getting sick of being made to feel as if she didn't have the guts to organise her own life, and after pushing a few errant hairs back into place she went determinedly downstairs again.

This time, Robert met her at the door of the drawing-room, his hand fastening possessively about her arm as she came in. 'Where have you been?' he demanded aggressively, as if he hadn't disappeared for the best part of half an hour earlier in the evening.

'I found I needed some air, too,' replied Fliss, with unaccustomed arrogance. 'And now I'm leaving, with or without your permission.'

Robert frowned. 'Is something wrong?'

'No.' Fliss had no intention of voicing her grievances here. 'I just want to go home, that's all. Now, if you'll let me go, I'll say my goodnights.'

Robert gazed at her. 'OK.' He moistened his lips as he released her arm. 'I'll just tell my mother we're leaving and then I'll get the car.'

'No.' Fliss looked up at him coldly. 'You've been drinking, Robert. You can walk me home, if you like, but you obviously can't drive.'

'Now, wait—'

'What's going on here?'

As if sensitive to her son's mood, Mrs Hastings appeared beside them, and Robert turned to her with ill-concealed fury. 'Did you tell Fliss I couldn't take her home?'

Flashing her future daughter-in-law a malevolent glance, Amanda Hastings clicked her tongue. 'I may have done,' she said quietly. Then, to Fliss, 'I was just about to ask Brian—'

'Vasey?'

'Is something wrong?'

Rose Chen joined them then, her curiosity evidently getting the better of her, and Mrs Hastings regarded her with tight lips. 'No,' she said, forcing herself to speak cordially. She glanced at Oliver Lynch who had appeared behind the Chinese woman. 'Oh—are you leaving?'

'We thought we might,' Rose Chen agreed, slipping her arm through Oliver's, as if she felt the need to hold on to him. 'It's been a delightful evening, Mandy. I do appreciate it.'

'Think nothing of it,' said Mrs Hastings, looking as if she had just swallowed a lemon. 'We must do it again.'

'No. Next time you must let us entertain you,' declared Rose Chen, including Oliver in the invitation deliberately, Fliss was sure. She looked at the English girl then. 'Lovely to see you again—um—Fluff.'

There was a moment's silence, when they all acknowledged the slight that had just been delivered, and then Oliver said levelly, 'Perhaps we can give you a lift home, Fliss. I believe I heard you say something about walking, but I was sitting by the window, and I believe it's started to rain.'

'Oh, I—'

'I'm sure—Fliss—would rather her fiancé escorted her home,' inserted Rose Chen quickly, but for once Mrs Hastings chose not to take her son's part.

'That sounds like a very good idea,' she said, ignoring the outraged face her son turned in her direction. 'Don't you agree, Fliss?'

And, although Fliss had sworn never to be put in such a situation again, there was absolutely nothing she could do.

CHAPTER EIGHT

THE Mercedes moved smoothly beneath his hands, the thick leather cool beneath his jean-clad thighs. Although he knew it was crazy, and he was quite aware that he was breaking the speed limit, he let the powerful vehicle make its own pace, the road passing beneath the big car's wheels at an ever-increasing rate.

It felt so good to be out on his own, away from Rose Chen's cloying presence, and if it wasn't really her fault that he felt this way it was easier to blame her than acknowledge what was really wrong with him.

Yet he was acknowledgeing it, Oliver thought drily. By just being on the road, heading for Sutton Magna, he was tacitly accepting that the reason for his uncertain temper was a cool almost-blonde temptress, whose eyes and lips, and lush, golden body, were threatening his hard-won impassivity.

He could imagine how Lightfoot would react if he knew his errant operative was in danger of blowing the whole deal on account of his hormones. If he even suspected that Oliver was risking the relationship he had built up with Rose Chen because he could think of little else but burying his aching sex in another woman's slick moist sheath, he'd have a seizure.

But God, it was years since he'd lain awake nights, imagining how it would feel to make it with some special woman. Hell, he'd been a kid when that happened, still bemused by his own feelings and eager to lay every chick in sight. Until Louise, and that abortive teenage marriage, that had taught him there was more to a relationship than relieving his frustration. He was too wise now to act like a lovesick moron; too old to have wet dreams.

The fact remained, he was risking everything for a woman who hated his guts. Or acted as if she did, anyway. A woman who was already involved with another man. And that man, moreover, who was one of the prime suspects in his investigation.

He thumped the wheel with the flat of his hand, his jaw hardening as he unwillingly considered the facts of the case again. If Robert Hastings wasn't involved, then he was more sinned against than sinning. But could he really be that naïve? He was James Hastings' son, for pity's sake! Who should have been more equipped to take his father's place than his only son? The twins were obviously too young, and there was no one else. Except Rose...

Oliver's mouth compressed. So far, he had no real evidence to connect Rose Chen to the operation. But, unlike her half-brother, there was nothing naïve about her, and Oliver had no doubt now that she had been involved. Was still involved, for all he knew.

For instance, he suspected she was only one, apart from James Hastings himself, who knew what was on the computer disk he had seen her reading after the office contents from a distance, but it had looked like a spreadsheet. He guessed it contained at least some of the information he was looking for. If only he'd had the chance to read it.

Chance, he mused wryly. So much of life—so much of his work—relied on chance, and he was a great believer in taking whatever was offered you. It was only chance that had brought him to the office, looking for Rose Chen; only chance that he'd come upon her using one of the firm's computers, when until then he hadn't even known she could operate one.

And it hadn't taken a great leap of intelligence to realise that this could be the break he was looking for, and the fact that Rose had quickly closed down the programme and turned off the computer had only confirmed his suspicions. Yet, to someone not looking for trouble, her attitude had been merely apologetic, the face she turned to him entreating his understanding that she had simply forgotten the time.

He believed that. He believed she had been so involved with what she was reading that she had forgotten the time. But she had made a mistake in drawing attention to herself; had proved she had something to hide in the hastiness of her actions.

Still, so long as she trusted him, she wouldn't suspect he might use the information against her. So far as she was concerned he had been more concerned with missing his dinner than wondering what she was doing. He was just one of life's drifters, after all. Why should he care if she acted a little nervously? What was it to him if she slipped the disk unobtrusively into her handbag?

Since then, he'd not seen the disk again. Even though he'd searched her apartment quite assiduously, and rifled the desk in her office. And it was a precarious business, making sure he left everything as he found it. Particularly at the office, when he had known he could be disturbed at any time.

But he'd chosen an afternoon when Rose had been entertaining Maurice Willis, of Willis antiques, ostensibly one of the firm's largest clients, who took many of the gold and bronze artefacts Hastings' imported into the country. Only Oliver knew Willis was not one of their largest clients—at least, not in the business with which James Hastings had amassed his fortune. His big clients were grey, unassuming men you'd pass in the street without noticing, not bluff, noisy giants who called Rose 'little lady' and drank more than was good for them.

Even so, his investigations had all been for nothing. He'd

found nothing of a suspicious nature, and he'd come to the conclusion that if Rose still had the disk she was either concealing it about her person or keeping it in her handbag. Besides, he had no concrete proof that the disk bore any incriminating evidence whatsoever. James Hastings had survived in this business for more than fifteen years that they knew of, and he hadn't done that by being indiscreet.

Which was the reason why he was in England, Oliver acknowledged grimly. The colonel wasn't a fool either, and he knew that his best chance of nailing the operation was by getting someone so close to the source that they themselves became incriminated. *Ergo,* Oliver's increasingly reluctant relationship with Rose Chen. And although that evening when he had seemed close to confiding in him hadn't been repeated, he knew if he played his cards right it was only a matter of time before she trusted him completely. If Robert Hastings wasn't involved, who else did she have? However sick it made him feel, she was in love with him.

He sighed. Yet he was jeopardising the whole project by pursuing a woman who'd rather he didn't exist. He had no illusions about what Fliss thought of him. She might respond to his kisses, might lose that cool composure in the undoubted heat of their lovemaking, but she'd fight him every inch of the way. She was content with her life here. She didn't want an affair that exploded all the careful myths she'd cultivated about herself. But, whether she liked it or not, her world was already changing, and once the authorities were given the proof they needed, Robert, Amanda, and the other Hastingses couldn't help being caught in the crossfire.

So what was he doing here? he asked himself harshly. Whatever happened, Fliss was unlikely to want to see him, before or after the holocaust. Dammit, she was just as likely to blame him for what happened. Whatever he thought of her relationship with Robert Hastings, she thought she loved him, and she wouldn't forgive anyone for destroying what was left of his inheritance.

Oliver scowled. He knew all this; he knew a washed-up Vietnam vet had absolutely nothing in common with an English vicar's daughter, yet he couldn't leave her alone. He was risking his relationship with Rose, his job, maybe even his life, if the men who controlled the British end of the operation thought he knew too much for his own good; and there was nothing he could do about it.

It was a little before eleven as he drove along the high street in Sutton Magna. The traffic in the village wasn't heavy, but there were one or two cars parked outside the general stores, and a handful of dogs vied for ownership of the green while their owners stood gossiping. No one appeared to take any particular notice of the Mercedes. He just hoped Amanda Hastings didn't do her shopping in Sutton Magna.

The church was at the end of the village, standing in its own grounds, which in turn adjoined the garden of the vicarage. An elderly man was busy trimming the hedge that fronted the old Victorian building, and as it was a fairly warm day he didn't mind at all when Oliver parked the car and came round to speak to him.

'Miss Hayton?' the man said, wiping his sweating forehead with the kind of coloured kerchief Oliver had always thought was reserved for neck-ties. 'Oh, you mean Fliss. Yes, she's about somewhere. Just brought me a cup of coffee, she did.' He nodded towards the empty mug residing on his wheelbarrow. 'Just what I needed, you know. Cold drinks don't cool you down, did you know that? It's proven fact—'

'I'll just go and see if I can find her,' Oliver broke in politely, thinking that a long cold beer would suit *him* very well. 'Thanks,' he added, opening the gate. Then, because he felt guilty at having cut the garrulous old gardener short, he indicated the hedge. 'Good job!'

'A *hot* job,' amended the old man, taking off his cap for a moment, and wiping the kerchief over his balding pate. He frowned. 'You that American who was here having tea with the vicar a week or so ago?'

Oliver gave an inward groan. He'd forgotten how small towns—*villages,* in this country—wanted to know everything about you. In Maple Falls, Virginia, you couldn't paint your fence without someone giving you advice about the colour.

'Yeah. Right,' he agreed, starting up the paved path, and although he was sure the gardener would have liked to continue the conversation he deliberately refrained from looking back.

Fliss herself answered his ring, and he could tell at once that she had known it was him before she opened the door. And why not? he asked himself wryly. He hadn't exactly disguised his arrival. She must have seen him from the window, and she was breathing rather fast, as if she had run down the stairs to prevent either her father or the housekeeper from intercepting him.

'Hi,' he said, thinking how pleasant it was to find a woman who didn't spend all her days in trousers. Her full-skirted print dress was rather longer than he could have wished, hiding as it did those gorgeous legs. But its strappy top exposed her arms and shoulders, and they were a delicious shade of honey. She had tied her hair back today. A french braid exposed the delicate curve of her profile, and the fine strands that had escaped at her hairline were dewy with moisture. 'Surprised to see me?'

'Not exactly.'

It wasn't quite the greeting he had hoped for, but he was nothing if not a realist. 'Is that good or bad? Were you expecting me?'

Fliss's tongue circled her upper lip, and Oliver quelled the urge he had to capture its pink tip between his teeth. 'I was afraid you might come back,' she said coolly. 'What do you want?'

Oliver put one foot on the step that led up to the porch, and tucked his thumbs securely in the back of his belt. 'Do I have to answer that?' he asked ruefully, aware of her wary withdrawal. 'How are you? How's your father?'

'I hope you don't really expect me to believe you care,' she exclaimed. 'But—' as good manners got the better of her '—he's very well, actually. As I was until I saw you.'

Oliver's lips twitched. 'You don't pull your punches, do you?' He grimaced. 'I guess you're still mad at me for the other evening. I thought you'd be glad of a lift. As you didn't even have a coat.'

Fliss took a deep breath. 'Your concern was overwhelming. It didn't occur to you that I might not want to get into a car with that—coarse female you call a girlfriend?'

'Rose?' He shrugged. 'I admit, she can be a bit bitchy at times.' He paused. 'She's just jealous.'

Fliss gasped. 'You arrogant—'

'Of you,' he informed her flatly. 'Rose has never met anyone like you before.' His lips twisted. 'I guess I could say the same.'

'I bet you could.' Fliss's face had filled with becoming colour. 'And if you think flattery—'

'Damn!' The word was out before Oliver could prevent it, and with a gesture of self-loathing he dragged his gaze away from her face. Then, trying to compose himself, 'I didn't come here to have an argument.'

'What did you come here for?'

'To see you,' he snarled, and her hand shook as it sought the frame of the door, grasping it defensively, as if she was afraid he might physically attack her.

There was silence for a few moments, and Oliver cursed

himself anew for having come here. He had really blown
it this time. She'd never believe he meant her no harm after
this.

'You'd better come in.'

Fliss's taut voice broke into his self-flagellation. As if
she had just noticed that the old gardener, who, if he
couldn't actually hear what they were saying, was taking
an inordinate interest in their exchange, she raised a hand
to the man, and then stepped backwards away from the
door.

'My—my father's not here. He's at the church,' she
added, in the same strained voice. 'He—he conducts a communion service for his older parishioners on Wednesday
mornings. He won't be back until twelve.'

Oliver hesitated only briefly, before crossing the tiled
porch and entering the vicarage. Fliss stepped behind him
to close the door, and then leaned back against it, her palms
flat against the wood. Oliver turned from an involuntary
appraisal of an antique chest and umbrella stand, to find
her golden hair haloed by the bottle-glass panels behind
her.

His heart thumped. She was so beautiful to him, so pure.
He wanted to hold her, and possess her and keep her safe.
Not just from Robert and Rose, and the mess James Hastings had left behind him. But from him, from himself. He
was so afraid he was going to hurt her.

He knew she was aware of him, knew that inviting him
inside had been an act of supreme bravery, risking as it did
her behaviour's becoming a talking point in the village. The
old man—the gardener—had already proved he enjoyed a
good gossip. His visit here was, in its way, as dangerous
to her reputation as it was to his.

But right now all that mattered was that he was here and
so was she, and God help him, he couldn't keep his hands
off her. Refusing to respond to the censure of his con-

science, he moved towards her, supporting his weight on hands that imprisoned her within the obstruction they created, bending his head to brush her lips with his tongue.

Her breath escaped against his mouth, soft and warm and sweetly scented. She was breathing rather quickly, and although he resisted the urge to slide his hand beneath her breast and feel the rapid beating of her heart for himself, he could see the pulse palpitating at her jawline. Dammit, his own pulse was beating just as rapidly, and the womanly scent of her body only accentuated his attraction to her.

'You knew I'd come, didn't you?' he murmured, tipping one slender strap off her shoulder, and lowering his head to kiss the silken skin. His tongue moved against the soft flesh and she quivered. 'I haven't been able to think about anything else but you for the past ten days. Hell, before that. Ever since we met, actually.'

Fliss drew in an unsteady breath. 'I can't believe that,' she said tremulously, but although he moved in closer, she made no attempt to get away.

'It's true,' he told her. 'Just because I acted like an idiot that night at the Hastingses', don't think I wasn't remembering how it was between us.'

'But Rose—'

'To hell with Rose,' he muttered recklessly, bringing up his hand to run his knuckles over the downy curve of her cheek. 'I was jealous. Didn't you realise that? Whenever that—ass-hole touched you, I wanted to put my gun between his ribs.'

'No—'

'Yes.' He was adamant. He cupped her face in his hand, rubbing his thumb insistently over the sensitive skin beneath her ear. 'And you know it. That's why we're here— why you're not fighting me any more.'

Fliss swallowed. 'I'm confused—'

'That makes two of us.' Oliver's lips took on a ruefully

sensuous curve, and his thumb found her mouth. 'Oh, baby, I want you—'

'No—'

'Yes.' His eyes followed his thumb, as it smeared wetness over her lips. 'I know you're engaged to that stuffed shirt, but, isn't this more important?'

He'd gone too far. He knew it as soon as the words were uttered, and a look of distaste crossed Fliss's face. Unwittingly—unwillingly—he had reminded her of her obligations to Robert, and she stiffened automatically, pressing back against the door.

'No,' she got out unevenly. 'No, this is not more important. I don't know what you want from me, but I was a fool to let you in here and an even bigger fool to think I could trust you.'

Oliver briefly closed his eyes. 'You can trust me.'

Fliss snorted. 'To do what? To make me betray Robert? To jeopardise my marriage, just because you—you've got some kind of vendetta against him?'

Oliver groaned. 'I've got no vendetta against Hastings,' he protested. But hadn't he? Wasn't that exactly what he did have?

'Well, whatever.' Fliss moved her stiff body away from the door, and Oliver found himself straightening, pushing his hands into his pockets, letting her get past him. 'I want you to go.'

She had a dignity he couldn't fault, an hauteur he couldn't deny. And he knew if he let her walk away from him now, he might never get another chance to talk to her alone.

'Wait,' he said, taking one hand out of his pocket, and making a helpless gesture. 'Don't—don't do this.'

'Do what?' She turned to face him again, and he guessed she thought the danger was over. 'You've said what you came to say, Mr Lynch. You've succeeded in humiliating me—yet again. Aren't you satisfied?'

Oliver's mouth curved. 'No,' he said, realising as he did so that he was going further—much further—than he had ever intended. 'Not nearly,' he added, using her momentary confusion to cover the space between them. Then, ignoring the horrified look that entered her eyes as she realised what he intended, he cupped the tops of her arms with hard, determined hands. Concentrating on her lips, he pulled her towards him, and before she could turn her head away he covered her mouth with his.

Her mouth was soft and sweet—so sweet—and Oliver's head swam at the first taste of her lips. For all her opposition, he could feel the button-hard thrust of her nipples, taut against his chest, and although her hands came up to press him away her palms were hot through the thin cotton of his shirt.

Was she wearing a bra? he wondered. Probably one of those strapless, half-cupped items, that did little to contain the lush fullness of her breasts, he decided, resisting the impulse to rush things. He badly wanted to touch her breasts. He wanted to hold them and lift them, and feel those throbbing nipples against his palms, but for the present he contented himself with ravaging her mouth. He'd already had two chances with her, and he'd blown them both. He had no intention of blowing a third.

All the same, he didn't know what message she thought she was conveying, as her fingers curled and spread against his midriff. God, he was already as hard as a rock, and if she brushed her hips against his one more time he was going to explode.

Capturing her face between his palms, he tantalised her quivering tongue with his, and she uttered a helpless little moan that told him more about the way she was feeling than any helpless attempt to hold him off. Whatever she wanted to believe, she wanted him just as desperately as he wanted her. She wasn't fighting him, she was fighting her own feelings, and he felt an exultant sense of pride that he could do this to her. He had the feeling Robert had barely scratched the surface of her emotions, and the wild hunger she was feeling was as powerful as it was unfamiliar.

As his mouth continued its drugging assault on hers, Oliver let her hands slide from her cheeks, down the sides of her neck to her bare shoulders. As he bit softly at her lips, sucking the tip of her tongue into his mouth, his thumbs tipped the straps of her dress down over her arms. The loosened bodice revealed the creamy rise of her breasts, and he caught his breath as he glimpsed their swollen perfection.

He longed to peel the dress, and the lacy half-bra he had exposed, away from her, but as far as he knew, Mrs Neil could be in the kitchen, and liable to interrupt them at any times. He couldn't risk that kind of embarrassment, he thought ruefully, but when Fliss's tongue brushed sensuously against the roof of his mouth he was unbearably tempted. Who knew when—or even if—he would be allowed to see her again?

His hands moved down her back to her waist, his thumbs meeting across her flat stomach. She had a deliciously small waist, and the swell of her hips was both satisfying shapely and sensuous. He couldn't resist the urge to press her softness against the aching thrust of his sex, and he groaned at the pleasure even that small capitulation gave him. He could imagine how much more satisfying it would be without the frustrating barrier of their clothes, and his limbs ached at the thought.

He uttered another groan, and Fliss, who had seemed content to let him nibble at the silky skin below her ear, lifted her head, as if in enquiry.

Controlling himself with a supreme effort of willpower, Oliver lifted his head, too. 'Mrs Neil?' he asked, dreading her reply, but Fliss's eyes were dark and slumberous.

'No,' she answered, half blankly, shaking her head. 'She's not here. Her sister—she was ill, so—'

Her voice trailed away as her eyes focused on his dark face, and Oliver tensed himself once again to face her resistance. But, it didn't come. Instead, she lifted her hand and ran her palm over the already roughening skin of his jawline. A look of confusion crossed her face, as if she wasn't entirely sure of what she was doing, but then her gaze settled on his mouth and a purely sensual expression touched her lips.

With a tentative finger she traced the moulded line of his mouth, and although Oliver was tempted to bite that tantalising invader he restrained himself. He sensed it would be wise to let her make her own pace, a feeling that was reinforced when she reached up to brush his lips with her own.

'Kiss me,' she commanded huskily, when he didn't immediately respond to her tasting, and it was beyond his powers of reason to resist. Besides, it was the first time she had invited him to touch her, and he didn't need any further encouragement.

'Let's find somewhere more comfortable,' he said thickly, swinging her up into his arms, his mouth hot and urgent against her throat. And because he only knew where the kitchen was on the ground floor, he started up the stairs.

It was a simple matter to find Fliss's bedroom. Only two doors stood open on the first landing, and the first of them was ovbiously her father's. Oliver felt an unfamiliar twinge of guilt when he saw one of Matthew Hayton's clerical collars residing on the drressing-table, but he squashed the feeling of betrayal it made him feel. He couldn't afford to have a conscience, he told himself grimly. Consciences were for fools and cowards; he had learned that in the jungles of South-east Asia, too.

Fliss's room was predictably feminine. Although he only gave it a cursory glance, his gaze was charmed by the lace-trimmed curtains at the open windows, and the assortment of bears and other soft toys that adorned the window seat. The walls were hung with a creamy striped paper, and the bed was gratifyingly large and quilted in a matching fabric.

The quilt was soft beneath his hand as he lowered Fliss onto the bed, and he spared a moment to kick off his boots before joining her on the soft coverlet. 'Beautiful,' he said huskily, cradling her slightly flushed face between his palms. 'You're beautiful. But you know that, don't you? God, you're the most beautiful creature I've ever seen.'

Fliss licked her upper lip, and Oliver gave in to the urge to do the same. 'I—I'm not beautiful,' she got out breathily, and he could tell from the glazed expression in her eyes that she was no longer in control of either herself or her emotions. Either she was an amazing actress, or she was totally at the mercy of her sexual needs, and Oliver was pretty sure it was the latter. As before, he had the sensation of dealing with someone who was wholly inexperienced, and he wondered what Hastings was thinking of to neglect her so.

But he didn't want to think about Robert Hastings now. For the first time he could remember, he was in danger of forgetting his own identity here, and while the hazards of that were apparent, he could no more have resisted his urges than she could.

He wanted her. God, how he wanted her! He couldn't wait to feel her slick muscles enfold him, and if that was a painful admission for someone like him to make, then so be it.

Covering her face with hot, insistent kisses, he allowed his hands to do what they had wanted to do for what seemed like forever. With the utmost care, he drew the folds of her bodice down to her waist, and then unclipped the frivolous bra.

Her breasts were every bit as full and luscious as he had imagined, the nipples knotted and distended, an irresistible invitation to his lips. Controlling his hunger with some difficulty, he lowered his head and took one of the dark, swollen areolae into his mouth, sucking on it so strongly that Fliss moaned and clutched his head. Her nails raked his scalp, and her fingers tangled in his hair. But she was totally unaware of it, arching helplessly against the pillows.

Not until he had tasted both breasts did he give in to the hands that were now tearing at his collar. With a skill learned in too many beds, he tore his shirt open, almost ripping off the buttons in his haste to shed his clothes. But it was worth the haste to feel her body against his, to see the fine hair that arrowed down his chest dark against her skin.

But it wasn't enough, not nearly enough. He had to see the rest of her, too, and propping himself up on his elbows, he tugged the dress down to her ankles. He thought he might have torn it. There was an ominous pause before the material gave way. But he tossed the garment on to the floor without contrition. He'd buy her a dozen new dresses, if only she'd let him.

She was wearing lacy briefs that matched the bra he had discarded earlier, but that was all. Her glorious legs were bare, and a delicious cluster of honey-coloured curls was visible through the silk.

Oliver was trembling. He knew it, and he knew why. He could hardly contain himself as he bent his head and pressed his face against that silky mound. His own erection was straining for release, and the scent of her arousal was like nectar to his senses.

She uttered a sound—it might have been a protest, he

couldn't be sure—but she lifted her hips obediently when he tugged the briefs away. She even parted her legs to facilitate his efforts, apparently unaware of the provocation of her actions.

But Oliver was aware of it; aware, too, that if he didn't touch her soon he was going to disgrace himself completely. Even so, he couldn't resist the opportunity to put his hand where her briefs had been, cupping her mound possessively, and finding the damp core of her with his finger.

She flinched when he toucher her, and for a moment he was afraid she was going to prevent him from going on. Her hands came to cover his, as if in some kind of belated protest, but when he eased his finger inside her, her hands fell away.

'Oh, God,' she moaned, giving voice to her emotions for the first time since he had brought her upstairs, and she shuddered half convulsively as he prevented her from pressing her legs together again.

'Just take it easy,' he told her softly, even though he was cursing under his breath because the button at his waistband refused to open. But at last the button gave way, and he released his aching sex, kicking the jeans away with an impatience born of necessity.

Yet, when he saw her eyes were closed, conversely he held back. Even though his needs were paramount, it was important that she should look at him; that she should know who had brought her to such a state of abandonment. For she was abandoned lying there, her limbs splayed, her hair coming loose from its braid and tumbling about her shoulders. She was the epitome of everything he had ever wanted in a woman, and he wanted her to look at him and know she wanted him, too.

Taking one of her hands, he brought it to him, steeling himself not to lose control as he wrapped her fingers about him. The feeling was unimaginable, the desire to move against her almost irresistible. But he forced himself to watch her face and not the erotic movements of his body.

And her eyes opened, almost immediately. She blinked for a moment, and then looked down the point where they were joined, and caught her breath.

'You're—so big,' she breathed, half withdrawing her hand, but then seeming to change her mind again. 'Oliver—'

'So you know it's me,' he said huskily, and she gave a jerky nod.

'I know,' she whispered, lifting her free hand to his face. 'Do you want to kiss me?'

'I'm afraid I'm going to have to do much more than that,' Oliver uttered on a breathy sigh. 'Oh, Fliss—I can't wait any longer. I've got to be inside you...'

CHAPTER NINE

'DID you type up those notes I gave you, Felicity?'

Matthew Hayton ran restless fingers through the pile of papers on his daughter's desk, succeeding in sending most of them fluttering to the floor. It wasn't often Felicity let him down, but this morning she was just sitting staring at her typewriter, making no effort to transcribe the hand-written manuscript he had left with her the night before.

Fliss blinked, and forced herself to attend to what her father was saying. 'I beg your—'

'The notes,' said the Reverend patiently. 'You remember? I gave you the folder last evening. Did you do them already?'

'What? Oh, no.' Fliss felt her cheeks deepen with colour. 'I'm sorry.'

Her father frowned. 'Are you ill, Felicity?' he asked, with some concern, laying a cool hand against her temple. 'Heavens, you're hot! Are you sure you're all right?'

'I'm fine, Daddy.' Fliss made a concerted effort to gather her thoughts, and rescued the file of notes from the bottom of the pile. 'Um—here they are. Do you want them?'

'Not if they're not typed,' replied her father, containing his frustration. 'But as you know, the bishop's coming to lunch, and I had hoped to show him what I was doing.'

Fliss sighed apologetically. 'I'll do them right away—'

'No, that won't be necessary.' Matthew Hayton patted her shoulder reassuringly. 'Whatever you say, I can see that you're not feeling on top form this morning. I'll just show him my notes, if he's interested. If he can't read my writing—well, I'll worry about that if it happens, hmm?'

'Oh, Daddy!'

Fliss felt terrible. And not just because she had let her father down. For heaven's sake, on a scale of one to ten, not typing the notes had to figure fairly low on the list. But, being unfaithful to Robert, making love with Oliver Lynch in her *own* bed—that was betrayal of a totally different kind.

God! How could she have been so foolish? She should never have invited him into the house. She'd known what he wanted, what he was doing there. She wasn't a fool—well, she hadn't thought so before. But to let him touch her, to let him make love to her, to give him that kind of hold over her—that was really stupid.

Yet, if she was honest—and Fliss generally was—she had to admit she had never shown a great deal of common sense where Oliver Lynch was concerned. When she was with him, she seemed to lose what little composure she had, and the fact that he had no respect for her or her position as Robert's fiancée seemed to show a lack of judgement on her part rather than his.

The awful thing was, she had always thought herself such a controlled individual until he came along. Her father, especially, would never have recognised his emotionally restrained daughter in the wild-eyed wanton Oliver Lynch had tumbled on her bed. Even now, it was hard to imagine herself as she had been then, and only the prickling of her breasts and a pulse beating in an unmentionable part of her anatomy when she reviewed what had happened convinced her it was real.

In some ways, it still seemed like a dream. Had she really let Oliver Lynch do that to her? No matter how often she thought about it, it seemed incredible that she had actually participated in her own downfall. After holding Robert off all these months, why had she let a man she barely knew make love to her?

The answer eluded her, though in her heart of hearts she knew it had something to do with the fact that no matter how she might despise herself for it, she was attracted to Oliver Lynch, just as he had said.

It would certainly explain why she had always been so nervous around him. Had she always sensed he could be dangerous to her? Had she been afraid even then he might expose her relationship with Robert for what it was?

But no. Whatever perverse fascination she might have for the other man, she *loved* Robert. She didn't love Oliver Lynch. She despised him. Despised him and herself for creating such a ghastly situation.

Yet, at the time, she hadn't cared about the consequences. She had been so caught up in her own emotions, she hadn't thought about the damage she was doing. All that had seemed important was that Oliver should go on kissing her, and touching her, and inciting her wilful body to even greater heights of passion, making her practically beg him to satisfy her needs.

And he had, she thought unwillingly, recalling the sleek thrust of his powerful body with a sudden weakness. Dear God, he had driven her nearly wild with excitement, taking her to the edge of madness so many times that, when she finally tipped over the brink, the sensations she had experienced were out of this world.

She had clutched him then, her nails digging into his shoulders, uttering little incoherent protestations that he seemed to find absurdly erotic. He'd encouraged her to voice her feelings, feeding on the moist sweetness of her lips. And when her muscles had convulsed he'd groaned, too, spilling his seed inside her.

It was no dream, she thought now, remembering how she had felt when she had awakened to find him gone. Even without her clothes strewn about the room, and the feeling of lethargy that had gripped her, she had known it had really happened. Oliver's scent was still on her sheets, even if he'd abandoned her.

She closed her eyes for a moment as she recalled how quickly delight had turned to disillusion. The marvellous feeling of well-being she had had when she awakened had only lasted as long as it took her to remember what she'd done. The fact that Oliver wasn't there, that he had left her as soon as he'd got what he came for, had made everything seem so sordid. Had he guessed that Robert had never made love to her? Had he gloried in her inexperience because it had signalled Robert's defeat?

She'd wanted to die then. She'd wanted to pull the covers over her head and never come out again. She hadn't even got the consolation of knowing he'd used a contraceptive. He'd asked her if she wanted him to, but she'd been so desperate for him to take her, she'd only shaken her head.

God, she had been so stupid! She had known he was still involved with Rose Chen, that he was unlikely to do anything to jeopardise their relationship, yet she had surrendered to his demands like a foolish virgin. To him, it had meant nothing. For some reason, she had intrigued him, and it had amused him to prove to her—and to himself—that he could do it. He didn't care who he hurt in the process. Just as long as he wasn't disappointed.

It had been her father's voice, as he chatted with Mr Hood before coming into the house, that had forced Fliss to take stock of the situation. She couldn't have her father see this room and guess what had been going on. She couldn't put that kind of burden on him. It was her problem, and she would have to deal with it, in whatever way she could.

So, by the time he came in, her tearstained cheeks were washed, her hair was brushed, and the dress Oliver had torn as he ripped it off her was hidden at the bottom of her wardrobe. Another dress had taken its place and, as she had expected, her father didn't notice any change in her appearance.

However, that was yesterday. After a virtually sleepless night, today Fliss was less able to hide her feelings. She had the feeling she was suffering a delayed case of shock, and the knowledge that she'd be seeing Robert in a few hours was making it difficult to concentrate on her work. She'd forgotten all about her father's notes, and she hastily scanned her appearance, half afraid she might have forgotten to put on her shoes or button her shirt.

'Um—you and Robert haven't fallen out, have you?' her father asked suddenly, coming back into the room with the file of notes still in his hand. 'I mean, I don't want to pry or anything, but with Lynch turning up again yesterday, I did wonder if it had caused a problem.'

'Oh—no.' Fliss managed to sound amazingly casual. She hadn't had to tell her father about Oliver's visit. Mr Hood had done that for her, and somehow she had put him off without an adequate explanation. She'd let him think Oliver had been hoping to see him, and if her conscience had troubled her on that score, it had seemed such a minor sin compared to the others she had committed.

'You didn't see Robert last night,' the Reverend pointed out now, and Fliss made a display of putting a carbon between two sheets of typing paper to avoid having to look at him.

'I told you: Rob was staying in London last night. There was some sort of meeting at the office this morning, and he wanted to be there early. You know Mr Hastings used to stay up in town sometimes, when he was involved in meetings.'

'You also told me that Robert was complaining about not being involved in the running of the company,' replied her father mildly. 'There's nothing you're not telling me, is there, Felicity? Hastings hasn't got himself into some sort of mess?'

Fliss gasped, and now looked at her father. 'Mess?' she echoed. 'What kind of mess?'

Matthew Hayton shrugged. 'You tell me.' He paused. 'I just got a feeling—when I was talking to Lynch, the other day—that he knew something I didn't.' He shook his head. 'I'm probably imagining things. But with him coming to see me yesterday...'

Fliss's lips tightened. 'It was only a courtesy call, Daddy,' she exclaimed, inwardly cringing at the absurdity of her words. There had been nothing courteous about Oliver Lynch's behaviour. 'If he'd had anything—important—to talk to you about, he'd have stayed, wouldn't he?'

'Perhaps.' Her father frowned. 'Yes, you're probably right. But if he calls again, do try and detain him. I enjoyed our conversation. He's an interesting man.'

Fliss made some guarded rejoinder, and thankfully her father didn't pursue the subject. With the bishop coming for lunch, he had things to prepare, and with some relief she abandoned the typing and escaped to the garden, and the undemanding task of weeding.

Robert arrived in the late afternoon. Fliss was in the kitchen when she heard a man's voice in the hall, and for a moment her knees turned to jelly. It wasn't that Robert's voice was anything like Oliver's, but she hadn't been expecting him until the evening. He was supposedly coming to take her to an art exhibition in Market Risborough, and his arrival now, some two or three hours before time was disturbing.

'It's only Mr Hastings,' said Mrs Neil, noticing how she had lost colour, and Fliss thought how ineffectual she was at hiding her feelings. But she couldn't help wondering if

Oliver had been at the London meeting, and what he had said to her fiancé.

'I know,' she said now, making a pretence of checking her hair to give herself time to compose herself. After all, she had conducted herself perfectly naturally while the bishop was here. And he should have been far more intimidating than the man she was going to marry.

To her relief, her father was with Robert when she joined them in the sitting-room. It was a little late for tea, but Matthew Hayton was offering his guest a glass of sherry. 'I'm afraid we don't keep any spirits in the house,' he was saying, and Fliss wondered what had happened to make Robert need stronger fortification.

'Thanks,' Robert responded, and although he saw Fliss in the doorway he swallowed the contents of his glass in a single gulp before greeting her.

'Ah, there you are, my dear,' her father observed, with an evident effort. 'Robert's here.'

'Yes. So I see.' Fliss managed to sound suitably surprised. 'Is—er—is something wrong?'

'What could be wrong?' asked Robert harshly, handing his glass to the Reverend in a mute appeal for a refill. He came towards her, and before she could guess his intention he had jerked her towards him and bestowed a wet, sherry-scented kiss on her mouth. 'I just couldn't wait to see you, that's all.'

Fliss's eyes sought her father's over Robert's shoulder, begging his indulgence, and although he would have obviously preferred to leave them to it Matthew Hayton poured his guest another sherry.

'Robert,' he said peremptorily, holding out the glass, and the younger man was forced to release Fliss to take it.

'Did—did you go to your meeting?' she asked warily, aware that Robert's behaviour was not typical. Something had happened. She was certain. But whether it was to do with her, she couldn't be sure.

'Oh, yes,' said Robert now. 'Yes, I went. It was most—enlightening.'

Fliss's stomach tightened. 'Really?'

'Yes, really.' Robert finished his second sherry, looked as if he might ask for a third, and then seemed to think better of it. He took a steadying breath. 'I've been recruited to the board.'

Fliss caught her breath. 'Oh! Oh, Rob—that's wonderful!'

'Is it?' His expression was sardonic.

'Well, isn't it?' She licked her lips. 'I—I thought that was what you wanted.'

'Yes. So did I.' Robert's lips twisted. 'Funny how wrong you can be.'

Fliss looked at her father, her own confusion plain, and clearing his throat, the older man stepped forward to take the empty glass. 'Um—does this mean you're going to be running the London end of the business from now on, my boy?'

Robert frowned. 'I'm not sure. I suppose I could be.'

'Oh, Rob!' Fliss's relief that her fiancé hadn't come here to accuse her of betraying him with Oliver Lynch made her more effusive than she might otherwise have been. 'Rose Chen must have great confidence in you.'

'Mmm.' Robert didn't sound as if that news filled him with delight. 'At least that bastard Lynch wasn't at the meeting. According to Rose, he's not involved in the operation.'

'No?' Fliss swallowed.

'No.' Robert's mouth hardened. 'He's just a hanger-on, as I always thought. But if he thinks he's got Rose in his pocket, he's way off base, as they say in his country.'

For the first time since Fliss had entered the room, Robert smiled, but it was not a pleasant expression. Whatever had happened in London, it was Robert who considered he had got the better of the other man. And, although Fliss couldn't suppress a totally unnecessary twinge of concern on Oliver's behalf, she was relieved that she hadn't been involved.

'I didn't get that impression,' Matthew Hayton remarked suddenly, and Fliss, who had been congratulating herself that the danger was over for the moment, cast him an anxious look. 'Lynch,' went on her father, when Robert looked blank. 'He didn't strike me as a—what was it you said? A hanger-on? I found him a very intelligent human being. Did you know, for instance, that he studied law when he was younger? I'd say he'd make a very fine student.' He paused. 'I should add that he didn't volunteer this information to impress me. I questioned him about his education, and he was obliged to admit that he had abandoned his career to join the army. He served in Vietnam, you know. An experience which damaged quite a number of young men, I believe.'

Robert's smile had disappeared now, and he looked resentfully at the older man. 'Are you saying that's an excuse for living off my sister,' he demanded.

'No.' Matthew Hayton drew himself up to his full height. At a little under six feet, he was still a couple of inches shorter than Robert, but his presence was impressive. 'I'm saying that someone who's lived a fairly comfortable existence all his life shouldn't jump to totally unfounded conclusions.'

'Now, look here—'

'Oh, please.' Fliss put herself between the two men, realising, if Robert didn't, that he was in danger of alienating her father completely. Besides, she had no wish to have to explain why Oliver had come here a second time, not unless it was absolutely necessary, of course. 'Does it matter what either of you thinks of him? As you've just said, Rob, he's not involved. Let's leave it at that.'

Robert looked as if he would have liked to continue the argument, but Fliss's intervention had reminded him of his obligations, and he had no wish to fall out with his future father-in-law. 'Suits me,' he said, albeit a little off-handedly, and the Reverend inclined his head in a gesture of acceptance.

'I'd better go and prepare for choir practice,' he said, addressing himself to no one in particular, and Fliss let her breath escape on a thankful sigh as he departed the room.

As soon as he had gone, Robert reached for her again, but Fliss managed to evade his possessive hands, and went to open the french doors into the garden. It was probably her, but the room seemed airless suddenly, and she couldn't wait to get outside. She stepped out on to the terrace, knowing Robert would follow her, and put the width of the wicker garden table between them, before he could approach her again.

'So,' she said, hurrying into speech so he wouldn't notice her nervousness, 'what happened?'

Robert frowned. 'What do you mean?' he asked, evidently diverted, as she had hoped.

'Well—you didn't seem exactly thrilled with the new arrangement when you arrived,' she pointed out carefully. 'Did Rose Chen give you a hard time?'

Robert hunched his shoulders, pushing his hands into the pockets of his jacket. He was still wearing the navy business suit he had worn at the meeting, and although he had unloosened his collar, he still looked hotter than she felt.

'Rose is OK,' he said, after a moment, and Fliss, who had been expecting anything but this, widened her eyes.

'She is?'

'Well—' Robert gave a careless shrug, no doubt remembering the invective he had previously used to describe his half-sister. 'I suppose she is family, whether I like it or not.'

Fliss hid her amazement. 'I see.'

'I know what you're thinking. You're thinking that because I've been invited to join the board, I've had a change of heart.'

'Well—'

'Well, that's not it.' Robert flushed. 'You don't understand. It's not as—simple—as I thought. Rose has had a pretty tough time since my father died, and it's up to us— my mother and me—to take some of that burden from her.'

'Oh.' Fliss hoped she didn't sound as horrified as she felt. But the idea of Rose Chen being accepted as part of Robert's 'family'; of her staying at the Grange, as a welcome visitor; of her becoming not just a business partner but his 'sister', filled her with alarm. For Rose Chen, she read Oliver Lynch, and the thought of seeing him again, maybe even on a regular basis if Rose Chen had her way, was unthinkable.

'What's wrong?'

Robert asked the question now, and Fliss realised that once again she was letting her emotions show. 'N-nothing,' she stammered, desperate to escape a prolonged postmortem of her feelings. 'I'm just surprised, that's all. I didn't think you liked her.'

Robert hesitated. Then, 'I don't,' he admitted, and she realised that what he had said before had been just self-justification. 'But I've got to work with her, Fliss. She holds the purse-strings. And what does it matter where the money comes from, as long as there's plenty of it?'

Fliss looked at him curiously now. 'What's that supposed to mean?' she asked, and Robert's eyes flickered uneasily.

'Nothing,' he said impatiently, and his momentary show of conscience might never have been. 'It means nothing. I was only thinking aloud, that's all. Now, why don't we drive into Market Risborough and get something to eat there, before going to the exhibition?'

Fliss shrugged. 'All right.'

'Good.' Robert looked at her expectantly. 'Well? Aren't you going to get ready?'

'Now?' Fliss stared at him in some confusion. 'But—' She looked at his suit which was creased from his journey. 'Aren't you going to get changed?'

'No, I don't think I will.' A faint trace of colour entered Robert's fair cheeks as he made his excuses. 'I—er—I can't be bothered to go back home just now.' He glanced down at his appearance. 'I'll do, won't I?'

What could she say? Fliss made a helpless gesture, and moved towards the house again. 'But—won't your mother expect to see you, to talk to you, to hear what happened?' she asked finally, and Robert sighed.

'My mother was at the meeting,' he said flatly. 'I dropped her at the Grange on my way here.' His lips thinned. 'Now, are we going out or aren't we? I'd really like to know.'

CHAPTER TEN

'AND you think he's been told what's going on?' Colonel Lightfoot sounded thoughtful. 'If it's true, isn't Rose taking a God-awful risk?'

'That depends.' Oliver considered the options. 'She could have been lying all along, of course. She and Robert could both have been playing a double game, but I don't think Hastings is clever enough for that. I think this is a calculated move on Rose's part.' He paused. 'What I've yet to discover is why. She's not the type to take chances. Not when there's so much at stake.'

The colonel made a sound of assent. 'So, what's your guess?'

Oliver shrugged, shifting the phone to his other ear. 'I don't have one. Not one I'd care to air yet, anyway. I'll wait and see what transpires. I've told Rose I want to return to Hong Kong by the end of next week, so—'

'What the hell did you do that for?' The colonel erupted into a frustrated tirade. 'For God's sake, man, do you want to lose whatever ground you've gained?'

'No.' Oliver kept his tone mild with an effort. It would be all too easy to vent his feelings in his present frame of mind, but he had no intention of giving Lightfoot another goad to lash him with. 'It's because I don't want Rose to get suspicious of me that I'm putting a deadline on the time I stay here. Don't let's forget, I'm supposed to be involved in deals of my own. What kind of jerk would I seem if I was prepared to hang about indefinitely? As far as she knows, I'm just wasting my time here. Who knows? Maybe it'll persuade her to offer me a reason to stay on.'

'Huh.' The colonel didn't sound convinced. If there was any merit in the idea, he wasn't about to admit it. 'Well, I hope you're right.'

'Yeah. So do I,' drawled Oliver evenly, aware that Colonel Lightfoot would very likely burst a blood vessel if he found out how his supposedly professional operative had been spending his time. 'I'll call you again, when I've got something to report.'

'In two days, Lynch,' said Colonel Lightfoot pedantically, but Oliver wasn't listening. He put down his receiver without acknowledging the order.

However, with the connection broken, and the rest of the day at his disposal, Oliver was less inclined to be arrogant. Whatever he'd told the colonel, his association with Rose Chen had never been at a lower ebb. Although Rose didn't know it, his infatuation with Fliss Hayton was the reason for the deterioration in their relationship, and after the row they had had last evening it was highly unlikely that she'd be offering him any kind of inducement to stay.

The knowledge angered him. He wasn't used to any kind of interference in his professional activities. Even his affair with Rose Chen had been carefully orchestrated, and at no time had he ever felt out of touch with his objective. He had been doing a good job, making good progress, and now he was allowing his feelings for Fliss to foul up not just his job, but his life.

He didn't like it. He liked what he'd done even less. What was wrong with him, for God's sake? Was he having some kind of mid-life crisis slap damn in the middle of a surveillance operation? And what would old Archie think if he told him he couldn't go on because he was emotionally involved with one of the principals?

He groaned. He could imagine what Archie would say all right, and it wouldn't be complimentary. And who could blame him? Dammit, he wasn't just acting out of line, he was acting out of character. He didn't get emotionally involved with women—any women. But least of all a vicar's daughter, for Pete's sake!

But he had—and that was what was eating him up. Cheating on Hastings didn't bother him. He'd dismissed the arguments on that days ago. He'd told himself then, he couldn't afford to have a conscience. In his line of work, a man used any means in his power to gain the upper hand, and if it meant compromising his own morals then so be it. It was Fliss who was causing him to question his motives—because he knew that, whatever excuses he might give himself, what he'd done he'd done for his own gratification and nothing else.

Which was why he'd been in such a filthy mood when he'd got back from Sutton Magna the day before. It wasn't just the risks he'd taken with his relationship with Rose Chen, though God knew, if she was as ruthless as her father had been, it might not just be his job he was putting in jeopardy. It was the realisation that he felt only contempt for his own actions. Fliss had trusted him, and look how he had repaid her.

And for once, the argument that he was only doing a job didn't hold any water. Seducing Hastings' fiancée had not been part of his brief, and the memory of how he had used her own inexperience against her filled him with shame. It was no consolation that what had happened had disturbed him equally as much as it had disturbed her. She didn't know it was the first time in his life he had actually lost control of his emotions. She probably thought he had used her, as he had used so many other women before, and she'd never forgive him for that.

But did he want her to forgive him? Wasn't it better, for both of them, if she continued to regard him as the bastard he was? He didn't need her understanding. He wanted no distractions to what he was being paid to do.

Nevertheless it had been a salutary lesson in how not to behave. Remembering how he had even failed to protect her from his lust only added to his sense of self-disgust. He wasn't a boy, for God's sake. He should have been capable of restraining himself long enough to take the usual precautions. But he hadn't. His need to fuse his body with hers had blinded him to all normal considerations, and even now, in the midst of his soul-searching, he could feel himself hardening at the thought.

God! He swore angrily. The trouble was, what had happened hadn't achieved the result he'd expected. No matter how crazy he knew it to be, once had simply not been enough. The way he felt at the moment, he doubted a lifetime would be long enough to slake the hunger Fliss had aroused in him. How the hell was he supposed to concentrate on his own safety, when all he could think about was how he could contrive to see her again?

But he mustn't see her again, he told himself savagely. For her sake, as well as his own. Whatever fleeting satisfaction they had shared, she was still going to marry Hastings. And, looking at it objectively, if he had alerted her to the sensuality of her nature, then her fiancé ought to thank him. He had the feeling Robert was somewhat short on sensitivity.

He snorted suddenly. Who was he kidding? His lips twisted. God, was he really that arrogant? Was he actually making a case for his own redemption, when what he should really be doing was acknowledging that the thought of Fliss in the other man's arms was tearing him to pieces? She had been his, dammit. And the truth, if he was man enough to admit it, was that he wanted more from her than just a hasty tumble in the sheets.

But that way lay madness, and defeat. However he might

kick against it, Fliss Hayton was not for him. It had been an enlightening experience, but that was all. He had to get the whole thing into perspective and start concentrating on the real reason he was here.

Which meant getting back into Rose Chen's good graces. If he wasn't careful Hastings would succeed in poisoning her mind against him, too, and he couldn't allow that. He had come too far, sacrificed too much. He wasn't going to lose out now.

'But who are these people, Rob? And why do I have to meet them? If it's business—'

'You met my father's business associates from time to time,' Robert interrupted her shortly, and Fliss, who had been hoping to avoid any further involvement with either Oliver or Rose Chen, wanted to scream.

'Even so—'

'Look: it's what I want,' her fiancé broke in again. 'You ought to be glad I'm being involved in the business at last. At least I know what's going on now. And—well, these people like to know who they're dealing with.'

'What people?' Fliss gazed at him. 'And if you wanted to entertain them, why haven't you invited them to the Grange?'

'So many questions!' Robert strode impatiently around the sitting-room at the vicarage. 'What's the matter? Don't you trust me enough to spend the night with me?' His lips curled. 'No, I'll rephrase that. Don't you trust me to book you a room of your own at the hotel?'

'Oh, Rob—'

'What? What is it with you, Fliss? Don't you want to support me in this? Can't you see that it's what I've got to do if we ever hope to have a life of our own?'

Fliss gazed at him anxiously. Was it just her own guilt feeding her uncertainties, or were Robert's explanations growing progressively more ambiguous? Ever since he had told her he had joined the board of Hastings', he had seemed to have a meaning deeper than the actual words he used.

For a while she had entertained the possibility that somehow he had found out about her and Oliver, and this was his way of telling her. But it was several days since the traumatic events of that morning, and, knowing Robert as she did, she couldn't believe he would conceal his feelings for so long. Besides, it was becoming increasingly obvious that it wasn't her behaviour that was on his mind, and this invitation to attend a private dinner party in London was obviously important to him.

But as soon as he had told her that Rose Chen would be there, Fliss had been desperate to avoid the confrontation. Rose Chen meant Oliver, and she didn't think she could face him again. Not now, not yet. Not until she had had time to recover a little of the pride he had so cruelly robbed her of.

'So?' Robert prompted now, and Fliss realised she had spent far too long mulling over her own situation. He was looking at her now with scarcely concealed irritation, and if she wasn't careful she would give him reason for questioning her motives.

'I don't know if I can,' she mumbled, pulling the dead stem of a carnation out of a vase, and folding it up between her fingers. It was slimy, and she pulled a face, before adding lamely, 'Daddy may need me.'

'*I* need you,' retorted Robert harshly. 'Come on, Fliss. If we're ever going to make a go of our relationship you've got to start deciding where your priorities are.'

Fliss bit her lip. She knew that. She knew she was being unforgivably selfish. But the trouble was, she didn't know what her priorities were any longer. She'd thought she did. She'd thought that marrying Robert would give her every-

thing she had ever wanted from her life, but now she was
not so sure.

Of course, she was being foolish. Ridiculously foolish in
the circumstances. It wasn't as if she wanted to marry anyone else, after all. She wasn't stupid enough to believe that
she had any future with Oliver Lynch. Even if he'd wanted
it, she had more sense than to ally herself to a man who
treated her sex with so little respect.

She wondered if he'd told Rose Chen what he'd done.
She doubted it, remembering how possessive the Chinese
woman had been, but it was always possible. She'd read it
was how some people kept their relationships alive.
Though, judging how fiery Rose Chen's response to him
had been, she doubted they needed any artificial stimulant.
She felt sick every time she pictured them together, and no
amount of self-analysis could alter the fact that she hated
them both in equal measure.

'All right,' she said now, realising that whatever their
future might hold, she couldn't let Robert down. 'But I
hope you know what you're doing.'

'What's that supposed to mean?'

Robert's response was instantly defensive, and Fliss
sighed. 'Nothing,' she said. 'I'm just not sure that working
with—with that woman is making you happy.'

'Happy?' Robert gave her an odd look. 'What's
"happy" got to do with anything? She's going to make me
rich. That's what matters, isn't it?'

Fliss wasn't so sure. She was very much afraid that
Robert was willing to do almost anything to sustain his
position in the company. From the beginning his main concern had been that he shouldn't get his fair share of the
business, and now that Rose Chen had solicited his help he
seemed desperate to justify her acceptance.

Still, as she got ready to leave the following afternoon,
Fliss decided there was no point in worrying about it. What

could Rose make him do, for heaven's sake? Falsify records? Condone the sale of some item of doubtful provenance? She had no doubt it happened, and not just with Hastings'; the antiques business was as open to fraud as any other. And the fact that James Hastings had lived in comparative luxury all his life seemed to point to the fact that he had either been amazingly fortunate or amazingly clever. Either way, Fliss would have believed anything of that cold, unfeeling man. He had had no heart, just a superficial charm—which she supposed was a fair description of his eldest daughter, too.

Her father was waiting to bid her farewell. He smiled his approval as she came down the stairs, but she sensed he wasn't entirely happy with the arrangements. He thought it very remiss of Robert to expect her to drop everything and travel up to London with him at a moment's notice, and although she had had slightly longer than that, Fliss could understand his feelings.

'You will phone after you're installed at the hotel, won't you?' he said, as they heard Robert's car pull up outside. 'And if you have any problem—any problem at all—don't hesitate to let me know.'

'I'm only going to be away one night, Daddy.' Fliss tried to make light of it. 'And I'm sure you'd rather Rob didn't drive home if he's going to be drinking.'

'Of course, of course.' Matthew Hayton pushed his hands into the pockets of his worn corduroy trousers and regarded her ruefully. 'I'm just an old worry-wart, that's all.'

'Well, I'm sure there's no need.' Fliss bit her lip. 'I'm only going to be with Rob, you know. You trust him, don't you?'

'I suppose so.' Her father looked a little discomfited now. He paused, and then added, 'I've just had the feeling lately that you've been having—well—second thoughts about him yourself.'

Fliss caught her breath. 'About Rob?'

'I actually wondered if Oliver was to blame,' her father continued steadily. 'Whether he'd made you a little—restless.' He shrugged, as Fliss struggled to control her colour. 'It was just a thought.'

'No.' The doorbell rang, and Fliss glanced half furtively towards it. 'I mean—no, I'm not having second thoughts, Daddy. And—and definitely not about Oliver Lynch!'

'OK.' Her father made a dismissing movement with his shoulders as the doorbell rang again. 'You'd better answer that. Patience has never been Robert's strong point.'

Fliss stared at him, unmoving, for another few seconds. She'd known that Robert and her father had had their differences in the past, but she'd never realised how deep-rooted they were. When had Matthew Hayton begun to actively dislike her fiancé? And where had he got the notion that her relationship with Oliver might be more or less than it appeared?

The bell rang for a third time, and the Reverend shook his head. 'The door,' he prompted, and with a feeling of bemusement Fliss went to answer it.

Robert was predictably terse. 'Doesn't this bell work or something?' he demanded, before he saw Fliss's father behind her in the hallway. He coloured. 'I thought it must be out of order,' he added, for the older man's benefit. 'I've rung it half a dozen times.'

'Three actually,' corrected Matthew Hayton evenly, and then turned to give his daughter a kiss. 'Now, remember what I said,' he murmured, giving her cheek an affectionate pat. Then, to Robert, 'Drive carefully.'

Robert stowed Fliss's holdall and the suit carrier containing her dress, into the back of the car, and then got into the seat beside her. He was very tense; she could feel it. And she didn't think it was just her father's attitude that had sparked his temper, though he chose to pretend it was.

'Dammit, you'd think I was a schoolboy, the way he talks to me,' he complained angrily, as they headed for the motorway. 'And what was all that about you remembering what he'd said? Is he afraid I'm going to jump you the minute I've got you to the hotel?'

Fliss sighed. 'Of course not.'

'Why "of course not"? Doesn't he think I've got it in me to seduce my own fiancée?'

'Rob!'

'Well, it's true.' Robert hunched his shoulders over the wheel, and Fliss guessed they were in for a fast ride to London. 'I know he doesn't approve of the arrangements, so don't pretend he does. Just wait until we're married. He won't be able to call the shots then.'

Fliss sighed again. 'Rob, he's not like that.'

'He's exactly like that.' With a swift depression of the accelerator Robert cut in front of a slow-moving wagon, causing it to break and blow its horn furiously. 'And you,' he muttered, giving the other man an uncomplimentary gesture. 'Bloody professional drivers! They think they own the road.'

'He was trying to keep a reasonable distance between him and the car in front,' said Fliss carefully. 'You closed the gap.'

'When I want instruction from you, I'll ask for it,' retorted Robert aggressively, opening his window, and throwing his elbow over the rim. 'I'm sick to death of people giving me orders. If you can't say anything pleasant, don't say anything at all.'

Fliss drew a deep breath, refusing to respond to his ill humour in kind. At times Robert *was* like a small boy, and this was one of them. She already had doubts about this evening, and his behaviour was only adding to her misgivings.

'Anyway, we've got to talk about other things,' he muttered, and, if it wasn't an apology, at least he didn't intend to sulk all the way to London. 'I may have to go to Hong Kong in a couple of months myself, and my mother thinks we should get married before I go.'

'What?'

Fliss turned a startled face towards him now, but Robert refused to look at her. 'Well, we were planning on getting married at Christmas, weren't we? If we bring it forward a couple of months, what does it matter?'

'We're talking about four months, at least,' exclaimed Fliss hotly, and then, realising she was panicking, she forced herself to calm down. 'If—if you do have to go to Hong Kong, then I think it would be more sensible if you got that out of the way before we got married. We could always postpone the wedding.' She despised herself for the relief she felt at the prospect. 'There's no urgency about it, is there?'

'Not for you, perhaps,' muttered Robert dourly. 'My God, I sometimes wonder if you've got a sexual urge in your body! Besides—' he took his eyes from the road for a moment to cast her a glowering look, and then had to brake fiercely to avoid another collision '—it's not an either-or situation,' he growled. 'You don't seem to understand. The reason we have to get married before I go to Hong Kong is simple. I don't know how long I'm going to have to stay there. I'm going to run the Hong Kong office. If it works out, it could be months; years, even. Naturally, you'll come with me. As my wife—'

'No!' Fliss was horrified. 'I—I—what about Daddy?'

'What about *Daddy*?' Robert was sardonic. 'You surely

knew when we got married he'd have to manage on his own.'

'Well, yes, but—'

'But, what? But not with you in Hong Kong, hmm? Well, I can't say I'm particularly excited about the prospect myself. I'd always imagined I'd have charge of the London office, as I told you. But—well, Rose thinks I should take over the Far East operation for a while.' He grimaced. 'I guess I can see her point. If she involves me in every aspect of the business, there'll be no chance that I'll—that is—' He broke off abruptly, and Fliss sensed he was rephrasing what he had been going to say. 'Make a hash of it,' he went on eventually. 'I'll be fully equipped to understand what's going on.'

Fliss's breath escaped in a rush. 'And—and when do you expect us to get married?' she ventured, knowing even as she asked the question that his answer would mean nothing to her. She was here, and she was committed to spending this evening with him, but as far as marrying Robert was concerned her father was right: she was having second thoughts. Particularly if he thought he could rush her into it.

Robert's expression lightened. He evidently thought her enquiry meant he had convinced her. 'Oh, I don't know. Shall we say six weeks? I may have to fly out to Hong Kong in the meantime, but that should give you enough time to organise everything. After all,' he grinned, 'it's not as if we have to make an appointment to see the vicar and book the church, is it?'

Fliss said nothing. This was not the time to air her doubts with him. She wanted to discuss the matter with her father first, and if that was an indication of how her feelings towards Robert had changed, then so be it.

All the same, she was not unaware of the enormity of her decision. Until these last few weeks she had anticipated the prospect of her coming wedding with the usual expectancy of any young bride. If she had had any misgivings about their relationship, she had submerged them beneath the belief that what she was doing was right; that Robert loved her, and she loved him.

But James Hastings' death had changed a lot of things, not least her interpretation of Robert's character. Even without her unholy association with Oliver Lynch, she had learned things about her fiancé she had previously not known—or perhaps had ignored. He could be selfish and self-pitying; he could be rude and aggressive—even with her father; and he was also weak where money was concerned, willing to sacrifice his lofty principles, too, if his way of life was threatened.

And that was why she was hesitating, Fliss assured herself grimly. Not because of Oliver Lynch, or through any hope that he cared anything about her. Her opinion of him hadn't changed. She hated and despised him. But she knew she'd never forget him—and that was the hardest cut of all.

CHAPTER ELEVEN

OLIVER accompanied Rose Chen to the club that evening with a curious feeling of detachment. Sitting in the back of the chauffeur-driven limousine, he was aware that he should have been in excellent spirits. After all, he had achieved all he had expected to achieve, and he should have felt elated. But he didn't. He felt cold, ambivalent; indifferent to the success he had contrived.

Which was some admission for a so-called professional to make, he thought wryly. He was actually anticipating the end of this mission with real relief. He had had enough of being Lightfoot's animal. He wanted to be in control of his own life again.

In a fit of nostalgia he had even spoken to his father the day before. The old man had sounded almost emotional over the transatlantic link, and when he'd heard that his son was coming home he'd been genuinely delighted. Oliver had been away for far too long, he said. Both he and his mother couldn't wait for him to settle again in Maple Falls.

Oliver hid a grimace. He didn't really know whether returning to Maple Falls was what he wanted. The truth was, he wanted something he couldn't have. Fliss had taught him there was more to life than death or glory, and a home, and family—even if he had to settle for second-best—had to be better than what he had now.

His only consolation was that Fliss wasn't involved in this rotten business. If she had already been married to Robert Hastings she would have been regarded as guilty by association. As it was, she had a chance to make her life again—even if it wasn't with the man she loved.

He supposed James Hastings' one redeeming feature had been his decision not to involve his son. Or perhaps Robert's free-wheeling lifestyle had saved him from corruption. Either way, James Hastings hadn't considered his son a suitable candidate for the organisation. Rose Chen had been a much more noteworthy advocate, and the fact that she was also his daughter must have lent the arrangement a certain piquancy.

Certainly Rose had proved herself a worthy successor, Oliver reflected now. No one in the London office questioned her orders, and that after only a few short weeks. Which might explain why her father had kept their relationship a secret from her. Had he been afraid she might supersede him? She was obviously less scrupulous, and ruthless to a fault.

She hadn't hesitated before telling her brother the facts of life. Although Oliver hadn't been present at the meeting, the fact that Robert was now involved in the decision-making process had proved that she had seen his ignorance as a danger. Rose worked on the premise that everyone was as self-seeking as herself. Oliver guessed Robert had been warned that threatening Rose was ultimately threatening himself.

In a way, Oliver pitied the younger man. He had looked pretty sick the last time he'd seen him at the office. If he had been as ignorant of what was going on as Oliver now suspected, it must have been a bitter pill to swallow. But weakness was no excuse for complicity.

From Oliver's point of view Robert's involvement was a fairly unimportant development. The computer disk he had copied, and which was presently in the hands of the Royal Mail, was a far more interesting coup. The names and figures it contained might have been meaningless to him, but they were no doubt invaluable to the relevant authorities. It was that which would give Lightfoot the information he needed, which would grant Oliver his freedom.

He sighed. If he had any doubts at all, they concerned the way he had acquired the disk. It had seemed almost too easy. And yet, remembering the things Rose had had on her mind that morning, was it really so surprising that she should have overlooked that one small detail?

The call, saying that the *Oriental Princess* had just docked after being escorted into the Pool of London by Her Majesty's Coastguard had caused the panic. The Chinese vessel, with its consignment of jade and porcelain, gold and Chinese carpets, had been involved in a collision with another vessel in Blackwall Reach, and the Customs and Excise people were showing an inordinate interest in its cargo.

Oliver had pitied the poor captain of the vessel. He knew that the last thing Rose wanted was anyone examining the cargo too closely. She didn't want anyone telling her that the items she was paying so highly to import were not the ancient artefacts she was declaring. The success of the operation depended on the fact that for years no one had suspected that someone who dealt in items that attracted such a swingeing duty could be involved in smuggling.

In consequence, Rose had rushed away to deal with the matter personally, leaving the disk she had been using in the computer. And, taking one of those chances that his life seemed to be composed of recently, Oliver had extracted the disk, carried it into one of the empty offices, and copied it. By the time Rose returned, it was safely back in the computer, and Oliver was somewhere else.

In any case, she trusted him, didn't she? Since he had convinced himself that Fliss was never going to forgive him—not just for taking advantage of her, but also for being involved in Robert's eventual arrest and conviction—he had expended a good deal of time and energy in con-

vincing Rose their relationship hadn't changed. He had
worked hard to suppress his real feelings. Why shouldn't
she trust him? So far as Rose was concerned he was as
ignorant of her real activities as he had ever been. Which
was probably why he was still around, he reflected ruefully.
Anyone who crossed Rose could expect swift retribution,
and if she'd suspected his real motives he might well have
returned home in a body bag.

Nevertheless, Rose was becoming increasingly arrogant,
and it had been only a matter of time before she took complete control of the operation. Her importance to the company, and the fact of her relationship to James Hastings,
had given her an added advantage, and Oliver doubted she
would have allowed Robert to snap at her heels for long.

Oliver gave an inward sigh. It was just as well he was
getting out. His own involvement with Fliss was threatening his objectivity. He was even feeling sorry for Robert,
poor bastard. He was weak and mercenary, no doubt. But
was that really grounds for complete emasculation?

Still, for tonight, at least, he had no choice but to be on
his best behaviour. This dinner party was important to
Rose, and although he suspected the men they were about
to meet were the real criminals here, nothing could alter
the fact that Rose, and Robert—and Amanda Hastings, too,
he suspected—had been perfectly willing to supply a market whose only traffic was in misery.

But meeting these men meant little to Oliver. He could
do nothing to stop them; not personally, at any rate. He was
not foolish enough to think he could be a hero. If these
men disappeared, others would take their place. What
Oliver—and Lightfoot—were trying to do was cut off the
trade at source.

'What are you thinking about, lover?'

Rose Chen's hand on his thigh reminded him of where
he was, and Oliver dragged his thoughts back to the pres-

ent. Until he could leave, until he could get on the plane
back to Hong Kong, he had to continue playing his part. It
wouldn't do to make her suspicious, even if the muscles of
his thigh threatened to reject her possessive fingers.

'Home,' he said swiftly, and not altogether untruthfully.
'I shall miss you when I go back to Hong Kong.'

'Then we'll have to see if we can find you something to
do here in London,' murmured Rose Chen softly. 'Did I
tell you I'm sending Robert to Hong Kong? He and that—
sweet—fiancée of his are going to have to bring their wedding forward. Robert wants to take her with him, naturally,
and I don't think her father would approve of anything
else.'

Oliver swallowed the instinctive retort that rose into his
throat, and then said carefully, 'You're sending Robert to
Hong Kong? Is that wise?'

Rose shrugged. 'It's—expeditious,' she replied, with a
secret smile. 'I'll ask Suntong to keep an eye on him.'

'Mmm.' Oliver could hardly hide his anger. 'I've no
doubt you will.'

'You're not jealous, are you, lover?'

Rose was watching him closely as she spoke, and Oliver
could feel the beads of sweat fairly bursting to break out
on his upper lip. But, 'Jealous?' he managed, with just the
right inflection. 'Of Robert Hastings? Do me a favour.'

'Of his relationship with the Hayton woman,' inserted
Rose impatiently. 'Don't tell me you haven't noticed her,
because I won't believe you.'

Oliver made a supreme effort and forced a reminiscent
smile. 'Oh,' he said, and, realising there was no point in
being unnecessarily obtuse, his lips twisted. 'That.'

'Yes, that,' said Rose tensely. 'Did you sleep with her?'

'Rose!' Oliver gazed at her with wounded eyes, amazed
at his own capacity for deceit. 'What do you take
me for?'

'I take you for an oversexed animal who's had far too much time on his own lately,' declared Rose acidly. 'And don't look at me like that. I know I've been neglecting you. But that's going to change.'

'Is it?' Oliver couldn't believe his luck. Rose was so conceited, she actually believed *she* had been neglecting *him*, and not the other way about.

'Yes,' she said, lifting her hand and cupping his face with strong aggressive fingers. 'I'm thinking of making you my personal assistant. That way, you can stay in London, and I can keep an eye on you.'

'But I thought we were having dinner at the hotel,' Fliss protested, peering out of the grimy windows of the cab. The streets beyond the windows were unfamiliar to her, and, although it should still have been light, a lowering sky and the occasional patter of rain on the windscreen was heralding a wet evening.

'I don't believe I said where we were dining,' replied Robert impatiently. Then, taking a calming breath. 'Besides, I didn't make the arrangements. Rose chose the venue. Blame her if you're not happy.'

Happy!

Fliss pressed her shoulders back against the worn leather upholstery, wishing she had refused to come at all. If only she had known that Robert was going to spring this Hong Kong trip on her. If only she had realised how she really felt, before she'd got herself into this mess.

And there was still the prospect of meeting Oliver to face. How was she going to look at him, and talk to him, without being overwhelmingly aware of how he had last seen her? What had he thought, when he'd left her there among the tumbled bedclothes? Did he despise her now as much as she despised herself?

'What's the matter?' Robert had taken her silence for

sulkiness and, shifting his position, he put his arm along
the back of her seat. 'Did I tell you, you look stunning?'
he asked, deliberately changing tactics. 'Wait until my
mother sees you. She's always asking me what I see in
you. Well, now she's going to know.'

Fliss stiffened, refusing to be disarmed by his attempts
at flattery. As a matter of fact she had decided she disliked
her dress violently. Its amber folds were too revealing, and
the taffeta was too rich.

In fact, she knew the dress suited her very well. Too well
for her to hope to remain unnoticed. But the situation had
changed since she had chosen the dress. Then, she had had
some crazy notion of making Oliver jealous, of showing
him what he'd lost. She'd wanted him to see how unimportant he was to her. Now, all she wanted was for the
evening to be over.

'I didn't know your mother was going to be there,' she
said now, shrinking away from his attempted embrace, and
Robert sighed.

'Well of course she's going to be there!' he exclaimed,
flinging himself back in his seat. 'As one of the major players in this drama, where else would she be?' His lips
twisted. 'Oh, yes, Mama will be present. You don't suppose
she's prepared to give Rose any advantage, do you?'

Fliss frowned. 'But I thought—I mean, that night at the
Grange, your mother seemed to be trying to make
friends—'

'Friends?' Robert snorted. 'Oh, Fliss, sometimes I despair of you, I really do. Do you really think my mother
wants to be friends with someone who's halved her income
at a stroke?'

Fliss shrugged. 'I don't know.'

'No. That's right. You don't,' said Robert flatly. He gave
her a pitying look. 'But you will, soon enough.'

'What do you mean?' Fliss felt anxious. 'Why are you looking at me like that? What's going on?'

Robert dragged his gaze away from her. 'You'll find out,' he said, and then, before Fliss could ask any more questions, he leant forward. 'This is it,' he told the driver. 'You can drop us here.'

Fliss looked about her warily as they got out of the cab. She didn't know what she'd expected when Robert had said they were dining at a club in Chelsea, but she could understand now why he hadn't wanted to bring his own car here. This dingy backwater, with the Thames lapping only a few yards from the end of the alley, was not the salubrious neighbourhood she had imagined. Instead of a doorman and a canopied entrance, there was only a neon sign indicating that the building opposite was indeed a nightclub, and her spirits sank as she anticipated what it must be like inside. What were they doing here? Who could they possibly be going to meet in such sordid surroundings?

'Come on.'

Robert seemed to have no such misgivings, and she had no choice but to follow him across the road, and down the flight of concrete steps that led to the basement entrance.

It crossed her mind as she did so that she was really putting herself in Robert's hands this evening. It was obvious that if she wanted to leave she wasn't going to be able to pick up some passing taxi in this run-down area. Maybe on the Embankment she'd have more luck, but somehow the thought of walking down that alley alone filled her with alarm. No, for her sins, she was compelled to follow her fiancé's lead, and she hoped he had the good sense to keep his wits about him.

They were admitted to the club by a man who could only be described as a bruiser. His scarred and pitted face matched a body as thickly muscled as a boxer's, and his completely bald head was absurdly threatening. Fliss had

the feeling she was having some peculiar kind of nightmare, that this couldn't possibly be happening—not to her.
But although she pinched herself hard she didn't wake up,
and she followed Robert into the club with a fast-beating
heart.

Amazingly, once they were through the rather battered
door, the atmosphere changed completely. Instead of a
smoke-filled room, with worn carpets and grubby table-
cloths, Fliss found herself in a brightly lit foyer, where a
uniformed hat-check girl took their coats. Robert lifted the
velvet cape she had worn to protect herself from the rain
from her shoulders, and handed it over, pocketing the ticket
with a wry smile.

'Not what you expected, is it?'

Fliss had to concede that it wasn't. 'It's very—nice,' she
said lamely, aware of a smell of good food and fine tobacco
emanating from the door to the right. Ahead of them, a
richly carpeted corridor led away to what appeared to be a
casino, and there was muted laughter and low-voiced conversation to calm her fears.

'Nice,' agreed Robert drily. 'Yes, it is, isn't it? Shall we
find the others?'

They found Rose Chen in the elegant bar that adjoined
the dining-room. She was perched on a high stool, swinging
her slim legs; holding court, Fliss thought briefly, and then
felt the air leave her lungs as her eyes encountered Oliver's.

He was propped beside Rose, supported by his elbows
resting on the bar behind him, but it was the sudden darkening of his expression when he saw her that arrested her
breathing. She had thought he would be expecting to see
her. After all, this was a *family* occasion, and she was almost family. But the scowl that crossed his face, and the
sudden chill that entered his eyes, almost froze her where
she stood. He hadn't expected her to be here tonight, that
much was obvious. He hadn't wanted her to be here. He

was looking at her as if he wished he'd never seen her before, and she longed suddenly for the floor to open up and swallow her.

With an effort she forced herself to look at Rose Chen instead, and saw to her relief that the Chinese woman was too busy introducing Robert to the two other men present to have observed that telling exchange. In a scarlet tunic, slit beyond her knee, and embroidered with dragons, she looked foreign and exotic. No man in his right mind would reject Rose's alien fascination in favour of her own milk-and-water colouring, thought Fliss raggedly. She was almost relieved when Amanda Hastings appeared, and gripped her arm in a painful grasp.

'Well, well, you've certainly made an effort this evening, Fliss,' she remarked, in some surprise. 'Is this all for Robert? Or do you find Mr Lynch as fascinating as I do?'

Fliss tried to sound casual. 'I don't know what you mean.'

'No?' Mrs Hastings looked sceptical. 'Well, no matter. Rose isn't likely to let him go. And you'll be safely out of reach in Hong Kong, while Oliver will be staying here in London.'

Fliss wanted to ask her what she meant by that, but before she could ask her to explain, Robert himself grasped her arm and drew her away. 'My fiancée,' he said, and she realised she was being introduced to the two strangers. 'Fliss, this is—'

'Just call me Tony,' the older of the two men interrupted him easily. 'And this is Vinny,' he added, nodding towards the younger man. 'We're business acquaintances of your fiancé and his family.' He smiled, his rather swarthy features not unattractive in the subdued lighting of the bar. 'It's good to meet you—Fliss, isn't it? I'm pleased to see Jamie's son has his father's good taste.'

'Thank you.'

Fliss smiled and acknowledged the compliment, but she wasn't happy being the centre of attraction. Rose was watching her now, and she could feel Oliver's eyes too, boring into her back.

She accepted a glass of white wine, and then positioned herself well away from the hub of the gathering. Robert had a glass of whisky in his hand, and that seemed to give him all the confidence he needed. Conversation became general, and it wasn't necessary for her to take any part in it. She was quite content to let the others do the talking, listening only desultorily when Robert took the floor.

All the same, she didn't think she liked the way he was attempting to sell himself to the two men, Tony and Vinny. They weren't representative of Hastings' usual clients, she was sure, and she could only assume Rose Chen had invited them to join them. The business acquaintances James Hastings had invited to Sutton Grange—the ones Fliss had met anyway—had been like him: vain, perhaps; pompous, certainly; but basically respectable people. Tony and Vinny weren't like that. They weren't like that at all.

It was strange, because she didn't exactly know what they were like, except that she didn't like them. They were respectably dressed. Their suits were immaculate, their linen whiter than a soap powder commercial. Oliver looked positively sinister beside them. Yet, she'd trust him before she'd trust the others.

'What the—hell—are you doing here?'

Oliver's voice sounded absurdly loud in her ear, and the hesitation before that rather mild epithet was a measure of what he had really wanted to say.

Fliss glanced anxiously at her fiancé, convinced he must have heard Oliver, too, but Robert was too busy ingratiating himself with their guests. He and Rose seemed to be competing for the two men's attention, the Chinese woman's eyes scornful as she watched her half-brother struggling to gain an advantage.

No one appeared to have noticed Oliver's casual removal of himself from one end of the bar to the other. Or if they had, they didn't connect it with Fliss. A quick glance up into his dark face elicited the information that he wasn't even looking at her as he spoke, and Fliss's pulse raced alarmingly as she acknowledged her helpless awareness of his nearness.

'I don't think it's anything to do with you what I do,' she replied at last, in low terse tones. 'And don't worry. I'm not here to tell your girlfriend you've been unfaithful to her!'

It was a calculated risk reminding him of that. By turning the tables on him, she hoped to gain the advantage. If he thought he could intimidate her, he was mistaken. He had just as much to lose as she had. More, in fact, if what Robert said was true.

Oliver swore then, making no concession to her sensitivities this time. 'Believe me,' he said, permitting himself a scathing glance at her shocked face, 'that's the least of my worries.'

Fliss swallowed a mouthful of her wine. 'You don't expect me to believe that.'

'Don't I?' Oliver's mouth curled. 'Trust me, Fliss. I know what I'm talking about.'

Fliss gave him a resentful look. 'I suppose you think she's so infatuated with you, she wouldn't care,' she exclaimed, and Oliver swore again.

'No—'

'Well, I don't believe you. I've seen the way she looks at you. If she knew—'

'Dammit, Fliss, will you quit talking about something of which you know nothing!' Oliver breathed heavily in her ear, and then, calming himself, he went on, 'I don't give a

damn what Rose thinks.' He paused, and then continued,
'I should. It's what I'm paid to do, goddamit. But I don't.
It's you I care about. Now—do you want to tell me what's
going on?'

Fliss stared at him, open-mouthed. 'Oliver—'

'Stop it,' he muttered. 'Stop looking at me like that, and
get to the point. I want to know what you're doing here.
What did Hastings tell you, for God's sake? Did he inform
you who these men are?'

Fliss's throat closed up. 'I—Tony and Vinny,' she said
helplessly, trying to instill some strength back into her
bones. What had he meant? He *cared* about her?
Particularly when he'd just admitted that Rose was supporting him.

'I know their names,' he grated, raising the glass he was
holding to his lips. 'I meant, do you know the purpose of
this meeting?'

'What do you—?'

'Forget it.' Oliver gave her a warning look. 'Just tell me
you've never met them before.'

'But—why?'

'Have you met them before?' His pale eyes narrowed,
and she shivered, as much in apprehension at his expression
as anything else.

'No,' she conceded at last. 'As far as I know, they're
just clients.' She hesitated. 'Rob seems to like them. And—
and Rose is practically falling over herself to be polite.'

'Yes.' Oliver finished his drink, and set the empty glass
on the bar. 'I noticed.'

Fliss's stomach twisted. 'You're jealous!' she exclaimed,
aware as she said the words that, whatever kind of relationship he had with the other woman, she was jealous too.

But Oliver only gave her a pitying look. 'As if,' he said,

pushing his hands into his jacket pockets. He looked down at her searchingly for a moment, and then shook his head. 'Nice dress,' he commented mockingly, before walking back to Rose.

CHAPTER TWELVE

FLISS closed the door of her hotel room behind her and turned the key with trembling fingers. Then, dropping her handbag on to the bed, she walked unsteadily into the bathroom.

She reached the basin just in time. She was sick, violently sick, and even after the awful retching had ceased she could hardly lift her head. Oh, God, she thought, wiping her mouth with shaking fingers. Oh God, what was she going to do? Hastings' weren't just importing antiques, they were importing heroin. Robert's father hadn't made his fortune from selling Chinese porcelain, he'd made it from selling drugs.

She couldn't believe it. She didn't want to believe it. Pushers, dealers, addicts; they were words that belonged to another world. The ruthless men who exploited human suffering for their own gain were gangsters, criminals, villains of low repute. They corrupted people's lives, and were themselves corrupted in the process. But the law was there to deal with them. There was nothing any ordinary citizen could do.

People like her—people who lived decent, honest lives—didn't get involved with such things. They read about them in the morning newspapers, they discussed them over the cornflakes. But they didn't really understand what was actually going on.

God! Fliss drew a trembling breath. It didn't seem possible that people like the Hastingses, who appeared to be so respectable, who lived in the heart of the country and invited the local magistrate to dinner, could participate in such a business.

And yet, with hindsight, she could imagine James Hastings enjoying the deception. It must have given him a great deal of pleasure over the years. However dubious his claim to being lord of the manor had been, the fact remained that Sutton Grange had been bought with tainted money. While the villagers had thought he'd been desperate for acceptance, James Hastings must have been laughing at them behind their backs.

And no one had found out. No one had suspected he was anything other than what he seemed. But he had obviously recognised that his son was an unlikely prospect to follow in his footsteps. What a pity Rose Chen hadn't done the same. If she hadn't involved Robert, Robert couldn't have involved her.

Fliss dragged herself up and stared at her reflection in the mirror. God, she looked awful! She doubted even her father would recognise her if he could see her now. She looked so pale and hollow-eyed. She looked like an addict herself.

She sighed. She was fairly sure Robert hadn't intended to be so indiscreet. But, as far as he was concerned, the evening had gone so well that he had drunk more than he could handle.

Rose Chen had realised the danger. Long before Tony and Vinny—was that really their names?—had exhibited any intention of drawing the evening to a close, she had been making it clear that she thought Robert had had enough. Remarks like, 'I think Fliss is getting bored,' or 'Don't you think Fliss looks tired?' were pointed suggestions to take his fiancée back to the hotel. But Robert had been having such a good time, he hadn't wanted to leave.

And he hadn't said anything precisely incriminating in their company, Fliss remembered unwillingly. With

Oliver's—as well as Rose's—eyes upon him, he had been careful not to blot his copybook. In any case, she had been so busy coping with her own chaotic feelings, she'd scarcely paid attention to what he had said. But she'd sensed no air of tension as they'd bade them all goodnight.

For herself, she'd been glad to be leaving. The private room, the expertly cooked dinner, the wine which, although she had had little of it, was evidently from a distinctive vineyard, had meant nothing to her. It was the devious game Oliver was playing that had occupied her thoughts. And why, when he'd admitted in so many words that Rose paid his bills, did she care what he did?

Then, on the way home in the chauffeur-driven limousine Tony had lent them, her world had fallen apart. In Robert's boastful ramblings she had heard her father's name disparaged, and when she'd cautioned him about it he'd exposed how he really felt.

It had been disjointed, at first. The resentment Robert felt towards her father mixed up with assertions of the success he was going to make of the business. Matthew Hayton was going to feel pretty sick, he said, when he found out how important Robert really was. *He* wasn't just some poxy country vicar, he added. He had real power.

Of course, Fliss had made excuses for him at first. He had had too much to drink, he was over-excited, and although she'd protested that her father would have nothing but praise if Robert did make a success of his life, she'd consoled herself with the thought he was going to feel pretty sick himself in the morning.

Then Robert's meanderings had taken a different turn. Fumbling in his jacket pocket, he had produced what appeared, in the passing street lights, to be a lacquered snuff box. It was small, and oval-shaped, with a painted lid and a release catch on one side.

Leaning towards her, he had extended the hand holding

the snuff box, and tapped his nose conspiratorially. 'Wanna try the merchandise?' he'd asked, with a defiant glance at the chauffeur, and Fliss, who'd assumed at first it must be a valuable item, had resignedly taken the box from him.

'Open it,' Robert directed eagerly, his whisky-laden breath unpleasantly close to her ear, and Fliss obediently pressed the catch.

She didn't know what she had expected might be inside. Snuff, perhaps; or a precious jewel. Either way, she wasn't particularly interested when she opened it, and the sprinkling of white power that spilled onto her lap as she did so was just an irritation.

It took Robert five seconds to disabuse her of that notion. His smothered oath, as he snatched the box back from her, and his added, 'Be careful, can't you?' were powerful deterrents. She'd never seen a narcotic substance in its purest form before, but she had seen pictures. And the way Robert was glaring at her was explanation enough.

'Is that—?'

'What do you think?' snapped Robert impatiently, as the chauffeur glanced curiously over his shoulder. 'One hundred per cent pure, and you throw it about like confetti! For God's sake, Fliss, this is the breath of life to some poor bastard!'

Fliss couldn't clearly remember what she'd done next. The idea that Robert and his family might be involved in smuggling drugs had seemed too incredible to be true. She thought she'd looked at him with a little of the horror she was feeling in her face, and Robert had seemed to realise— belatedly—that he might have gone too far.

With an impatient shake of his head, he'd slipped the box back into his pocket, and started talking about something else. By the time the chauffeur dropped them at the hotel, she could almost believe she'd imagined the whole thing.

Almost…

As soon as Robert left her—he needed a nightcap, he said, and the bar was still open for residents—the enormity of what had happened had swept over her. Going up to her room in the lift, the nausea that had later become a reality had gripped her. Did he know what he'd done? she wondered. Or was he too full of Scotch to care? Would he remember what had happened in the morning? If she challenged him and he denied it, she had no proof.

She looked down at her skirt suddenly, but the tiny grains of—of what? cocaine? heroin?—had all disappeared. In any case, no one would believe her. Even if she went to the authorities, it was only her word against his.

She shivered suddenly as another thought struck her. If Robert was implicated, Oliver must be implicated, too. It seemed fairly obvious that Rose Chen was at the heart of it. And anyone who lived with her had to know what was going on.

Her breath escaped on a long sigh. Oh, God! Was it only a matter of hours ago that she'd thought the only problem she had was telling Robert she couldn't marry him? How could she tell him now? What was he likely to say? He'd be sure to think it had some bearing on what had occurred this evening. He might not let her go, knowing he had betrayed himself to her.

There was an element of farce to the whole affair, she thought tremulously. But the wild laughter that bubbled in her throat was pure hysteria. Things like this just didn't happen, she told herself unsteadily. Not to women like her, who just wanted a quiet life.

She wished she could blame Oliver. She would have liked to convince herself that this was all his fault. And it was true that until he and Rose Chen came along she had led a fairly placid existence. But it was James Hastings who was the real offender. James Hastings, whose death had set these wheels in motion.

She wondered suddenly how long Robert had known about his father's imperfections. Not long, she suspected, remembering the day of the London meeting, and the strange expression he'd worn when he'd told her he'd been offered a seat on the board. Her father had said that James Hastings had never taken his son seriously. Or perhaps he'd never trusted him to keep his mouth shut.

Whatever, the knowledge that Oliver had made a fool of her, not once but several times, was what hurt the most. As she turned away from the mirror and stumbled back into the bedroom, she wondered why he'd bothered to take the time. Unless—as she'd thought before—it was his way of fooling Robert. It must have given him a great deal of satisfaction to take what Robert had never had...

When someone knocked at the door, Fliss nearly jumped out of her skin. The last thing she had expected was that Robert would trouble her again tonight, and she didn't know if she could even speak to him without betraying how devastated she felt. There was no question of her opening the door. Apart from anything else, she had no desire for anyone to see her in her present state. But tomorrow morning she hoped to have her emotions under control again.

The knock came again, more imperative this time, and she realised she couldn't allow him to wake up the whole floor. This was a respectable hotel, and she had no wish for the management to think that she was anything less than respectable.

She hesitated only a moment, and then went unwillingly nearer. 'Go away, Rob,' she said, in clear, if slightly unsteady tones. 'I'm going to bed.'

'It's not Rob,' a woman responded impatiently and Fliss's lips parted as she recognised Rose Chen's voice. 'I want to talk to you. Open the door.'

Fliss swallowed. 'Um—no—' Her eyes darted desperately around the room, as if looking for a way of escape. 'We've got nothing to say.'

'I disagree.' Rose rattled the handle, and Fliss could imagine how angry she must be to find her way thwarted. 'Open the door, Fliss, unless you want me to cause a scene. I'm quite prepared to say I'm your lover and you won't let me in.'

'You wouldn't!'

Fliss was against the door now, her cheek pressed to the panels, and she distinctly heard Rose's scornful laugh. 'Wouldn't I?' Rose taunted. 'Do you want to take that risk?' Then, 'For pity's sake, open the door. I'm not going to hurt you.'

Fliss straightened. 'What do you want?'

'Let me in and I'll tell you.'

'Robert's not here.'

'I know that.' Rose uttered an impatient sigh. 'You ordered him away, remember? And before you ask, he's not with me.'

'Where is he?'

'Does it matter?' Rose was getting more and more frustrated. 'Drowning his sorrows in the bar, I should imagine. Isn't that usually what he does when he's in trouble?'

'In trouble?'

'Open the door.' Rose was through with trading arguments. 'This is your last chance, Fliss. Any more delay, and I'm going to start shouting.'

Fliss swallowed hard. Then, aware that Rose had her over a barrel, she unlocked the door and opened it. Apart from her own fears, her father would never survive the kind of publicity that would ensue if Rose made good her threat.

Rose was alone. As she stalked into the hotel room, Fliss realised she'd never asked her if she was. For all she knew, Oliver could have been with her.

'Close the door.'

Aware that, for the present, Rose was calling all the shots, Fliss did as she was told. But when she turned around she felt a sudden surge of resentment. This woman wouldn't have caused a scene. She had too much to lose. She'd got in here under false pretences, and Fliss was all kinds of a fool for believing her.

However, Rose's first words prevented the accusation that sprang instantly to her lips. 'You look ghastly!' she sneered scornfully. 'If I didn't know better, I'd say you were desperate for a fix!'

Fliss caught her breath. 'And you'd know, wouldn't you?' she declared recklessly, realising as soon as she'd done so that she'd played right into Rose's hands.

'Would I?' she said, adjusting the fur boa she was wearing across her shoulders. 'Now why would you think that, I wonder? Could it be that my dear brother's been a little indiscreet?'

Fliss took a deep breath and tried to slow her thinking down. No matter how provocative Rose might be, she had to control her panic. She wasn't used to playing this game, whereas Rose knew all the moves.

'I don't know what you mean,' she said now, aware that it was hardly a satisfactory response. 'What do you want? What are you doing here? I'm tired. I'd like to get some sleep.'

'Would you?' Rose regarded her with pitying eyes. Then, tucking the black clutch bag she was carrying beneath her arm, she shrugged her shoulders. 'Well, we don't always get what we want. At least, not in the way that we want it.'

Fliss straightened her spine. 'Is that supposed to mean something?'

'It might.' Rose's lips twisted. 'Don't get clever with me, Fliss. You don't know any of the answers.'

Fliss tried to look confident. 'And you do, I suppose.'

'More than you,' agreed the other woman wryly. 'Though even I don't pretend to know everything.'

'You surprise me.'

Fliss's words were muffled, but Rose heard them, and her eyes glittered dangerously. 'Wait until you hear what I have to say, before you make any more mistakes,' she warned harshly. 'I don't believe you're stupid, and you've got such a lot to lose.'

Fliss pressed her lips together. 'Is that another threat?'

'No. It's the truth,' replied Rose evenly. 'Now—I assume your present appearance is down to your fiancé. And as he's far too drunk to get it—well—' She broke off mockingly. 'Let's just say he hasn't got romance on his mind tonight.'

Fliss coloured. She couldn't help it. It wasn't that what Rose had said had shocked her. It was simply an acknowledgement of her own less than competent state.

'Right.' Rose took her silence for assent, and continued smoothly, 'So we have to suspect that something else has happened to disturb you. And, although I can imagine many things my brother might say which would cause me to want to throw up, you must see him differently. You're going to marry him.'

Am I? The words trembled on Fliss's tongue, but this time she had the sense not to say them. She told herself she wasn't scared exactly, but Rose's coming here had unnerved her. If Hastings' were involved in drug smuggling, it would be unwise to make any unwary statements. She'd already made one mistake. She mustn't make a second.

'He did say something, didn't he?' Rose prompted, after a moment, and although Fliss felt safer on her feet, she forced herself to perch on the end of the bed.

'Perhaps,' she conceded at last, realising there was no point in prevaricating. But her knees felt even weaker, now

that she was sitting down. She should have remained standing. She doubted she could get up again even if she'd
wanted to.

'You don't have to lie to me, Fliss,' Rose exclaimed, and
now she offered the other woman a mocking smile. 'Joe—
Tony's chauffeur—' she inserted, by way of an explanation
'—he heard everything. The idiot showed you the snuff
box, didn't he? I warned him to wait until you were married, but Robert never did have any sense. If you'd heard
what his father—what *my* father—used to say about him!'
She grimaced. 'Oh, well, I suppose it takes all sorts. One
day you must tell me what you see in him. I'd really like
to know.'

Fliss kept silent with a supreme effort. Rose was clever,
she'd give her that. This cosy conversation was not just an
attempt to gain her confidence. Mixed in with a kind of
homespun tolerance were comments designed to promote a
response. If she damned Robert, she damned herself, but if
she defended him, would Rose believe her?

'Well?' the Chinese woman demanded at last. 'I'm right,
aren't I? Robert did show you the stuff. Do I take it you
can't handle it?'

Fliss swallowed. It was hard, harder than she could have
imagined to find the right approach. Any casual reaction
was obviously faked, but she mustn't behave as if it meant
her engagement was over.

'You'll have to give me some time,' she said finally. 'It
was a—shock.'

Rose's eyes narrowed. 'I'll bet.'

Fliss waited for her to say something else, but she didn't.
And, realising it was up to her to try and convince the
woman she wasn't about to go screaming for the police,
she added, 'I never suspected, you see. Rob—Rob's father
was so—discreet.'

'That's one way of putting it.' Rose hesitated. 'You see

now why I want you and—Rob—to go to Hong Kong. He has told you about going to Hong Kong, hasn't he? I think it could be the making of him.'

Or the breaking of him, Fliss thought, with a pang. If it didn't work out, there were ways of dealing with him. Oh, lord, she thought hysterically, was she really thinking that?

'He mentioned it,' she admitted now, hoping Rose wouldn't ask what her response had been. Oh, God, oh, God! What was she going to do?

'Good.' To her relief, Rose seemed to accept her offering, and then, with one of her sudden swings of mood, she said harshly, 'I'm glad you're being so astute. I'd hate to have had to involve your father. From what Oliver tells me, he's a rather sweet old man.'

Fliss's jaw sagged. 'What does my father have to do with anything?' she exclaimed, forgetting for the moment that she had determined not to say anything rash, and Rose regarded her coldly.

'Why—he's our safeguard, of course,' she replied, a long red nail flicking carelessly at her fur coat. 'A—hostage to fortune,' she added without emotion. 'I believe that's the current phrase. I'll have Oliver keep an eye on him. While you're all those miles away.'

CHAPTER THIRTEEN

'No—' The word slipped out. Fliss couldn't stop it. It was just impossible to imagine marrying Robert now, with or without the prospect of living in Hong Kong. 'That is—' She struggled to control her panic, striving desperately to find the proper words. 'My father isn't involved in this. I don't want him to know.'

'Oh, he won't.' Rose uttered a short laugh. 'At least, not so long as you're a good girl. Robert may be foolhardy, but I assure you I'm not. No, I hear your father likes Oliver. They're becoming quite good friends.'

Fliss felt sick. 'You think so?' she said bitterly, hardly knowing what she was saying in her distress. Was that why Oliver had insinuated himself into their lives? Had his intention only been to neutralise the opposition all along?

'What do you mean?'

Rose's sudden reversion to menace was frightening. Taking a step towards Fliss, she fixed her with an inimical stare, her red mouth thin and threatening.

Fliss licked her lips, unaware at first that she had caused this aggression. 'I don't know what you're talking about,' she said blankly, gripping the edge of the bed with nervous fingers. 'If—if you've said all you came for, I'd really like you to go.'

'I bet you would.' Rose stepped nearer, and to Fliss's dismay, she took a hold of her arm. 'What did you mean when you implied there was some doubt about Oliver's friendship with your father? Is there something more behind it? You'd better tell me, because I mean to find out.'

166

Fliss gulped. 'Let go of me.'

'When I'm ready,' Rose's fingers were amazingly strong, her nails digging into Fliss's flesh. 'Come on, damn you, tell me the truth! What are you hiding?'

'Nothing!' But Fliss was a little scared now. She dreaded to think what Rose would do if she found out that she and Oliver had...

'I don't believe you.' Rose was persistent. Her dark brows descended. 'If I thought your father suspected the truth—'

'Daddy?' Fliss's breath escaped on a strangled laugh. 'You're not serious!' Her relief was such that she was in danger of over-playing her hand. 'I mean—it's not possible. He's a vicar!'

Rose was not convinced. 'You thought Jay-Jay was just an antique dealer,' she reminded her. 'Few of us are what we seem.'

Fliss trembled. 'Who—who is Jay-Jay?'

'Robert's father, of course.' Rose was not diverted. 'So, if your father is just a vicar, why shouldn't I believe Oliver when he tells me your old man is a pushover?'

Fliss's lips tightened. Was that really what Oliver had said? That her father was a pushover? But, perhaps he hadn't been talking about her father at all...

'I haven't said you shouldn't,' she muttered now, seemingly incapable of saying anything that wouldn't evoke an aggressive response. If only Rose would go.

Her nails dug into Fliss's arm suddenly, drawing blood, and she couldn't suppress the cry of protest that escaped her. There was an expression of such malevolence on Rose's face that for a moment she thought she was going to strike her.

But Rose's voice was almost conciliatory when she spoke. 'I know,' she said softly. 'You're afraid I'll find out about your little affair with Oliver.' Her lips were mocking.

'Oh, Fliss, what a lot you've got to learn. I know all about *that*!'

Fliss felt sick. Even though she wouldn't have believed it possible in the circumstances, nausea welled like a bitter bile in the back of her throat. Oliver had told her! He had told Rose all about their sordid little coupling. Oh, God, how could he? And still pretend to care about her?

But, lost in her misery as she was, she wasn't paying any attention to Rose's reaction to her silence. For as if that silence was an admission in itself, the older woman suddenly issued a hoarse cry. 'I knew it,' she grated. 'I knew the bastard couldn't keep out of your bed!' And, with a sudden switch to violence, she brought her hand back and slapped Fliss full across the face.

'I shouldn't do that again, Rose.'

The hard male voice startled both of them, and Fliss, her head still ringing from the blow, was hardly relieved to see someone who at that moment seemed to be the instigator of all her troubles.

But at least Oliver's appearance caused Rose to release her, even if any reprieve she had had was only likely to be temporary. With an angry exclamation, the Chinese woman turned on her erstwhile lover like an enraged tigress, glaring at him savagely, and spitting out a stream of invective that happily Fliss couldn't understand.

Oliver, who had been propped against the doorpost, pushed himself upright, and allowed the door to swing closed behind him. Fliss didn't know how long he'd been there, but he seemed unperturbed by Rose's tirade, his eyes moving briefly over her flushed and dishevelled appearance before returning to the woman before him. He was a bastard, she thought painfully, covering her burning cheek with a protective hand. He actually seemed to be enjoying this.

'That's humanly impossible, Rose,' he remarked finally, giving some indication of what his girlfriend had been saying. 'Now, why don't you calm down, and we'll talk about this like civilised people?'

'Civilised!' Rose fairly choked on the word. 'Don't talk to me about civilised! If it wasn't enough that that fool brother of mine had spilled his guts, now I have to deal with you as well.'

Oliver's eyes narrowed. 'Robert's told someone else?' he asked evenly and Rose gave him a wary look.

'Someone else?' she echoed faintly. 'What are you talking about?'

Oliver took a deep breath and, having successfully diverted her attention from Fliss, pushed his hands into the packets of his trousers. 'Nothing,' he denied carelessly. 'I always thought it was a mistake to trust him, that's all.'

Rose stared at him intently. 'What would you know about it?' she exclaimed. 'You know nothing about antiques.'

'No.' Oliver conceded the point. 'But I know about heroin, and that's what we're really talking about here. Face it, Rose. I wasn't born yesterday.'

The Chinese woman continued to stare at him in silence, but Fliss guessed Rose's brain was working as energetically as her own. Of course, Fliss had assumed Oliver knew what was happening all along. But it didn't make any difference. They were all implicated really—the Hastingses, Rose, Oliver—and the various levels of their involvement didn't mean a thing.

'How did you find out?' Rose asked at last. 'Did Robert tell you?'

'No way.' Oliver regarded her impatiently. 'I was in Vietnam, Rose. I learned to live by my wits. And not knowing who your enemy is is the quickest way to lose your life.'

Rose frowned. 'You think I'm your enemy?'

'No.' Oliver was quick to deny that. 'But your father

was. You know he never liked me, Rose. He was always looking for some way to separate us.'

Rose seemed to have forgotten there was anyone else present, and Fliss wished she could just slip out of the door and escape. She didn't want to hear this. She didn't want to know how long Oliver had been Rose's lover, and how he had outwitted her father. She didn't want to hear this. She just wanted to go home, and forget any of this had ever happened.

'You knew about us, before my father died?' Rose was saying now, and although Fliss knew in some curious way that Oliver didn't really want to admit it, he nodded his head. 'You knew about my father?'

'And if I did?'

'Why didn't you tell me?' Rose was sounding less shocked than disbelieving now, though there was no denying her attention was totally focused on the man. 'Lee, if you knew, why didn't you let me know before we came to London. You knew I needed some support. You could have helped me.'

'It's a long story,' said Oliver flatly, and Rose gave him a scornful look.

'It must be,' she agreed, with sudden anger. 'Where did you get your information? And why do I get the feeling I don't want to know?'

Oliver drew a breath. 'I have my sources, Rose. You're not the only one in Hong Kong with a line on what's going down. Think about it, can't you? Do you really believe I can't recognise the signs?'

Rose scowled. 'I'm not a user!'

'No? But I was.' Oliver's mouth curled. 'Come off it, Rose, Hastings knew exactly what he was doing.'

Rose moved her head from side to side. 'I don't believe this.'

'Why?' Oliver appeared to be gaining confidence, and

Fliss, who was still reeling from the shock of his confession, closed her eyes against the triumph in his face. 'I think it's time you offered me a piece of the action. I've certainly got more—' he looked at Fliss, and amended his words '—guts—than your brother.'

What happened then seemed afterwards to happen in slow motion. Fliss saw Oliver pull his hands out of his pockets, and Rose, who must have believed he was carrying a gun, groped awkwardly for her bag. It was ludicrous really, because all Oliver did was spread his hands towards her, but the bullet that caught him in the chest was all too unhappily real.

'Bitch!' he said chokingly, falling back against a chair, and then the door was flung open behind him, and three other men with automatics burst into the room...

Fliss's father collected her from the hospital the following morning. The authorities had wanted to contact him the night before, but she had insisted on them waiting until it was light. She was all right, after all. They had only kept her in the hospital overnight for observation. She was tired, and a little shaky, but not injured. Well, not in body anyway, she amended. Her mind—her psyche—was something else.

Matthew Hayton didn't say anything until they had cleared the city centre, concentrating on his driving, and giving his daughter time to marshall her thoughts. He was more concerned with her white face than with any physical pain she might have suffered. He had the feeling it would take her more than twenty-four hours to recover from the shock.

But, when they were safely on the M40 heading westward, he felt compelled to say something, *anything*, to bring some life back into her pale features. However loath she was to discuss what had happened, she really ought to talk about it. Bottling it up was not going to help, and not everyone would be as understanding as himself.

She'd already been told that the police would want to speak to her again within the next couple of days. She had made a preliminary statement, but there was more, much more, that they would have to discuss with her. Not least, how much she had known about her fiancé's business; and why she hadn't called the police as soon as she'd learned the truth.

'Tough night,' commented Matthew Hayton softly, and Fliss turned a strained face in his direction.

'Mmm,' she murmured, finding it difficult to speak at all without breaking down. 'Um—thanks for coming to get me. You don't know how good it is to—to—'

'I can imagine,' her father interrupted her gently. 'I'm just sorry I didn't see this coming. It's not as if I haven't heard gossip about Hastings in the past. But a man in my profession is only supposed to see the good in people. And casting doubts on a man's character does seem a rather un-Christian thing to do.'

'Oh, Daddy!'

'Well.' He sighed. 'It's over now. From what the officer told me, I gather both Robert and his mother have been arrested. They'd apparently been suspicious of their operation of some time. The arrival of the daughter only accelerated the proceedings.'

'Yes.' Fliss didn't really want to discuss it. The success of the police operation, and her own rescue at their hands, meant nothing. All she could see was Oliver's face when Rose Chen fired her gun.

'It was a shame anyone had to be injured,' went on Matthew Hayton ruefully. 'Although I suppose Lynch was as guilty as the rest.' He paused. 'Whatever you say, I know you liked him, Felicity. But you could never have had a life with a man like him.'

'Do you mind if we don't talk about it?' Fliss stared blindly through the car's window, trying to make some sense of her mixed emotions. She hadn't cared about Oliver Lynch, she'd despised him. So why did she mourn him now that he was dead?

'If you insist.' Matthew Hayton gave her a sideways glance. 'But you're going to have to talk about it soon, darling. I'm sorry, but it won't just go away.'

Fliss bent her head. 'I know.'

Her father hesitated. 'That bruise, on your cheek—did Lynch do that?'

'No!' Fliss lifted her hand and laid her palm along her jawline. 'I—it was Rose—Rose Chen.' She licked her lips, and then added in a muffled voice, 'Oliver prevented her from hitting me again, actually. If—if he hadn't followed her back to the hotel, who knows what might have happened.' She sniffed, and then murmured barely audibly, 'Who knows? He might have got away.'

'And you'd have been glad if he had?' her father suggested, proving his hearing was still as sharp as ever, and Fliss gave him a defensive look.

'Perhaps.'

'In other words, you were attracted to him,' Matthew Hayton declared forcefully. 'Oh, Felicity, the man was a criminal!'

'So was—is—Robert,' she retorted painfully, and her father shook his head.

'Even so…'

Fliss stifled a sob. 'Well, it doesn't matter anyway, does it?' she asked him unsteadily. 'As you've just said, it's over. At least you won't have to worry about me ever seeing him again.'

CHAPTER FOURTEEN

'I'M LEAVING now, Felicity. Are you sure you don't want to change your mind and come, too?'

'Quite sure, thanks.'

Fliss looked up at her father and endeavoured to appear apologetic and nothing else. It wouldn't do for him to think she was still depressed. In the last two weeks, since she had learned there was to be an epilogue to her relationship with Oliver, she had made a concerted effort to assuage her grief.

'Well, if that's your final word...' Matthew Hayton regarded his daughter with a disturbingly shrewd gaze. Whatever she thought, he knew she was still suffering. And there was something she wasn't telling him, of that he had no doubt.

'It's so cosy here,' exclaimed Fliss, from the comfortable depths of her father's armchair. She spread the skirt of her navy pinafore dress over her legs, and smiled appealingly. He couldn't know that the book in her hand was unread. The picture she presented was surely convincing enough. 'It's raining,' she added. 'You go and enjoy the play. You can tell me all about it when you get back.'

Her father looked as if he might object but, then, with a resigned shake of his head, he buttoned his overcoat. 'I suppose it isn't the most exciting prospect,' he agreed. 'Amateur dramatics aren't really my line either, and the church hall isn't the warmest place on a chilly autumn evening.'

'I'm sure you'll enjoy it,' Fliss assured him firmly, and he pulled a wry face.

'I just don't like leaving you alone, that's all.' He shook his head, and then went on reluctantly, 'Whatever you say, I know you're still fretting over—over that man, Oliver Lynch.'

'Oh, Dad!'

'I know I'm right.' Matthew Hayton gave in to the urge to seek her confidence yet again. 'Ever since the authorities decided you couldn't help them any more, you've refused to talk about what happened, about *him*. I'm sure it would be better if you—'

'Not now, Dad.' Fliss spread the folds of her skirt over her knees, realising she would have to talk to her father sooner or later. 'Um—you're going to be late—'

'Do you think I care?' Her father gazed at her worriedly. 'You're not deceiving me, you know, Felicity. Was he really worth all this soul-searching?'

Fliss sighed. 'No,' she admitted, after a moment. She concentrated on the glowing embers burning in the grate. 'No, I don't suppose he was. But give me time, Dad. It is only three months.'

'Three months.' Matthew Hayton raised his eyes heavenward. 'It seems like three years!'

'Oh, Daddy.' Fliss looked at her father for a moment, and then unfolding her legs, she got to her feet. 'I love you,' she said, going to kiss his cheek. 'And we will talk, I promise. Maybe tomorrow, hmm?'

'Tomorrow,' he agreed warmly, hugging her in return. 'I won't let you forget.'

'OK.' She accompanied him to the door. 'Now—enjoy your evening. I intend to enjoy mine.'

But after her father had gone Fliss trudged back into the living-room on rather heavier feet. It wasn't easy trying to behave as if it was only a matter of time before she snapped out of her misery. The way she felt at the moment, it was hard to believe she'd ever get over it.

To begin with, she had had a lot to occupy her. The police investigation, the interviews, the questions; they might not have helped to ease her pain, but they had given her something else to think about. But that was all over now. The court case was still pending, of course, but it didn't look as if her evidence was going to be needed. Robert had broken down during his interrogation, and his evidence had gone a long way in implicating his mother. They were both in custody now, the house was closed up, and the twins, whom Fliss had felt sorry for, had been despatched to distant relatives in Scotland.

Of course, she knew Rose Chen had been arrested too, but in her case the charges would include murder. Oliver's murder, she thought, with the agonising ache she always felt when she thought of him. Whatever else Rose was convicted of, his death would always be on her conscience.

The urge to weep swept over her, but she forced herself not to give in to her tears. Tears wouldn't help her. They wouldn't help the tiny pulse of life that lived inside her. Her father was right. They had to talk. He might not be able to forgive her when he knew.

Looking down, she shaped the curve of her stomach with searching hands. As yet there was little to see. Certainly nothing was visible through her clothes. But when she was naked, when she stood in front of her dressing-table mirror and studied her body, it was a different story. The solid little mound of her pregnancy was unmistakable.

Dropping her hands, she moved back to the chair and picked up her book. It was just as well her father was used to seeing her in loose shirts and dresses. As yet he'd made no point of the fact that she'd stopped wearing trousers. But it was nearly four months now. She would have to tell him soon.

She sat down, and the book dropped unheeded from her

fingers. A baby, she thought, still with a certain amount of incredulity. Oliver's baby. He never would have the chance to learn that he was going to become a father. Would it have made a difference? Would he have asked her to wait for him until he was free?

More to the point, would she have done it? she wondered unhappily. But it was only a fleeting thought. She knew that if Oliver had asked her, she'd have followed him to the ends of the earth.

It was ironic really. When Robert had asked her to go with him to Hong Kong she'd instinctively fought against it. Yet she knew she'd have lived anywhere with Oliver. With him, she'd learned what loving someone could mean.

Did that make her a bad person? she wondered. How would her father feel when he learned what she had done? Nothing could alter the fact that she had betrayed her promises. And he was going to have to face his parishioners in the face of her disgrace.

Of course, everyone would think it was Robert's baby, and that was something else she was going to have to deal with. There was no way she was going to let her child grow up not knowing who his real father was. Oliver's death might not have been an heroic one, but he had been protecting her.

The sound of a car drawing up outside brought a look of anxiety to her face. Obviously someone didn't know her father was attending the amateur dramatic society's production at the church hall this evening. And, as Reverend Matthew Hayton's services were rarely needed in the evenings except in emergencies, she got up at the first ring of the bell.

She had turned on the hall light, so that when she opened the door the man sheltering in the porch outside was immediately visible. His dark hair flecked with raindrops, his collar turned up against the weather, he stood waiting patiently for her to recognise him.

And she did. Oliver's features, though gaunt, were instantly identifiable, and a wave of dizziness swept over her. The rain was driving down beyond the roof of the porch, and although she cast a panic-stricken look up and down the street there was no sign of another living soul.

But Oliver wasn't living, she reminded herself unsteadily. He was dead, and whoever it was standing here on her porch it was not Oliver. She was either blind or hallucinating, and she clutched the doorpost weakly in an effort to control her fears.

'Hello, Fliss.'

The voice was the same. It was Oliver's voice, Oliver's lips that twitched in sudden ruefulness, Oliver's hand that reached to cover hers where it rested on the wood.

'Don't.'

Fliss pulled her hand away before he could touch her, pressing both hands together over the slight rise of her stomach, as if in protection of her unborn child. She wasn't sure, but she didn't think she'd ever fainted before, yet she knew she was near to it now. Standing here, staring at a dead man's face, she felt the first flicker of darkness nudging at her temples.

'It's me, Fliss.' Oliver took her obvious withdrawal for repugnance, but he didn't disappear as she'd hoped, or show any signs of going away. 'I know it's late, but I didn't get in from the States until a couple of hours ago. This weather isn't confined to England, and the flight was delayed—'

'Go away!'

Unable to stand it any longer, Fliss tried to close the door against him, but somehow his foot was in the way, and she fled on panicky feet back into the living-room. She half expected to see herself, as you did in nightmares, fast asleep by the fire, but her chair was empty. And footsteps were coming along the hall, undeterred by her attempt to thwart him.

'Fliss,' he exclaimed wearily, appearing in the doorway like some malevolent ghost. 'For God's sake, Fliss, will you listen to me? It's really me. I'm alive. The news of my death was faked!'

Fliss came round to find herself lying comfortably on the couch. For a moment the awareness of where she was confused her. Hadn't she been sitting in her father's chair? She frowned. She must have moved because she was tired. She certainly felt a little shaky at the moment.

She blinked, and as she did so, she caught sight of a tall, dark figure standing on the hearth. It was a man, but it wasn't her father. And suddenly the whole terrifying scenario swept over her again.

At once, she struggled to sit up, but Oliver's tired voice arrested her. 'Relax,' he said heavily. 'I'm not going to touch you. I'm sorry if I frightened you earlier, but it wasn't meant to be that way.'

Fliss ignored his instructions, and pushed herself up against the cushions. 'You're not dead,' she ventured unsteadily, still not prepared to believe the evidence of her own eyes, and Oliver sighed.

'Not nearly,' he agreed flatly. 'The reports were, as they say, an exaggeration.'

Fliss stared at him. 'But—the police said—'

'I know what the police said,' Oliver interrupted her wearily. 'They said what they were told to say. It suited everyone's purpose if I was assumed to be deceased.'

Fliss swallowed. 'Whose purpose? Aren't you—aren't you wanted for—for questioning?'

'Oh, I've been questioned,' Oliver assured her drily. Then, glancing round, 'Can I sit down? I guess you deserve an explanation. Though it's just possible you may not like it.'

'You mean you turned informer,' Fliss exclaimed, capable of no other interpretation for his being here, and Oliver sighed.

'In a manner of speaking,' he said, making little effort to defend himself. 'I certainly told them what I knew. It was fairly futile as it happens. Hastings condemned them all as soon as he opened his mouth.'

Fliss shook her head. 'But why are you here? Why aren't you—?'

She broke off, and Oliver gave her a rueful look. 'In prison, like the rest of them?' he suggested drily, and she nodded.

'Well—you were involved, weren't you? I mean—you told Rose you knew what was going on.'

Oliver glanced behind him, and then lowered his weight into her father's chair. In the light from the fire behind him, Fliss could see the lines of strain that bracketed his mouth. Whatever had happened to him, it hadn't been as easy as she thought.

'I guess it looked that way, didn't it?' he said now. 'But appearances aren't always what they seem.'

Fliss's hands trembled. 'But you were with Rose. You were—*her*—lover.'

Oliver spread his legs, and linked his hands together in the space between. 'I slept with her,' he amended evenly. 'Until I met you, it was no problem.' Then, as Fliss's stomach quivered he added carelessly, 'But you have to know I didn't *love* her. When we were together, love simply didn't come into it.'

Fliss pressed her shoulders back against the cushions. 'Is that supposed to be an explanation? Do you really expect me to believe you weren't part of that whole drug scene?'

She caught her breath. 'For God's sake, Oliver, I was there, remember? Don't expect me to forget the things you said.'

Oliver shrugged. 'I gave up expecting anything a long time ago, Fliss,' he said flatly. 'But, for what it's worth, I never was involved. I was working for the United States government. I was recruited in Hong Kong many years ago.'

Fliss gasped. 'You're not serious!'

'Funny.' Oliver gave her a telling look. 'I thought I was.'

Fliss swung her feet to the floor and sat up. 'It's not possible.'

'I'm here.'

'Yes, but—' She sought for an explanation. 'You said yourself that you'd been an informer.'

'I said in a manner of speaking,' corrected Oliver, regarding her with weary, hooded eyes. 'I know it wasn't a pleasant job I was doing. But if you'd seen the victims of the trade, you might have more compassion.'

Fliss moistened her lips. 'So—' She couldn't get the words out at first, and she had to try again. 'I—why didn't you—?' She had been going to say, 'let me know', but she realised that was too presumptuous and changed it to, 'let anyone know?'

'As I said before, it was easier if I was believed dead.'

'But why?'

'Fliss, we're not dealing with choirboys here. These men are dangerous. I doubt my life would have been worth a plugged nickel in the days before Robert confessed. And even then—'

'So you—went back to the United States?' Fliss was trying to make sense of what he was saying, and Oliver gave her a wry smile.

'Not initially, no.' He paused. 'I had a bullet wound to contend with. The doctors wouldn't let me travel, until I was out of Intensive Care.'

Fliss gulped. 'You really were shot, then?'

'I really was shot,' he agreed drily. 'I'll show you the scar some time. They patched me up real good.'

Fliss pressed a hand to her stomach. 'I can't take this in.'

'No.' Oliver looked sympathetic. 'Well, I guess it is a lot to handle right away.' He paused. 'Do you want me to come back tomorrow? I wanted to speak to your father, but I see he doesn't appear to be around.'

'He's—he's at a play. In the church hall,' said Fliss quickly, feeling a hollowing in her stomach at the realisation that Oliver must have come here to see her father and not her. 'He won't be back for a couple of hours.' She hesitated. 'Are—are you staying in the village?'

'I just got off Concorde,' Oliver reminded her quietly, pressing down on the arms of the chair, and getting to his feet. 'I may just drive back to London. I don't feel like being sociable this evening.'

Fliss got up, too, and for a moment there was only a hair's breadth between them. But then, as if unwilling to give her the wrong impression a second time, Oliver moved away, running a hand through his rain-splashed hair, and heading unmistakably for the door.

'Um—you could stay here,' Fliss found herself saying hurriedly, and Oliver turned to give her a wary look. 'Well, we do have plenty of room,' she defended herself quickly. 'And—and I'm sure my father would like to see you.'

'But not you, hmm?' Oliver murmured softly, and she stared at him disbelievingly as his gaze sought hers.

'I—didn't say that,' she protested, shaking her head. 'I—of course I'm pleased to see you. I—I thought you were dead, for heaven's sake! Finding out you're not, I—I just don't know what to say.'

'Can you forgive me?'

'Forgive you?' Fliss's mind spun wildly in all directions,

trying to ascertain what he was meaning. 'Oh—you mean for what happened between us? Well—I suppose that was as much my—my fault as yours.'

'That's not what I mean.' Oliver turned fully to face her. 'I meant for deceiving you; for being involved in your fiancé's arrest and eventual conviction. Dammit, Fliss, I'm sorry. I didn't mean for you to get hurt.'

Fliss trembled. 'Robert—Robert and me—that was over before—before I found out about—about—'

'About what was going on?'

'Yes.'

Oliver stared at her. 'Why?'

'Why?' Fliss caught her lower lip between her teeth, wishing she knew how to answer him. 'Well—I suppose because I realised I didn't love him. He—he asked me to go to Hong Kong, and that's when I knew it was over.'

Oliver took a step towards her. 'You mean you'd changed your mind before he was arrested?'

'Yes.' Fliss cleared her throat. 'My father guessed before I did. He—he thought it was because of you.'

Oliver caught his breath. 'And was it?'

Fliss bent her head. 'I didn't want to think so.'

'But was it?' Oliver's voice was taut.

'Does it matter?'

'God, of course it matters.' With a smothered oath, he covered the last few feet that separated them, and took hold of her shoulders. 'Are you saying that my making love to you meant something to you? If it meant half as much to you as it did to me, I might believe I stand a chance.'

Fliss looked up at him. 'Oh, Oliver…'

'Tell me,' he exhorted her fiercely. 'Come on, Fliss. I need to know.'

Fliss pressed her lips together for a moment. 'Yes,' she said simply, incapable of denying him. 'But you didn't come back to hear that, did you? You came back to see my father.'

'Don't talk—'

The rest of what he said was muffled against her lips, and Fliss was in no state to demand an answer. Besides, she had her answer in the welcome possession of his hands, and the hungry affirmation of his mouth.

He kissed her many times, long, drugging kisses that took her breath and bruised her lips. His tongue invaded her mouth, seeking its own fulfilment, and she clutched his neck eagerly, half afraid even now that she was dreaming.

But when his hands moved down her body, drawing her closer, making her instantly aware of the pulsing heat of his arousal, Fliss was forced to resist him. Much as she wanted to give in, to yield to him, to feel again the hard strength of him inside her, there was still so much that hadn't been said, so much she had to know.

And Oliver, sensing her withdrawal, allowed her to put an inch of space between them. 'I know,' he said, resting his forehead against hers. 'I'm not going to rush you this time. Don't worry, love. We have all the time in the world.'

Fliss took a trembling breath. 'Yes, but—'

'And I know your father's quite likely to come back soon,' he added, 'particularly if someone happens to tell him there's an unfamiliar car at your gate. Relax, sweetheart. I don't expect you to climb into bed with me—at least—' his lips twisted '—not yet, at any rate. I realise I still have some explaining to do, so why don't we sit right down and do it?'

'Do what?'

'Talk,' he said, giving her an old-fashioned look. 'Don't tease me, Fliss. It's not easy behaving like a sane and sensible guy. These last three months have been hell, believe me.'

And for me, thought Fliss ruefully, but she didn't say it.

For the moment, it was enough just to try and absorb the fact that Oliver wasn't dead, that he cared about her, that her baby might have a father after all.

But, for a while after Oliver had shed his jacket and they had settled on the sofa, there was an intimate silence in the room, punctuated only by little sighs and murmurs, and the satisfying melding of mouths and tongues. It was difficult to be sensible when they had so much time to make up, but after Oliver had taken her hand and pressed it to the throbbing hardness of his body Fliss at least knew something must be said.

'Tell me about what happened,' she murmured, ducking out of any explanations she had to make, and with a brief closing of his eyes, and a final arching of his hips against her, Oliver gave in.

'You know most of it already,' he said, settling her head on his shoulder, and resting his head back against the cushions. 'I was supposed to keep close to Rose, to find out how the merchandise was being distributed in England. We knew some of it was finding its way to the States via London, and my boss was hoping Rose would make me her confidant.'

Fliss bit her lip. 'And did she?'

'Not really. Rose was too wary for that. Her only mistake was involving Robert. James Hastings had recognised his son's weaknesses early on.' He shrugged. 'But I was able to keep my boss informed of her movements, even if the computer disk I copied and sent him turned out to be no use.'

'Go on.'

'What I didn't know was that the British authorities were working alongside us. That was something Archie chose not to tell me, obviously in case I made any mistakes. But that meeting at the club was exactly what they wanted. Only, when they moved in, our mutual friend had gone.'

'Rose?'

'Yeah, Rose.'

'So—when she came to the hotel—'

'God knows what she intended. Of course, she didn't know the police were involved, though I know she was suspicious of me.'

'Why?'

Oliver hesitated. 'It was a job, Fliss. And it was no real hardship to begin with. Rose is a beautiful woman, and I'd be lying if I said I objected to the assignment in the beginning. But—after I met you my relationship with Rose became an anathema to me. It was all I could do to speak to her, let alone anything else.'

'But you did go on—going to bed with her, didn't you?'

'Would you believe me if I said no?'

'I don't know.' Fliss lifted her shoulders. 'Try me.'

Oliver sighed. 'Rose and I weren't living together. Not in Hong Kong or London. We each had our own place. I admit, things were different in Hong Kong. But after we came to London she was too wrapped up in the business to feel any sense of neglect.' He grimaced. 'Actually, she thought she was neglecting me.' He paused. 'Except when she saw us together.'

'Is that true?'

He held up one hand. 'I swear.'

Fliss snuggled closer. 'That night—the night you were shot—did you know the police were following you?'

'Hell, no. All I was concerned about was you.' He shook his head. 'I knew I had to do something to stop Rose from hurting you, but when she pulled out that gun I thought I'd had it.'

'I thought you had, too,' murmured Fliss, in a muffled voice, remembering the horror she had felt when Oliver had slumped, bleeding, to the floor. The arrival of the men who had rescued her and arrested Rose had meant little compared to the anguish she had felt when she'd thought Oliver was dead. She'd wanted to die as well.

'Well, as you can see, I didn't,' Oliver murmured now, nuzzling her cheek. 'They whipped me off to a safe hospital, and I spent the next four weeks recovering from my injuries. They wouldn't let me see anyone or talk to anyone. Even my own parents were kept in the dark. Then Archie had me shipped out to Hong Kong, and I flew to the States from there.'

Fliss frowned. 'Who is Archie?'

'Colonel Archibald Lightfoot. He was my controller. It was he who insisted on complete confidentiality, until he had Rose safely back in Hong Kong.'

'I see. But Rose can't be charged with your murder now.' She paused. 'Does she know you're not dead?'

'She does now.' Oliver grimaced. 'She wasn't very happy about it. But then, Rose never was a good loser.'

'But won't she—?'

'Fliss, Fliss. What they have on Rose will put her away until she's a very old lady. She had used that gun before, you know. She wasn't an amateur.'

Fliss shivered. 'You're not still going to work in Hong Kong, are you?' she ventured, and to her relief Oliver shook his head.

'That was another reason why I wanted to visit the States before I came here. I wanted to know if I had a job to go back to. My father—he's a judge, by the way,' he added modestly, 'thinks he may be able to put in a good word for me.'

'I see.' Fliss licked her lips. 'And that's important to you?'

'More important than you, you mean?' Oliver suggested, guessing immediately what she meant. 'No, my love, no one's more important than you. But until I got here, until

I looked at you and saw that you could forgive me, I honestly didn't know if I stood a chance.'

'Well, you do,' mumbled Fliss, burrowing against him. 'Oh, Oliver, I'm so glad you came back. I—there's something you don't know, you see. Something I have to tell you. I just hope you'll understand. I'm not very good at making confessions.'

Oliver frowned now, and because he was looking so intently at her, Fliss felt obliged to straighten up. 'It's—it's just—this,' she said awkwardly, and grasping his hand, she laid it on the swelling mound that marked her waistline.

Oliver's eyes darkened. 'You're pregnant!'

'Mmm.' Fliss swallowed. 'I'm sorry.'

'You're *sorry*?' Oliver scowled. 'Isn't it mine?'

Fliss gazed at him with indignant eyes. 'I—I—' she spluttered. 'Of course, it's yours. I don't. I haven't—'

'I know.' Oliver pulled her eagerly back into his arms. 'But when you said you were sorry—' He groaned. 'God, don't be sorry about our baby.' He gave a short laugh, but she could tell he was almost as stunned by the news as she had been by his appearance. 'I'm going to be a father! I can't believe it! Wait until my parents hear about this!'

Fliss gazed up at him. 'You don't mind, then?'

'Mind?' He gulped. 'My love, I'm delighted. You're going to have to marry me now. I won't take no for an answer.'

Their son was born five months later. Benjamin Lynch came into the world without too much effort on his mother's part, and Oliver, who had stayed with Fliss throughout the long night preceding the birth, was there to hand the baby to his wife.

'He's like you,' said Fliss, at once, studying the baby's dark features with a marvellous feeling of well-being. 'Can you see? He's got your nose.' She smiled. 'I wonder what he's thinking now.'

'He's wondering who that beautiful creature is who's making such a fuss of him,' declared Oliver drily, unable to resist brushing her damp hair back from her forehead. 'How do you feel? Are you tired?'

Fliss smiled up at him. 'Do I look tired?'

'You look gorgeous,' Oliver averred, wedging his hips on to the bed beside her. 'But we won't do this too often, hmm? I don't think I can stand the strain.'

'Silly.' Fliss stroked her husband's rough cheek with a caressing finger. 'It was easy. I could do it all again.'

'Well, I couldn't,' said Oliver. 'And I'd like my wife to myself for a while. As soon as junior's old enough, we're going to have that honeymoon I promised you.'

'We had a honeymoon.'

'I mean, when there's just the two of us,' replied Oliver wryly. 'With nothing to come between us. Not even Ben.'

'Ben.' Fliss smiled again. 'Benjamin Matthew Lynch. I like it.'

'I'm sure your father will like it, too,' said Oliver, bending to kiss her cheek. 'He always says he knew what was going on before we did.' He shook his head. 'Oh, baby, do you know how much I love you? I'm never going to let you go.'

'That's good.' Fliss reached up to kiss him. 'Because you know what? I feel exactly the same.'

DARK APOLLO

by

Sara Craven

CHAPTER ONE

'BUT he loves me.'

'I wouldn't count on it.' Camilla Dryden spoke more brusquely than she'd intended, and repented instantly as she saw her sister's eyes cloud with bewildered hurt.

'Katie, love,' she went on more gently, 'you hardly know each other. It was a holiday romance. Just—one of those things.'

She could hardly believe her own ears. One cliché was following another, and she wasn't surprised to see Katie shaking her head.

'It wasn't like that. I knew as soon as I met Spiro that there would never be anyone else. And he feels just the same about me.'

Camilla winced inwardly. 'Then why wasn't he on that flight? Or any of today's other flights, for that matter?'

'I don't know. Something must have happened to prevent him—delay him.'

Camilla could make a cynical guess what that 'something' might be. Spiridion Xandreou had probably remembered, just in time, that he had a fiancée—or even a wife—already.

This is what comes, she thought seething, of al-

lowing an impressionable eighteen-year-old to spend
Easter in Greece.

It had seemed a perfectly acceptable invitation at
the time. Lorna Stephens, Katie's best friend, was
going to Athens to visit her aunt, married to a Greek
businessman. The two girls had been working hard
for their public examinations, and deserved a break
from their studies.

How could Camilla have guessed that Lorna's
aunt was the kind of irresponsible idiot who'd allow
her niece and her niece's friend to be chatted up by
personable Greek waiters?

If only it had stopped at chat, Camilla thought
with a silent groan. Or if Katie had been sophisticated enough to realise she was being spun a line
by an experienced charmer.

On her return, she'd informed her elder sister that,
although she was still prepared to take her A levels,
they no longer mattered because she was engaged
to be married.

Camilla had taken a deep, steadying breath, and
done some gentle probing.

What had emerged was hardly reassuring. Spiro,
it seemed, worked in a marvellous and famous restaurant where Katie had gone for a meal with the
family party. Spiro had served at their table, and the
following evening Katie and Lorna had managed to
return to the restaurant alone.

'Of course, he's not really just a waiter.' Katie's
eyes had been full of stars, and a new womanly

awareness which had struck a chill to Camilla's heart. 'His family own the restaurant, and masses of other things beside—hotels, even a shipping line. From what Spiro says, they must be amazingly wealthy. Isn't it incredible?'

'It certainly is,' Camilla had agreed, but Katie had been oblivious to the irony in her voice.

'When my exams are over, Spiro's flying over to meet you, and ask formally if he can marry me.' She had smiled tenderly. 'He's very old-fashioned.'

Well, he'd certainly chosen the right route to Katie's heart, Camilla had thought savagely. Katie was old-fashioned too, a shy, gentle girl, who before that Athenian spring had had her heart set on university and an academic career. First love should have come gently to her too, not force-fed under a Greek sun by some plausible Lothario.

She'd thought, She's going to be so hurt.

But, to her surprise, letters with Greek stamps had begun to arrive regularly and frequently.

Perhaps Spiro Xandreou knew Lorna's rich uncle, and assumed Katie came from the same kind of background.

Little does he know, she'd thought, looking round their small flat. When he realised that Katie's only relative was an older sister working for a busy secretarial agency to keep a roof over their heads, this so-called engagement would be a thing of the past.

Camilla had never been to Greece, but she had a shrewd idea that marriages there were still very much tied up with property, and the size of a bride's potential dowry. Katie had no financial qualification to recommend her to the family of a young waiter on the make.

For a time, it had seemed as if Katie was having second thoughts about her romance as well. She had been silent and preoccupied, and spent a lot of time alone in her room. She'd lost weight too, and there were shadows under her eyes.

But then another letter arrived, and Katie, bubbling with renewed happiness, had revealed that Spiro was flying to London at the end of June.

But his flight had landed without him, and Katie had eventually returned to the flat alone, almost distraught with worry.

And now Camilla had to make her see reason.

'Surely he'd have sent word if he'd been delayed,' she said. 'I think,' she added carefully, 'we're going to have to accept, darling, that he's simply changed his mind...'

'He can't have done.' Bright spots of colour burned in Katie's cheeks. 'We're going to be married. He—he has to come here. Oh, Camilla, he's simply got to.'

Camilla looked at her in sudden horrified understanding. She didn't have to ask why, she thought. It was all there in Katie's tear-bright eyes and trembling mouth, in the curious blend of dignity and shame in her face as she looked back at her sister.

Her voice broke. 'Oh, no, Katie. For God's sake—not that.'

'It's quite true. I'm going to have Spiro's baby. But it's all right, because he loves me, and we're going to be married as soon as it can be arranged.'

Camilla's voice was weary. 'You've actually told him you're pregnant?' She gave a mirthless smile. 'And you wonder why he wasn't on that plane.'

'You're not to say that.' Katie's voice shook with intensity. 'You don't know him. He's decent and honourable.'

'So decent, so honourable he couldn't wait to seduce a girl on her first trip abroad.' Camilla shook her head, her throat aching with grief and bitterness. 'Oh, Katie, you fool.' She sighed. 'Well, now we have to decide what to do for the best.'

'I know what you're going to say.' Katie's face was suddenly pale. 'Don't even think it, Milla. I'm having this baby.'

'Darling, you haven't thought it through. You've got your university course—your whole life ahead of you. You can't imagine what it would be like trying to cope with a baby as well…'

'But that isn't what I've chosen. I'm going to marry Spiro. It isn't the life I'd planned, I agree, but it's the life I want—the only one, now and forever.'

'Katie—you can't know that.'

'Mother knew it, when she met Father. And she was younger than me,' Katie said unanswerably. 'And you can't say they weren't happy.'

No, Camilla thought. She couldn't say that. Her parents had loved each other deeply and joyously until a jack-knifing lorry had brought that love to a premature end, leaving her at nineteen with the sole responsibility for a vulnerable adolescent.

And what a hash I've made of it, she castigated herself. She needed her mother's wisdom to tell her how to support Katie through this crisis. I don't know what to do, she thought, and felt a hundred years old.

She felt even older when she woke the next morning. It had been a terrible evening. Katie had managed to telephone the restaurant in Athens, only to be told with polite but impersonal regret that Spiro no longer worked there. Nor could they say where he'd gone.

I bet they can't, Camilla had thought, seething. They're probably inundated with calls like this.

All night long, Camilla had heard the sound of Katie's desolate sobbing through the thin partition wall. She'd tried to go to her, but Katie's door was locked. Besides, what could she do, or say—she who had never been even marginally tempted to fall in love herself? She was the last person in the world to know what comfort or advice to offer, she'd told herself unhappily.

To her surprise she found Katie already up, and making breakfast in the tiny kitchenette. Her sister looked wan and red-eyed, but her face was set with determination.

'I'm going to find him, Milla,' she said.

'But you can't trail round every restaurant and taverna in Athens asking for him. It would be like searching for a needle in a haystack.' Dismayed, Camilla took the beaker of coffee Katie handed her.

'Not Athens.' Katie shook her head. 'Spiro comes from an island called Karthos. It's in the Ionian Sea, south of Corfu. I shall go there. His family must know where he is.'

Camilla took a wary sip of the strong black brew. 'Katie,' she said hesitantly, 'has it occurred to you that Spiro may not—want to be found?'

'That's not true,' Katie said calmly. 'If it were, I'd know it here.' She put her hand on her heart.

The simplicity of the gesture and the profound trust it implied made Camilla's throat ache with unshed tears.

He's not worth it, she thought savagely.

There were a thousand arguments she ought to be able to use to stop Katie embarking on this crazy and probably fruitless quest, but somehow she couldn't think of one.

Instead, she said, 'Then I'm going with you.'

'Milla, do you mean it?' Katie's face was transfigured. 'But what about the agency? Will Mrs Strathmore give you the time off?'

'I've a whole backlog of leave I haven't taken.' Camilla gave her a reassuring smile. 'And Mrs

Strathmore can lump it. She won't sack me. She relies on me to handle the ghastly clients the others won't work for. I'll call in and explain on the way round to the travel agency.'

She tried to sound positive and encouraging, but her heart was in her boots.

What the hell will we do if we don't find him? she wondered. Or, even worse, supposing we find him and he doesn't want to know?

She sighed silently. They would cross that bridge when they came to it.

'We'll find him.' Katie seemed to have read her thoughts. Her voice and face were serene. 'It's fate. The Greeks have always believed in fate.'

And in the Furies, Camilla thought grimly. The so-called Kindly Ones inexorably pursuing the erring, and wreaking their vengeance on them.

Well, she would be a latter-day Fury, trailing Spiro Xandreou, no matter how well he might have covered his tracks.

She said, 'There's no such thing as fate,' and surreptitiously crossed her fingers under the kitchen table.

The Hotel Dionysius was small, fiercely clean, and frankly basic. Camilla sat at a plastic-covered table in a corner of the outside restaurant area, a tall glass of freshly squeezed orange juice in front of her. She was sheltered from the glare of the midday sun by a thatched roof, interwoven with a sprawling and healthy vine. Beyond the hotel's tiny garden with its hibiscus hedge lay the main square of Karthos town.

The island was only a remote dot in the Ionian Sea, but it was bustling with tourists. So far Camilla had heard French, German and Dutch being spoken, as well as English, and she and Katie had been lucky to get the last two vacancies at the hotel.

She'd left Katie sleeping in their white-washed shuttered room on the first floor. She was beginning to feel the effects of her pregnancy, and had been miserably sick on the flight to Zakynthos, and the subsequent long ferry trip. The temperature on Karthos was already up in the eighties, and she'd agreed with little fuss to Camilla's suggestion that she should rest and leave the initial enquiries for Spiro to her sister.

Camilla had been sorely tempted to cancel this whole wild-goose chase after a reluctant telephone call to Lorna Stephens' Greek uncle. She'd explained, without going into detail, that she was anxious to trace a young waiter from the restaurant Clio, and wondered if he could help.

To judge by the cynical sigh, and muttered, '*Po, po, po,*' no further explanation was needed. 'You know the name of this man, *thespinis*?'

'He's called Spiro Xandreou.'

'Xandreou?' Across the miles, she heard the sharp intake of breath. Then, 'I regret I cannot assist you. But I advise you most strongly, *thespinis*, to proceed no further in this.' A pause. 'Most strongly.' And

he'd rung off, leaving Camilla with a host of un-
answered questions.

She'd been warned off, she realised uneasily. She
could only hope that Spiro wasn't some kind of
thug—a member of the Greek mafia, if there was
such a thing. Maybe he wasn't on Karthos at all, but
in gaol somewhere.

But how could she tell Katie her suspicions, and
burst the bubble of optimism and anticipation which
encircled her? Maybe she just had to let her find out
for herself, she concluded resignedly.

Camilla sighed silently as she finished the iced
fruit juice.

But where on earth should their search start?

'You enjoy?' Kostas, the hotel's burly proprietor,
arrived to clear the table. He had a thick black moustache, a booming laugh, and he smoked incessantly.
But the warmth of his welcome had been quite un-
feigned, and to Camilla's relief he spoke better than
rudimentary English. The questions she needed to
ask were omitted from the usual phrase books.

She nodded vigorously. 'It was delicious, thank
you. Just what I needed.'

'To travel in this heat is not good.'

As he turned away, she said, 'Kostas, do you
know a family called Xandreou—with a son named
Spiro?'

The genial smile vanished as if it had been wiped
away. He looked startled, and almost apprehensive.
'Why do you ask?'

She said lightly, 'Oh, our families used to be—acquainted. I believe they come from here, and I'd like to see them again. That's all.'

There was a silence, then, 'Xandreou, you say?' Kostas shook his head. 'I don't know the name. You have come to the wrong place, I think, *thespinis*.'

'I don't think so.' She gave him a level look. 'You're sure you haven't heard of them?'

'Certain.' He paused. 'You are on holiday, *thespinis*. You should relax. Go to the beach—enjoy the sun—drink some wine. Make other friends—and don't waste time looking for these people.'

And if that wasn't an oblique warning, she'd never heard one, Camilla thought, watching him walk away between the tables, which were already filling up for lunch.

It was the same message she'd got from Athens: keep away from the Xandreou clan.

Everyone knows them, but they don't want to talk about them, she thought, a prickle of wariness running down her spine. Yet, somehow, for Katie's sake, she had to penetrate this wall of silence.

She picked up her bag, and walked to the steep outside stairway which provided an alternative access to the bedrooms.

There'd been some cards on the reception desk advertising car and motorbike hire. She'd rent a scooter and take a preliminary look round. The brochure on the island had warned that most of the best beaches were out of town, and it might be pleasant to find some deserted cove and laze around for a while before the real business of their trip began.

'Journeys end in lovers meeting', she thought. I only hope it's true.

She was halfway up the steep outside staircase that provided an alternative access to the bedrooms when a voice below her said urgently, '*Thespinis.*'

Glancing down, she saw one of the hotel waiters, who'd been serving an adjoining table while she spoke to Kostas. He gave her an ingratiating smile. 'You want Spiro Xandreou?'

'Why, yes.' Her heartbeat quickened in swift excitement. 'Do you know him?'

'Since boys.' He touched a fist theatrically to his chest. 'I too am a man of Karthos.'

'Then can you tell me where to find him?'

The young man shrugged, sending a slightly furtive glance back over his shoulder. 'Is not easy for me, you understand…'

Camilla understood perfectly. She extracted a thousand-drachma note from her wallet, and handed it over.

He whispered hoarsely, 'He is at his house—the Villa Apollo.'

'Is that near here?'

'*Ochi.*' He gestured towards the craggy hills which formed the island's hinterland. 'Is long way.'

'Is there a bus?'

'No bus. Nothing there—only villa. You get car,

or motorbike.' He handed her one of the cards dis-
played in Reception. 'My cousin rent—very cheap.'

With you on commission, no doubt, she returned
silently. But she thanked him politely, and went on
up the steps.

'*Thespinis*,' he hissed again, and she paused.
'*Thespinis*, whatever occur, you don't say to boss I
told you, *ne*?'

'Not a word,' she said, and watched him vanish
into the hotel.

Katie was still out for the count. Camilla wrote her
a brief note saying she was going to explore, and
replaced the simple button-through dress she'd worn
for the journey with white shorts and a sleeveless
top, with her initial in red and gold embroidery over
the left breast. She gathered her thick chestnut hair
into a barrette at the nape of her neck for coolness,
and slid her feet into comfortable canvas shoes.

She found the rental place easily enough. It was
basically a dirt yard, with chickens pecking round
between the scooters. Andonis, the owner, wore a
grubby singlet and a three-day growth, and had the
kind of gleam in his eye which made Camilla regret
she hadn't changed into something less revealing.

She was able to hire a scooter with a disturbing
lack of formality, although the actual cost was rather
more than she'd bargained for. She enquired about
a safety helmet, and Andonis stared at her as if she
were mad, then spat on the ground.

'Karthos roads are good,' he said flatly. Her request for a map of the island met with more luck, however. A photocopied sheet, dog-eared and much folded, was produced.

Camilla stared at the web of roads, wondering where she would find the spider.

'I'm looking for a particular house—the Villa Apollo,' she said. 'Can you mark it for me?'

He whistled through the gap in his teeth. 'You want Xandreou?' He gave her another lascivious look. 'So do many women. He's lucky man.'

Well, his luck's about to change, Camilla thought grimly. Andonis's remark, and the grin that accompanied it, had only confirmed all her worst fears. Katie's honourable lover was nothing more than a practised Casanova, she realised with disgust.

Andonis made a laborious pencil cross on the map. 'Villa Apollo,' he said. He gave her another openly appraising stare. 'You should tell me before. Maybe I make special price for Xandreou's woman.'

Presumably they arrived in convoys, Camilla thought with distaste.

She distanced Andonis, who was disposed to help her on to the scooter, with an icy look.

'You're mistaken, *kyrie*. I'm not—what you say.'

The grin widened, unabashed. He shrugged. 'Not now, maybe, but who knows?'

'I do,' Camilla said curtly, and rode off.

This was obviously what they'd all been trying to

warn her about, she thought, as she headed out of
town on the road Andonis had indicated.

Innocent Katie had given her heart and her body
to a worthless piece of womanising scum. Well, he
wasn't going to get away with it.

'Xandreou's woman', she thought with contempt.
What a tag to be branded with.

But I'll make him pay for it, she vowed under her
breath, if it's the last thing I do.

'Whatever occur'. The waiter's words sneaked
unexpectedly back into her mind.

An odd thing to say, she thought. Almost like
another warning. And, in spite of the intense heat,
she felt suddenly, strangely cold.

CHAPTER TWO

CAMILLA brought the scooter gingerly to a halt on the stony verge, and wiped the sweat from her forehead.

Much further, and she would run out of road. Already the surface had dwindled to the status of a track, yet there was still no sign of the Villa Apollo. Had Andonis deliberately sent her to a dead end?

She eased the base of her spine with a faint grimace. He'd certainly given her the maverick of his scooter collection. The steering had a mind of its own, and the brakes barely existed. If she had to do an emergency stop...

Not that there seemed much chance of that. So far she hadn't passed another living thing, except for a donkey, a couple of tethered goats, and a dog on a chain who'd barked at her.

The road, rising steeply, was lined on each side with olive groves, and their silvery canopy had protected her from the worst of the sun. Some of the trees, with their gnarled and twisted trunks, seemed incredibly old, but they were still bearing fruit. The netting spread on the ground beneath to catch the olives bore witness to that.

Camilla turned and looked behind her, as if to

remind herself that civilisation did exist. Below her, in the distance, glimpsed in the gaps between the clustering olives, were the multicoloured roofs and white walls of Karthos town, topped by the vivid blue dome of a church. And beyond that again, azure, jade and amethyst, was the sea.

I could be on a beach now, she thought wistfully, if I weren't riding this two-wheeled death-trap up the side of a mountain.

She sighed, as she eased the clinging top away from the damp heat of her body, imagining herself sliding down from some convenient rock into cool, deep water, salty and cleansing against her skin.

One more bend in the road, she told herself. Then I go back.

She coaxed the scooter back to life, and set off, trying to correct its ferocious wobble on corners. In doing so, she nearly missed the Villa Apollo altogether.

She came to a halt, dirt and gravel flying under the tyres, and stared at the letters carved into the two stone gateposts ahead of her. And beneath them the emblem of the sun—the sign of the god Apollo himself, who each day, according to legend, drove his fiery chariot through the heavens.

Camilla dismounted with care, propping her machine against the rocky bank. With luck, someone terminally insane with a death wish might just steal it.

Beyond the gateway, more olive trees shadowed a steeply lifting driveway.

Right, she thought, tilting her chin. Let's see this irresistible Adonis who causes such havoc in people's lives. Hands in pockets, she set off up the gradient, moving with a brisk, confident stride that totally masked her inner unease. Knowing she had right on her side did little to calm her nerves, she discovered.

And when the man stepped out in front of her, she only just managed to stifle a yell of sheer fright.

One glance told her that he wasn't the one she'd come to find. He was stocky and grizzled, with a walkie-talkie in his hand, and a gun, she noted, swallowing, in a holster on his hip. His face was unwelcoming, his stance aggressive as he barked a question at her in Greek.

Camilla stood her ground. 'I don't understand,' she said. 'My name is Dryden, and I have come from England to see Mr Xandreou.'

An armed security man, she thought. What am I getting into here?

The man stared at her for a moment, then spoke into his radio. He listened, then jerked his head at Camilla, indicating that she should follow.

The drive curved away to the right and Camilla saw that the olives gave way to lawns of coarse grass, and flowerbeds bright with colour.

And beyond them was the house itself, the Villa Apollo, large and sprawling, its white walls dazzling

in the sunshine. It was surrounded by a colonnaded
terrace, festooned in purple and crimson bougainvillaea, and a smoky pink flowering vine.

Camilla slowed, staring round her. What did a
waiter in an Athens restaurant have to do with this
frankly glamorous background? she asked herself.
Unless Spiro Xandreou was merely an employee,
and she was being shown to the tradesman's entrance.

The security man looked back, gesturing impatiently, and she moved forward reluctantly. Ahead
of her, she saw the clear turquoise sparkle of a large
swimming-pool. Around the edge were tiles in an
intricate mosaic pattern, and loungers and chairs
stood waiting under fringed sun umbrellas. There
was a table with a tray of drinks, and on the edge
of the pool a twin of the radio device carried by the
security man.

Otherwise, the place seemed deserted.

As she stared round her in bewilderment, a man's
dark head suddenly broke the surface of the water.
Camilla felt her heart beating slowly and unevenly
as he pulled himself athletically from the pool, and
stood for a moment, shaking the excess water from
his mane of black curling hair.

He was well above average height, she saw,
broad-shouldered and narrow-hipped, his bronzed
body lean, muscular and perfectly proportioned.

He was good-looking too, she recognised dazedly,
his almost classical beauty of feature redeemed by

the inherent toughness and strength of his mouth and chin. A man to be reckoned with.

'Like a Greek god.' She'd heard the phrase many times, but never expected to see it brought to life in front of her.

Especially as, like most of the ancient classical statues of the Olympians and heroes, he was completely naked.

Moving with the lithe grace of a jungle animal, he walked over to one of the loungers, picked up a waiting towel, and began to dry himself, casually and without haste, ignoring the presence of the new arrivals.

Camilla knew that displaying himself like this in front of her—a woman, and a stranger—was a calculated insult. But if he expected her to blush or faint, or run off screaming like some frightened nymph from mythology, he'd be disappointed, she told herself, and stood waiting in stony silence, refusing to let the deliberate affront get to her.

Eventually, he draped the damp towel round his hips, securing it with a knot. He reached for the thin, elegant platinum watch on the table, and clasped the bracelet on to his wrist, allowing his gaze, at last, to rest coolly and dispassionately on Camilla. His eyes were dark, long-lashed, holding an odd glitter.

Like cold fire, she thought.

He said, 'Who are you, and what do you want here?'

His voice was low and drawling, the accent only

slightly marked. But then Katie had told her his English was excellent.

Katie, she thought with a kind of despair. No wonder she'd fallen for him hook, line and sinker. But why should a sophisticated man of the world like this have encouraged her inexperienced sister, even for a moment? It made no sense at all. Unless he still wasn't the one she sought.

'Well?' His voice prodded at her impatiently. 'You have forced your way in here. Why don't you speak?'

She said slowly, gauging his reaction, 'I want to talk about—Xandreou's woman.'

He filled a glass with mineral water from one of the bottles, and drank. The security man, she realised, had discreetly faded away.

He said, 'I think you flatter yourself, Kyria…?'

'Dryden,' she supplied again. 'Please don't pretend you've forgotten the name.'

He shrugged. 'It is vaguely familiar.' He sounded bored. The brilliant eyes went over her, lingering on her breasts and thighs and long, slim legs, making her uneasily aware that the heat had made her scanty garments into a second skin.

His gaze met hers again. 'So, what do you want, Kyria Dryden? Or do you plan to spend the whole afternoon staring at me in silence?'

'I'm sorry.' What am I apologising for? she asked herself in disbelief. She pulled herself together with determination. 'You aren't exactly what I expected, Kyrios Xandreou.'

'Nor are you. But it isn't important.' His tone was dismissive. 'Say what you must, and go.'

All her worst forebodings were confirmed. He didn't care about Katie, or the baby. Her sister's sole attraction for him had been her innocence. Now it was gone, he didn't want to know. Katie was just another notch on a well-dented bedpost.

She said stonily. 'You know why I'm here. I think some kind of—reparation is called for.'

'For what? A pleasant interlude like so many of your countrywomen expect to enjoy in Greece?' The contempt in his voice lashed her.

Just because other girls might behave like sex-crazed idiots, there was no need to tar Katie with the same brush, she thought in furious anguish. Hadn't he realised that she was different—that she'd actually believed whatever corny seduction line he'd handed her?

'Unfortunately, this particular interlude has had consequences.' She hated the smile which twisted his mouth. 'Or had you forgotten there's a baby on the way?'

'There is nothing wrong with my memory,' he said. 'It is more a question of credulity, perhaps. A child with Xandreou blood might have a claim on Xandreou money. Is that what you think?' He shook his head. 'I am not a fool, Kyria Dryden. I am pre-pared to subject the paternity of this child to every test available to medical science. But can you afford to fight me?' The studied insolence of his gaze scorched her again. 'I don't think so.'

'No,' she said curtly. 'Nor would I dream of it. Obviously your responsibilities mean very little to you.'

'You are wrong. They mean a great deal. Which is why I will not submit to pressure from a girl who has behaved like a slut, and now wishes to benefit from her indiscretion.' His drawl intensified. 'Perhaps you are not aware that in Greek the name Catherine means "purity". It is something to consider— for the future, *ne*?'

Her hands curled into fists at her sides, and her voice shook a little.

'You've more than made your point, Mr Xandreou. I'd hoped you might have some shred of decency in you, but clearly I was mistaken. However, you won't be troubled again. The baby may not be brought up in the lap of this kind of luxury—' she gestured scornfully round her '—but it will be welcomed, looked after and loved, and that's far more important. It wasn't money I came for, but something more fundamental. Something you wouldn't understand.'

She paused, struggling to control her voice. 'And, hopefully, although the baby will be illegitimate, it will grow up without knowing what a complete bastard its father was.' She drew a deep and shuddering breath. 'I wonder how many more lives will be ru-

ined before you get your well-deserved come-
uppance?'

'You have the insolence to talk about ruined
lives?' He flung his head back, and she felt his anger
touch her like a blast of lightning. 'How dare you
say such a thing—speak to me like this?'

'It's quite simple,' she said. 'I just tell the truth.'

She turned and walked away from him, back rigidly straight, fighting the storm of angry tears which
threatened to overwhelm her.

Of all the hateful, disgusting things he'd said, it
was the gibe about Katie's name which, ridiculously, had got to her most.

He must have known she was untouched, yet he'd
set out deliberately to deflower and destroy, using
all the potent virility and sexual charisma he possessed in such abundance to undermine her resistance.

My God, I was aware of it myself, she thought,
shame mingling with anger. And I was only with
him for a few minutes. If I'd met him in different
circumstances—if he'd been charming, or even marginally polite...

She blotted out that line of thinking instantly.
Spiro Xandreou clearly regarded himself as some
latter-day Apollo, a sun god to whom every woman
was a potential victim for conquest, and she dis-
graced herself by even acknowledging his attraction.

But what had he been doing, working in that restaurant? she asked herself. Waiting on tables for a bet—or some other kind of sick joke?

If so, why go on with the pretence once Katie had returned to England? Promising to come over—claiming they were going to be married. All those letters—all those lies.

Unforgivable, she thought as she dragged the despised scooter upright, and kicked it into grumbling life. She wanted to get away from the Villa Apollo, and its owner, as fast as she could—breathe some untainted air.

And decide what she could possibly tell Katie, she thought despondently as she steadied her temperamental machine for the first bend.

The open-topped sports car was upon her instantly, racing up the hill on the wrong side of the road. Camilla caught a stunned glimpse of a girl's face, olive-skinned and pretty behind the designer sunglasses but transfixed by sheer horror. Then she pulled the bike over in a kind of desperation, striving to avoid the inevitable collision.

The scooter hit the loose stones on the verge, and went out of control, running up the bank. Camilla was thrown off, landing painfully on her side. She lay still for a moment, feeling sick and dizzy with shock.

She heard the sound of running feet, and the girl bent over her. '*O Theos.*' There was panic in her voice. 'You are hurt. Are you broken anywhere?'

Into several pieces by the feel of it, Camilla

thought, as she pulled herself to her feet. There were no actual fractures, she was sure, but there was a deep graze on her bare leg, and another on her arm, blood mingling with the dirt on her torn blouse.

'I did not expect anyone else on this road.' The girl was practically wringing her hands.

'So I gathered,' Camilla forced from her dry throat.

'You need a doctor.' The girl took her uninjured arm, urging her towards the car. 'With me, please. Come.'

Camilla shook her head. 'It's all right.' Her voice sounded very small and far-away suddenly. 'I—I'll be fine.' She saw the road, the car, and the newcomer's anxious face dip and sway, then everything descended into a dark and swirling void.

Somewhere, a storm must be raging. Camilla could feel the splash of rain on her face and hear a distant rumble of thunder. But she herself seemed to be floating on some kind of cloud.

She opened unwilling eyes, and stared up at a face she'd never seen before, female, elderly and wrinkled with concern. Nor was it raining. She was simply having her face bathed with cool water.

I hurt, she thought, wincing, as she looked around her. She was in a large room, lying on a vast luxurious sofa the colour of rich maize.

And the sound of the storm was Spiro Xandreou, who was standing a few feet away conducting a low-voiced but furious argument with the girl from the car.

Oh, my God, Camilla thought with horrified alarm. She's brought me back here—to his house. I can't bear it.

She tried to sit up, only to be vociferously restrained by the old woman attending to her.

Spiro Xandreou swung round, frowning, and came striding over. He'd exchanged the towel, Camilla noticed, for a pair of white shorts almost equally revealing. Still competing for the Stud of the Year award, no doubt, she thought, hating him.

'My sister has told me what happened,' he said harshly. 'You must remain where you are—keep still until the doctor has made his examination.'

'I'll do nothing of the kind.' Camilla's head swam as she put her feet gingerly to the floor. But she was becoming more aware of her surroundings. One entire wall of the room was made from glass, a series of sliding doors pushed open to admit the sunlight, and a breeze bringing a hint of flowers and citrus.

The floor was tiled in creamy marble, veined in blue and gold, and the same blue was echoed in the colour of the walls, which were bare except for a few modern abstract paintings, clearly original and probably valuable.

Ironically, the one thing Spiro Xandreou hadn't lied about was his wealth, Camilla thought sourly. She was in the lap of luxury here. The sofa she was lying on was one of a pair flanking a wide marble fireplace, which was presumably for use in the winter months but was now screened by a large bronze sculpture of a sunburst.

The whole effect was airy and spacious, yet somehow welcoming, so presumably the owner had had no hand in the décor.

She glared up at him. 'There's no need for all this fuss. I want nothing from you, Mr. Xandreou. I thought I'd made that clear.'

'Unfortunately, neither of us has a choice. You are not leaving here, *thespinis*, without medical attention.'

'What are you afraid of? That I'll sue?' His autocratic tone needled her. She tried to smile past him at the girl, who was standing looking sullen, her arms crossed defensively in front of her. 'I shan't. I've a few grazes, that's all.'

'You cannot know that. And in the circumstances we can afford to take no risks,' he said grimly. He issued some low-voiced instructions to the old woman who left the room instantly.

'Arianna tells me you were riding a scooter,' he went on. 'Are you quite crazy?'

'Only on a part-time basis,' Camilla said wearily. 'Look—just get me a taxi, and I'll go back to my hotel. My sister will be wondering where I am, and I don't want to cause her unnecessary worry,' she added pointedly.

'She knows of your activities, then—and she permitted them?' Spiro Xandreou raised clenched fists towards the ceiling. 'Unbelievable.'

'No,' Camilla said, with a sigh. 'This was all my own idea. And clearly a bad one.'

'At least we agree on something,' he said silkily.

The old woman in her black dress and snowy apron came back into the room, carrying a bowl of steaming water, a bottle of antiseptic, and some cotton wool.

Camilla eyed them with misgiving. 'There's no need...'

'There is every need,' he contradicted flatly. 'This is not England, Kyria Dryden. Grazes such as this carry a risk of infection, and need immediate attention.'

He knelt beside the sofa, his face coolly intent, soaking a swab of cotton wool in the antiseptic solution.

Camilla wanted to draw away. He was altogether too close for comfort, she thought, dry-mouthed, as she absorbed the clean, fresh scent of his sunwarmed skin. His bare shoulder brushed against her knee, and she felt a sharp pang deep inside her that had nothing to do with pain.

She said huskily, 'No—please...'

He gave her a look of withering contempt and began to swab the dirt and grains of gravel from her leg. She bit her lip, her body tautening instinctively at his touch.

He looked up at her, his mouth slanting sardonically. 'If it's only a graze, *thespinis*, you're not being very brave about it.'

She said between her teeth, 'Maybe I'd prefer to wait for the doctor.'

He shrugged. 'The Hippocratic oath is not needed for simple first aid,' he returned. 'I am not enjoying this either, Kyria Dryden.'

The oath, she thought, that the medical profession still used. 'I swear by Apollo...' And Apollo himself was here, or so it seemed, kneeling at her feet.

He was deft enough, and even quite gentle, she was forced to admit, but some of the dirt was deeply embedded, and there were tears in her eyes before he'd finished, although she kept her teeth firmly fastened in her bottom lip.

But the smarting was only part of it, she realised. The truth was she didn't want to accept this kind of intimate service from him.

When he had cleaned her arm, he hesitated. 'The shirt is already ruined, I think, so...' He put two fingers in the jagged tear at the side, and ripped it completely down to the hem.

Camilla gasped, dragging the torn edges together. 'How dare you...?' Her voice was unsteady. For one brief instant, his fingers had brushed the curve of her bare breast, and his touch had scalded her.

'So modest?' His voice taunted. 'Your fellow-tourists show more on our beaches every day.'

'But I don't,' she said huskily.

The old woman stepped forward, gesturing him

imperatively out of the way. With another shrug, he got to his feet, and walked to the window, turning his back while Camilla's scraped ribs were bathed.

'Arianna,' he tossed over his shoulder, 'you will provide Kyria Dryden with a blouse from your wardrobe as a temporary measure.'

'Of course, I shall be pleased. She can come upstairs to my room, and choose. Petros can examine her there too.'

He frowned. 'Is that necessary?'

'But of course.' Arianna Xandreou looked scandalised. 'Such a procedure requires privacy.'

His frown deepened. 'Then stay with her—all the time, you understand?'

He'd spoken in English, so presumably Camilla wasn't to be left in any doubt either.

'What the hell are you implying?' she demanded.

'I intend to ensure you do not turn this accident to your advantage, *thespinis*.'

'What do you think I'm going to do—steal something?' Camilla pulled away from the old woman's restraining hand, her eyes blazing. 'God, you've an almighty nerve.'

'And I think the same of you, *thespinis*. You will play no tricks in this house.'

Her lips were parting to tell him unequivocally what she thought of him, when the door opened and a young man, swarthy and stockily built, wearing glasses, walked in. He paused, surveying the tableau in front of him.

'I understand I have a new patient,' he remarked. 'A road accident, *ne*? Thank you, Eleni.' The old woman stepped back, and he inspected her handiwork critically, and nodded. 'You are lucky, *thespinis*. I have known similar incidents where skin grafts have been needed. But you, I think, will be left without a scar. A shot, maybe, to protect against infection and you will be as good as new.'

Spiro Xandreou took him to one side, and said something softly in Greek.

'*Po, po, po.*' The doctor's brows lifted sharply. 'Then I should examine without delay. Eleni can act as chaperon.'

'This is ridiculous,' Camilla protested. 'I'm fine.'

The doctor smiled at her. 'I'm sure that is true. You seem a perfectly healthy young woman. But your pregnancy is in its early stages. We need to establish that all is well.'

'Pregnancy?' Camilla stared at him stupidly. 'What are you talking about? I'm not pregnant.'

'So you lied.' Spiro Xandreou's voice was almost gloating. 'I knew it.' He walked to the door of the *saloni*, and threw it wide, his face a mask of icy anger. 'You will leave my house, *thespinis*, and not come back.'

His voice dropped to pure menace. 'And you will never trouble me or mine again. That is, if you know what's good for you. Now go.'

CHAPTER THREE

CAMILLA stared at him.

She said quietly, 'I think you must be insane, Kyrios Xandreou. Or has your womanising now reached such proportions that you can't even tell one girl from another?'

'How dare you speak to me like that?' His voice was molten. 'How dare you...?'

Camilla met his gaze. Eyes dark as obsidian, she thought with a strange clarity, and as hard as flint. But with a small flame burning...

Just as she was burning inside.

'Oh, I dare.' She drew a deep angry breath. 'Because it wasn't me that you—seduced and abandoned in Athens a few months ago. It was my younger sister, Katie.' A sob rose in her throat. 'And you can't even remember what she really looks like—you bastard.'

Her words fell into a silence so profound it was almost tangible.

It was broken by the doctor, his face expressionless. 'I think, my dear Nic, there has been some misunderstanding. Now, if you'll excuse me, I will go up to my other patient.'

As he turned away, Camilla caught his arm. 'Just a moment—please. You called this man—Nic?'

'*Ne, thespinis*. Is something wrong?'

She swallowed. 'You mean—he's not—Spiro?'

The doctor looked astonished. 'Spiro is Kyrios Xandreou's younger brother, *thespinis*. He was also injured in an accident, a short while ago, rather more seriously than yourself. In fact, I should be with him now. If you will call at the clinic in town tomorrow morning, I will prescribe some medication for you—as a precaution only, you understand,' he added kindly, misunderstanding the sudden pallor of her face. 'Infection breeds fast in our climate.'

He nodded briskly, and left the room, Arianna sliding after him.

Camilla found herself alone with Nic Xandreou.

She ran the tip of her tongue round her dry lips. 'You thought I was Katie,' she said. 'I thought you were Spiro. We've been at cross purposes from the start.'

'So it would seem.' His voice was even.

'But Katie's only just eighteen,' she protested. 'You must have known I was older than that.'

He shrugged. 'I thought Spiro had been deceived.' His glance flicked over her. 'There was also the initial on your shirt—a C, presumably for Catherine.'

She said quietly, 'My name is Camilla.' She looked down at the tiled floor. 'I've said some pretty harsh things. I'm sorry, but I was just so upset for Katie.'

'You are loyal to your family,' he returned flatly.
'I don't blame you for that. It's a quality I share.'

'Was Spiro badly hurt in the accident?' she asked
in a low voice.

He shrugged again. 'He has a broken leg and a
bump on the head. Time and rest will cure them
both.'

She tried a small smile. 'Well, it could have been
very much worse.' She paused. 'That's why he
never turned up at the airport. I just wish someone
had let us know. Katie will be so relieved when she
knows the truth.' She waited, but he said nothing.

She tried again. 'I'll go straight back to the hotel,
and explain.'

'Not,' he said, 'like that, I think.'

She realised where his gaze was directed and
dragged the torn edges of her top together again,
flushing.

'Well, perhaps not.'

He said curtly, 'I will take you to my sister's
room. Come.'

Camilla took a step forward and faltered, her legs
shaking under her.

He turned at the door, staring back at her. 'What
now?' he demanded impatiently.

'Just reaction, I think.' She tried to force a smile.
'If you could—give me a moment.'

He muttered something succinct and angry under
his breath, and came striding back. Before she could
guess what he intended, he had swung her off her

feet into his arms, and was carrying her across the *saloni* and out into a large hall.

'What the hell are you doing?' Camilla gasped furiously. She braced her hands against his chest, but it was like trying to overturn a brick wall. Except no wall had ever been so warm—so smooth—so sensuous to the touch. She could feel, she realised with an unnerving tingle of awareness, his heart beating under her fingers...

She said breathlessly, 'Put me down at once.'

'Be still,' he snapped back.

He was very strong. She was slim, but no featherweight, yet he went up the wide, shallow sweep of the marble staircase without a pause.

In the gallery above, he shouldered open a door and went in. It was a large, light room, all pale wood and floating pastel drapes. Arianna was not there, and Nic Xandreou clicked his tongue in sharp annoyance before depositing Camilla without particular gentleness on the edge of the wide, soft bed.

She watched him walk to the tall wardrobes which lined one wall, and fling open a door. He took a shirt, classic in heavy white silk, from a hanger and tossed it to her.

'You can use this,' he ordained.

'I think I'll stay as I am,' she returned quickly. The shirt was clearly very expensive, and the thought of having to struggle to remove her ripped top over her sore shoulder and arm didn't appeal at all. There were some pins in her bag, she remembered. She could make herself decent until she had Katie to help her change.

Nic Xandreou frowned slightly. 'You are in pain?' he guessed.

'Stiffening up a little,' she admitted.

Nic extended his arms in front of him. 'Can you still do this?'

'I think so.' Camilla raised her own arms slightly in imitation.

Nic leaned down, and in one swift movement whipped the torn top over her head and off, baring her to the waist.

'Oh.' Camilla snatched up Arianna's shirt, and held it as a shield in front of her naked breasts, as a wave of frantic embarrassed colour engulfed her. 'How—how dare you?'

'There was no question of daring.' He sounded almost bored. 'You needed assistance, and there was no one else.'

'But that doesn't give you the right...'

A faint smile twisted the corners of the firm mouth. He said softly, 'In my house, Kyria Camilla, I assume whatever rights I choose. Now, I will await you downstairs.'

At the door, he paused, looking back at her, the smile deepening with disturbing mockery.

He said, 'I am glad to know you will not be scarred. Your body is very beautiful.'

And he walked out of the room, leaving Camilla, lips parted in shock, staring after him.

It took her a while to recover her composure. She had never been treated like that in her life before—never been made to feel so vulnerable—so frighteningly aware of her womanhood.

Nic Xandreou wasn't just a powerful and attractive man, she decided grimly. He was dangerous in all kinds of ways she'd never envisaged.

She might have said some harsh things to him, but he'd more than redressed the balance with that parting shot of his, she thought as she struggled into Arianna's shirt, her fingers fumbling the silk-covered buttons into their holes.

From now on she would be ultra-careful in any dealings she had with him.

There was a tiny tiled shower-room opening from the bedroom, which also contained a washbasin. Looking in the mirror, Camilla realised for the first time that her face was smeared with dirt from her fall, and her hair was tangled and dusty, and she found that she wanted very much to burst into tears.

But that was just foolish weakness, she told herself as she washed swiftly and dragged a comb through her hair. For a moment, she was half tempted to leave it loose on her shoulders. It framed her face appealingly, making her look softer—more relaxed, she thought, lifting some of the heavy chestnut strands in her fingers.

She stopped right there. What on earth was she thinking of? She wasn't there to relax, or make any kind of impression—particularly on someone like

Nic Xandreou, she thought with self-disgust. She
pulled her hair back severely, securing it almost savagely with the barrette.

She came out on to the gallery, and stood for a
moment, looking around her. There were a number
of other doors on both sides of her, all inimically
closed, and between them alcoves had been carved
into the walls to display special ceramics and other
precious objects.

Camilla's eye was caught by one figurine in particular, and she walked down the gallery to take a
closer look. It was a bronze, about three feet high,
of a young man with a face as proud and beautiful
as an eagle's.

The god Apollo, she wondered, or just the owner
of the house, and could anyone tell the difference
anyway? But it was a powerful and arresting piece,
to say the least.

In fact, the whole villa was quite magnificent, she
thought, and maybe that was the trouble—because
it was more a showplace than a home, expensive but
oddly cold and empty.

She heard the sound of an opening door, and
turned to see Arianna and the doctor emerging together from one of the rooms. They walked away
from her towards the stairs, too absorbed in conversation to notice her, and disappeared downstairs and
out of sight.

So that must be Spiro's room, she realised, swallowing. Spiro whom she'd never even seen.

Impulsively, she went to the door, and knocked. There was a pause then a weary voice said, '*Peraste*,' and she went in.

Spiro Xandreou was lying on a couch near tall windows opening on to a balcony. He was a younger, gentler version of his brother, his good looks muted by pain and shock. He was leaning back, his eyes closed, and the snowy cast on his leg, coupled with the greyness beneath his tanned skin, gave him an air of acute vulnerability.

She said quietly, 'Spiro?' and he opened dazed dark eyes and stared at her.

'*Pya iste*?' he demanded.

'I'm Camilla—Katie's sister.' She smiled at him. 'We arrived on Karthos today to look for you.'

He went on staring at her, his brows drawing together. '*Then sas katalaveno*,' he said. 'I do not understand,' he added in English. 'What do you want?'

'I've come here with Katie,' she said. 'She must have mentioned me.'

He shook his head, his anxious look deepening. 'I do not know you. I do not know any Katie.'

Camilla's heart sank. 'Of course you do.' She tried to sound encouraging. 'You met her in Athens at Easter, and you were coming to London to see her. Only you had this accident, so we've come to you instead.'

'What are you saying?' His voice rose. 'Who are you?'

As Camilla hesitated, uncertain how to proceed,

the door behind her was flung open, and Nic Xandreou's voice, molten with anger, said, 'This is intolerable, *thespinis*. My brother must have peace. How dare you intrude on him?'

He took her sound arm, and urged her out of the room, not gently.

Camilla tried to hang back as she was hustled towards the stairs.

'I'm sorry if I've trespassed in some way,' she said. 'But it was Spiro, after all, I came here to see in the first place.'

'In my house you see no one without my permission.'

Camilla lifted her chin. 'And, if I'd asked for permission, would it have been given?'

'No,' he said curtly. 'I only hope your intervention has done no actual harm.'

'I fail to see how a few words from me could affect a broken leg,' she said angrily. 'I know you're concerned about him, but I have my sister to think of.' She paused. 'I also thought Spiro might appreciate some news of her.'

'And did he?'

'Well, no.' Camilla found herself being escorted swiftly and inexorably out of the house, with no chance of saying goodbye to Arianna or asking the doctor about Spiro's condition, she realised with vexation. 'He seemed—confused.'

Nic's firm mouth tightened as he assisted her without particular finesse into the passenger seat of a serviceable-looking Jeep waiting at the front entrance. Her bag, she saw, was waiting for her on the seat, depriving her of any excuse to return. He seemed to think of everything.

'Spiro's recovery will not be assisted by any kind of harassment,' Nic Xandreou said as he started the engine.

Camilla sighed. 'I truly didn't intend that. I just wanted to say—hello.'

'Well, now you have done so,' he said dismissively. 'So let that be an end to it.'

But it couldn't be the end, Camilla thought as the Jeep swung down the drive. It was only the beginning...

She stiffened as she caught sight of the scooter at the side of the road. 'Oh, what am I going to do about that?'

'You will do nothing,' he said grimly. 'I have examined the machine, and it was not fit to be on the road even before the accident. Where did you get it?'

'From someone called Andonis.' She produced the card from her bag. 'I got this from the hotel.'

He shot it a frowning glance. 'Ah, yes, the Dionysius. Of course.' He hit the steering-wheel with an exasperated fist. 'I should have known. How many times has he been warned in the past?' He shook his head. 'Never again.'

'I'll go along with that. No matter what it costs, I'll rent a car.'

'You intend to remain on Karthos?' He shot her an unsmiling look.

'Of course. Katie will naturally want to spend every moment with Spiro, and I can enjoy a normal holiday.'

He said bleakly, 'I regret that will not be possible.'

'Why—does Karthos only cater for eccentrics?' Camilla tried to make a feeble joke, to dispel the sudden cold feeling inside her.

'It would be better for you to return to your own country, and take your sister with you.'

She said huskily, 'You mean while Spiro recovers. But he isn't that badly hurt, and Katie will want to help look after him.'

'Her services will not be necessary.' He did not look at her. His attention appeared to be concentrated on the corkscrew road they were descending.

'That's not for you to say.' Camilla kept her tone level. 'You seem to have forgotten that she and Spiro are engaged to be married...'

'I have sanctioned no such engagement,' he returned harshly. 'Nor shall I. It is you that has the poor memory, *thespinis*. We have resolved the mistaken identities, perhaps, but nothing else has changed, believe me.'

'What do you mean?'

His fingers beat an irritable tattoo on the wheel. 'I thought I had made it clear. I do not accept that your sister or her unborn child has any claim on my family. A girl who is over-generous with her favours before marriage must accept the consequences,' he added damningly.

'While the man escapes scot-free?' Camilla drew

a deep, angry breath. 'What a wonderful double standard.'

Nic Xandreou hunched a shoulder. 'Spiro is young,' he said flatly. 'I will not allow him to ruin his future for one foolish lapse.'

'And what about Katie's future?'

'Your sister is clearly a clever young woman. She'll make out.'

'But you can't dismiss it like that.' Camilla's heart was hammering sickly and painfully. 'They're in love.'

His mouth twisted cynically. 'The first of many times for them both, I have no doubt.'

For Spiro, perhaps, she thought, hating him—hating all the lordly Xandreou males. But not steadfast Katie. She had chosen her mate and given her heart. A rejection like this could scar her for life.

She drew an unsteady breath. 'Has Spiro himself no say in all this?'

He paused. 'He knows he has been at fault,' he said. 'I am the head of our family, and ultimately he will do as he is told.'

'A life sentence.' Camilla's tone was biting.

Nic Xandreou shrugged again. 'I have my own plans for Spiro,' he retorted. 'They do not include your sister, *thespinis*.'

'An arranged marriage, no doubt.' It was chilling to have her original fears confirmed.

'A marriage, certainly, based on proper foundations, with real values and a shared culture.' His profile looked as if it had been cast in bronze. 'Spiro will be a wealthy man one day. He will not throw himself away on the first pretty face to catch his eye.'

'So, if Katie were rich, it would be a different story,' Camilla said bitterly.

'I did not say so. Spiro's wife should, firstly, be a woman of discretion.'

She bit her lip. 'People in love don't always behave very sensibly. Haven't you ever fallen head over heels for someone, Mr Xandreou? Or are you like that bronze statue at the villa—all surface glamour but no heart?'

'You presume altogether too much, *thespinis*.' His voice was ice. 'And my emotions are not at issue.'

'But they must meet—to talk about the baby. You can't prevent their seeing each other for that,' Camilla said desperately.

'There would be no point.'

'That's just your opinion. Spiro may have other ideas,' she said tautly. 'Katie certainly will.'

'The matter is not open to discussion. You serve no purpose by remaining on Karthos, *thespinis*, neither you nor your sister. Go back where you belong.'

'Not until Katie has seen Spiro,' she flung back at him. 'You have no right to keep them apart in this high-handed way. I can understand now why "tyrant" is a Greek word,' she added angrily.

The first buildings of Karthos town were beginning to line the road.

'We will not discuss my rights, if you please,' Nic Xandreou said coldly, 'or call me names. Spiro has no wish to see your sister. In fact, he doesn't even remember her name, or that she ever existed.'

'I don't believe that.' Her voice shook. 'You're just afraid to let them meet each other again. You don't want to lose your influence over Spiro—or let him lead his own life.'

'They could meet a dozen times, I promise you, and it would make no difference.' Nic Xandreou swung the Jeep into the square and brought it to an abrupt halt outside the hotel.

'Why should I listen to any promise of yours—or anything you say, for that matter?' Camilla found the passenger door being wrenched open, and herself being lifted down to the narrow pavement.

'Because that bump on the head has given Spiro amnesia, *thespinis*.' His hands were hard on her shoulders. The dark eyes glittered down at her. 'He remembers nothing and no one before the accident. Are you satisfied now?'

'Oh, no.' Camilla lifted a distressed hand to her mouth, her hazel eyes enormous suddenly. 'It can't be true.'

'You think I would lie about something so serious?' His voice rasped.

'No.' She shook her head. 'Oh, God, poor boy. What are we going to do?'

'You will do nothing,' he said. 'I shall nurse my brother back to health and strength alone.'

'That's what you think.' Camilla tensed with new purpose. 'I won't allow you to dismiss Katie from his life like this.'

He said, 'You think to dictate to me, *thespinis*? A woman, to impose her will on Nic Xandreou?' He laughed harshly. 'Never.'

His hands tightened, and he jerked her towards him. Camilla's swift yelp of pain as he touched her grazed arm was as suddenly silenced by the forceful pressure of his mouth on hers.

She felt the cruel dazzle of the sun on her face, beating against her closed eyelids, as his kiss deepened, taking control, teasing her lips apart to admit the invasion of his tongue.

Her breasts were crushed achingly against his chest. She recognised the taut muscularity of the body pressed against hers with every fibre of her being—as if she'd always known in some secret recess of her soul exactly what it would be like to be in Nic Xandreou's arms. As if she'd been born for this moment alone...

Then, with the same suddenness, she was free. He was breathing unevenly, the dark gaze that burned into hers as hot and relentless as the Greek sun.

He said harshly, 'Don't cross me again, Camilla Dryden—if you know what is good for you.'

He swung himself lithely back into the Jeep, and drove off, leaving her staring after him, a hand pressed in disbelief to her ravaged mouth.

CHAPTER FOUR

CAMILLA'S legs were shaking under her as she made her way through the restaurant area to the outside staircase.

She'd never been kissed so publicly before. In fact, she hadn't been kissed that much at all, and Nic Xandreou's deliberate ravishment of her mouth had been a profound and shattering experience.

Particularly when conducted under the gaze of the hotel staff and half the population of Karthos, she thought, shame and resentment fuelling her anger. She was all too aware of the grins and nudges between the waiters who were preparing the tables for dinner. She heard someone say, 'Xandreou's woman,' and laugh.

What on earth had possessed him? she raged inwardly as she went upstairs, avoiding a sullen look of disapproval from Kostas's wife Maria, who was hosing down the courtyard.

A gesture of contempt, perhaps, for the sister of a girl who'd allowed herself to be too easily seduced? Well, he'd misjudged both Katie and herself, as he'd find out to his cost, she promised herself wrathfully.

And if he imagined he could humiliate her into running away, he'd think again about that too.

In the meantime, she'd decided it was best for Katie to remain in the dark about what was going on. She would reunite her sister with Spiro somehow, she was determined about that. But it would serve no purpose to worry Katie unnecessarily, for the time being.

When she went to the clinic in the morning, she would ask the doctor about Spiro's amnesia, its treatment and likely duration. At least then she'd know what they were dealing with.

Nic Xandreou's intransigence was another matter altogether. She'd no idea what could cure that, she thought as she went into the bedroom.

The splash of the shower ceased as she entered the room, and Katie emerged from the small bathroom, a towel wrapped sarong-like around her, running her hands through her damp hair. Her eyes widened when she saw her sister.

'Milla—what's happened?'

Which particular incident did she have in mind? Camilla asked herself in silent irony. Aloud she said, 'I did a really stupid thing, love. I hired one of the local scooters, and fell off.'

Katie looked horrified. 'But you could have been killed.'

'Could have been, but wasn't.' Camilla kept her tone light. 'I'm now cured of living dangerously.'

Or I hope I am, she added silently. 'What have you been doing?'

'I slept for ages.' Katie began towelling her hair. 'Then I walked down to the beach and had a swim. The water was wonderful. You should have been with me.'

'Yes.' Camilla collected a handful of fresh undies and started for the shower. 'I really wish I had been.'

'The beach was really crowded,' Katie went on. 'I kept thinking how wonderful it would be if I looked up and saw Spiro coming towards me, just like that first time.' Her voice was very tender, and slightly wistful. 'Falling in love with him was so simple—and right. Now, suddenly, it's all difficult and complicated.'

'But not impossible,' Camilla said bracingly. 'And that's a promise. Now, you decide what I'm going to have for my first Greek meal.' She paused. 'Shall we eat here or at one of the tavernas?'

'Here, I guess.' Katie sounded suddenly listless, her shoulders slumped defeatedly. 'It doesn't really matter.'

Camilla felt her hands clench, and wished they were fastened round Nic Xandreou's throat.

She showered swiftly, flinching as the water touched her grazed skin, but glad at the same time to wash away any lingering contact with Nic Xandreou's mouth and hands. Although the actual memory of the kiss might not be so easy to dismiss, she realised unhappily.

She dressed in a simple jade-green dress with a full wrap-around skirt, brushing her hair out on to her shoulders.

Downstairs, Kostas welcomed them exuberantly, and showed them to a table.

'To drink, ladies?' He handed them menus.

'Orange juice for me,' decided Katie, who'd perked up a little, to Camilla's relief. 'And retsina for my sister.'

'Good, good,' he approved. 'And to eat, may I recommend lamb baked in the oven with tomatoes, garlic and fresh herbs?'

Both girls agreed that that sounded wonderful, and he went off, bellowing noisy instructions towards the kitchen.

'What's retsina?' Camilla asked suspiciously, noting Katie's dancing eyes.

'Resinated white wine. Very Greek. Spiro told me it gets its flavour from the casks it's stored in. You'll love it,' Katie promised.

At first, Camilla found the flavour odd, but her palate soon adapted, and by the time a beaming Kostas brought them appetisers of deep-fried *kalamari*, accompanied by *tsatsiki*, a dip made from yoghurt and cucumbers, she was entirely won over.

The lamb, which came with sliced fried potatoes and green beans, was tender, robustly flavoured and delicious, and Camilla noted thankfully that Katie ate every scrap of her generous helping. Both girls

declined the sweet pastries offered for dessert, opt-
ing simply for coffee served *sketo*, without sugar.

With the coffee came complimentary glasses of a
liqueur tasting of tangerines, served by Kostas who
informed them that the entertainment was about to
begin.

'Tonight, *thespinis*, we have live bouzouki, and
also dance.'

'That sounds like fun.' Katie's face had that wistful look again. 'Spiro took me to some wonderful
bouzouki clubs in Athens.'

Camilla couldn't judge the standard of performance when the trio of musicians started up, but the
music was lively with an infectious rhythm, and she
found herself clapping in time with the beat along
with everyone else at the surrounding tables.

A beaming Kostas led off the dancing, with some
of the waiters, moving in a slow, almost stately se-
quence, in line, their hands resting on each other's
shoulders.

'That's the *syrto*,' Katie told her. 'It's incredibly
old and there are only about six basic steps, but the
leader always supplies his own variations.'

Like many burly men, Kostas was agile, and light
on his feet, as he dipped and swayed to the music,
sinking down to one knee before leaping upright
again.

Camilla noticed Maria watching from the hotel
doorway, her face sullen and unsmiling. Her whole
attitude was in total contrast to her husband's ge-

niality. If theirs had been an arranged marriage, Kostas seemed to have the worst of the bargain, Camilla thought with faint amusement.

The beat of the music had changed, and more people were joining in the dancing, moving and turning in a chain which wound between the tables.

Camilla shook her head regretfully when Kostas beckoned. Her bruised side was aching too much for that kind of exertion, but Katie jumped up eagerly.

'Do you think you should?' Camilla put out a detaining hand.

'Just this once.' There were dreams in Katie's eyes. 'It brings back so many memories.'

She was young and healthy, Camilla thought as she sipped her drink. It was wrong to try and wrap her in cotton wool. And she needed all the cheering up she could get.

Everyone in the restaurant was watching the dancing, absorbed in the colour and movement, but Camilla was suddenly aware, with a little shiver of unease, that someone was watching her instead.

The music seemed to fade to a distance, and the dancers became a blur. She put the tiny glass down carefully, because her hand was shaking, and sent a studiedly casual glance towards the restaurant's trellised entrance.

Nic Xandreou was standing there, hands on hips. He looked taller than ever in pale grey trousers, and a shirt in the same colour with a soft, silky sheen. Across the space that divided them, his dark eyes met hers in a direct challenge she felt down to her bones, then switched quite deliberately to where Katie was dancing, her face shining with animation.

Camilla saw his brows lift, and the faint contemptuous smile which twisted his mouth, as he registered the scene before him. He glanced back towards her table. Is this the innocent child, pregnant and broken-hearted? his cynically accusing gaze demanded, louder than any words.

Then he turned, and vanished back into the dark street as silently as he'd come.

Camilla found her heart was hammering, and her mouth suddenly dry. What was he doing there? she asked herself. If he'd come to see Katie, he couldn't have chosen a worse moment. He'd be convinced now that she was just another silly, pretty English girl hell-bent on a good time. She could have screamed with vexation.

The music ended, and Katie returned, glowing.

'That was wonderful,' she said. 'Spiro would be proud of me.' She gave her sister a swift hug. 'Everything's going to be all right. I know it is.'

Camilla returned her smile, but with constraint. With a sinking heart, she thought, I wish I could be so sure.

The next morning found her climbing the steep cobbled street that led up through the centre of town to the clinic.

To her relief, Katie had not pressed her initial

offer to accompany her, agreeing to see her later on the beach.

Quite apart from her various aches and pains, Camilla had found sleep elusive the previous night. She had lain listening to Katie's gentle breathing, trying to make plans—to decide principally what to do if the doctor refused to help them.

It was a possibility she couldn't discount. He was clearly a friend of the Xandreou family, and might well agree with Nic Xandreou that Katie was a minor indiscretion, easily brushed aside.

She sighed as she traversed the crowded pavements, where shop displays overflowed into the open air. She found herself edging round stands of beautifully tooled leather bags, woven rugs in traditional patterns and cascades of embroidered linens and wall-hangings. At any other time, she would have lingered for a closer look at the goods on offer, but she had the uneasy feeling that there wasn't a second to be lost.

Nic Xandreou was a powerful man, with the island in his pocket. And she and Katie were outsiders, totally isolated. She couldn't forget that for a minute.

Nor could she forget the scorch of his kiss on her mouth—nor, more fundamentally, his parting warning. For her own peace of mind, she should keep out of Nic Xandreou's way, and common sense suggested a strategic retreat back to England.

But, in spite of her personal misgivings, it was

Katie's interests she had to consider, and those of her unborn child. Katie had come to Karthos to be reunited with the man she loved.

And I've promised to help, she thought. I can't go back on that now simply because Nic Xandreou alarms and disturbs me.

The clinic was housed in an old building, its bell-tower revealing it as a former monastery. But once inside the rather forbidding entrance Camilla found the facilities were a dream of ultra-modernity. Petros, in an immaculate white coat, was standing talking to the receptionist, and he came across to Camilla at once.

'How are you today, *thespinis*?' His smile was friendly. 'No ill effects from your fall—no raised temperature, or headaches?'

'I'm a bit stiff and sore, but otherwise fine. I really don't need any antibiotics.' She paused. 'But I would like to consult you about something else.'

'Of course.' He opened a door, and waved her ahead of him. Camilla walked in, and paused, half dazzled by the blast of strong sunlight which greeted her, turning the rest of the large room to shadow. The room was dominated, she saw, by a huge desk, and, straight ahead of her, long windows stood open, giving access to a walled garden with a colonnaded walkway, presumably once used by the monks.

'My office,' Petros told her as he closed the door. 'For my sins I am also the clinic director.'

'You've certainly chosen the loveliest room.'

Camilla looked with open delight at the central square of grass, where a small fountain danced from the cupped hands of a discreetly veiled stone nymph, while surrounding the fountain were roses, great, shaggy, untamed masses of them in every shade from crimson and deep copper to the palest cream.

'Sit down, *thespinis*. How may I help you?'

Camilla took a deep breath. 'I want to ask you about Spiro Xandreou's amnesia,' she said. 'I suppose you know why my sister and I are on Karthos?'

'The matter has been mentioned.' The doctor's face was discreetly enigmatic.

'Then we're very much at your mercy. Please—how long will it be before Spiro remembers things again?'

He shook his head. 'You ask me something I cannot answer. Sometimes the condition changes slowly. In other cases, a jog to the memory can restore it suddenly and completely.' He sighed. 'But Spiro fights his condition. It frightens him to realise that much of his past has become a blank, and this increases his confusion.'

Camilla grimaced. 'Then my visit yesterday really didn't help. I wish I'd been told what was wrong.'

'The family does not wish his condition generally known. This is a small island with simple people. A broken leg is understood, something in the mind less so.'

Camilla nodded. 'You mentioned a jog to his

memory. Do you think, maybe, seeing my sister again could be just the jolt he needs?'

Petros's face sobered. 'It is certainly possible,' he said, after a pause.

'Then can you arrange it?'

He spread his hands in apology. 'I regret it is not permitted. Nic—Kyrios Xandreou—has given orders that neither you nor your sister is to be admitted to the villa, or allowed to see Spiro. I'm sorry.'

'Oh, God.' Camilla, speaking through gritted teeth, hardly recognised her own voice. 'The bastard.'

She remembered the searing pressure of his mouth on hers and thought, Judas.

Petros looked shocked. 'You must not say such a thing, *thespinis*. You do not understand. Since Nic was quite young, he has had to be the patriarch to his family, and it has not been easy. He seeks only to protect them.' He paused, looking uncomfortable. 'Perhaps to keep them from mistakes that he knows will only lead to great unhappiness.'

'I'm sure the mighty Mr Xandreou has never put a foot wrong in his life,' Camilla said bitterly. 'He's the golden boy through and through.'

The doctor shook his head. 'Not always, *thespinis*,' he corrected gently. 'The loss of his parents—then his marriage, and the death of his wife— all these were tragedies for him. And they have left their mark, I think.'

Camilla gasped. 'He's a widower?' she asked huskily. It was the last thing she'd expected to hear. She bit her lip, remembering how she'd accused him of being without a heart—without feeling. Clearly that had not been true—once. But surely it should make him more understanding of Katie and Spiro...

She said, 'Couldn't you talk to him—from a medical point of view? Convince him that letting Katie see Spiro would be worth trying at least?'

'I can try,' he said. 'But I guarantee nothing. Nic is my friend—and a friend to everyone on Karthos.' He gestured around him wryly. 'He provided this clinic at his own expense. But, like his father and grandfather before him, he is an autocrat. His word has always been law, and he expects no argument with his decisions.'

Camilla got to her feet. 'Then perhaps it's time there was,' she returned crisply.

His brows rose. 'You are a brave woman, *thespinis*.' The internal telephone rang on his desk, and he lifted the receiver. As he listened, Camilla saw him begin to frown. He said something quietly in his own language, and rang off.

He said, 'There is something I must see to, *thespinis*, if you'll excuse me.' He paused, looking faintly embarrassed. 'I hope I may offer you some coffee before you go?'

'There's no need.' Camilla hesitated, glancing at her watch.

'No, it is my pleasure. One moment only, please.'
The door closed behind him.

Camilla walked over to the window, and looked out. The sun-warmed scent of the roses, carried on the faint breeze, seemed to fill the room. Their fragrance and colour caught at her throat—lifted her heart.

She thought, I was right to come here. He's made no promises, but at least he's held out a glimmer of hope.

She heard the door behind her open again.

She said, 'I can't tell you how grateful I am. I'm sure, between us, we can persuade Mr Xandreou to change his mind.'

'Such certainty, *thespinis*.' The silken mockery of an all too familiar voice assailed her ears. 'Now I wouldn't count on a thing.'

For a moment, Camilla stood, frozen to the spot, then slowly she turned and looked across the shadows of the room to the tall man who stood by the doorway. Blocking, she realised, her means of retreat.

'*Kalimera*,' said Nic Xandreou, and smiled at her.

CHAPTER FIVE

CAMILLA said, 'What are you doing here?'

'I knew you were due to see Petros Deroulades here this morning.' The dark gaze went over her coolly, absorbing the pale blue button-through dress, as if its chain-store origins were quite apparent to him. 'I thought perhaps we should talk—on neutral territory.'

'And he just went along with it,' she said bitterly.

'You must not blame poor Petros,' he said. 'I have—a certain influence here.'

'So he told me.' Camilla drew a breath. 'You're quite the philanthropist, Mr Xandreou. Someone should have told you that charity begins at home.'

'Which is exactly what I wish to discuss.' He moved to the desk and sat on the corner of it, lithe and relaxed. 'Won't you sit down again?'

'I'll stay where I am,' she said curtly. 'Are you telling me you're prepared to lift your embargo on Katie's visiting Spiro?'

'No,' he said. 'I'm sure you know better than that.'

'Then there's no more to be said.' She walked past him to the door, head held high, and twisted the heavy carved handle with mounting frustration.

He said, 'Save your energy, *thespinis*. There is a security device in operation.'

So, for the moment she was trapped. The realisation dried her mouth. She looked at him lounging there, totally the master of the situation, and anger shook her voice.

'Will you let me out of here?'

'When you have heard what I have to say.'

'I'm not interested,' Camilla said huskily. 'Until your attitude changes over Katie, there is nothing to discuss.'

'We will see.' The dark eyes were hooded, enigmatic. 'Where is your sister?'

'At the hotel.' Camilla looked at her watch again. 'And she'll be wondering where I am.'

His mouth twisted. 'I am sure she will have found entertainment.'

'What do you mean by that?'

'As you know, I saw her dancing last night.' His smile was edged. 'She seems to have an affinity with my countrymen. An uninhibited performance.'

'Then your brother must be a good teacher,' she returned, refusing to take the obvious bait. 'He showed her all the steps in person.' One mark to our side, she told herself silently as she saw his lips tighten.

She hurried into speech. 'As a matter of interest, why was he working in that restaurant? It seems an odd way for a future millionaire to earn a crust.'

'You think a man should take his inheritance

without effort—without responsibility?' His voice was suddenly harsh. 'That he should enjoy the fruits, and remain in ignorance of how the harvest has been grown?' He shook his head. 'No, Spiro will work, as I have done, in every branch of our business undertakings, and at every level, from the lowliest menial job to top administration.' He paused. 'Good management comes from knowledge and understanding.'

'Of which you have so much, of course.' It nettled her that what he was saying made so much sense; that he was determined not to let Spiro degenerate into just another member of the idle rich. 'So Athens was just part of the menial phase.'

'Yes, but don't pity him too much. There are worse jobs, I promise you,' he added sardonically.

She could believe it, although for the life of her she couldn't imagine Nic Xandreou himself, in spite of his claims, waiting on tables, or emptying garbage. Someone would have been around to flatten his path, and make sure he didn't roughen his hands too much on his way to the boardroom.

She found herself suddenly remembering those hands as they'd touched her. Powerful, she thought, and strong as steel, but the long fingers strangely sensitive.

Her own were small and workmanlike, as they'd had to be. She found she was spreading them against the door behind her, as if seeking reassurance from its solidity and weight.

She said, 'And your sister Arianna—will she take her turn as a chambermaid?'

'No. For a woman, it is different.'

She thought, Not where I come from.

Aloud, she said, 'And I suppose you have a nice dynastic marriage worked out for her too.' She shook her head. 'Don't you ever get tired of dominating people—controlling their lives?'

He said tautly, 'I care for my family, *thespinis*. I am responsible for them, and for all those who depend on me. I cannot afford to become weary or indifferent to these responsibilities.'

'And Arianna's just content to—go with the flow.' Camilla found it hard to believe. She remembered the petulance in the dark eyes, the sullen curve to the girl's mouth.

'She knows where her duty lies,' he returned flatly. 'And so does Spiro. So, do not hope, or allow your sister to do so. She has no place in his life.'

'And if Arianna were in the same situation as Katie, Mr Xandreou—what then?' she demanded.

She looked at him, and he was darkness against the brilliance of the sun.

He said softly, 'I would find the man, and kill him with my own hands.'

The words died away, but their menace remained almost tangibly. It was suddenly difficult to breathe. She needed air, and she ran, almost stumbling in her haste to the open glass doors and the escape they seemed to offer.

But even that was an illusion. The garden was totally enclosed in its high walls.

The heat beat down on her like a clenched fist. The scent of roses was almost overpowering, and the air was heavy with the hum of working bees, and the ceaseless rasp of unseen cicadas. She walked to the fountain, and let the cool water play on her wrists, as she strove to calm her errant pulses.

This might have been a monastery once, she thought, her heart hammering unsteadily, but there'd been something altogether older and more primitive than Christianity in that room just then. And it was around her now, in this blazing sun, and bleached walls, reminding her that Greece was a country where once pagan gods had ruled with their own savage codes of blood and vengeance.

She'd come to Karthos as a latter-day avenging Fury, but now the tables were turned, and in some strange way she was the quarry, not the pursuer.

In one shady corner, she saw the spreading branches and glossy leaves of a laurel. Apollo's tree, she thought. Sacred to him because it was supposed to hold the spirit of a girl he'd loved—the river nymph Daphne who'd run from him, and turned herself to wood to escape capture.

Had she hated him or simply been afraid of the power he exerted? Either way, Camilla could understand that kind of desperation. Because her own dark Apollo had followed her now, and was standing watching her, hands on hips. He was more formally dressed than she had ever seen him, but he'd discarded the jacket of his light suit, and the sleeves of his white shirt had been turned back to reveal his tanned forearms. His tie, too, had been loosened, as if he'd grown impatient with its constriction. As if the normal trappings of civilisation were only a veneer, easily discarded. As well they might be...

His gaze was almost meditative, lingering on the loose waves of her chestnut hair, the quiver of her parted lips, and the thrust of her rounded breasts against the thin material of her dress. She was covered from throat to knee, but she might as well have been naked, she realised dazedly.

She'd never been so physically aware of any man in her life before, or so helpless in controlling her own reactions. She was actually beginning to shake under the dark intensity of his eyes.

The silence between them was charged—dangerous.

She took a step back, and found herself caught fast, anchored to the spot by the trailing briar of a bush of deep crimson roses.

'Oh, no.' She twisted, struggling to free herself, shying away with a yelp as Nic walked across to her. 'I can manage.' Her voice sounded oddly breathless.

'Keep still, and don't be a fool,' he cautioned sharply. 'I don't need another torn garment of yours laid to my account.' With infinite care, he detached her skirt from the clinging tendrils. 'Nor any further marks on your skin,' he added quietly.

'Thank you.' Camilla swallowed, smoothing the snagged fabric over her thighs.

'*Parakalo.*' There was a note of veiled amusement in his voice. He leaned past her, deftly picking a rose, a folded bud of dark velvet, from the offending bush.

'So soft, *ne*?' His voice was almost teasing. 'So beautiful.' He brushed the dusky petals against her cheek. 'So exquisitely scented.' The rose touched the corner of her startled mouth, forcing a gasp from her. 'But beware,' he added silkily. 'Like a woman, this beauty hides sharp thorns.'

He was altogether too close to her. She could almost feel the warmth of his body, as if he were touching her in earnest, drawing her against him, holding her near.

Instead of just—stroking her with that damned flower. He was brushing it against the pulse in her throat now, and down to the demure rounded neckline of her dress. And down further to the first soft swell of her breasts...

She could feel herself shivering suddenly, her nipples hardening in anticipation against the thin, revealing fabric.

Oh, God, she thought. What am I doing? What's happening to me?

He was playing some kind of game with her, and she knew it, even if she didn't fully understand what it was. She was supposed to be the cool one, the girl who was practical and in charge, and she couldn't allow him to destroy her equilibrium like this.

Because, like him, she was the head of her family, and she had to face him, challenge him on equal terms.

She stepped away, deliberately out of range. 'Did you arrange this interview just to discuss horticulture?'

'Is that what we were doing? It was not my purpose—however enjoyable.' He paused, the dark eyes glinting, letting her know he'd been well aware of her body's involuntary reaction to his teasing. He was still holding the rose, turning it slowly in his fingers. He said, 'I have a business proposition to put to you.'

'Oh.' Camilla stiffened. 'What kind of proposition?'

'A financial deal. I realise on reflection that I was over-ready to dismiss your claims. But your appearance at my home took me by surprise, you understand.'

'You thought Katie would just let Spiro vanish from her life?' she asked incredulously. 'That she'd make no effort to find him?'

He shrugged. 'She would not be the first to find that a holiday amour can have—repercussions. She might have decided to cut her losses—put it down to experience.'

'But it wasn't like that,' she said desperately. She

beat her clenched fist into the palm of her other hand. 'I wish Katie were here to convince you.'

'It would prove nothing.' He paused again. 'Would she have been so anxious to trace my brother, I wonder, if he'd been simply a waiter in a restaurant? If he hadn't told her that he was a Xandreou?'

'She didn't believe his claims,' she said wearily.

'And now?'

'Nothing has changed.' Camilla hesitated. 'I've mentioned nothing about you, Spiro, the villa—any of it.'

'Why not?'

'To protect her from the hurt of knowing she's not considered good enough for your family.'

His mouth tightened. 'Do you have no man to speak for you?' he asked. 'No father—no brothers?'

'We're alone.'

'Then any negotiation must be with you.' He paused. 'I am prepared on certain conditions to settle a sum of money on your sister, which, suitably invested, will provide support for her child.'

Camilla tensed. 'Conditions?' she repeated. 'What conditions?'

'They are simple,' he said. 'She will receive the money through an agreement drawn up by our respective lawyers only if she promises to leave Karthos immediately, and makes no attempt to contact Spiro in the future.'

She couldn't believe what she was hearing. Nic

Xandreou was proposing to write Katie out of Spiro's life, as if she were some unimportant tax loss.

She said, 'And if Spiro himself tries to contact her—when he recovers?'

'He will not.'

A few brief words, she thought shakily, to pass sentence of death on a love-affair.

She said, too evenly, 'As simple as that.'

'That's how it has to be,' he said. 'Or no deal. I want the matter over, before more harm is done. And be thankful I offer this much,' he added icily. 'I saw her last night at the Dionysius. If she behaved with equal freedom in Athens, Spiro may not be the only candidate for the fatherhood of her baby.'

Camilla's face flamed. 'How dare you say such a thing?'

'Because it's true,' he flung back at her. 'She is no saint. Like all the rest, she comes to Greece looking for romance—a little adventure with a man. And you, Camilla, you are no different either.'

He tossed the rose away from him suddenly, as if it had burned his hand. 'Let us speak the truth to each other—the truth our bodies have already uttered. If I wanted you, I could take you, and we both know it.'

His words fell into a hot and stinging silence.

The blood was pounding in Camilla's head. She drew back her arm, and slapped him hard across the face. His head fell back in shock, and he swore briefly and violently in Greek, as his hand went up to touch his bruised cheekbones.

She saw anger and disbelief flare in his eyes, then he reached for her, and she dodged past him, and ran for the open glass doors.

Although there was no sanctuary there in the locked and shadowed room, she thought, her heart pounding as she realised he was coming after her. No friendly laurel tree either to transform and protect her from his pursuit.

But, like a small miracle, the office door was standing open. And there were people there—Petros Deroulades, and beside him Arianna Xandreou, their faces pictures of sheer astonishment.

Camilla said breathlessly, '*Kalimera*,' and kept running.

Her legs were still shaking under her when she arrived back at the hotel. Fortunately she'd managed to hail a cruising taxi just outside the clinic, and she huddled in its back seat, resisting the impulse to peer over her shoulder to see if Nic Xandreou was still chasing her.

She found herself wondering, absurdly, what would have happened if the original nymph had stood her ground and cracked Apollo as hard as she could. Maybe he'd have abandoned his seduction, and she could have gone on happily swimming in her river.

And maybe not. It was never a good thing to cross the ancient gods. Or Nic Xandreou, for that matter, although his slap across the face had been fully deserved.

Presumably he was so used to women going down like ninepins under the force of his sexual charisma that he'd taken her compliance for granted.

Well, he could nurse the realisation that he was wrong about her along with his bruised face.

He was wrong, too, if he thought that Katie could simply be bought off.

There isn't enough money in the world, Mr Xandreou, she thought savagely as she paid off the taxi driver.

Maria was at Reception when she called for the room key. The older woman gave her a venomous look, then disappeared behind the beaded curtain behind the desk which led to the family quarters. A moment later, Kostas appeared, wiping his moustache. His normal dazzling smile had disappeared, and his expression seemed stuck at some halfway mark between wariness and embarrassment.

'Kyria Dryden.' He weighed the key in his hand. 'I regret there is a problem. A mistake in reservations. Your room is needed for other people—a prior booking, you understand. I must ask you to vacate it tomorrow.'

Camilla felt as if she'd been poleaxed.

'But you can't do that. We have a fortnight's booking, paid in advance,' she protested.

He spread his hands in a sketch of an apology.

'All your money will be refunded. I am sorry for the inconvenience.'

'Inconvenience, you call it.' Camilla's voice shook. She was angrily aware that Maria was watching with sour triumph from behind the curtain. 'If you've made a mistake, the least you can do is find us another room.'

Kostas looked uneasier than ever. 'That would be difficult for me, *thespinis*. I don't want trouble. It would be better if you left Karthos, I think. Take the ferry—go to Zakynthos. I have a friend with a hotel in Alikes—very pretty, very quiet.'

'Oh, I see.' Camilla was getting more furious by the second. 'You don't just want us out of the hotel but off the island too. Tell me, Kostas, would Mr Nic Xandreou have any hand in this?'

A dull flush showed under his skin. '*Thespinis*, this is not easy for me, but it is impossible you stay in my hotel. I give you back your money, and you go, *ne*?'

Camilla picked up her key with all the dignity she could assume. She said, 'Don't worry. We wouldn't dream of staying on.'

She was near to tears as she went upstairs. She hadn't escaped from Nic Xandreou at all, nor scored even a moral victory. That had been illusion. Even at a distance he had the power to harm her.

One phone call from the clinic was all it had taken. An act of spiteful retaliation for that slap on the face. And Kostas, like a good vassal, was carrying out the orders from his overlord.

I should have kept my temper, she berated herself as she unfastened the shutters and stepped out on to the balcony. Let him think I was prepared to negotiate. Bought us some more time here. Now I've blown it completely.

We'll have to go back to England, she thought, and get the best legal advice we can afford. Which means that Katie's love-affair is going to be distorted into a sordid wrangle over child support. And Spiro, in his blank, confused world, won't even know.

And now she would have to find Katie and break the bad news to her—all of it.

She was turning away, when she saw a familiar figure walk into the restaurant area below, and stand looking round her, hand on hip, head arrogantly high.

Arianna Xandreou, she thought. Sent by big brother to check we've got our marching orders. She picked up the silk blouse she'd laundered the night before, and left the bedroom.

On the stairs, she met Arianna on her way up. The Greek girl treated her to a mischievous smile.

'So,' she said. 'You called up the storm and survived. I am all admiration.'

'Oh.' Camilla paused, taken aback. 'You—you know what happened?'

'Not everything, and I did not dare ask. I don't

have your courage, *po*, *po*, *po*. My brother is not
accustomed to opposition.'

'Then he'll have to get used to it.' Camilla drew
a furious breath. 'Because I'll go on fighting him
every step of the way—even if he does get me de-
ported from Karthos. And you can tell him so.'

Arianna shrugged a slim shoulder. 'I don't think
so,' she said drily. 'But what is this ''deport''? You
are leaving Karthos?'

'Not of my own free will.' Camilla bit her lip.
'Your brother tried to buy us off, and when I—refused he instructed the hotel to throw us out. We're
homeless as from tomorrow.'

Arianna's brows snapped together. She said flatly,
'No, Nic would not do such a thing. He would despise it. It is the action of a man with a small mind,
and though he has many faults he is not that.'

'But Kostas didn't deny it when I asked if your
brother was involved,' Camilla argued. 'And I did
make him very angry.'

'Yes.' Arianna's tone gloated. 'More angry than
I can remember. With Spiro there are often explo-
sions. But Nic—always he stays as cold as ice. So
it is good for him that someone does not do as he
wants—and even better when that someone is a
woman.' She nodded. 'Come, we will talk together.'

Camilla hung back. 'I don't want you to get into
trouble with your—family.'

Arianna's smile was impish. 'No problem. And

you need me, Camilla Dryden, if your sister is to see Spiro—and make him remember.'

Astounded, Camilla found herself seated at a table, sipping iced peach juice, fresh and tangy in tall glasses.

She said in a low voice, 'You mean you're prepared to help? But why?'

Arianna shrugged. 'Spiro is my brother, and I love him. I want him to be happy, but in his own way, not that of Nic,' she added emphatically. 'And maybe, one day, you can also help me, *ne*?'

'If I can, perhaps,' Camilla agreed warily. The lovely Arianna was clearly up to something, but she couldn't figure out what it was.

'So Nic offered you money.'

'Yes.' Camilla flushed stormily at the memory.

'Do not blame him too much,' Arianna said calmly. 'Life, I think, has taught him that everything and everyone has a price. But you refused him?'

Camilla drank some peach juice. 'Not in so many words,' she said guardedly. 'I just—lost my temper.'

'That is good.' Arianna gave a vigorous nod. 'Because that gives you an excuse to stay—to have more discussions with Nic.'

'I don't think so.' Camilla paused. 'Your brother won't want to see me again.'

Arianna smiled. 'No?' She glanced past Camilla. 'See for yourself.'

Camilla twisted round in her chair in time to see Nic Xandreou, with a face like thunder, stride under the vine-clad archway, and head straight for their table.

The storm she'd summoned up was about to break.

CHAPTER SIX

CAMILLA pushed her chair back and got to her feet, aware that she was trembling.

'Come to evict us in person, Mr Xandreou?' she challenged as he reached them.

Nic Xandreou frowned, his dark gaze stormy as it flicked over her. 'No, *thespinis*, to find my sister.' He looked down at Arianna who was toying with the straw in her glass. 'I saw your car in the square,' he said flatly. 'What are you doing here?'

Arianna shrugged. 'I decided to save Kyria Dryden the trouble of returning the shirt you lent her.' She held up the garment in question. 'Remember?'

'Yes,' he acknowledged after a brief pause. 'I remember.'

It occurred to Camilla exactly what he was recalling to mind, and sudden warmth invaded her face.

'And now we are having a farewell drink together,' the Greek girl added pointedly.

Nic Xandreou turned back to Camilla. 'You are truly leaving?'

He had the unmitigated gall to sound surprised. Camilla's gaze dwelt vengefully on the reddened

82

mark on his cheek. Her only regret was that she hadn't given him a black eye.

She said, clearly and coldly, 'You should know, *kyrie*. You arranged it, after all.'

'I?' His frown deepened. 'Naturally I welcome the wisdom of your decision, but what has it to do with me?'

'Because of you, Camilla and her sister have been told to leave the hotel,' Arianna supplied.

'Nonsense.' He gave Camilla an ironic look. 'You credit me with more influence than I possess, *thespinis*.'

'Naturally you'd deny it,' she returned tautly.

'I am not in the habit of lying.' His mouth tightened. 'Nor have I reason to do so. However I will speak to Kostas Philippides so you may judge for yourself.'

Kostas arrived, his face sullen. Camilla could understand little of the conversation which followed, but the hotel-keeper was clearly on the defensive, hands waving as he gesticulated angrily towards the hotel.

Nic dismissed him with obvious impatience, and gave Camilla a grim look. 'It is Maria, his wife, who demands your departure, *thespinis*. Because of you, a member of her family has been insulted, and she refuses, in consequence, to allow you to stay.'

'Because of me?' Camilla sank back into her chair. 'But that's ridiculous. I've done nothing.'

'You hired a scooter,' Nic reminded her. He

sighed angrily. 'I spoke to Andonis about it—warned him he would be reported to the police if he continued to rent out machines in that condition.' His mouth twisted. 'It was not a friendly interview.'

'Andonis is related to Maria?' Camilla asked blankly.

'Her nephew.' He paused. 'Another works here as a waiter.'

'Yes,' she said. He told me how to find you, she thought. And he was the one who called 'Xandreou's woman' after me yesterday.

'Andonis has complained to his aunt. She witnessed your return to the hotel yesterday, it seems, and has told Kostas you are a trouble-maker and also morally suspect.'

'But that's absurd.' Camilla pressed her hands to her hot face as the memory of that parting insult of a kiss tormented her once more. 'She wouldn't turn us out—just for that, surely?'

Nic shrugged. 'She has lived all her life on Karthos,' he said flatly. 'It does little to broaden the mind, believe me. But the root cause of her anger is my threat to Andonis. I have assured Kostas you are blameless, but Maria has a bad temper and a wicked tongue, and his life will be a misery to him unless he carries out her wishes.'

'So, in fact it is true. Camilla and her sister are being turned out of the hotel because of you!' Arianna exclaimed, her eyes glinting.

'I suppose—yes.' He gestured angrily. 'But I

could not know that my words with Andonis would
have such a repercussion.'

Arianna leaned back in her chair. 'Then we must
make amends, Nic.'

'What do you mean?' His tone was biting.

She looked back at him blandly. 'We cannot let
two girls, one of them pregnant, be turned on to the
streets. We are responsible, my brother, so we must
help.' She paused. 'They must stay with us at the
Villa Apollo.'

Camilla heard Nic's sharp intake of breath, and
froze in shock.

'No,' they both said, in sharp and explosive
union.

Arianna laughed. 'So, you agree on something, if
only to disagree.' She lifted a graceful shoulder.
'But I think there is no choice.' She paused. 'If not
the villa, then the sea house. It is never used, and
Soula can look after them.'

'There's no need,' Camilla protested into a loaded
silence. 'All we need is another hotel room somewhere…'

'That is not so easy.' Arianna pulled a face.
'Karthos is full at this season. And, besides, what
has happened to you is an outrage against *philox-
enia*—the welcome we Greeks give to the strangers
among us.' She turned to Nic. 'Tell her, brother.'

He looked as if he'd been carved from stone.
'Arianna is right,' he said icily. 'You have been
wronged because of me, and I must make reparation.

I offer you our—hospitality for the remainder of your stay.'

She said between her teeth, 'I'd rather sleep on the beach.'

'But that would not be good for your sister,' Arianna pointed out. 'Also the tourist police do not allow. Better you come to us.'

There was a silence. Nic's face was expressionless, but Camilla had the sensation of harsh emotion barely under control.

At last, he said tautly, 'The sea house is at your disposal, *thespinis*. You will be transferred there tomorrow.' He paused. 'It is at a distance from the Villa Apollo, so we shall be able to respect each other's privacy.'

The warning was unequivocal, Camilla realised. The villa and Spiro were still strictly out of bounds.

'I understand.' She lifted her chin.

'I thought you would.' Nic nodded curtly. 'Now I shall go and make the necessary arrangements.' He looked at his sister. 'And you, Arianna?'

'I have still some shopping.' Her face was guileless.

'Then I'll see you later.' His tone was clipped as his glance flicked once more to Camilla. 'Until tomorrow, *thespinis*.'

Camilla watched his tall figure stride away, and collapsed back in her chair. She said wanly, 'Arianna, you've put me in an impossible position. I—we can't accept this offer.'

'You wish to stay on Karthos, *ne*?' Arianna's smile was cat-like. 'Then that is the important thing—not your pride, or even this quarrel with Nic, which made him hold his hand to his face when he followed you from the garden today,' she added slyly.

Camilla bit her lip. 'Your brother and I are better apart, believe me,' she said constrictedly.

'So, the sea house will be perfect,' Arianna said with a shrug. 'Because Nic never goes there. It was where he spent his honeymoon, so it has bad memories for him.'

'Oh, God,' Camilla said huskily. 'This gets worse all the time. Katie and I are the least people he'd want in a place with such—personal associations.'

'All the more reason for him to keep away,' Arianna returned caustically. 'And Soula will be happy to have someone to look after again. She was our nurse when we were children, and has been with us in America and Australia, so she speaks English.' She leaned forward, eyes gleaming. 'And once you are living in the sea house it can be arranged for your sister and Spiro to see each other again. No problem.' She pushed back her chair. 'Now it would be good if Katie and I met, *ne*?'

Camilla said mechanically, 'Yes, of course. We'll go and find her.'

Her legs were shaking as she got to her feet. The full implications of what she'd agreed to were just starting to sink in. She was about to become the guest of Nic Xandreou, resident on his property, if not actually under his roof.

'No problem'. The phrase—the Greek panacea for everything—echoed mockingly in her mind.

Camilla shivered inwardly. My God, she thought, if only it were true.

They found Katie on the beach. She listened in grave silence while Camilla, with certain prudent exceptions, recounted everything that had happened since their arrival on Karthos.

Katie went very white when she heard the details of Spiro's accident, and its effects, but seemed to accept Arianna's assurance that he was expected to recover fully in time.

'But I should be with him,' she said anxiously. 'He needs me.'

'Of course.' Arianna patted her arm. 'Unfortunately, little one, we now have to persuade my stubborn older brother too.'

Katie gave her a wavering smile. The two girls had taken to each other on sight, rather to Camilla's surprise. Arianna was light years ahead of Katie in sophistication, and, Camilla suspected, guile. They shouldn't have had a thought in common. However...

'A young sister,' Arianna had laughed. 'Just what I always wanted. Spiro told me I would love you.'

'He spoke about me?' Katie asked wistfully.

'Of course. He knew I would be happy for him.'
Arianna sighed. 'But Nic was a different story.' She
shook her head. 'My God, what a quarrel. The whole
of Karthos must have heard it.'

Katie looked troubled. 'Spiro told me there might
be—difficulties.'

'My brothers have always fought,' Arianna said
serenely. 'It's nothing. But Nic has strong views on
marriage. He says like must marry like, or there can
be no happiness. And he'd planned a bride for
Spiro,' she added almost casually. 'Already there'd
been discussions with the girl's family, so he was
not pleased when Spiro said he'd made his own
choice.

'After all, it was only what Nic had done himself,
as Spiro was quick to remind him.' She pulled a
face. 'He was so angry. Even after five years, there
is still pain for him when he remembers.'

'Well, that's understandable,' Camilla said constrictedly. Although Nic Xandreou was hardly the
pattern of the grieving widower, she thought, wondering what his wife had been like. Some gentle
doe-eyed Greek girl, no doubt, who'd treated him
like a god.

She said, 'If he wants this marriage so much, why
doesn't he marry the girl himself?' and was surprised at the sharpness in her voice.

Arianna shrugged. 'There is a saying, *ne*, that
once burned you fear the fire?' Her smile was
worldly. 'Besides, Nic amuses himself very well.

There is a girl in Athens, and another, I think, in New York. Why should he choose one dish, when a banquet is waiting?'

Why indeed? Camilla thought hollowly.

She got to her feet. 'I'd better start packing if we're moving tomorrow.'

'Shall I help?' Katie sat up.

'No, stay where you are.' Camilla forced a smile. 'Enjoy the sun.'

'And I will stay too,' Arianna said. 'We will talk, Katie *mou*, become friends as well as sisters. Make Spiro happy.'

Arianna certainly knew the right things to say, Camilla thought as she walked back to the hotel. And she was clearly going to be an important ally in the battle to reunite Spiro and Katie.

So why do I feel there's more going on than meets the eye? she wondered restively. Beware the Greeks when they come bearing gifts. That was the old saying, although it seemed ungrateful to remember it.

The hotel seemed totally deserted as she threaded her way between the tables in the courtyard, but she had the oddest feeling that she was being watched as she went up the outside stairway to the room. She glanced back over her shoulder, but could see no one. Perhaps the malignant Maria's evil eye was operating at a distance, she thought, deriding herself for being over-fanciful.

The room was cool and shady, the shutters closed, and the thin tan-coloured drapes drawn too. Camilla reluctantly lifted the empty cases on to one of the beds. She hadn't bargained for packing up so soon. But then, if she was honest, she hadn't envisaged anything that had befallen her on Karthos so far. Anything—or anyone.

The image of Nic Xandreou rose in her mind so clearly and sharply that he might have been there, standing in the small shadowy room beside her. So near that she had only to turn to touch him—to feel the warmth of his skin under her hand...

She felt her whole body clench in a sudden shock of sheer yearning, and stopped, appalled at herself. What was the matter with her? How could she let her mind stray like this, in directions which should have been—and had to be—strictly taboo?

Just remember, she adjured herself savagely, that you're not alone. Exactly the same fantasies are probably being indulged in Athens and New York at this very moment—and they're only the ones you know about.

Xandreou's women, she thought with contempt, marching into the little shower-room, and turning on the water. She needed to cool off. To remember her pride and wash Nic Xandreou out of her mind and senses, she thought as she pulled off her clothes and stepped under the shower, lifting her face to the full force of the water.

She felt refreshed and more in control of her errant senses when she emerged, the enveloping towel anchored sarong-like just above her breasts, her hair hanging damply to her shoulders.

The rap on the bedroom door startled her. Katie was back sooner than she'd suspected. Judging by the way they'd had their heads together, she'd imagined that her sister and Arianna were on the beach for the duration, she thought drily as she opened the door.

But the smile died on her lips when she saw who was standing there.

It was Maria's nephew, the one who waited on tables. But out of uniform now—and out for mischief, her brain telegraphed the swift warning. The smile that slid over her was knowing—insolent, and she wished to God she were wearing more than just a wet towel.

She said curtly, 'Yes? What do you want?'

'I came to visit you, *thespinis*.' He peered past her. 'You are alone?'

'Yes, and I don't want company.' She tried to push the door shut, but he was too quick for her, shouldering his way into the room.

'Unless it's Nic Xandreou, *ne*? Tomorrow you go to him—live in his house—sleep in his bed. You thought no one would know?' The smile became a leer as he studied her shocked expression. 'Xandreou himself has told Kostas Philippides that you are leaving, and where you go.' His voice became insinuating. 'You should thank me, *thespinis*, for telling you where to find him.'

'You've already been thanked.' She was frightened now, but determined not to show it. 'Now get out before I tell your aunt.'

'You think she cares?' He laughed. 'She knows what you are. A little English whore to warm Xandreou's bed. But he is not the only man on Karthos.' He took a step nearer, the dark eyes hot and greedy on her bare shoulders and the first swell of her breasts above the towel. 'Who would know if I also tasted the honey Xandreou has chosen for himself?'

'I would know.' Nic Xandreou's voice was icily grim as he appeared with devastating suddenness in the doorway behind them. 'And also how to punish such a thief.'

'Kyrios Nicos.' The young Greek's swarthy skin was tinged with grey, and his tongue ran round his lips. 'I—I meant nothing. It was a joke…' He slid out into the passage, almost flattening himself into invisibility in his eagerness to escape.

Nic Xandreou followed, and Camilla heard the sound of a scuffle, a thud and a yelp of pain before he returned, rubbing his knuckles.

'You—hit him?' Camilla asked faintly.

Nic shrugged. 'He has a sore mouth,' he countered flatly. 'He will think before using it to insult another woman.'

'But nothing actually happened,' she protested, relief warring with mortification inside her.

'No thanks to you.' He looked her over, his brows

snapping together ominously. 'Are you quite mad to permit such a one as that to enter your room—when you're unclothed? Or perhaps he was welcome.' His voice hardened. 'Maybe my own arrival was the real intrusion.'

'How dare you?' Camilla flared. 'You know that isn't true.'

'What do I know?' The dark eyes glittered at her as he put a wry hand to his cheek. 'You did not offer him the treatment you gave me.'

'I didn't get the chance,' Camilla said crossly. 'And I thought it was Katie at the door, or I'd never have opened it. I never dreamed it would be him—or that he'd think…' She halted, aware that she was blushing. 'Well, you heard him.'

'Yes.' He was silent for a moment. 'That was why I came back—to tell you that it might not be safe for you to remain here tonight. That there might be some form of harassment.'

'What made you think that?'

His mouth twisted. 'An absurdity. I thought—it was almost as if I heard you call out—cry for help.'

You did, Camilla thought with horror as she remembered how she'd conjured up his image, here in this room. But not in fear, she mused with a shiver.

'So I thought it best to return,' he went on. He gestured brusquely at the cases. 'Pack your things, *thespinis*, and come with me now. You cannot stay here any longer.'

She gasped. 'I'll have to fetch Katie. She's on the beach,' she added with a certain constraint, not wishing to mention Arianna's presence there too. Nic Xandreou would not approve of this newly hatched intimacy, she thought.

He frowned again. 'I will send Kostas to find her. And tell him too it is time he controlled his wife's relations, and became master in his own house,' he added harshly.

Camilla drew a breath. 'Isn't that rather a chauvinist viewpoint?'

'You can ask that—after what you have just experienced here?' His voice was hard.

'I'd say it in any circumstances,' Camilla hit back. 'And you don't seem to impose too many limitations on your own conduct,' she added shakily. 'It's thanks to you we're in this mess, after all. If you hadn't been so high-handed—and—mauled me in front of Maria, we'd be staying here. Instead we're moving to accommodation that belongs to you, and people will draw the obvious conclusion.'

'You will be there for a little less than two weeks,' he said tersely. 'Is that really so great a hardship?'

'Yes, it is.' She glared at him. 'When I know I'm going to be regarded as just another in a long line of—willing women,' she added bitterly.

Nic Xandreou took a swift harsh breath. 'No one,' he said. 'No one has ever dared speak to me as you do.'

'Then it's time someone did,' Camilla lifted her chin. 'Full time someone told you how—arrogant and unfeeling you are,' she added passionately, and burst, to her own consternation, into overwrought tears.

Nic Xandreou muttered some expletive half under his breath. Camilla found herself guided to the nearest bed, and seated on its edge, a handful of tissues from a box beside the bed pushed into her hand. Discovered, too, that her head was pressed against his shoulder, while his hand gently stroked her damp hair, and he murmured quietly and soothingly to her in his own language.

Self-consciously she drew away, scrubbing her face with the tissues. She mumbled, 'I'm sorry.'

'And I too regret—more than you can imagine,' he said with a touch of grimness. He put a hand under her chin, and lowered his mouth to hers. His lips were warm, almost gentle, but their touch was sensuous, bringing every pulse, every nerve-ending in her body to throbbing urgent life.

When he put her away from him, she could have cried out in disappointment. She stared up at him, watching his mouth slant in sardonic acknowledgement.

'Young Stavros was right,' he said. 'You are honey, *agape mou*. Honey and wine, and ripe, sweet fruit. All the things to tempt a man.' His fingers feathered delicately over her bare shoulder, and came to rest a brief millimetre away from the curve of her breast. 'But I,' he went on softly, 'am not in the market for such temptation. Especially as in two weeks you will be gone forever. I hope that reassures you.'

He kissed her again, the caress swift, hard, and carrying a kind of strange finality. Then he got up and went to the door.

Camilla watched it close behind him. Her skin was tingling where his hand had rested, and it hurt suddenly to breathe. It hurt...

I have to dress, she thought, swallowing past the pain. And I have to pack. Before he returns, and I have to go with him.

'Xandreou's woman'. That was what they would all think—all say as she left. It was a label which would haunt her until she left Karthos, and perhaps beyond.

And it isn't even true, she thought savagely—and was suddenly aware, with a shame that scorched her, that Nic Xandreou was not the only one with regrets.

CHAPTER SEVEN

IT WAS late afternoon when they arrived at the sea house. It had been a largely silent journey. Camilla, huddled on her side of the Jeep, had tried to concentrate on the scenery, which was spectacular enough to warrant it, and not Nic Xandreou's profile, which she found even more disturbing. And Katie was equally quiet, lost in her own thoughts.

Her first meeting with Nic had been formal on his side and composed on hers. She'd shown little of the hurt and indignation she must be feeling, and Camilla had felt both surprised and proud at her forbearance, and the maturity of her reaction.

On one side of the narrow pot-holed road, hillside covered in scrub soared upwards towards the unclouded arc of the sky to become, in time, a tall bleached mountain, all jagged silver and violet peaks and deep agate corries. High above them a solitary bird hovered, motionless and predatory.

On the other side, there was an almost sheer drop to the sea, sparkling like a brazen mirror under the sinking sun.

It seemed very remote, but wasn't that the idea? she thought bitterly. They were to be hidden away in this inaccessible place, and forgotten there until their money ran out and they were forced to leave.

Money, she thought with a stifled gasp of distress. In the scramble to be ready she'd forgotten to get the money for their room back from Kostas.

'There is something wrong?'

He didn't miss a thing.

She hunched a shoulder. 'No.' He was the last person in the world who needed to know they had a cash shortage. That would be playing right into his hands. 'It's just—very beautiful,' she added, gesturing around her.

He nodded. 'Every man sees his island as the loveliest place on earth. I only wish I could spend more time here, but our business interests are world-wide and expanding.'

He said it quite casually. Money, and the power it bestowed, were things he took for granted. And, with so much under his control, the destinies of two young lovers would seem an annoying triviality to be disposed of between one deal and the next. Spiro's and Katie's happiness wouldn't feature on any of Nic Xandreou's balance sheets.

That was something she needed to remember—to build up the flame of her anger and resentment against him, and keep it burning. She couldn't afford any more weakness where he was concerned. No more aching yearning to feel his mouth exploring hers, or his hands spinning a web of sensual delight on her skin.

The kind of spell he knew so well how to weave. The way he'd enthralled other fools.

But not me, she vowed with passion. Never again.

The Jeep swung off the road, and began to wind its way down a track so narrow that the shrubs and bushes which bordered it reached out to brush the sides of the vehicle. Pollen, heavy and golden, showered down on to Camilla's bare knee.

The Jeep turned a corner, and there in front of them, occupying its own headland, was the sea house. It was small by the standards of the Villa Apollo—single-storey, and roofed in faded terra-cotta tiles, their colour repeated in the shutters that hid the windows—and surrounded by a tangle of overgrown garden.

Camilla thought, It looks lonely, and instantly derided herself for being sentimental. Of course it was lonely—that was the whole point. They were being dumped in the back of beyond for the duration. She hadn't seen another hamlet, let alone a village within walking distance, during the entire journey.

Soula was waiting at the entrance as Nic brought the Jeep to a halt. She was small and plump, clad in the inevitable black dress and headscarf, but her wrinkled face was wreathed in smiles, as she took Camilla's hand in both of hers.

'Welcome,' she said. 'You are welcome, Kyria Camilla, and you too, Kyria Catherine.'

'I'm afraid we're causing a great deal of trouble,'

Camilla said haltingly as Nic, his face set, unloaded their cases.

'No problem.' Soula gave a gusty sigh. 'At last life returns to this place.' She took both girls by the hand, tugging them forward. 'Come look.'

The house had been designed, Camilla realised, to capitalise on the views of the sea. Each room had its own superb vista, and the windows stood open to catch the breeze from the water, and the soft murmur of the waves.

A terrace had been built along the entire length of the house, overlooking the water, and from this a flight of steps led down, Soula told them, to a cove with a small sandy beach.

'Very private for the sun,' she added. 'Also good for swimming.'

The interior of the house was like walking straight into the heart of the sun. The floors were tiled in deep amber, the walls colour-washed in a paler shade of the same colour. The main living area was equipped with a sofa and several armchairs covered in a vibrant geometric print in shades of blue, gold and rust, with a separate raised dining area.

The room to which Camilla was shown opened directly on to the terrace, and was the largest of the bedrooms. She looked around slowly, assimilating the patina of the wood of the built-in furniture, and the enormous wall-hanging in rich earthy shades of bronze, copper and gold which supplied a dramatic background to the wide bed with its linen the colour of warm cream.

'You like?' Soula demanded anxiously.

'Like' was hardly the word, Camilla thought, drawing a breath. She said, 'It's—magnificent.'

Soula nodded her satisfaction, missing the touch of uncertainty in Camilla's voice. 'I bring you coffee,' she said. 'Kyria Catherine will rest until dinner. She has a little headache, I think.'

No, Camilla thought with an inward sigh. She has one enormous headache, which I share.

This had to be the master bedroom, she told herself tautly, when she was alone. This was where Nic Xandreou had brought his bride. And in that bed he'd made her his wife.

For a moment her mind ran riot, then she closed off the clamorous, disturbing images, her nails scoring the soft palms of her hands. Well, she couldn't—wouldn't sleep there. She'd swap with Katie, on whom all the implications of the room would be lost.

She felt stifled suddenly, and headed for the windows, pushing open the shutters as she sought the fresh air of the terrace.

But under the heavy canopy of bougainvillaea she paused.

Because he was there, she realised tautly, seated on the low parapet, his figure darkly silhouetted against the glitter of the sea, as he stared out at the horizon.

As if some silent signal had alerted him to her

presence, he turned his head and looked at her, his expression starkly, almost bitterly arrested.

She knew of course what he must be seeing— another girl emerging from the room they had once shared, standing for a moment, framed by flowers. That girl would have smiled, evoking memories of the night that had just passed, promising more pleasure to come. She would have held out her hands— walked across the terrace, and into his arms.

They said time healed, she thought, but judging by his face Nic Xandreou's bereavement must have inflicted a wound as deep as the whispering sea around them.

She moved hurriedly away from the bedroom window, and its connotations, forcing a smile, hastening into speech to conceal her own sudden pain.

'I can see why it's called the sea house.'

He nodded. 'My father built it. He loved the sea, and always kept a caique moored in the cove below. Later, when Arianna and Spiro were born, he sold our house in Karthos town, and started on the Villa Apollo. But this place was always a refuge for him—for all of us.' His fleeting smile mocked her. 'Quite separate from the main house.' He pointed across the small bay to the adjoining headland and to where the sun highlighted white walls amid a cluster of encircling greenery. 'Which is there.'

'So close?' Camilla was taken aback. 'I—I didn't realise.'

'But only by sea,' he said laconically. 'There is

no direct road between the two properties. One must go a considerable way inland, as you must have realised, and this has proved an inconvenience—in the past.' His brief pause told her the present was a different matter.

He picked a loose stone off the parapet, and tossed it down into the rippling dark blue water. 'Spiro and I used to swim from one house to another,' he went on almost musingly. A faint smile twisted his mouth. 'How strong a swimmer are you, Camilla?'

'Good enough,' she said shortly. 'But not so expert as to risk that distance.'

'I'm glad you are so conscious of your safety.' His smile widened, mocking her. 'It is always best, I think, to know one's limitations, and abide by them,' he added silkily.

'Oh, I've got the picture.' Camilla glanced round. 'Here we are, and here we'll stay. Isn't that it?'

'You are hardly prisoners,' he said sardonically. 'You are free to leave whenever you wish.'

'But on whose terms?' Camilla met his glance levelly.

He laughed. 'Again, I am sure you have the picture.' He paused. 'You should at least listen to my offer, Camilla. I am prepared to be generous—within reason.'

Camilla shook her head. 'No deal.'

'I am sure that is not your final word.' Nic's voice was silky. 'Here you will have leisure and tranquillity to think. And when you are ready to talk, you have only to let me know.'

'You'll wait a long time,' she said tersely.

'But I think my resources will outlast yours.' He paused again. 'Which reminds me.' He reached for his jacket, flung across the parapet beside him, and extracted a bulky envelope from an inside pocket. 'This is for you.'

The envelope was crammed with Greek drachmae in a variety of denominations. Camilla thrust it back at him. 'What is this? A down-payment on my ultimate co-operation? No way, Mr Xandreou.'

'Actually, the money is yours, Kyria Dryden.' His tone jeered at her own formality. 'The refund on your hotel room. Fortunately Kostas has a conscience as well as a bitch of a wife.' He closed her fingers round the envelope, and, despite herself, a swift burning tingle ran up her arm at the brush of his hand on hers. 'Take it,' he urged softly. 'You will need all the cash you can get if you seriously mean to prolong this battle between us.'

She looked down at the envelope. 'You didn't have to hand it over. You'd be quite entitled to keep it—as rent.'

The dark eyes flashed. 'Please do not insult me by such a suggestion,' he said. 'You are my guest here—you and your sister.'

'But I'd rather we paid our way,' she said stubbornly. 'You—you can't pretend we're welcome here.'

'Perhaps not, but it provides an opportunity to settle matters between us before you go home.'

She took a breath. 'You're really so sure you'll win?' she said bitterly.

'Oh, yes.' His voice was soft. 'One way or another.'

His glance seemed to touch her, lingering on her mouth, then sweeping down to the swell of her breasts, reminding her that his most lethal armament in this conflict was his virile, charismatic sexuality.

Whereas she had nothing to fight with but her own convictions and determination. Could they ever be enough?

Nic lifted himself lithely from the parapet, glancing at his watch. 'I must get back, I'm expecting a call from New York.'

'A personal call?' some demon prompted her to ask.

His mouth twisted. 'My sister has been busy,' he commented with a touch of grimness. 'But I don't think, *matia mou*, that is any concern of yours.' He paused. 'Think about what I have said, and remember I am prepared to reopen negotiations at any time.'

'I'll negotiate,' she said steadily. 'But only on condition that you let Katie see Spiro. Can't you see that she might be able to jog his memory? Isn't it at least worth trying—to have him cured—restored to the way he used to be with no blank spots in his mind?'

His face hardened. 'Spiro will recover in time. And if there are blanks—' he shrugged '—well, your sister's intervention in his life is best forgotten anyway.'

'That's cruel.' Camilla's voice shook.

'It is also practical.' His smile held no amusement. 'When you realise, finally, that you do not make conditions, you will be free to concentrate solely on the terms of our eventual bargain. There is no other real alternative, I promise you.'

He absorbed, with irony, the stricken look on her face. 'And now I wish you goodnight, Camilla.' The dark eyes glittered at her. 'Sleep well in my bed, *agape mou*—if you can.'

He inclined his head to her almost formally, and was gone, his parting words smarting like the lash of a whip across her consciousness.

'No problem,' Katie said cheerfully, tucking into her helping of Soula's delicious chicken in lemon sauce that evening.

Camilla stared at her. 'I wish I shared your confidence,' she said wearily. 'We're here, and Spiro might as well be at the end of the universe.'

Katie shook her head. 'He's not that far away,' she said firmly. 'Arianna says we must just be patient for a while—bide our time.'

'Really?' Camilla queried drily. 'Just remember, darling, that Arianna's a Xandreou as well. And it was her idea to strand us here, out of harm's way. Are you quite sure you can trust her?'

'Absolutely. Nic's trying to rule her life too— push her into marrying a man she doesn't love.'

'Oh.' Camilla digested this. 'And Arianna presumably has other plans?'

'Of course,' Katie said serenely. 'She's in love with Petros—Dr Deroulades.'

'My God,' Camilla said faintly. The young doctor seemed the unlikeliest of targets for someone as glamorous and worldly as Arianna. Yet there was great kindness in his face, she thought slowly, and integrity in the gaze behind his spectacles.

I knew she was up to something, she thought, but not this.

'And he loves her too,' Katie went on. 'They've known each other all their lives. In fact the Xandreou family paid for Petros's medical training. But he's not rich or powerful, of course, so Nic wouldn't even consider him as a suitable husband for Arianna.' She sighed. 'Arianna says if he had the least idea they were in love he would be terribly angry. Petros would lose his job at the clinic and be sent away from Karthos altogether, and she would never see him again. And Nic's vengeance would follow him wherever he went,' she added.

'I can imagine,' Camilla said grimly.

Katie pushed away her empty plate. 'So, they have to pretend when they meet in public, and see each other properly in secret.'

'She told you all this today?' Camilla asked, frowning.

Katie nodded. 'It's a mutual pact,' she said. 'She helps reunite me with Spiro, we do what we can for Arianna and Petros in return.'

'I don't like the sound of this.' Camilla shook her head. 'We have enough problems already. And Nic Xandreou may actually have a point,' she added grudgingly. 'Arianna seems an expensive proposition for someone on a doctor's salary. Maybe she needs a convenient millionaire.'

'Camilla.' Katie was shocked. 'You're surely not on *his* side?'

'I'm not taking sides,' Camilla said defensively. 'Just trying to be realistic. If we interfere, we could have Nic Xandreou's vengeance following us as well, and we don't need that.'

'You forget,' Katie said gently. 'We'll have Spiro to protect us.' Her eyes shone. 'Everything's going to be fine. I know it.'

Camilla could find nothing to say in the face of such sincere and passionate conviction.

Later, alone in her room, she found herself hoping that Katie was right—about all of it.

She looked around her with dissatisfaction. Her plan to swap accommodation with Katie had been forestalled firstly by Soula who had unpacked for her, and put all her things away. Any attempt at change now would inevitably become some kind of big deal, and might even get to the ears of Nic

Xandreou, who would draw his own all too accurate conclusions.

And I don't need that, she muttered to herself.

And then Katie had disclosed, starry-eyed, that she could see the lights from the Villa Apollo from her window, which made her feel that Spiro was close to her.

And after that, of course, there was nothing more to be said.

I shall have to bear it, Camilla thought. Even if I can't manage the usual grin.

She took the passports and the envelope of money Nic had given her, and looked round for a safe place to put them. The drawer in the night-table beside the bed seemed the obvious repository, but that was easier said than done, she realised with vexation, when the drawer refused to budge.

At first, she thought it might be locked, then she realised that something bulky had been put into the drawer and become wedged. After some manoeuvring with her steel comb, she managed to free the obstruction, and open the drawer.

She found herself holding a photograph in an ornate but tarnished silver frame.

It was the picture of a girl, the face radiant, almost flawlessly beautiful. Blonde hair tumbling on to bare shoulders. Full lips parting in a smile to reveal perfect teeth. Violet eyes, glowing a provocative invitation.

And all of it oddly but elusively familiar, Camilla thought wonderingly.

There was a scrawl of writing across the bottom left-hand corner. The words seemed to leap up at her. 'To Nic, on our wedding-day. Forever, Rachelle.'

Camilla drew a sharp breath. Of course, she thought. It was Rachelle Morgan, the actress. She'd blazed across the cinema world in a brief, stormy career, which had included an Oscar nomination as well as rows with leading men, and an eventual sacking from a film. She'd never made another, and Camilla remembered reading some years before of her death from a drugs overdose in some Los Angeles motel.

She sank down on the edge of the bed. This—*this* was the girl Nic Xandreou had married, she thought faintly. A far cry from the docile Greek heiress of her imagination. And clearly a very different marriage from the ideal he'd outlined to her. Perhaps she could now understand, if not condone, his reasons.

Rachelle Morgan had died alone a long way from Karthos, and the sea pavilion. In fact, Camilla could recall in all the attendant publicity about her career no mention of any marriage, or any husband left to mourn in the tragic aftermath.

No wonder Nic was bitter, nor that the scars of his loss had gone so deep.

For him, 'forever' had been over too soon. If it had even existed at all...

Nic Xandreou was no all-conquering god. Just a man, as Arianna had said, who'd been burned and now feared the fire in consequence.

Or was it Rachelle Morgan who'd been scorched instead? The thought struck her like a blow from a clenched fist. Had she, like some latter-day Icarus, flown too near the Xandreou sun, not comprehending its power, only to drop like a stone to earth in the ruin of her wings?

Who could say what demons had driven all that beauty and talent to destruction?

Hands shaking, Camilla put the photograph down beside her bed. She would keep it there, she thought, shivering, as a timely reminder. A warning even.

She felt suddenly cold. 'Dear God,' she whispered. 'He could destroy me too—so very easily.'

CHAPTER EIGHT

SLEEP did not come easily to Camilla that night. Huddled awkwardly under a single sheet at the edge of the bed, she found her search for temporary oblivion distorted and disturbed by unwanted thoughts and images which even pursued her into her dreams.

A tall man with skin like bronze, and eyes like a dark flame, moved through those dreams, lay beside her, shared her pillow.

She could feel the warmth of his body against hers, the fever of his lips, the frank enticement of his hands as they explored her. Found herself reaching out in turn, seeking him vainly in the still heat of the night. Only to realise, with a frightening sense of desolation, that she was alone.

She drew an angry breath, kicking away the imprisoning tangle of sheet from her overheated body. What was happening to her? How could she possibly feel these things about a man who was still virtually a stranger, and almost certainly an enemy?

'Damn you, Nic Xandreou,' she whispered into the darkness. 'I should never have come here, and now I'm trapped, and I can't get away.'

She escaped at last into a restless doze, only to be jolted back into wakefulness again by the certainty that she could hear something—someone moving on the terrace outside.

She sat up, pushing the hair back from her face, staring towards the shuttered windows, her heart thumping erratically. She'd thought the sea house too remote for intruders, but now...

She swung her feet to the floor, reaching for the white cotton peignoir trimmed with broderie anglaise which matched her nightgown.

The early morning air was fresh as she stepped out on to the terrace. The sky was pale, almost misty. The sea was a ripple of silver. A faint breeze stirred in the bougainvillaea above her head. There was no one there, of course, and yet...

'*Kalimera*.'

Camilla whirled with a startled cry. Nic Xandreou was standing, hands on hips, a few yards away outside the open window of the *saloni* from which he'd obviously just emerged.

He was wearing ancient denim jeans, hacked off at mid-thigh, and a short-sleeved black shirt, unbuttoned almost to the waist. He looked tough, virile, and devastatingly sexy—last night's dream come suddenly alive in front of her.

Remembering the precise nature of that dream, Camilla found colour mounting in her face, and her hand went to her throat to clutch the edges of her peignoir more tightly together.

'You!' she said unevenly. 'What are you doing here?'

His brows lifted, the amusedly cynical appraisal of his dark eyes telling her that neither the blush or the betrayingly defensive gesture had been lost on him.

'This is my property,' he reminded her drily.

'But you never come here,' she protested, then caught herself. 'At least...'

'That is what Arianna told you,' he supplied. 'She exaggerates. I come to visit Soula, naturally.'

'At this hour?' Camilla glanced at her watch.

'No, this morning I've been fishing so there will be fresh mullet for your dinner tonight.'

She said blankly, 'I don't believe it.'

Nic shrugged. 'The proof is in the kitchen. Do you wish to look?'

'No—I mean—I can't see you as a simple fisherman, alone in the dawn.'

He laughed. 'Yet to a Greek the sea is like the blood in his veins. And on a boat you have time to be alone—to think. Often, it's the only time.'

'A boat?' Camilla parodied astonishment. 'I thought you had your own shipping line.'

'I do,' he said silkily. 'But that is not the same thing at all. Like my father before me, I keep a caique for my own use.' He paused. 'However, I did not intend my visit to wake you. I apologise.'

She bit her lip. 'It doesn't matter. I didn't have a particularly good night, anyway.'

'No?' The dark eyes mocked her.

'No,' she returned tautly. 'This isn't exactly an easy situation—for any of us.'

Nic shrugged again. 'You can resolve it any time you wish,' he retorted.

'You mean—take the money and go.' She lifted her chin. 'Never.'

'That will not be your final decision,' he said. 'I can wait.'

'It isn't my decision to make—or yours. Spiro and Katie are the people concerned—or should be.'

'Unfortunately such sentimental notions have no place in real life.' He sounded bored.

'And what do you know about "real life", Mr Xandreou, shut up in your ivory tower of power and money?' Camilla's voice had an edge. 'You only have to wish for something and it's granted—snap your fingers, and everyone dashes to obey.'

'Naturally you exclude yourself from this fascinating picture of mass acquiescence,' Nic said grimly.

'Of course. You can't expect to own the whole world.'

'I've never wanted to.' His tone hardened. 'Once I thought, as you seem to do, that love could conquer all barriers. But not any longer. A collision between two different worlds can lead only to disaster.' His face was brooding, bitterly introspective, as he looked around him. 'This is a lesson I was forced to learn with the kind of pain I would wish on no one—least of all my young brother.'

'But you can't protect him from experience—or prevent him making his own mistakes,' Camilla protested. 'It doesn't work like that.'

'So you admit that Spiro and your sister would be a mistake.'

'No,' she said wearily. 'I'm trying to say that you and I aren't qualified to make judgements for them.' She took a deep breath. 'It's terrible—a tragedy that your marriage ended as it did—that someone so lovely, with so much going for her—' her voice faltered a little '—should be simply wiped out, but Katie and Spiro are still entitled to lead their own lives, whatever the cost.'

Nic Xandreou was very still, his tall figure suddenly menacing in the clear morning light.

'What do you know of my marriage?'

'Nothing at all, really.' She swallowed. 'But—but I found your wife's photograph, and realised who she was.'

'What are you saying?' His face was thunderous. 'Show me.'

Camilla turned and went back into the bedroom, uneasily aware that he was following. She picked up the photograph and handed it to him. 'It was in this drawer. It must have been pushed in there and forgotten.'

He said harshly, 'An unforgivable oversight. I gave orders for everything to be removed. I wanted nothing left here to remind me.' The dark eyes looked around him, taking in the disordered bed, the intimate clutter of Camilla's toiletries, and discarded clothes. 'Nothing,' he repeated slowly.

Her voice shook a little. 'But you can't easily forget—beauty like hers.'

'Yet you can try.' His mouth was set. He took the backing from the frame, which he tossed contemptuously aside, then ripped the print across, again and again, letting the torn fragments flutter to the floor.

Camilla gave a small distressed cry. 'Oh, no. Oh, how could you?'

'It was simple, believe me.' He swung back to her, his smile almost a snarl. 'This—this is the complication.'

His hands were hard on her shoulders as he pulled her towards him. Her startled eyes read the purpose in his face, but even as her lips framed a negation his mouth possessed hers, making no concession in its fierce demand. The scent of his skin, fragrant with sunlight and the sea, seemed to invade her senses—to fill her being with a harsh and undeniable longing.

She found she was kissing him in return with the same vibrant, consuming urgency, her lips parting eagerly to accept the thrust of his tongue.

Pinned against his body, she was aware of every bone, muscle and sinew in his taut, virile frame. Could feel the heat and strength of his arousal, mirroring the rising flame inside her.

Nic's hand shook as he pulled apart the ribbons of the peignoir, allowing his lips to traverse the vulnerable line of her throat, and the curve of her shoulder. His fingers slid under the strap of her nightgown, tugging it down, baring one rose-tipped breast to his caress.

His palm cupped the soft mound, his thumb brushing the tautening peak, piercing her with a shaft of bewildered pleasure bordering on pain.

The dark head bent to her, and he took the small engorged bud into his mouth, laving it with his tongue, his mouth like fire against her skin. She felt her body judder in anguished delight, her hands lifting to twist in the thick, crisp hair at the nape of his neck.

He lifted her on to the bed, and lay beside her. She was caught in the dream again, she thought dazedly, fright and excitement warring for mastery inside her.

She was sinking down into the softness of the mattress, the weight of his lean body imprisoning her, creating new hungers in every trembling inch of her as she strained towards him in this new and incomprehensible desperation.

He pushed down the other strap of her nightgown, his face absorbed, intent, his mouth hot and seeking against her fragrant flesh. His hands were urgent as they stroked her body through the thin fabric, pushing its hem up towards her thigh with swift and sensual purpose.

'*Se thelo.*' His voice was husky against the uneven beat of her heart. '*Se thelo poli.*'

And the alien words which instinct warned her spoke only of physical need, and no warmer, tenderer emotion, sent the dream shattering into sudden, cold reality.

She was insane, she thought with fear. She must be—lying here on the bed he'd once shared with his wife—a girl whose promise-filled life had ended in isolation and despair. Whose torn photograph was scattered at their feet in ultimate rejection.

And she was letting him touch her—oh, God—letting him *use* her like some sensual exorcism.

She braced her hands against his chest, pushing him away, her body rigid with panic and denial.

'*Matia mou*—what is it? What's wrong?'

'Everything,' Camilla said hoarsely. 'Let go of me—leave me alone. How—how dare you…?'

She scrambled off the bed, dragging the bodice of the nightdress up to cover her breasts, her hands clumsy with shame and remorse.

Nic lifted himself on to an elbow and observed her struggles, his eyes hooded, his firm mouth twisting cynically.

'There was no question of daring, *agape mou*. You wanted what was happening as much as I did. Perhaps more,' he added with swift, silky cruelty.

Camilla gasped, mortified colour burning her face. She said unsteadily, 'Get out of this room. Get away from me.'

'Are you sure?' There was deliberate insolence in his voice—in the look which raked her—stripped

her. 'Perhaps you should learn to be more accommodating—like your sister. You might find there
was more to be gained. That, in certain circumstances, I could be persuaded to be generous.'

She flung back her head. 'Become just another
"Xandreou's woman"?' Her voice was uneven.
'You over-estimate your attractions, *kyrie*. I'd beg
in the streets first.'

Nic's eyes narrowed, but he shrugged as he
swung himself off the bed. 'That is your choice, of
course. But I should warn you there is a time limit
to the terms I'm prepared to offer—all of them.' He
paused to allow the implication in his words to sink
in. 'Maybe it would be wiser, for your sister's sake,
to think again—and soon.'

He walked without haste to the open window,
turning to touch his fingertips to his lips in a parody
of a tender farewell.

He said softly, 'Send me word when you have
changed your mind.'

'About what?' Camilla demanded tautly.

His eyes swept her body again, and he smiled.
'Everything,' he said, and was gone.

It was another flawless morning, baking hot already,
even under the protection of a sun umbrella.
Camilla, ensconced on a lounger in a sheltered part
of the terrace, could hear the sound of voices from
the *saloni*, and guessed that Arianna had arrived for
her daily visit.

Her misgivings about the Greek girl had been un-
justified, she was bound to admit. Her presence at
the sea house was, for Katie, a much needed link
with Spiro, and also the outside world as the sea
house had no phone.

Three endless days had dragged by since that devastating encounter with Nic, and, although there had
been neither sight nor sound of him since, her emotions were still ragged, her senses in turmoil.

She had told herself a hundred times that this
crazy, unwanted infatuation with Nic Xandreou—for
that was all it was, all it ever could be—meant nothing. Absolutely and finally nothing.

Life in England might not have been easy, but
she'd coped—earned herself a reputation for being
calm and reliable. Yet now…

I don't know what's happening to me, she thought
desperately. I'm not in control any more, and I hate
it. I miss my peace of mind. I want it back.

But there would be no inner tranquillity for her
on Karthos. Living in the sea house was a constant
torment, with its reminders of the shadowed past Nic
had shared there with his beautiful young wife—and
those even more potent recent memories, from
which there was no escape.

The thought of his lovemaking still seared her
skin. His presence seemed to linger in the room,
evoking a strange trembling awareness she had no
power to suppress.

Soula had cleared up the torn fragments of the

photograph, her plump face sad, her mouth discreetly compressed. Her employer's marriage was a subject on which she was clearly not prepared to be drawn, although she would chat to Katie by the hour about the old days when both Nic Xandreou and his brother were boys.

Arianna had explained the situation to her, and she had taken Katie firmly under her wing, supervising her diet, and rationing her hours in the sun.

As for Nic himself, presumably he was staying aloof, awaiting her message to say she was ready to deal, Camilla thought bitterly.

But, even when he was absent, she was always aware of him, just the same. Sometimes, across the shimmering water, the Villa Apollo looked almost close enough to touch, and as she sunbathed or swam in the shallow waters of the cove she had the odd impression that unseen eyes were watching her, although she knew that was absurd.

The need to go—to get away before it was too late—had begun to obsess her. Part of her mind was saying that her mission to Karthos was hopeless, anyway. That maybe Nic did hold all the aces, and their best course would be to agree to some kind of financial settlement. But she knew any suggestion to Katie they should cut their losses and return to England would be indignantly resisted.

Katie, immersed in her own emotional maelstrom, had no idea of the confusion that was ripping her sister apart. Nor did Camilla want her to know.

'*Kalimera.*' Arianna appeared beside her, looking cool and elegant in a slim-fitting dress the colour of peppermint ice. 'Soula insists your sister must rest on her bed a little.'

'She's been very kind,' Camilla said rather stiltedly.

Arianna shrugged. 'She loves Spiro, and wants to see him happy. But how to achieve it, that is the problem.' She sat down on an adjoining lounger. 'Petros has promised he will bring Katie and Spiro together as soon as the coast is clear.'

She spread her hands. 'But Nicos is rarely away from the Villa Apollo these days, and when he is absent it is only for a short time—and he leaves Yannis to watch Spiro.' She frowned. 'We must find some way of drawing him from the villa, and keeping him away for several hours.'

Camilla said constrictedly, 'Surely he'll be going to Athens some time…'

'You mean to see Zoe?' Arianna gave a worldly shrug. 'Who knows? Nicos does not discuss such things with me, and he is too concerned with Spiro anyway. In fact—' she leaned forward '—he has told Petros that he may soon take Spiro to the States to see specialists there, and if he does…' she shrugged again '…I think that will be the end of your hopes. You could not afford to follow him there.'

'No,' Camilla said quietly. 'We couldn't. Does Katie know about this?'

'No. I thought it best to say nothing. But,' Arianna said briskly, 'it means there is no time to be lost. We must make a diversion somehow for Nicos. Get him away from the villa for half a day— a day even.' Her brilliant gaze switched to Camilla. 'This will be your task, I think.'

'Mine?' Camilla sat bolt upright on her lounger. 'What are you talking about?'

Arianna's smile was oblique. 'You tell Nicos you wish to meet with him, to make a deal, but away from here so that your sister will not know and be upset. And then you keep him with you,' she added, her smile widening. 'It will be no problem. He is an attractive man, *ne*, and you—intrigue him, I think.'

'No.' Bright spots of colour burned in Camilla's face. 'I'm sorry, but I can't—I won't. It's quite impossible.' Her heart was thumping against her ribcage. 'Anyway he wouldn't believe me. I've made it more than clear that I won't negotiate.'

'But isn't it also a woman's privilege to change her mind?' Arianna asked. 'That is something Nicos understands very well, I think.'

Camilla sank her teeth into her lower lip. 'I'm— sure he does. But I don't play those kinds of games.'

Arianna shrugged again, this time with an air of fatalism. 'Then we can do nothing. Spiro will go to America, and you will go home with a suntan and some money.'

Camilla groaned inwardly.

'I'd never get away with it,' she said desperately.

'Unless you try, how can you know?' Arianna demanded. 'Besides, Nicos has always said that an easy deal is one not worth making. He expects a fight.' Her eyes gleamed at Camilla. 'But not always the choice of battlefield—or weapons.'

There was a loaded silence.

At last Camilla said helplessly, 'All right—I'll try, but I'm not promising a thing.'

'Good,' Arianna approved with the familiar cat-like grin. 'Because now you could have the perfect opportunity.' She pointed a pink-tipped finger. 'My brother comes here, I think.'

Camilla saw that a blue boat, its tan sail neatly furled, had come round the adjoining headland, and was making for the cove.

'Oh, God.' The breath seemed to choke in her throat. She turned on Arianna. 'You knew already— didn't you?' she accused. 'That he was coming here. You've set me up.'

'No, I swear it. He said nothing at breakfast. But it is a chance we cannot miss, *ne*?' she went on pleadingly. 'For the sake of Spiro and your sister, tell him you wish to talk to him privately. Make him take you with him on the boat, wherever he is going—then keep him with you until the sun has set. Give us time.'

She rose gracefully to her feet. 'As soon as you have left with him, I will take Katie to the clinic to fetch Petros so that he may supervise their meeting, then we will all go straight to the Villa Apollo.' She put her cheek swiftly against Camilla's. 'Good luck to us all,' she whispered, and was gone in a cloud of warm fragrance.

Camilla looked at the approaching boat, and the dark figure at the tiller, then at the brilliant sky.

It would be a very long time until sunset, she realised numbly. And she would need more than luck to come through unscathed.

She said aloud, softly and despairingly, 'Oh, God, what have I just agreed to?'

CHAPTER NINE

CAMILLA waited for him on the small wooden jetty built out from the beach, standing slim and straight in the sleeveless, button-through sundress, with its deep scooped neck, which matched, and now covered, her jade-green bikini. Chin tilted slightly to conceal her nervousness, she watched him bring *Calliope* expertly alongside.

'*Kalimera.*' He tossed a rope to her, then swung himself lithely ashore. He was wearing brief white shorts which hugged his lean hips, topped by a sea-island cotton shirt striped in red and navy. 'I hope I haven't kept you waiting.'

'I wasn't aware that I'd sent for you,' she retorted, and caught herself. That wasn't the persuasive note Arianna had suggested.

He shrugged. 'But I knew it would only be a matter of time.' He was half smiling, the dark eyes narrowed and speculative.

'How?'

'Because whatever wrongs you feel your sister has suffered, you have to go back,' he said. 'You have a life to return to—a job which you need because times are hard.' His glance travelled with cool deliberation down her body. 'Maybe even a man.'

128

The inflexion in his voice made it a question rather than a statement.

'That,' Camilla said quietly, 'is none of your business.'

'Then let us discuss the real business between us. That is why you are here, *ne*? Because you are ready to negotiate a settlement?'

'I—I don't seem to have a choice.' Camilla avoided the intensity of his gaze.

'At last you see reason.' There was satisfaction in his tone. 'I will call on you this evening after dinner with details of my proposals.'

'Oh, no.' That was the wrong plan altogether, Camilla thought with alarm. 'I mean—I'd hoped to talk things over with you—privately, first—before I break the news to my sister.'

He shrugged. 'Very well—when?'

Camilla took a deep breath. 'There's no time like the present.'

'Now?' The dark brows lifted. 'That is not possible. I have only called to see Soula, to pay her some money for the house. Then I am going to Marynthos, a village on the other side of the island.'

Camilla's nails dug into the palms of her hands. 'Couldn't I come with you?' She saw a flare of surprise in his face and hurried on. 'Now that I've made up my mind, I don't want to let things—drag on. And, anyway, I've hardly seen anything of Karthos, and this could be my last chance. That is if you don't mind a passenger,' she added, challenging his lengthening silence.

'No,' he said at last, his smile crooked. 'I do not—mind. But you, *matia mou*—are you prepared to take the risk?'

'Risk?' Camilla glanced around her and shrugged. 'The weather seems set fair, and I'm a good sailor anyway.'

'That is not,' Nic said quite gently, 'what I meant.' As their eyes met, a faint shiver went through her, mingling fear and excitement. He laughed suddenly, and held out a hand to help her into the caique. '*Ela tora*. Come on, then, Kyria Camilla.'

So far, so good, Camilla told herself as he manoeuvred the boat away from the jetty and turned the bow towards the open sea. She risked one fleeting glance back at the sea house. Which, of course, he saw.

'Should you have left a message for your sister? Will she be concerned?'

'Katie's resting,' she said briefly. 'And I mentioned I might go out today—find out what the island has to offer.'

'Then I shall have to make sure you are not disappointed.' There was a vein of amusement underlying the courteous words that wasn't lost on her.

He thought she was a pushover, she realised with a swift smart of shame. That she'd come with him for a brief sexual adventure, although that was what she needed him to think, of course. She had to use all that superb male confidence against him, to bolster her own resolve not to fall into that sensual, charismatic web he knew so well how to weave, and become just another of Xandreou's women.

I'll be the one that got away, she assured herself. Oh, God, I've got to be...

'Would you like to steer?' His voice broke across her uncomfortable reverie.

'Is it safe?' she asked doubtfully, and Nic laughed.

'I won't let you sink us, *matia mou*.'

'Why do you call me that? What does it mean?' Camilla asked as she gingerly took the tiller.

'It means "my eyes",' Nic said, after a pause. 'When a woman allows a man to look into her eyes, Camilla *mou*, she offers him a key to the secrets of her heart.' He paused. 'Or so it is said.'

Her pulses quickened. She said flippantly, 'No wonder so many people wear sunglasses, in that case.'

'You do not.'

'Well.' Camilla shrugged. 'Perhaps I have nothing to hide.'

'No?' He took her chin in his hand, turning her gently but inexorably to face him. For a startled moment, she found his dark gaze burning into hers. 'I see anger, Camilla, and defiance, and anxiety, and behind these a mystery as deep as the sea.' He paused again. 'What I have never seen is laughter.'

'That's hardly surprising.' She freed herself with a swift jerk of her head. 'After all, I haven't found a great deal to laugh about since I got here.'

'Or before that, either, I think.' His voice was reflective. 'How long have you had the sole responsibility for your sister?'

'Three—nearly four years.' Her voice shook as she told him briefly about the accident. 'But—please,' she added hurriedly, 'you mustn't think it's been some kind of burden. Katie's a wonderful girl. She's never given me a moment's worry...' She stopped, feeling foolish.

'Until now,' he said drily.

Camilla shrugged. 'I didn't bargain for her falling in love.'

'No?' His smile was faintly cynical. 'Have you forgotten the power of a warm night under the moon?'

'No.' She wouldn't admit that she'd never experienced it. 'I just thought Katie was more—level-headed, that's all.'

She needed to find a less personal topic—defer any discussion about Katie for as long as possible, she reminded herself.

'Why are we going to Marynthos?' she asked brightly. 'Is there something special there?'

'Very special—a new baby—the son of my friend Dimitris Ioannides. He's asked me to be godfather.'

'And you've agreed?' She couldn't hide her surprise.

'Of course,' he said with slight hauteur. 'We Greeks take such a responsibility very seriously.'

'Oh.' Camilla swallowed. 'I didn't realise I'd be intruding on such a private occasion. I'm sorry.'

'If I thought you would intrude, you would not be here.' His tone was matter-of-fact.

'Oh.' She could easily, she realised, have been left standing on the jetty. 'Thank you—I think.'

'*Parakalo*.' His grin was swift, and oblique. His hand covered hers on the tiller. 'You have strayed a little off course,' he cautioned. 'Take care.'

Yes, Camilla thought grimly, feeling her flesh warm and tingle at the contact with his. I certainly will.

She removed her own hand, and said coolly, 'Perhaps you'd better take over. I don't want to end up on the rocks.'

'As you wish. Relax, then, and enjoy the trip. Feel the sun on your face.' He reached out and released the barrette which confined her hair at the nape of her neck. 'And the wind in your hair,' he added, tossing the barrette casually overboard.

'Why the hell did you do that?' Camilla demanded furiously, trying to control her chestnut mane with her fingers, and failing as the breeze gleefully whipped it into a tangle.

'Because today, *agape mou*,' Nic drawled, 'you are not the tied-back, buttoned-up, oh, so responsible sister. She is consigned to the oblivion she deserves. Today you will drink wine and taste life.' He paused. 'And your eyes will smile at me. Is it agreed?'

Camilla looked down at the vivid sea, sparkling and dancing round the boat, feeling its restless excitement thrill suddenly through her own veins.

Today. The thought was like a prayer to placate the ancient envious gods. One day out of all eternity. Was it so much to ask?

She flung back her head recklessly. 'Agreed,' she said.

An hour later, they reached Marynthos. It was only a small village—a straggle of white buildings with coloured roofs round a natural inlet where fishing boats bobbed. And a welcoming committee, Camilla noted, with an inrush of shyness.

She said, 'Shall I stay on *Calliope*?'

'By no means. Dimitris would be most offended if you failed to admire his son.'

He took her arm, urging her on to the narrow quay, responding to the noisy babble of greetings, putting names unerringly to the crowd of smiling faces which surged round them.

They were almost lifted off their feet on a wave of goodwill which carried them up the steep and narrow street. Here the women were waiting more decorously, the youngest children playing in the dust at their feet. The two grandmothers, wearing the inevitable black dresses and headscarves, offered a formal welcome, and then Dimitris Ioannides himself appeared, a neat, bright-eyed man, his teeth gleaming in a grin of pure delight under his heavy moustache.

The two men shook hands, then embraced, slapping each other on the back. Then Nic beckoned Camilla forward.

Her hand was taken and held for a moment by Dimitris. 'Welcome,' he said in careful English. 'You are welcome, *thespinis*.'

She was given a glass of wine, heavy and rather sweet, made, Nic told her, from Dimitris's own grapes, then was conducted into the house to see the baby.

Hara Ioannides was sitting up in bed, holding him in her arms. She was a pretty girl, her face wearily contented as she crooned to her child.

She greeted Nic shyly but with composure, and put the baby into his arms amid applause from the rest of the family clustering in the doorway.

Clearly a visit from such an important and respected figure as Nic Xandreou was an event in their lives, Camilla realised. The fact that he had agreed to be godfather was an additional honor.

And he talks of my responsibilities, she thought, when he's central to so many people's lives—the chief man of this island, quite apart from his business ventures.

He wasn't awkward with the baby, she saw. He handled the small bundle with complete assurance, instantly soothing an experimental wail of protest, lifting the baby to a more comfortable position against his shoulder, his smile softening to tenderness as the tiny angry face relaxed back into slumber.

She thought, with a pang, He should have children of his own, then paused, her throat constricting in self-derision. He was playing the part expected of him, that was all.

Nic Xandreou had already tried the obligations of marriage, and found them not to his taste, she reminded herself with an effort. His life belonged now in boardrooms and penthouses, and wherever else there was money to be made and pleasure to be enjoyed.

She glanced back, and found him looking at her, one eyebrow raised interrogatively. He said laconically, 'Hara wants you to hold him now.'

'Oh, no.' Camilla took an alarmed step backwards. 'I'd really rather not. I might drop him. I'm not used to small babies.'

'Then start accustoming yourself.' His quiet voice brooked no opposition. 'Sit on the bed, if you feel safer that way. You cannot hurt Hara by refusing.'

He pushed her down gently on to the edge of the mattress, and put the baby into her reluctant arms amid another chorus of approval.

She looked down at the shawl-swathed cocoon. One small starfish hand had emerged from the wrappings, and moved to splay against her breast. A tiny bubble escaped the pursed lips as the baby's head turned—seeking.

Strange anguish lanced through her as she wondered for the first time in her life what it would be like to bear a child to the man you loved. To be the focus, as Hara was, of his pride and adoration.

She thought, I wish—oh, God, I wish...and stopped dead, transfixed by the realisation of precisely what she wished.

As if magnetised, she looked up at Nic, her eyes widening, her parted lips tremulous. His face was sombre and aloof, a muscle working beside his mouth as if he was trying to control some angry emotion.

He probably resented the way she, a stranger, and an unwanted outsider at that, had been drawn into this intimate family moment, she thought painfully. Nor could she blame him, considering the deception she was practising on him.

He said softly, 'You are supposed to say something.'

She bit her lip, and turned to Hara. 'The baby's very handsome,' she said. 'Like his father.'

Judging by Hara's delighted beam as Nic translated, and the shout of laughter and acclaim from the others, she'd managed to find the right comment, outsider or not.

Hara bent forward, speaking rapidly in Greek, and Camilla shook her head in incomprehension.

Dimitris supplied the cheerful explanation. 'My

wife hopes that Xandreou's woman also bears many fine sons.'

Camilla felt a wave of helpless colour sweep up into her face. She did not dare look at Nic as he bent and took the baby from her, restoring him to his mother. But, to her relief, the room began to empty, and they were conducted outside where tables had been set with platters of bread, salad and sliced fruit, and jugs of red wine.

Nic was escorted ceremoniously to the place of honour, but Camilla was surrounded by the women, and pulled away to another table where she was subjected to a friendly but thorough scrutiny, everything from the colour of her hair to the material of her dress being examined and exclaimed over.

Her throat taut with embarrassment, Camilla managed to smile as she swallowed some grapes, and drank a glass of the wine, aware that Nic was watching ironically.

But she had only herself to blame, she thought. If she hadn't gone along with Arianna's suggestion and pushed herself on to him for the day, she'd have been saved all this discomfiture. She could only pray that back at the Villa Apollo everything had worked out, and that the end would, somehow, justify the means she'd chosen.

The celebration seemed endless, although she supposed she should be grateful for that. The longer it extended into the afternoon, the less time she would have to spend on her own with him, and the less opportunity there would be for the kind of self-betrayal she dreaded, she thought constrictedly.

She was conscious of him all the time. Above the laughter and chatter of the women there seemed to be a silent zone where the two of them existed alone. A place where she could look at him, and smile, and say the words of love and desire she dared not even think. Where his kisses burned on her parted lips, and her body bloomed under the touch of his hands. A secret place, she thought, which would haunt her for the rest of her life, tormenting her with all kinds of unfulfilled yearnings.

When she felt his hand curve round her shoulder in reality, she almost cried out in longing, but when she looked up at him his face was remote, his eyes guarded.

'It is time we went.' His tone was crisp, formal. 'Please say your goodbyes.'

Mechanically, Camilla began to assemble her few Greek phrases of thanks and farewell.

A stranger, she thought, not a lover. That was what he was, and that was how he must remain for her sanity's sake.

They were escorted back to the harbour, and helped enthusiastically on board *Calliope*. As they headed out of the bay, Camilla waved until the figures on the quay became mere dots.

'You enjoyed that?' Nic asked quietly from the tiller.

'Of course,' Camilla said with slight constraint. 'I felt very—privileged to be made so welcome.'

He was silent for a moment. 'They are simple people,' he said at last. 'I hope their—lack of inhibition didn't distress you.'

'No.' Her face warmed again. 'I suppose they were bound to draw the obvious conclusion.' She tried to laugh. 'Everyone else has.'

'Yes.' The monosyllable was clipped and curt, and she ventured no other comment.

The breeze had dropped, and the afternoon was still, the horizon a shimmer of heat. Camilla felt a trickle of sweat run down between her breasts. She put her hands to the nape of her neck, lifting away the heavy fall of hair.

It occurred to her suddenly that Nic had not turned *Calliope* back the way they'd come, but that they were sailing on round the island.

She looked at him. 'Where are we going?'

'I know a small bay where the swimming is good,' he returned. 'I thought we could anchor there for a while.' He paused again. 'And also—talk.' He slanted a smile at her, his eyes flicking over her breasts, and down to where the thin cotton dress clung to the line of her thigh.

'About what?' Camilla hunched a defensive shoulder, aware that her pulses had begun to thump erratically.

'We have negotiations to conduct,' he reminded her silkily. 'Or had you forgotten?'

'By no means,' she retorted. 'But I thought this was the time of day when all business stopped.'

His smile widened. 'That, *agape mou*, rather depends on the nature of the business—and its urgency.' He left the words tingling between them, and turned *Calliope* towards the shore again.

Camilla found herself staring blankly at the small horseshoe of pale sand sheltered by two stony outcrops that they were approaching. From the beach, the ground rose into a wilderness of bleached rock smudged by the occasional olive tree. It was very quiet—very lonely.

She swallowed. Keep him talking, she thought, touching her dry lips with the tip of her tongue. Make it formal—a discussion of terms. The problem was she hadn't had time to do her homework—to find out the kind of hypothetical sum she'd be expected to ask for on Katie's behalf. She had no real idea what bargaining power she could command.

But Nic Xandreou knew, down to the last drachma, and could call her bluff whenever he chose.

But what else did he know—or suspect? That was the real risk—the danger she needed to be on her guard against.

'*Matia mou*,' he had called her. And she must never let him look into her eyes again in case he saw the pitiful truth she needed at all cost to conceal: that, against all logic, reason or even sanity, she was in love with him.

CHAPTER TEN

NIC dropped anchor some hundred and fifty yards from the shore. With the noise of the engine stilled, there was only the creak of *Calliope*'s timbers and the soft lap of the sea to break the hot and heavy afternoon silence. To remind Camilla, if any reminder were needed, just how alone they were. Shading her eyes with her hand, she stared towards the beach as if mesmerised by it.

'Can you swim so far?' He was standing just behind her. He spoke softly, his breath fanning her ear.

'Of course.' She kept her tone brisk and bright. 'I'm not that much of a wimp.'

'No,' he said rather drily. 'That much is certain. But, all the same, we will take the boat ashore.'

Camilla watched as he brought the small dinghy alongside, loading it with towels, straw mats, a basket containing food and wine, and even a sun umbrella brought up from *Calliope*'s cabin.

All the gear for a successful seduction conveniently to hand, she thought, swallowing. But then she'd hardly be the first girl he'd have brought to this remote and lovely place.

She trailed her hand in the water as they rowed ashore. Shoals of small fish darted here and there, and soft fronds of weed billowed and danced in the shadowy depths.

Her feet sank into the hot sand as she helped him drag the boat up the beach. By the time they'd unloaded it, Camilla felt that her dress was sticking to her. Surreptitiously, she eased the cling of the fabric away from her thighs.

But he'd noticed, of course.

'Shall we cool off before we open our discussions?' Nic wedged the sun umbrella in place with a couple of large stones, and dusted off his hands. Camilla watched with misgiving as he unfastened the remaining buttons on his shirt. She was suddenly, forcibly reminded of the first time she'd seen him. Did he usually swim naked? she wondered, dry-mouthed. And, if so, would this occasion be any exception?

But to her relief he stripped off his shorts to reveal brief black trunks. He turned, encountering her scrutiny with a mockingly lifted eyebrow. The faint smile playing round his mouth was a challenge as he waited for her to fumble clumsily out of her dress, and drop it with self-conscious awkwardness on to one of the straw mats.

'Your scratches are healed now?' He took her arm, turning her slightly so that he could study the fading marks.

Flushing, Camilla pulled free. 'Completely.' She kicked off her sandals and ran past him down to the edge of the sea.

The water felt breath-stoppingly cool against her over-heated skin as she splashed through the shallows.

'Have a care.' Nic was beside her, overtaking her with ease. 'The beach shelves quickly and very steeply. You can soon find you are out of your depth.'

I found that out a long time ago. She thought it, but did not say it, as she watched him take a running dive, the lean, dark body cutting the water with hardly a splash.

She'd been out of her depth since the moment she arrived on Karthos. She'd been so sure of her ability to handle things, but looking back it seemed she might just have made the situation worse. Lending herself to this deception seemed the only way to make amends to Katie, but she had also to gauge the consequences to herself. Physical damage healed. Emotional scarring could be with you for life.

Other girls at the secretarial agency came back from foreign holidays giggling over brief flings with waiters, couriers or ski instructors, but for Camilla there could be no guilty secrets to be shared with a smile and sigh over coffee.

Because Nic Xandreou mattered, she thought as she slid down into the water, letting it take and lift her, closing her eyes against the dazzle of the sunlight. He was in her mind and her heart, part of the fibre of her being, and she hadn't the least idea how or when it had begun to happen. She'd been in too deep before she'd even seen the danger.

But what she needed to remember, above all, was that it wasn't mutual. She was an annoyance to Nic—a small problem to be resolved, and that was all. If he made love to her, it would be with cynical amusement at the ease with which his victory had been accomplished. A trifling bonus on another successful deal.

And the knowledge of that more than outweighed the transitory delight of being, for a few hours, Xandreou's woman. It had to.

She turned to glance at the shore, and saw with a shock of alarm that she'd let herself drift further out than she'd intended. She was a competent enough swimmer, but she was accustomed to the predictability of swimming-baths. Beneath her now were untold fathoms of the Ionian Sea. She trod water, breathing deeply and calmly, refusing to panic as she felt the pull of an unsuspected current.

She glanced around, but could see no reassuring dark head within hailing distance. Besides, she didn't want to call for help unnecessarily, especially when she'd been quite implicitly warned.

The boat, she realised, biting her lip, seemed marginally nearer than the beach. She would swim there first—make some excuse about preferring to sunbathe on board, which was probably a safer option anyway.

She was halfway there when she realised she was

in difficulty. The current seemed stronger, constantly hampering her progress, and her arms and legs were getting heavy.

She thought, This is stupid, and a small wave broke against her face, making her cough, increasing the frightened tightness in her chest.

One answer was to turn on to her back again and float, but that would leave her at the mercy of the current, and it seemed best to flounder on, fighting panic and fatigue.

She'd told him her swimming was 'good enough' but it seemed she'd overestimated her capabilities.

She opened her mouth to shout, swallowed more water, and almost submerged, choking. Through streaming eyes, she saw that *Calliope* looked further away than ever.

Suddenly there was a dark shape beside her in the water, the sea churned, and Nic was there, shaking the water out of his eyes, his face dark with anger. She heard him say something in furious Greek, then his arms went round her, lifting her up, holding her against him.

'Relax, little fool,' his voice bit at her. 'I have you now.'

He turned her effortlessly, supporting her as he used a smooth, powerful side-stroke to take them back to shore.

'It is safe now.' His voice was terse as his clasp slackened. He lowered her gently, and Camilla discovered sand and shingle under her feet, her legs buckling in sheer relief.

Nic muttered something under his breath, then his arms were round her again, and he was carrying her up the beach.

Camilla found herself deposited under the shade of the umbrella. She looked up at him. He was dark against the sun, sea-water droplets glistening on his tanned body. Her chest hurt, and she could taste nothing but salt, but all the same she felt a twist of hot, shamed excitement deep within her. She said hoarsely, 'I'm sorry.'

'I did warn you.' His shrug was almost impatient. 'But there was no real danger. Lie quietly for a while.'

Through half-closed eyes, she watched him busy himself with the food basket. Heard the subdued pop of a wine cork being withdrawn.

'Drink this.' The glass he gave her was crystal with a twisted stem. Just the thing for a beach picnic, the fragment of her mind still working normally noted drily.

Her teeth chattered against the rim of the glass. His hand came up to steady it, and the brush of his fingers against hers made her shiver.

The wine was cold, crisp and dry, but it brought warmth to the frozen, frightened place inside her, and steadied the uneven rush of her pulses.

When she had finished, he silently took the glass

from her hand, and replaced it with a fresh bread roll crammed with cold roast lamb.

She began, 'Oh, I don't think…' but he silenced her with a lifted hand.

'It is little wonder you tired so easily,' he told her curtly. 'At Dimitris's house, of course, you only pretended to eat.'

'I wasn't—I'm not hungry,' she protested without conviction. Actually she was ravenous. Maybe frightening yourself silly had that effect. But she doubted whether she could swallow a morsel.

She was too aware of him, of his proximity, the sheen of his bronze skin, the damp tendrils of hair curling on his forehead and at the nape of his neck, and above all his own unique male scent commingling with the tang of salt. Although he was no longer touching her, she felt as if she was being tied in knots. Fool, she castigated herself inwardly.

'I don't save a woman from drowning merely to watch her starve in front of me.' He was implacable.

Mutely, she bit into the roll, the slices of lamb were thick and juicy, enhanced by a sprinkling of salt, and there were big, firm-fleshed tomatoes as an accompaniment, with sharp black olives, and more of the wine. It was one of the simplest meals she'd ever eaten, and she would remember it, she thought, for the whole of her life.

She wiped her hands on a paper napkin. 'Thank you,' she said stiltedly.

'The thanks are due to Hara's mother,' he said

with a shrug. 'She packed the basket and put it on the boat for me.' He slanted a smile at her. 'She says you are too thin. That I should look after you better.' He paused. 'God knows what she would say about the events of the past half-hour.'

Camilla sat up straight. 'Nothing, I hope. I'm grateful for what you did, of course.' She steadied her voice. 'But it's not your business to look after me at all, and you should have told her so.'

'No,' he said. 'Because she would not understand. In her world, a woman belongs to a man. Her father first, then her husband.'

'How cosy.' Camilla lifted her chin. 'The twentieth century has clearly passed Karthos by.'

'Not all of it.' His voice was cool, and the firm mouth seemed to tighten in momentary bitterness.

She knew he was thinking of his wife. There were a hundred questions teeming in her brain, but she resisted them, lying back on her straw mat, and pretending to close her eyes.

'Don't fall asleep in the sun,' he advised drily. 'Or you could have third-degree burns to add to your other problems.'

Camilla grimaced swiftly, then rummaged for the protective lotion she used. She said lightly. 'I seem to be a walking disaster today.'

'Not just today.' The contradiction was flat, with an underlying note of anger. 'You have caused difficulties ever since you arrived here.'

'You're not so easy to deal with yourself.'

Camilla began to apply the lotion to her arms and legs, glad to bend her head and let her damp hair form a curtain against the brooding intensity of his gaze.

'I did not intend to be,' he reminded her. 'Yet here we are.' He paused. 'Shall negotiations begin?'

'Yes.' She was smoothing the lotion over the swell of her breasts above the brief bikini cups, and across the flatness of her abdomen, acutely aware that he was following every movement, a faint smile curling the corners of his mouth. There was reminiscence in that smile, and something altogether more edged and dangerous that she preferred not to analyse. 'At least, I—I suppose so.'

The smile widened. He held out his hand. 'Turn over, *matia mou*, and I will oil your back.'

'No, thank you, Kyrios Nicos.' She replaced the cap on the bottle very precisely. The last thing in the world she could afford was to feel his hands on her again, she thought, a sharp tremor running through her senses. 'As you've reminded me, I'm not here to sunbathe.'

'Such formality,' he mocked.

'A business meeting is a formal occasion.' She gave him a direct look. 'Although today you've let me see how kind you can be—to all sorts of people. I only wish you could spare some kindness for Katie, and Spiro.'

He shrugged. 'Sometimes the greatest kindness lies in cruelty. I'm sure you've heard that.'

'Yes,' she said. 'But I'm not sure I believe it.'

'Then you should,' he said softly. 'Also that you should not let your heart rule your head. That can lead only to—disaster.'

Camilla looked up at the fierce blue arc of the sky. She heard herself say, 'Was it here that you met her—your wife?' and braced herself for an icy snub, or, at worst, an explosion.

'Yes, it was here.' He looked away at the horizon. 'They used the north of the island as location for a film—a thriller.' His smile was wintry. 'Not a very good one. It never went on general release. And she was afraid, I think, that her career would never amount to more than films like that.' He shrugged slightly. 'She was ready for a change of direction—which I provided.'

Camilla's breath caught in her throat. She said, 'There must have been more to it than that.'

'Oh, at first, yes. There was certainly passion.' His voice slowed to a drawl. 'She was a beautiful, radiant creature, my Rachelle. To make love with her was to taste paradise. Every day was filled with sunshine. It was easy to forget that winter must follow.'

He looked down at the glass he held, twisting its stem in his lean, strong fingers. Hands that could crush, if they chose, Camilla thought, as well as rescue—and caress. His words were like bruises on her mind. 'A beautiful, radiant creature'. Quite the opposite to ordinary Camilla Dryden.

To her surprise, his voice went on. 'At first, she loved it here.' His tone was quiet, almost reflective. 'She thought it quaint. That should have warned me. It was the view of a tourist—someone passing through, who looks but does not see. She knew that I had other homes in other places, but this was my island—the place to which I would always return. She seemed to accept that. She seemed also to want, as I did, a settled life—children.'

His mouth twisted. 'I forgot, of course, that she was an actress. For a while it suited her to play the part of my wife—docile and devoted. Then she began to want more—always more. Whenever I went away, she insisted on going too, even though I'd warned her it would not always be possible—that there were times when I had to travel light and fast. Rachelle needed her entourage—her maid, a major domo to ensure fresh flowers and champagne in every suite, her personal chef. She needed to be centre-stage, but with me there were times when work had to come first, when I could not be there at the restaurants—the theatres—the parties.'

His voice was weary. 'She was like a child robbed of its toys. She was lonely—I neglected her. She was young and she would enjoy herself—with me or without me—'

'Please,' Camilla broke in urgently. 'You don't have to tell me this.'

'Ah, but I do.' For a moment the dark eyes glittered at her. His voice deepened. 'You asked the question; you must listen to the answer—all of it, if you wish to understand.' He looked away again, his brows drawing together as if he was in pain. 'It was at one of those parties I could not attend that Rachelle began to experiment seriously with the drug that eventually killed her.'

He sighed. 'I knew there had been earlier experiences, but she'd sworn her involvement had been minimal—that it was behind her. I was caught up in a deal, working day and night. I—missed the warning signs.' He tossed back the remains of his wine, and replaced the glass in the basket.

'Perhaps I didn't want to see them. When I realised what was going on, I arranged for her to have treatment. She wept, clung to me, swore it would never happen again. She was just so bored...'

He flung his head back, the muscles in his throat taut. 'I wanted so badly to believe her. I blamed myself for leaving her so much to herself. I had realised, of course, by then that our expectations of marriage were completely opposed. But I still thought a child might heal the breach—give some purpose to our lives.'

He paused. 'Then she told me her former agent had been in touch—that she had the chance of a major role.' His voice was hard as stone, and Camilla felt her heart twist in pity at the starkness in his face. 'I had my life, she said; she should be allowed to have hers. There would be plenty of time in the future for children, if we still wanted them.

In the meantime, she had been advised to play down her marriage altogether.'

He laughed bitterly. 'She could have said nothing more damaging to my pride—to my sense of family. I was angry. We quarrelled, and I left. I think I expected her to follow. But she did not. For a while she had all the success she had dreamed of. But it was never enough. She always wanted a new sensation—a new high—and there was one sure way to provide it.

'She continued to be treated for addiction. Although we were apart, almost completely estranged, I paid at first. Later it was the studio, until she became totally unreliable and they sacked her.'

He cleared his throat. 'She called me—told me she was going underground—renting a cabin in the hills while she tried to get her head together. That she needed to be alone.' He made a small sound in his throat. 'She was found in the motel room a week later. She had not been there alone—far from it—but none of her—companions ever came forward.'

'Oh, God.' Camilla forced the words from a dry throat.

He turned his head slowly and looked at her. 'You wonder why I have told you this—spoken of things I hoped were buried forever? It is to make you understand at last why I must protect my family—stop them from making the same mistakes as I did.' His shrug was cynical. 'Oh, you will tell me that Catherine is not Rachelle. That my wife carried within her the seeds of her own destruction. But it is not that simple.'

He beat a clenched fist into the palm of his hand. 'When you are young, you think love can solve everything—that it can tear down the barriers of background and culture. Overcome all difficulties and misunderstandings.' He shook his head. 'I know that is a fallacy. I had money, and power, but I could not offer Rachelle what she wanted, or save her from what she ultimately chose.

'And I will not have Spiro hurt as I was—constantly reaching for your sister across a widening abyss of bitterness and estrangement.'

It was all there in his voice—the anger, the regret, the underlying sense of desolation.

There was a loneliness, an isolation in the tense, dark figure beside her that caught Camilla by the throat. Although the things he'd spoken of were light-years from her own experience, the instinct to offer some kind of comfort, however inadequate, was overwhelming.

Kneeling beside him, she said his name. Put a hand tentatively on the smooth skin of his shoulder. Felt the hard muscle clench beneath her touch, and the harsh tremor which seemed to shake his whole body.

He turned to her swiftly, almost savagely, a dark flame in his eyes and burning on his mouth as it possessed hers. Camilla kissed him back, her lips parting to allow the urgent, aching dart of his tongue, her first shy response becoming ardent as the shackles of restraint fell away. Nic's arms went round her hard, tightening almost convulsively as if he was trying to fuse their bodies into a single entity, as the kiss went on, blurring reality into a fevered awareness only of themselves, and a need that could not be denied.

Camilla was breathing his breath, absorbed into the fierce hurry of his heartbeat. When his weight carried her backwards, downwards on to the straw mat, she had no thought of resistance. Her hands went up to hold him—to claim him as her man. To offer herself as his woman.

For a moment, he reared above her, his breathing ragged, his eyes searching her face. Then he said hoarsely, '*Matia mou*,' and bent to her.

Impatiently, he wrenched the fragile bikini-top apart, then cupped her bare breasts in his hands, lifting them so that his lips could explore their delicate roundness more fully. She felt her nipples harden in sensuous response, the joy of this remembered intimacy invading her like a warm tide. His mouth closed over one rosy tumescent peak, tugging persuasively at first, then more compellingly, forcing a husky moan of pleasure from her taut throat.

He laughed softly against her skin. 'Is that good, *pedhi mou*—my little one?'

Her voice cracked. 'Oh, God, you must know…'

'Yes,' he said on a breath of satisfaction. 'Now I know.' He began to kiss her again, his mouth feathering against hers, demanding, yet withholding, in a teasing but wholly inexorable arousal.

'Touch me, *agape mou*,' he whispered hoarsely. 'I need to feel your hands on me.'

She reached for him, hands framing his face, feeling the faint roughness along his jawline, then clung to his shoulders, her body arching like a cat's as his own fingers moved slowly down her body in soft, stroking exploration, tracing the gentle valley between her breasts, the fragile shell of her ribcage, the tender flesh inside her elbows, and down to the pulses fluttering like humming birds in her wrists, and across to the flat plane of her stomach, and the delicate thrust of her hipbones.

Where his hands moved, his mouth followed like sweet, dangerous fire, tasting her as if she were some exquisite banquet arrayed for his delectation.

Camilla moved restlessly, little helpless sounds breaking from her throat, as she strayed down her own tactile paths, her hands gliding over the strength of bone and fierce tension of muscle. There was a warmth inside her as potent as the great brazen sun above them, and an ache as deep as the restless sea. For the first time in her life, she was totally at the mercy of needs she had never imagined. The carefully structured barriers of control and reserve had splintered into sensation now, and yearning.

She was hardly aware that the caressing hands had stripped away her bikini briefs, until he touched her at the silken, molten core of her womanhood, the lean fingers stroking her, lifting her on to a dizzying spiral of blind, moaning acceptance.

Through half-closed eyes she saw him rear over her, head and shoulders gilded by an aura like flame. He was naked too now, a god of bronze and copper.

Apollo, she thought dazedly, whose sun was around her, and within her, devouring her—consuming her.

She felt the sleek velvet hardness of him between her thighs, seeking her. His hands were beneath her, raising her—challenging her to meet his urgency with her own.

For a moment, the tautness of her inner muscles resisted his penetration, and a small shocked sob rose in her throat. Nic bent his head, his mouth closing on hers, stifling the tiny sound, whispering soft words of reassurance, as, slowly and with forbearance, he coaxed her body to relax again, and yield up its last secret to him.

Sheathed within her, he held her close for a while, his lips soothing her with gentle sensuality, as she accustomed herself to the reality of this, the ultimate intimacy.

Then, still without haste, he began to move, smoothly, easily, luring her to join him, to echo the eternal rhythms of passion, so strange to her, and yet, at the same time, so right and familiar.

Pleasure began slowly to unfurl inside her like a leaf in spring, beckoning her to a deeper response. She clung to him, fingers digging into his sweat-slicked shoulders, legs locked round his waist, letting her body pulse in time with his, the sudden harshness of her breathing echoing, commingling with Nic's. All her being, mental and physical, was concentrated now—fixed, almost with bewilderment, on the flowering of these new, intense sensations deep within her.

With every powerful thrust of Nic's loins, she seemed to be carried nearer some nameless but attainable goal, driven on by instinct, seeking blindly for some surcease from the fierce maelstrom of craving he'd created in her.

Every nerve-ending was vibrating suddenly. She was gasping for breath, her head thrashing wildly from side to side, her mouth framing words of need—of entreaty.

'Yes.' His voice seemed to reach her from some vast distance. 'Yes, *agape mou.*'

She felt a faint judder, down in the depths of her being, a sweet, hot, ineffable trembling that was spreading, gaining momentum, taking possession of her, forcing her into an upward spiral of sharp, half-crazy delight.

She could hear herself moaning, her voice thick, like a stranger's, as the spiral deepened, intensified almost unbearably, keeping her on the screaming edge of some undreamed-of sensation.

Then, as she thought she could stand no more—that she was going to die—the spiral broke, and she was free, her body convulsed by tremors as strong as the earth, her mind torn apart by the exquisite savagery of her release.

As she fought for breath, for sanity, she heard Nic's breathing change, quicken hoarsely. She saw him fling back his head suddenly, the muscles in his throat like whipcord, his face strained, almost anguished. Then she felt, like silken fire, the molten reality of his own climax.

She held him close, floating down with him from one plane of golden, honeyed satisfaction to the next, as their bodies quietened and gave them peace at last.

CHAPTER ELEVEN

I LOVE you.

Camilla pressed her mouth to the damp, heated skin of Nic's shoulder, damming back the words which rang in her head, and sang in her heart. Words, she reminded herself, that he would not want to hear from her—ever.

The realisation chilled through the heavenly euphoria which had succeeded their lovemaking. Up to then, she'd been lying in his arms, head pillowed on his chest, enjoying the touch of his fingers as they lazily caressed the curve of her hip.

Now, she moved restively as awareness flooded back, alerting other emotions. Reminding her with merciless clarity precisely how far she'd allowed herself to stray from her self-imposed guidelines of morality and common sense.

She sat up abruptly, reaching for her bikini with hands that shook.

'What is it?' Nic lifted himself on to an elbow and studied her, a faint frown drawing the dark brows together.

'Nothing,' she said, then amended swiftly, 'Just that it's getting late, that's all.'

'Is that really all, *matia mou*?' He took her chin

in his hand, forcing her to meet his gaze. 'I think I see regret in your eyes.'

'Well, please don't worry about it.' Her voice was brittle as she jerked herself away from his grasp. 'I can't imagine I'm the first to be swept away by your fabulous technique, and come to her senses when it's too late.'

His gaze sharpened. 'You think I planned this? Let me remind you that you asked to come with me today.'

'I haven't forgotten.' Her laugh cracked in the middle. '"Those whom the gods wish to destroy, they first make mad." I should have remembered that.'

'Madness?' Nic shook his head. 'I think it was the hand of fate which brought us together here.'

'I don't believe in fate.' She'd said that before—a lifetime ago. Now fate had punished her lack of faith with the cruellest of revenges. She lifted her chin. 'You said you could have me whenever you wanted. It must be wonderful to be infallible.'

'Don't talk like a fool,' he said with sudden brusqueness. 'You must believe me, Camilla. I did not intend this to happen.'

'Oh, I do believe it.' Fighting for control, she laced her tone with scorn. 'Two paternity suits in one family might be too much to handle, even for you.'

'Is that all that concerns you?' His voice was very quiet. 'The legal—financial implications?'

'What else is there?' She felt very weary suddenly, and close to tears. 'That's what we came here to discuss in the first place.' She buried her teeth in her lower lip. 'Until, of course, I let myself be so expertly side-tracked.'

Nic reached for his own clothes, began to drag them on. 'Then perhaps all future discussions should be conducted by our lawyers,' he said harshly. 'Then there will be no danger of any—personal element intruding.'

'Our lawyers'. Camilla found herself thinking numbly of elderly Mr Cranshaw who had dealt so kindly with the aftermath of her parents' death. Was he up to the kind of hard-nosed legal battle which the Xandreou legal experts could enforce? Somehow she didn't think so.

Because she didn't yet know, of course, what had transpired at the Villa Apollo in their absence. They were all taking it for granted that if Spiro regained his memory he would still want Katie and acknowledge his baby. But nothing was certain in this hideously shifting world. Maybe Nic's undoubted influence over his brother would prevail in the end after all. Spiro might well decide he could not afford to disregard his brother's plans for his future.

I came here to help, she thought. And all I've managed to do is make everything a thousand times worse—not just for Katie, but for myself as well.

The possibility of a future as a single mother was

just too hideous to contemplate. But it was what she'd invited just the same.

Just the touch of Nic's mouth on hers, the brush of his fingers on her skin, and all her resolve seemed to melt away in a need that transcended common sense and logic. And she would have to live with the consequences, whatever they were.

Her life was in pieces, at any rate, she acknowledged with a kind of desperate clarity. Somehow she had to drag it into shape again. Dismiss this pitiful creature at the mercy of her own physicality. Find again the cool, sensible persona she'd once possessed.

If I can, she thought sorrowfully. If that girl still exists. Or is she now, no more, no less, for better or worse, simply Xandreou's woman?

The return trip was a silent one. Camilla sat in the bow, staring ahead of her. The sea had darkened into a faint swell, and the air seemed still and almost threatening—or was that merely the suggestion of her own inner tensions?

She'd presumed that Nic would return her to the beach below the sea house, but instead he turned *Calliope* towards the landing stage below the Villa Apollo. She turned questioningly, and saw him laying aside a pair of binoculars, his black brows drawn together in a frown.

A tremor of apprehension crept down her spine. Peering ahead, she could just make out a figure on the landing stage, his arms semaphoring for attention.

Yannis, she thought, swallowing. And no prizes for guessing the reason behind the frantic signals either. She straightened her shoulders, bracing herself mentally. Nic was angry enough as it was. When he found out he'd been duped...

Her heart was hammering. She found herself wordlessly begging Apollo the Healer to make it somehow all right.

They arrived at the landing stage, Nic throwing Yannis a rope as the other man burst into a flood of excited Greek. Nic listened tautly, his mouth set in grim lines. When Yannis paused for breath, he nodded curtly, then turned and looked at Camilla, the dark eyes narrowed, his face harsh with silent accusation. Helplessly, she gazed back at him, trying not to let him see that she was shaking.

He swung himself lithely on to the landing stage, and he and Yannis began to run up the sloping narrow path which led to the villa. Camilla had no choice but to follow. The leaves and twigs of unknown shrubs brushed her as she passed. Something with thorns caught her dress and she tore it free as she ran. In the distance, she heard the first faint rumble of thunder.

A storm, she thought, a bubble of hysteria welling up inside her. There was going to be a storm, and she needed to reach the villa before it broke. The path became steps, and she went up them, two at a time, breathless but driving herself on. There was a glimmer of turquoise ahead of her somewhere that she knew was the swimming-pool, and she pushed through the last of the encircling bushes, throat dry, heart hammering, hand pressed to the stitch in her side.

The little tableau had been established on the terrace outside the *saloni*.

Spiro was in a chair, his injured leg supported by a stool. Katie stood beside him, her hand in his. It was as simple as that, but their tranquillity, their happiness, their sense of total belonging was almost tangible.

Camilla halted, her throat tightening, tears stinging at her eyes. They looked so right together, she thought. Surely Nic would be able to see that, and forgive.

But he didn't look particularly compassionate, she saw with a pang. He was quietly, furiously angry, colour burning along his cheekbones, his mouth a straight line.

He was a powerful man. His rage could be destructive, and Spiro and Katie were so young, so vulnerable. She wanted to get between them, to use herself as a shield.

He said softly in English, 'So, little brother, your memory has returned. God be thanked.'

'Yes.' Spiro spoke in the same language. 'And, with Providence, you must also thank Katie, who is soon to be my wife.' The words were calm, measured. He lifted Katie's hand and pressed it to his cheek in a gesture of tender possession, then gave Nic a level look. 'I hope, Nicos, our marriage will have your blessing, but I must warn you it will happen anyway, whatever you decide.'

'Then you have not recovered your senses along with your memory. A pity.' Nic's voice was harsh.

'Nic.' Arianna, who had been standing in the shadow by the long windows with Dr Deroulades, and an anxious Eleni, interposed herself. 'Katie has given Spiro back to us—like a miracle. You must accept their love, approve it—welcome Katie to our family.'

'Be silent.' He didn't even look at her. 'Go to your room, Arianna. I shall not forget your part in this. Or yours, Petros,' he added as Arianna, unwontedly subdued, turned away into the house, her fist pressed to her mouth.

The doctor said quietly, 'That was a risk I had to take for Spiro's sake. I must always think it was worth it. And now your brother should rest.'

Nic's body was taut as a bowstring. 'Of course.' He looked at Katie. 'Yannis will drive you back to the sea house, *thespinis*. You—and your sister.'

'No.' Spiro shook his head, his tone suddenly fierce. 'Katie stays here. My mistake was ever to allow her out of my sight.'

'And my error was to allow you out of mine.' The retort was hard, but Nic walked over to the chair, bending to draw his brother into a fierce embrace. For a long moment they held each other in silence.

Camilla found herself choking back a sob. Over the sea a streak of fire forked through the darkening sky, to be followed almost at once by an ominous growl.

She watched Spiro helped up on to his crutches, Katie assisting, her young face furrowed in concern, as the small procession wended its way into the villa.

Leaving her alone with Nic in the gathering storm.

'Quite a conspiracy.' His tone was deceptively laconic. The hooded eyes told her nothing. 'Was anyone not involved, I wonder, apart from Yannis and Eleni?'

She touched her tongue to her dry lips. 'I—I didn't want to deceive you, but there seemed no other way to give Katie and Spiro their chance.'

'And I played right into your beguiling hands,' he said softly, his mouth curling in contempt. 'My congratulations. You were most—convincing in your efforts to hold my attention—even to making the ultimate sacrifice.' He shook his head in cynical wonderment. 'Can sisterly devotion ever ask more?'

His voice cut her like a whip. She flinched and stepped back.

'It wasn't like that. You know that.'

'No?' His brows lifted. 'Then tell me how it was,

honey girl, with your saint's eyes and sinner's body.'

I loved you, she thought. I wanted to make up to you for all the pain—all the loneliness. And now I've brought it all down on myself instead, because I can't tell you.

'Well?' he said too gently. 'I am waiting.'

Camilla bit her lip. 'You talk as if I planned it somehow…' She stopped abruptly, colour rushing into her face as she realised he was laughing soundlessly.

'No, no, *agape mou*. You forget. That was what you accused *me* of doing. Quite a master-stroke, all that injured, ruined innocence. The seducer reproached by his victim.' His voice deepened in harsh mockery. 'A second accomplished actress to add to my collection, and I never guessed.'

Another lightning flash flickered in the sky, the accompanying thunder closer, louder.

'I wondered what you were hiding from me, *ma-tia mou*,' the relentless voice went on. 'And now I know—the corruption behind the mask of virtue. The lies behind the appearance of candour. No wonder you didn't want me to look into your eyes.'

The sky was pressing down on her. The air felt thick, making it difficult to breathe.

She saw that Yannis had returned, and was waiting, hands on hips, for Nic's orders. Orders that would take her back to the sea house and away from him forever.

Here, she thought unsteadily, here, where it had begun, was where it would end in acrimony, bitterness and misunderstanding. The wheel had come full circle.

She said huskily, 'You must believe what you want. I thought I was acting for the best. And please don't punish Katie for my mistakes. Just remember—she reached for Spiro across the abyss—and brought him to safety.'

She turned and walked away, moving almost blindly, as the first heavy drops of rain began to fall.

Camilla folded a white cotton shirt and laid it on top of her case then glanced round the room, checking the empty cupboards and drawers. But no trace of her brief occupation remained.

It was very quiet in the sea house. Soula had gone to visit her sister in a neighbouring village, and Yannis was driving Katie and Spiro into the mountains for dinner at a romantically remote taverna.

'Come with us,' Katie had urged. 'Darling, you can't spend your last evening on your own.'

'Oh, but I can.' Camilla had smiled at her. 'I've no intention, my pet, of playing gooseberry. Anyway, I've far too much to do this evening. I'm catching the early ferry, remember.'

In spite of Katie's protests, Camilla had insisted on returning to England before the wedding.

'I can't try Mrs Strathmore's patience any further,' she'd said. 'I need that job. And anyway, now that Spiro's hopping around on crutches, you'll be off to the mainland to meet the rest of the Xandreou clan.'

'Yes.' Katie had grimaced slightly. 'The aunts in the Peloponnese sound a bit formidable.'

'You'll have them eating out of your hand in no time,' Camilla had reassured her. 'Then, before you know it, you'll be married.'

But for all her brave words, the last thing in the world she'd wanted was her own company tonight. But making a third with Katie and Spiro, being on the edge of their coruscating happiness, was more than she could handle, she thought wretchedly.

It had undoubtedly been the worst week of her life.

She'd returned to the sea house on the night of the storm, wandering through the rooms, unable to sleep, or even relax, while it raged itself out.

She'd been hollow-eyed and on edge, in contrast to the calm serenity of the following morning, hoping and praying for some message from Nic. But there had been nothing.

The things he'd said, the way he'd looked at her with such contempt, seemed to be seared across her consciousness.

It had been almost a relief to hear from Arianna that he'd gone to Athens.

'And I hope his Zoe puts him in a better temper,' she'd added sourly. 'He is still barely speaking to me. Of course he is pleased about Spiro, but he cannot bear to be wrong.'

'I shouldn't imagine it happens very often,' Camilla had said drily, biting her lip until she tasted blood as an image of Nic, naked with a sinuous Greek beauty in his arms, had impinged on her imagination.

'Oh, well,' Arianna had shrugged. 'He will come round.'

Camilla had decided she wouldn't hold her breath waiting for it to happen. Nic would never appreciate being made a fool of, but that had seemed a risk worth taking in the circumstances. What he would find impossible to forgive, however, was the belief that she had duped him sexually. Used her body as bait as she got him to confide in her about his relationship with Rachelle.

He opened the door to me on his private nightmare, she thought desolately. He'll hate me for that.

Once, in those first hopeful days, she'd seen *Calliope* in the bay, under sail, and had thought for a few heart-stopping moments that she was heading for the sea house, only to watch the caique's tan sail disappear round the headland, and out of sight.

She wondered if she would manage to find the emotional strength to come back for the wedding, once the break with Karthos had been made. Maybe by then she'd have pulled her life together—stopped hurting quite so much, she thought. Although that would largely depend on whether or not she was expecting Nic's baby, she reminded herself unhappily.

She looked at herself in the mirror, noting almost objectively her shadowed eyes and the hollows beneath her cheekbones.

No doubt about it, Dryden, you're an all-round mess, she told herself.

The sudden bang of the main door made her jump. She heard the click of heels across the tiles, then the door of her room crashed open and Arianna stood there, dishevelled and out of breath.

'Camilla.' Her voice was almost hysterical. 'You must help me—save me from Nicos.'

And she burst into tears.

'What are you talking about?' Camilla looked past her, half expecting to see a vengeful Nic close on her heels.

'Nicos came back from Athens an hour ago—perhaps more,' Arianna vouchsafed between sobs. 'He was quiet—strange. He sent for me—told me that when Katie goes to the Peloponnese I must accompany her—and stay there with our aunts until my own marriage has been arranged.'

Her pretty face was haggard. 'I argued with him—but he would not listen. And I shall die in the Peloponnese. Indeed, I would rather be dead than marry some stranger he has chosen for me.'

Camilla groaned inwardly. 'You know you don't mean that.'

'I do. Without Petros, my life is nothing. And

Nicos means to send him away—to ruin him for disobeying his wishes over Spiro.'

'I'm sure he didn't mean that.'

Somehow, Camilla got the near-hysterical girl into the kitchen and coaxed her to drink some coffee.

'You don't know,' Arianna said, blotting her face with a handful of tissues. 'Nicos is hard—like a rock—like ice.' She looked pleadingly at Camilla. 'So you will help us, *ne*?'

'I think I'm the last person your brother would listen to,' Camilla said with a sigh.

'Not that—not talking,' Arianna said impatiently. 'I want to leave Karthos—to go to England with you, Camilla. Later, Petros can come for me there, and we will be married. And I will never see my brother again.'

Camilla put her cup down with care. 'I don't believe you've thought this through,' she said. 'For one thing I leave in the morning…'

'I know that.' Arianna tapped her soft leather shoulder-bag. 'I have my passport, also money. No problem.'

'There's the small matter of a seat on the plane,' Camilla reminded her drily.

Arianna gave her a haughty look. 'I am a Xandreou. They will make room for me.'

And I'll be the one left standing on the tarmac, Camilla thought.

'What are your plans if you get to England?' she asked.

'I shall stay with you,' Arianna said promptly. 'You can hide me when Nicos comes to search for me—as he will.'

It sounded like a scenario for a nightmare.

'You realise he'll be worried sick as well as damned angry,' Camilla said curtly. 'You can't treat him like this.' She took a breath. 'Go back and talk to him, Arianna. Tell him how unhappy you are, and why. You may find he understands better than you think. But confrontation won't help, and neither will running away.'

Arianna bounced to her feet. 'You're saying you won't help?'

'It wouldn't be any use to do what you're asking. I'd just make matters worse, and I've done enough of that already.' Camilla kept her voice steady. 'I really think you should go back to the Villa Apollo.'

'Never,' Arianna flared. 'He would lock me in my room until we left for the mainland.'

It occurred to Camilla that Nic might have a point. 'Does he know where you are now?'

'No, of course not,' Arianna said scathingly. 'He will not know I am gone until tomorrow.'

'Then go back the way you came—and sleep on it,' Camilla urged. 'You'll both have calmed down tomorrow, and feel more prepared to be reasonable.'

'*Ochi*.' The Greek girl's face was stormy. 'If you

will not help, I make my own way, and to hell for you.'

'With you,' Camilla corrected automatically, and with one last furious glare Arianna whirled out of the kitchen.

Camilla chased after her. 'Where are you going?'

'Away, now—tonight,' the other flung over her shoulder. 'Where no one will find me.'

'Please speak to Nic first,' Camilla appealed. 'Or I will.'

'I don't think so.' Arianna was triumphant. 'There's no telephone here, and you don't have a car. It's a very long walk, I think, and by the time you get there I will be gone—forever.'

'Damnation,' Camilla exploded in frustration as Arianna drove off.

She should have stopped her somehow, and she knew it. Arianna was quite capable of driving to the port and catching the last ferry to Zakynthos, from which there'd be regular flights all over Europe. It would be all too easy for her to disappear.

She felt cold suddenly. Arianna might be spoiled and wilful, but she'd led a sheltered life, and that, coupled with her beauty, made her vulnerable.

I can't just let her vanish into the night, she thought frantically. But I can't follow her either—not on foot, or from the back of beyond.

But she must do something. Nic thought badly enough of her as it was, and nothing could change that, but she couldn't let Arianna charge unhindered down a road to self-destruction.

Whatever Greek men might do with their lives, Camilla had already deduced that the rules which applied to women were very different. And a headlong flight by Xandreou's sister was just the thing to set malicious tongues wagging.

If Arianna broke the code, however unreasonable it might seem to an outsider, the Xandreou family pride and prestige could be damaged, perhaps irrevocably. And Arianna and Petros would become exiles, with no way back.

She thought, I can't let it happen.

From the terrace, she could see the lights of the Villa Apollo shimmering across the silken calm of the sea. They looked almost close enough to touch, but she knew that was an illusion.

But they were within swimming distance. Nic himself had told her so, a lifetime ago, when things were still simple between them.

She stood very still for a moment, thinking. She'd swum regularly in the bay, and never come across any potentially dangerous currents there. And there was no breeze tonight. If she took it steadily, she could make it.

She didn't allow time for second thoughts. She dragged her one-piece blue swimsuit out of the case, and put it on. It was the one she wore to the local baths at home.

I'll pretend that's where I am—seeing how many

lengths I can do, she told herself determinedly, ignoring the nervous flutters in her stomach.

She left her wrap and sandals at the foot of the steps, then, taking a deep breath, ran down to the edge of the sea.

CHAPTER TWELVE

THE water felt chilly against her warm skin. Camilla waded in till it was chest-high, then struck out smoothly, deliberately not hurrying.

It was a totally different experience, somehow, swimming at night. The dark water was mysterious, full of whispers and movement. Once something seemed to brush past her, and she bit back a cry, reminding herself of the shoals of fish she'd swum among in daylight. It could even have been a strand of weed, or just her imagination playing tricks.

As soon as she felt tired, she turned on to her back and floated for a while until she was rested enough to go on. There was a brief sickle of a moon above her now, like a friendly beacon, lighting her way towards her lover—her enemy.

She changed her stroke to a crawl, cutting easily through the water. She seemed to be making real headway now, with the lights from the Villa Apollo appearing much closer at last. She must be well past the point of no return, she thought, her heart jumping nervously.

Don't think about that, she adjured herself. Concentrate on your breathing, and moving your arms and legs correctly to take full advantage of every stroke. Textbook stuff.

But she needed more than theory to get her through tonight. A fair helping of luck wouldn't come amiss, she thought, treading water to get her bearings. This time, to her dismay, her destination seemed as far away as ever. Maybe she was doomed to swim forever, like some ill-fated mermaid, while the Villa Apollo, like Nic himself, stayed always out of reach.

I was crazy to have started this, she thought, suddenly aware of how cold she was getting, how increasingly difficult it was to maintain that first easy rhythm.

But she mustn't think like that. It wasn't just defeatist, but downright dangerous. Somehow she had to go on. The choice was out of her hands.

All the choices had been out of her hands since the moment she'd first set foot on Karthos. She realised that now. She'd been the plaything of fate since day one.

And if she went down into the sea—the wine-dark sea—that would be fate too. And it would be so easy. She felt the drag of the water at her weary limbs. And then remembered what had brought her this far.

Nic, she thought dazedly, pushing her aching body forward. She had to see him—to tell him— something. What exactly didn't seem to matter any more. The important thing was to see him—to hear

his voice—to touch him once more before she left—
before the old, drab life closed over her head like
the sea.

In her head, she seemed to hear him calling her,
urging her on. Eyes closed, arms and legs like lead,
she concentrated every nerve, every muscle, every
scrap of will on survival.

She was hardly aware of the light at first. It was
only a faint blur behind her tired eyelids, but with
every stroke it seemed to swell and grow until it
filled the universe. And there were voices too—
men's voices, shouting something.

Her flailing arms brushed something solid—
planking, she realised dazedly—then something
seized her, held her, pulling her up into the light.

She cried out in fright, and pain as her muscles
protested. When she opened her eyes, she found herself lying on *Calliope*'s deck, with Nic bending over
her.

She barely recognised him. His face was grey, his
voice hoarse. 'What have you done?' he demanded.
'In the name of God, why are you here? Are you
insane?'

She wanted to put up a hand and smooth away
the haggard lines beside his mouth, the crease between his brows. Her heart cried out, I love you.
Her mouth tried to form the words.

From a great distance she heard her voice, husky
and laboured, say, 'Arianna's run away. You—you
must stop her.' Then she fainted.

*   *   *

She was in the sea again, the water lapping round her, loading her down, enclosing her so that she couldn't breathe—and she was struggling, fighting her way to the surface.

'Be still, *pedhi mou*. You are safe now.'

She forced open her weighted lids, and looked up into Nic's grave face. She was lying in a bed, she realised, with blankets wrapped round her, swaddling her. That was why she'd felt she couldn't move.

'You have to rest—keep warm,' he said quietly. 'Petros's orders must be obeyed.'

'Petros?' Camilla frowned as memory began to nudge at her. 'Is he here? But surely...'

'He is downstairs with Arianna.' He paused for a moment. 'After she left you, she went to him, it seems, and he brought her back.'

'Oh, thank God.' Camilla felt sudden tears scalding her eyes. 'Please—don't be angry with her. She's so unhappy.'

'Indeed?' The dark brows lifted quizzically. 'When I saw her last, she was smiling and drinking champagne in celebration of her engagement.'

'Engagement?' Camilla ran her tongue round her dry lips.

'To Petros, naturally.' Nic's gaze bored into her. 'Or did you think I was blind to what was going on?'

'But she said you had plans for her—an arranged marriage.'

He shrugged. 'I was testing her,' he said flatly. 'I wanted to discover if she really loved Petros, or was simply enjoying the drama of a secret romance. He is too good—as a man, and as a friend—to be at the mercy of her whims and fancies, if she had no serious intentions towards him.' He smiled faintly. 'But as she was prepared to abandon everything for a hand-to-mouth existence with him on the other side of Europe, I had to believe her sincerity.'

He sighed. 'I only hope he knows what he is taking on,' he added drily. His smile became slightly crooked. 'So true love triumphs over circumstances again, Camilla. You should be delighted. Another victory for you.'

'I had nothing to do with it,' she protested, suddenly and uncomfortably aware that she was naked inside the cocoon of blankets. 'But I'm glad that everything's worked out for them,' she added rather stiltedly. 'Even if I did make that swim for nothing.'

'Ah, yes,' he said softly. 'That swim.' He paused, and Camilla felt tension crackle in the air. 'You crazy little fool. Don't you know you could have drowned?'

She forced a smile to trembling lips. 'It did occur to me—several times. But I had to tell you—to warn you what Arianna intended.'

There was a silence, then he said, 'Was that the only reason?'

She felt a wave of betraying warmth sweep over

her. 'There was no other way to reach you,' she prevaricated.

Nic shook his head. 'That was not what I asked, *matia mou*, and you know it.'

She said in a little rush, 'I couldn't bear to see you hurt again. I knew if Arianna talked to you, told you how she felt, you'd understand.'

'You had more faith in me than she did,' he said with a touch of grimness.

She didn't look at him. 'Perhaps you don't see things too clearly when you're in love,' she said in a low voice.

'No.' His voice was reflective. 'So—it was just for Arianna's sake that you chose to risk your life?'

She picked at the edging of a blanket. 'Not—totally.'

'So?'

She sighed. 'I didn't want to leave—with all this misunderstanding between us.'

'Tell me something.' Nic's fingers closed round her chin, tilting it so that he could study her flushed face. 'When you came with me to Marynthos—and afterwards—was it only so that your sister could meet with Spiro?'

'No,' she said. 'At least—I wouldn't have pushed myself on to you as I did—but if you'd asked me I'd have gone with you.' She stopped, confused and miserable. 'You were right all along, you see. I was—yours for the taking, only I didn't want to admit it.' Her little laugh cracked in the middle. 'Just another of Xandreou's women after all.'

'You flatter me,' he said with irony. He released her. 'I'll carve another notch on the bedhead, and we'll part friends. Is that what you want?'

What I want? she could have shrieked at him. Body, heart and soul, I ache—burn for you.

She said, 'I—hope we can be friends, certainly. Maybe one day you'll come to see that Katie and Spiro are happy together, and that the end has justified the means.'

'You thought I was angry because I'd been made a fool of,' he said. 'But that was only part of it. I was frightened, Camilla. Scared that when Spiro regained his memory I might lose him.' He sat for a moment, looking down at his hands, his face brooding.

'We quarrelled, you see, before the accident,' he went on. 'I said cruel things—damaging things about your sister. Made assumptions that he resented. I have never seen him so angry—so determined. He said he was going to her, and there was nothing I could do to stop him. That if his marriage to her meant a complete breach between us, then that was how it would be.'

He shook his head. 'We were both furious—emotional. I knew he was driving to the ferry—I should have stopped him—calmed him down. He wasn't fit to be in charge of a car, and I knew it. But—I let him go.' His voice broke. 'When I saw the car, crumpled against a tree, Spiro slumped over the wheel, I knew I could never forgive myself.'

His voice sank almost to a whisper. 'I feared that when Spiro remembered it would only be the anger—the bitterness. Both he and Arianna—I have had to be responsible for them for so long—more like their father than their brother. I suppose I wanted to protect them both—too much.'

'I felt the same with Katie,' Camilla confessed. 'I wasn't overjoyed when she first told me about Spiro, believe me.'

He smiled faintly. 'I do, *pedhi mou*. We both—underestimated them perhaps.' He threw his head back. 'I came to realise that while Spiro had that blank in his memory he belonged to me—depended on me again, and I was disgusted at my own selfishness—my own cowardice.'

'But in reality you had nothing to fear,' Camilla said softly.

'No,' he admitted. 'Spiro has been—generous. Your sister also.' He reached out and took her hand, staring at her fingers as if he was committing them to memory. 'If I had chosen her myself, I could have found no better match for him. I—see that now.'

She bit her lip, feeling tears sting at her eyes. 'You can be generous too, Kyrios Xandreou.'

'I need to make amends, Kyria Dryden.' His mouth smiled at their formality, but the dark eyes were serious.

'And now it's my turn.' She swallowed. 'I did

agree to keep you out of the way that day, but only because I felt I had no choice. I felt such a fraud when your friends were so nice to me. I found I wanted the day to be real, with no pretence—no hidden agenda.'

'And it was real?' His voice was harsh suddenly. 'When we were together, a man and a woman with nothing but our need for each other? Or was it more pretence—and pity?'

'Pity?' she echoed in shock. 'Oh, God, do you really think I could have behaved like that—given myself to you—because I thought you'd had a raw deal with your marriage?' She shook her head. 'You don't know me very well.'

'And that is something I mean to change.' He put her hand against his mouth, his lips grazing her skin, sending a shiver of sensuous yearning through her body. 'Where do you think I was going in *Calliope* tonight, *agape mou*, when I pulled you from the sea?'

'Going?' She frowned. 'I don't know.'

'No?' He smiled at her, a tenderness in his face that she had never seen before. 'To the sea house, my Camilla. To ask you to stay—on my knees, if I had to.'

She said with a catch in her voice, 'I thought you went to Athens to get away from me.'

He grimaced. 'So did I. But you've been with me every moment of this endless, damnable week, invading my thoughts all day, torturing my dreams at night in spite of myself.'

She looked at him under her lashes, swiftly and shyly. 'In spite of Zoe too?'

Nic looked resigned. 'My beloved sister, no doubt. I shall instruct Petros to beat her regularly when they are married. Yes, my sweet devil, in spite of Zoe, who found me poor company on the one occasion I took her to dinner. However, I don't know which of us was more surprised when I suddenly heard myself telling her I would not be seeing her again.

'That moment was like a catalyst. I knew then what I had been fighting so desperately to deny.' He framed her face very gently in his hands. 'That I love you, *matia mou*, my sweet girl who gave me the innocence in her eyes.'

Camilla said with a little sob, 'Oh, Nic.'

'Hear me out, *agape mou*. When Spiro called me to say you planned to leave tomorrow, I cancelled my meetings and flew back. I could not let things rest as they were between us. I had to see you—to tell you what was in my heart—to ask you if we could cancel out the unkindness, the mistrust, and begin again.'

He smoothed back a strand of still damp hair from her forehead. 'I also need to know, my dear one, if you can love me.'

She smiled at him, eyes shining, lips tremulous. 'I lost my battle long ago, *kyrie*. Why else would I swim further than I've ever done in my life, if not to be with you?'

He was very still for a moment, then with a groan he lay beside her, gathering her into his arms as carefully as if she were made of spun glass, planting swift, sweet kisses on her hair, forehead and eyes.

'I really knew,' he told her softly, 'that day when I saw you with Hara's baby in your arms. It came to me, like a bolt of thunder, how much I wished to see you holding our child.'

'That's a wish that might be granted sooner than you think,' Camilla said ruefully.

'The possibility troubles you?'

'No.' She shook her head. 'But I'd better cut out the strenuous exercise from now on, just in case.'

'Yes,' he said grimly. 'You will. Dear God.' He smothered a groan. 'How easily I could have lost you.'

'Never.' She was laughing now, warmly, glowingly provocative as she eased herself out of the encircling blankets and watched the answering fire kindle in his dark eyes. 'Darling Nic, it was all fate. I was born to be Xandreou's woman.'

'No, *sigismos mou*,' he said softly as he bent to her, mouth and hands sensuous against her skin, drawing her against the vibrant beat of his heart. 'Xandreou's wife.'

DARK FIRE

by

Robyn Donald

CHAPTER ONE

WHEN Paul came to pick her up, Aura Forsythe's heart swelled with pride.

He looked so good, the black and white of his evening clothes setting off his fair hair and skin. But she didn't love him for his blond handsomeness. Aura knew, none better, that good looks and regular features had little to do with the person beneath the fleshy veneer.

It had been his smile that first caught her attention, and his air of calm, confident good humour. However, very soon after meeting Paul McAlpine she had realised that he was utterly, completely reliable. It made him irresistible. Over the past three months she'd come to understand him very well, this man she was to marry in a fortnight's time. Bathed in the warmth of his love, her turbulent search for some measure of peace in her life was transformed into serenity. She had never been so happy.

'We're meeting Flint at the restaurant,' he said as he opened the door of his expensive car for her. 'He wants to shower and change, but he'll probably be at Quaglino's before we are.' Flint Jansen was to be best man at their wedding in two weeks' time.

'Where does he live?'

'In Remuera, but he's staying with me.'

'Oh. Why?'

'His place is being redecorated. Wet paint everywhere, so he's going to stay with me for at least a week, and possibly until the wedding.'

He lifted her hand to kiss the slender fingers. Aura's full mouth curved into a smile.

'You look very pretty tonight,' Paul murmured as he released her.

'Thank you. I like this dress.'

Although compliments still made her uneasy, experience had trained her to handle them with poise. And compliments from Paul were no threat.

The dress was one she had had for some years, but the rich, muted green silk played up hair the colour of good burgundy wine and ivory skin, darkened and emphasised her huge green eyes.

'So the fabled Flint Jansen is here. It seems odd that I haven't met your best friend yet,' she said, deliberately steadying her voice as she changed the subject with automatic skill.

Paul laughed softly. 'He was saying the same thing. I told him that if he insists on staying in Indonesia for months at a time he must expect things to happen while he's gone.'

Suddenly a car roared across the intersection in front of them. Paul reacted swiftly and without alarm, but Aura was flung forward on to the seatbelt.

'Are you all right?' he asked sharply.

She flashed him a reassuring smile. The way he looked after her, as though she were a precious piece of porcelain, made her feel safe and cherished.

'Yes, I'm fine. You've got very fast reactions.'

His mouth turned up at the corner. 'Not so fast as Flint's. He's like greased lightning. We went hunting in the Uraweras once and he stopped me from going over a cliff.' He paused, then finished enviously, 'Man, did he move! Faster than a king cobra and stronger than a horse. I'm no lightweight, but he hauled me back out of the air as though I were made of balsa wood.'

'He sounds very macho.' Her voice was cool and non-committal.

Paul laughed. 'It's not the way I'd describe him. Macho

has a ring of fundamental insecurity to it, whereas Flint is honest right through. And completely self-sufficient.'

'Honesty,' Aura said cynically, 'can be a much overrated quality.'

Paul's smile was tender and tolerant. 'Don't try to shock me, darling, I know your little tricks. Although I must admit Flint's complete self-assurance does antagonise people— mostly people who envy it!'

'Well, we all envy the things we haven't got,' Aura agreed, thinking of the many qualities she yearned for.

'How would you know? You've got everything.'

Aura's snort was followed by a smile. 'I'm glad you think so. You and he don't seem to have much in common.'

'We don't, but Flint's the best friend I've ever had. He doesn't suffer fools gladly—if at all—he's about as yielding as granite bedrock, and he has the sort of ominous patience that makes a cat hunting a mouse look testy. But I like him, and I think you will too. He'll certainly be impressed by you. He has an eye for a beautiful woman.'

I'll just bet he has, Aura thought wearily. A cold foreboding sandpapered her nerves. She didn't want to meet Flint Jansen; she already knew she wasn't going to like him.

'He hasn't had much sleep these last few days,' Paul went on. 'He's been tidying up a very hush-hush situation in Indonesia and he strode off the plane looking like something piratical and fierce from the South China Sea.'

'He must be exhausted! Perhaps we should have skipped tonight, and just met at the party tomorrow night.'

'He's tough enough to cope.' Paul smiled indulgently. 'It's inborn. I remember when he first arrived in primary school he was given a rugged time—kids can be little heathens, can't they?—and we've been friends ever since.'

Aura already knew that Flint Jansen and Paul had gone to the same expensive boarding school. She was surprised to hear the rest, however. From the few allusions that Paul had made to his best friend, she'd visualised him as being born able to deal with anything the world threw at him, an iron baby who'd progressed inexorably into an iron child, then hardened more as he grew into an iron man.

'Why did he have such a bad time at school?'

Paul's shoulders lifted. 'Family scandal. His father decamped with a vast amount of other people's money—turned out he'd been spending it on a rather notorious woman who was his mistress. There was a luridly salacious fuss in the newspapers, ending in a court case and even more gaudy revelations. Some of the people his father had defrauded had kids at school. The whole thing got out of hand a bit. Mind you, Flint gave as good as he got, but it was an unhappy couple of years for him.'

'How old was he?'

'Only eight. Old enough to know what was going on, too young to be able to protect himself from older boys who tormented him. Although he tried.' He laughed reminiscently. 'Lord, he must have fought every kid in the school who even looked sideways at him. He didn't care what size they were, and a fair few of them he beat, too.'

Only too well Aura knew what it was like to find no haven from a tormenter. Unwillingly, a pang of fellow feeling softened her attitude. She, too, had been eight when her father had deserted his wife and child to go as a missionary doctor to Africa. Even now, fifteen years later, she felt a shadow of that old grief and bewilderment.

Sighing silently, she told herself that a friend of Paul's had to have a gentler side. At least she and Flint would have something in common: their mutual affection for the man who was to be her husband.

But her first sight of the formidable Flint Jansen changed her mind completely. There was not a hint of softness in him. At least three inches taller than Paul, he had to be six foot four, and, with a thin scar curling in a sinister fashion from his left cheekbone to the arrogant jut of his jaw, his image seared into her brain, leaving a dark, indelible imprint.

A discord of emotions jostled her, confusing her into silence; only gradually did she realise that the most predominant was a turbulent, piercing recognition.

Which was ridiculous, because she had never seen this man before, not even in a grainy photograph in a newspaper. If she had, she'd have known him; he was not a man easily forgotten. Beneath the black material of his dinner jacket his shoulders were broad and powerful. A crisp white shirt contrasted with skin the bronze of an ancient artefact. Those wide shoulders and long, heavily muscled legs beneath smoothly tailored trousers combined with a lithe grace of movement to make him instantly, lethally impressive.

Dark brown hair, conventionally cut, waved sleekly beneath lights that spun a dangerous red halo around his head. He had a starkly featured buccaneer's face, hard and unhandsome, yet it was Flint everyone was watching from beneath their lashes, not her good-looking Paul.

The man was awesomely conspicuous, the power of his personality underlined by a barely curbed, impatient energy that crackled like lightning across the richly furnished room.

Whatever he might have been like at the age of eight, Aura thought dazedly as Paul, beaming and endearingly pompous with pride, introduced them, Flint Jansen certainly didn't need sympathy now; he was more than capable of dealing with anything life threw at him. Except that this man didn't deal with anything; he conquered. Flint Jansen made his own terms, and forced the world to accept them.

Smiling stiffly, Aura extended her hand, felt it enveloped by long, strong fingers. It took an effort of will to persuade her unwilling lashes up, and when she did her gaze was captured by golden eyes as clear and startling as a tiger's, with a predator's uncompromising assumption of power and authority, eyes fixed on her face in a gaze that stripped away the superficial mask of her beauty to spotlight the woman who hid behind it. A premonition ran with swift, icy steps through her body and mind.

'Aura,' Flint said in a deep, subtly raw voice that played across her nerve ends with sensual precision. 'Paul's told me several times that you are beautiful, but I thought it was just the maunderings of a man in love. Now I know he understated the case.'

Long past the age when praise for her beauty gave her more than a mild pleasure, Aura winced under a stab of stupid disappointment.

It seemed, she thought ironically, that in spite of that unrestrained magnetism, the fierce, lawless penetration of his glance, Flint Jansen was no more perceptive than other men. The physical accident of her features, the legacy of her ancestors, fooled him as it did most others into believing that her beauty was all she was.

Hoping her maverick chagrin didn't show, she smiled. 'Thank you,' she said aloofly.

His hand was firm and warm and hard, and for a moment the conventional grip felt like some kind of claim, a staking of ownership, a challenge. It took all her self-command not to flinch and pull away.

And then it was over. Their hands relaxed, dropped; Flint turned with a comment that made Paul laugh, and Aura was left wondering whether the shivers that tightened her skin were simply attributable to a cold winter's night and the fact that she, with typical vanity, was wearing no more than the barest essentials beneath her green silk dress.

Of course they were.

Yet as they walked towards the table she felt Flint's probing regard, and once again that eerie sense of dislocation cut her adrift from her usual composure.

Casting a quick upward glance at Paul's pleasant, handsome face, she wondered what on earth her kind, reliable, trustworthy fiancé had in common with this arrogant, intolerant man; it must be one of the mysterious masculine friendships that women couldn't fathom.

Apart from their schooldays, the only attributes they seemed to share were intelligence and ambition. Perhaps they were enough to sustain a friendship.

Paul was rapidly heading for the top of his profession, and people spoke of Flint Jansen as being right in line for position as the next chief executive officer of Robertson's, the big conglomerate he worked for. Paul, a partner in a big City law office, knew a lot about the City, and had told her that the present CEO trusted him implicitly.

Aura understood why. Her first look had convinced her that Flint possessed enough concentrated, effortless authority to take over any organisation, even one as big as Robertson's, and run it with the decision and uncompromising strength that such an enterprise needed.

By the time they arrived at their table tension was jagging through her, snarling up her thought processes, pulling her skin taut. She retained enough presence of mind to smile at various acquaintances, but her whole attention was focused on the man who walked behind her. Although she couldn't see him, she knew when he nodded a couple of times at people who greeted him with transparent interest.

Smiling her thanks at the waiter, Aura allowed him to seat her. As the two men sat down, the little buzz of conversation that had greeted their progress across the room died back to the normal low hum.

Aura drew in a deep breath, purposefully commanding her thudding pulses to slow down, using her considerable willpower to control her wildly unsuitable reactions. Unfortunately, she wasn't given much time to re-erect the barriers of her self-possession.

The formalities of ordering their meals barely over, Flint asked her with a smile that didn't reach his eyes, 'What do you do, Aura? For a living, I mean?'

Talk about throwing down the gauntlet! Clearly, like most of Paul's friends, like his mother, Flint believed that Aura looked at the man she was going to marry with greed rather than love in her heart.

For a fleeting second she wished she had a high-powered, important job to throw in his teeth.

But she hadn't, and it was no use playing for sympathy. Flint Jansen was too hard, too dynamic, too much master of his own destiny to understand the clinging bonds that entangled her.

It wasn't her fault she had no job. In spite of opposition and ridicule she had worked damned hard for her double degree, and if circumstances had been kinder she would already be on the first rungs of her chosen career. Nevertheless, Flint's expression revealed that she wouldn't get anywhere by pleading for understanding.

So with nothing but limpid innocence in her face and voice she looked directly into eyes as clear and sharp as golden crystals, and said, 'Nothing.'

He lifted uncompromising black brows. 'Not a career woman, then.'

There was no scorn in his words, nothing more apparent than mild interest, but the invisible hairs on Aura's skin were pulled upright by a sudden tension.

Cheerfully, yet with a hint of warning in his tone, Paul interposed, 'I know dynamic, forceful, professional women are your cup of tea, Flint, but Aura was brought up the old-fashioned way, so don't you get that note in your voice when you're talking to her. Until the end of last year she was at university. Unfortunately, she also has—responsibilities.'

He and Aura exchanged a glance. Paul not only understood her situation with her mother, he approved of her handling of it.

'Resposibilities?' Flint was smiling, but thick, straight

lashes covered the tiger eyes so that it was impossible to see what emotions hid behind that rugged façade.

'A mother,' Aura said lightly, 'and if you think I've been brought up the old-fashioned way, wait till you meet Natalie. She's straight out of the ark.' She primmed her mouth. 'She had a very sheltered upbringing. Her father believed that women were constitutionally incapable of understanding matters more complicated than the set of a sleeve, so he didn't bother to have her taught anything beyond womanly accomplishments like playing the piano and running a dinner party with flair and poise. Consequently she's as sweetly unconcerned about practicalities as a babe in arms.'

'It sounds a considerable responsibility,' Flint agreed in his slightly grating voice. 'Will she be living with you after you—after the wedding?'

At the look of sheer horror that spread over Paul's face, Aura bubbled into laughter. 'No,' she said demurely.

Recovering his equanimity, Paul told him, 'She'll be living quite close to us, so we'll be able to keep an eye on her.'

'I see.' Flint sounded remote and more than a little bored.

Aura asked, 'What are you doing in Indonesia, Mr Jansen?'

'Flint,' he said, smiling with an assured, disturbing magnetism that made every other man in the big, luxurious room fade into the wallpaper. 'I was tidying up a mess.'

'Oh?'

'Don't ask,' Paul advised kindly, directing a purely masculine look at the man opposite. 'He won't tell you anyway. Flint's work is highly confidential.'

Thoroughly irritated by the unspoken male conspiracy, Aura fluttered her lashes and cooed, 'How fascinating. Is it dangerous, too?'

'Sometimes,' Flint said, the intriguing, gravelly texture in his voice intensifying. 'Does danger excite you, Aura?'

From beneath half-closed eyelids he was watching the way the light shimmered across her hair. Uneasily she shook her head; an unknown sensation stirred in the pit of her stomach. Perhaps, instead of letting her hair float around her shoudlers in a gleaming burgundy cloud, she should have confined it into a formal pleat.

'No, far from it,' she said, trying to make her tone easy and inconsequential. 'I'm a complete coward.'

'Aura,' Paul said, touching her hand for a second, 'is not into risk.'

As she turned her head to give him a quick, tender smile, she caught in the corner of her eye the ironic movement of Flint's lips.

'Yet you're getting married,' he said speculatively. 'I've always thought that to be the greatest risk in the world, giving another person such power in your life. Unless, of course, the other person is too besotted to be any threat.'

'Ah, you've guessed my secret,' Paul retorted, his blue eyes warmly caressing as they rested on Aura's face.

Without reason, Aura was hit by a wave of profound disquiet. Her gaze clung a moment to Paul's, then slid sideways as the wine waiter appeared.

When the small business of handing the drinks out was over, Paul began talking of a political scandal that had erupted a couple of weeks before. Hiding an absurd relief, Aura listened to the deep male voices, sipping her wine a little faster than usual because something was keeping her on edge.

No, not something; *someone*, and he was sitting next to her. If she lowered her eyes she could see Flint's long fingers on the round tabletop, his bronze skin a shocking contrast to the white, starched damask cloth. He had a beautiful hand, lean and masculine and strong.

He had to spend a lot of time in hot sunlight to acquire a tan like that, she thought vaguely. Of course, he had just returned from the tropics, but, even so, he was far darker skinned than either her or Paul. It was one of the reasons those glittering golden eyes were so spectacular, set as they were in black lashes beneath straight black brows.

The hum of conversation receded, became overlaid by the sudden throbbing of her heart in her eardrums. From beneath her lashes Aura's gaze followed his hand as he lifted his wine glass and sipped some of the pale straw-coloured liquid. When he'd greeted her the rough hardness of calluses against her softer palm had made her catch her breath, and set up a strange, hot melting at the base of her spine. It had receded somewhat, but now it was starting all over again.

She didn't know what was happening to her, although instinct warned her it was dangerous. With a determined attempt to ignore it, she joined in the conversation.

To share a meal with someone who disapproved profoundly of her was nothing new; hatred she could deal with.

But Flint Jansen despised her. He had taken one look at her, and for a frightening second contempt had flickered like cold flames in the depths of his eyes. The moment her eyes had focused on that harshly commanding face, an intuition as old as her first female ancestor had warned her that he was no friend of hers, that he never would be. For some reason they were fated to be enemies.

And Paul hadn't noticed.

She looked up at him, half listening as he expounded some interesting point of law to the other man. Apart from her cousin Alick, Paul was the most intelligent man she had ever known, yet he thought they were getting along well.

Flint's textured voice dragged her glance sideways. He was smiling, and even as she tried to jerk her eyes free his gaze snared hers.

For the length of a heartbeat green eyes and gold clashed. His mouth curved in the smiling snarl of a tiger playing with something small and not worthy of it.

A question from Paul shattered the tension, his beloved tones both an intrusion and a shield. As Flint answered, Aura breathed deeply.

Stop it, her brain screamed. But she had no idea what *it* was. Her reaction was totally new to her; it seemed that a new person had moved in to inhabit her body, a bewildering renegade, a woman she didn't know.

She had to calm down, reimpose some sort of control over her wayward responses.

Something Paul said brought a smile to Flint's face, revealing strong white teeth that did more uncomfortable things to the pit of Aura's stomach. Snatching at her slipping self-possession, she concentrated fiercely on the words, not the man; on the occasion, not her reactions.

He had excellent manners. He was entertaining in a dry, wittily cynical fashion. When Aura spoke he listened attentively with nothing more obvious than lazy appreciation in his hooded eyes, yet she felt the track of his eyes like little whips across the clear ivory of her skin. And she sensed his contempt.

Oh, he was clever, he hid it well; he was a man whose feelings were caged by a ferocious will. But Aura had spent too many years noting hidden, subliminal signals to be fooled. This was not the casual disdain of a man faced by a woman out to feather her nest. Flint Jansen's anger burned with a white-hot intensity that made him more than dangerous. And all that savage emotion was directed at her.

It bewildered her and upset her, but the most astonishing thing was that in some obscure way it was exciting. She looked across the table to the shadowed, clever face slashed by the scar, a countenance almost primitive in its force and power, and a feral shudder ran down her spine, set off warning signals all through her, flashpoints of heat and light leaping from cell to cell.

Shaken, at the mercy of forbidden and equivocal sensations, she managed to disguise her response with a sparkling glow of laughter and bright conversation, while Paul watched her with pride and the tiniest hint of possessive smugness. Amazingly, the secret, seething undercurrent of ambiguous emotions appeared to swirl around him without touching him.

She didn't begrudge him his pride; all men, she knew, wanted to stand well in the eyes of their fellows. It was at once one of their strengths, and rather endearingly childish.

'Paul tells me we're having a party tomorrow night,' Flint said coolly while they waited for dessert.

Natalie had insisted that as mother of the bride she owed friends and relatives a drinks party. Behind Aura's back she had wheedled Aura's cousin, Alick Forsythe, into paying for it, and because she refused to entertain in the small unit she and Aura lived in now it was being held at Paul's apartment.

Aura nodded, hoping her irritation didn't show. 'Yes.' She sent Flint a sideways glance.

His eyes darkened into tawny slits, and for one pulsing second he watched her as though she'd started to strip for him. Then his lashes concealed eyes cold and brilliant as the fire in the heart of a diamond.

Aura's mouth dried. 'You'll meet my mother and my bridesmaid, and an assortment of other people. It should be fun.'

'I'm sure it will be.'

Aura resented his bland tone, but more the sardonic quirk of his lips that accompanied it. Although she had fought against the whole idea of this wretched party, now that it was inevitable she was prepared to do what she could to make it a success.

By the time the evening wound towards its close Aura was heartily glad. Every nerve in her body was chafed into painful sensitivity, her head ached dully and bed had never seemed so desirable.

By then she knew she would never like Flint Jansen, and

found herself hoping savagely that his job kept him well away from them. The less she saw of the beastly man, the better. Fortunately the feeling was mutual, so she wasn't likely to be plagued with too much of his presence after she and Paul were married.

She expected to be taken straight home, but as Flint held open the car door for her with an aloof, studied smile Paul asked, 'Do you mind if we go back to the apartment first, darling? I'm expecting a call from London, and I'd like to be there when it comes.'

'Yes, of course.'

Halfway there she yawned. Instantly Paul said, 'Poor sweet, you're exhausted, and no wonder. Look, why don't I get off at home, then Flint can drive you the rest of the way? That way you'll be tucked up in bed at a reasonable hour.'

'Oh, no, there's—'

Aura's swift, horrified, thoughtless answer was interrupted by Flint's amused voice from the back seat. 'Sounds like a good idea to me,' he said lazily. 'Where does Aura live?'

Bristling, but recognising that protests would only make her antagonism more obvious, Aura gave him her address.

'Really?'

The hardly hidden speculation in his tone made her prickle. 'Yes,' she said stiffly.

'I know how to get there.'

The hidden insolence in his words scorched her skin with a sudden betraying flush. Aura's tense fingers clasped the beaded work of her fringed Victorian bag. She most emphatically did not want to be cooped up with Flint for the twenty minutes or so it would take to get her home. However, as there was no alternative she was going to have to cope as well as she could.

'Goodnight, sweetheart. Try not to push yourself too hard tomorrow,' Paul said when the transfer of drivers had

een effected. He bent down and kissed her gently. 'I'll see
ou tomorrow night.'

She watched him walk across the footpath and in through
he door of the elegant block of apartments where they were
oing to live until they had children.

Aura bit her lip. She had always thought Paul big, but
eside Flint Jansen he was somehow diminished.

With a suddenness that took her by surprise Flint set the
ar in motion. Aura turned her head to look straight ahead,
attered by a ridiculous sense of bereavement, almost of
anic.

She searched for some light, innocuous, sophisticated
omment. Her mind remained obstinately blank.

The man beside her, driving with skill and control if
lightly too much speed, didn't speak either. Aura kept her
lance away from his hands on the wheel, but even the
hought of them turned her insides to unstable quicksilver.
A shattering corollary was the image that flashed into her
nind, of those lean tanned hands against the pale translu-
ence of her skin.

Aura stared very hard at the houses on the side of the
oad. Lights gleamed in windows, on gateposts, highlighted
ardens that bore the signs of expensive, skilful attention.
Although it was winter, flowers lifted innocent blooms to
he shining disc of the moon, early jonquils, daisies, the
ristocratic cornucopias of arum lilies. To the left a wall of
olcanic stones fenced off a park where the delicate pointed
eaves of olive trees moved slightly, their silver reverses
himmering in a swift, soon-dead breeze. Beyond them rose
he sharp outlines of a hill.

Aura said sharply, 'This isn't the way.'

'I thought we'd go up One Tree Hill and look at the city
ights,' Flint said in his cool, imperturable voice.

Aura's head whipped around. Against the glow of the
treet-lights his profile was a rigorously autocratic silhou-
tte of high forehead and dominating nose, the clear state-

ment of his mouth, a chin and jaw chiselled into lines of power and force.

Speaking evenly, she said, 'Thanks very much, but I'd rather go straight home.'

A blaze of lights from the showgrounds disclosed his half smile, revealed for a stark moment the narrow, deadly line of the scar. He looked calculating and unreachable. 'That's a pity,' he said calmly. 'I won't keep you long.'

Aura felt the first inchoate stirrings of fear. 'I'm actually rather tired,' she confessed, keeping up the pretence of reluctantly refusing a small treat, trying to smooth a gloss of civilisation over a situation that frightened her needlessly to hide her uncalled-for alarm and anger with poise and control. 'Organising a wedding is far more exhausting than I'd expected it to be.'

His unamused smile held a distinctly carnivorous gleam

Oh, lord, she thought frantically, keep things in perspective, Aura, and don't let your imagination run away with you. The man is a barbarian, but he won't hurt you. After all, he's Paul's best friend.

'I'm sure it is,' he said, 'especially at such short notice but a few minutes spent looking down on the most beautiful city in the world won't hurt you. Who knows, it could even recharge your batteries.'

'It might be dangerous up there,' she said quickly, although she had never heard of anything unpleasant happening on top of One Tree Hill.

His laughter was brief and unamused. 'I don't think so.'

She didn't think so, either. For other people, possibly but not the ruthlessly competent Flint Jansen.

Opening her mouth to object further, she cast a fulminating glance at that inexorable profile then closed it again He was a man who made up his mind and didn't let anyone change it.

The exact reverse of her mother, Aura thought acidly trying to fight back the fear that curled with sinister menace through her. Natalie's mind was like a straw caught in a summer wind, whirled this way and that by each small eddy, held only on one course, that of her own self-interest.

Flint Jansen was bedrock, immovable, dominating, impervious, a threat to any woman's peace of mind. Even a woman in love with another man.

Aura pretended to look about her as they wound up the sides of the terraced volcano and along the narrow ridges. For centuries the Maori settlers of New Zealand had grown kumara in the fertile volcanic soil of the little craters below, but the rows of sweet potato were long gone and now sheep cropped English grasses there.

At the top the car park was empty. Nobody looked down over the spangled carpet of city lights, no one gazed up at the obelisk past the lone pine tree, past the statue of the Maori warrior, past the grave of the pioneer who had given this green oasis to the people of Auckland, nobody gazed with her into the black infinity that ached in Aura's heart, the unimaginable reaches of space.

Switching off the engine, Flint turned to look at her. The consuming heat of his scrutiny seared her skin, yet banished immediately the haunted isolation, the insignificance she felt whenever she looked at the night sky.

Tension crawled between her shoulder-blades, tightened every sinew in her body, clogged her breath and her pulse, made her eyes dilate and her skin creep. When he spoke she recoiled in nervous shock.

'I assume,' he drawled, 'that you know what you're doing.'

She ran the tip of her tongue along dry lips. 'I assume so, too. In what particular thing?'

'Marrying Paul.'

It had to be that, of course. So why did she feel as though they were talking about two different subjects? She was letting him get to her. Calmly, and with a confidence that sounded genuine, she said, 'Oh, yes, I know exactly what I'm doing.'

'I do hope so, pretty lady. For everyone's sake. Because if you do to him what you've done to two others and jilt him, you're in trouble. Paul may be too besotted to deal with you properly, but I'm not.'

For a moment Aura couldn't speak. Then she returned haughtily, 'I presume you've been snooping through my life.'

'Yes.' He sounded as though her naïveté amused him.

Aura felt sick, but she managed to keep her voice steady, almost objective. 'Mr Jansen—'

His smile was cold and mirthless. 'You've been calling me Flint all evening. Reverting to my surname now is not going to put any distance between us.'

She said aridly, 'Flint then. I won't hurt Paul in any way, if that's what you're afraid of. I'm going to make him very happy. This time it's real.'

'I suppose each of the other poor fools you were engaged to thought it was real, too.' He paused, and when she didn't reply, added, 'And presumably that you'd make them very happy.'

The obvious sexual innuendo made her feel sick. She stared sightlessly ahead. 'Paul knows about them,' she said.

'So it's none of my business?'

'Exactly.'

'Not even when he finds out—as he's bound to do—that you're not in love with him?'

Aura said angrily, 'I love him very much.'

He laughed softly, an immense cynicism colouring his tone. 'Oh, I have to admire the languishing glances, the smiles and the gentle touches. But they didn't look like love to me, and if Paul wasn't so enamoured that he can't think straight he'd know that what you feel for him is not the sort of love that leads to a happy marriage.'

'You'd know all about it, I suppose.' Struggling for control, she caught her breath. 'I love him,' she repeated at last, but the conviction in her voice was eaten away by a sense of futility. One quick glance at Flint's unyielding profile and she knew that whatever she said, she couldn't convince this man.

'Just as you'd love your older brother, with respect and admiration and even a bit of gratitude,' he agreed dispassionately. 'But that's not what marrige is all about, beautiful, seductive, sexy Aura. It's also about lying in a bed with him, making love, giving yourself to him, accepting his body, his sexuality with complete trust and enthusiasm.'

Her small gasp echoed in the darkened car. She searched for some reply, but her mind was held prisoner by the bleak and studied impersonality of his tone.

After a moment he continued, 'When Paul looks at you it's with love, but I don't see much more in you than satisfaction at having got what you want: a complacent and easygoing husband.'

Stonily, Aura said, 'I want to go home.'

'I'm sure you do.' He sounded amused, almost lazily so, and satisfied, as though her reaction was just what he had expected. 'But you're going to stay here until I've finished.'

'What gives you the right to talk like this to me?'

The words tumbled out, hot with feeling, shamingly defiant, giving away far more than was wise. Aura tried desperately to curb the wild temper that used to get her into so much trouble before she found ways to restrain it.

'Paul is my friend,' Flint said coolly. 'I care about him and his happiness. And I'd hate to see him tied to a calculating little tramp when a few words could save him. That's what friends are for, surely?' The last question was drawled with mockery.

She didn't intend to hit him. In fact, she didn't even realise she had until the high sweep of his cheekbone stopped her hand with such implacable suddenness that every bone in her arm ached with the impact.

Gulping with shock and pain, she snatched her hand back, cradled it to her stomach and said in a voice she had hoped never to hear again, 'Don't you call me a tramp. Don't *ever* call me a tramp.'

He hadn't moved. For long, taut seconds the imprint of her hand, white in the darkness, stood out with stark, disgraceful precision.

So coldly that it congealed even her righteous indignation, he said, 'Why not? You're selling yourself to him. That's what tramps do. Money for sexual services.'

'I am *not* selling myself to him.' Her voice cracked, but she rushed on, hurling the words at him, 'And it's not just sex, damn you, you ignorant swine, there's more—'

'Not much more. For you it's security, for him love. You need his money, he wants to spend the rest of your life making you happy. And, not so incidentally, sleeping with you. If that's the bargain it's fair enough, I suppose. Just don't renege on it, Aura, when he's so far under your spell that the poor sod can't crawl out.'

It took a vast effort to moderate her tone, to summon the cadences of bored sophistication, but Aura hoped she managed it. 'Paul is thirty-two—old enough, don't you think, to fall in love without needing someone to vet his choice?'

'Paul is a romantic,' he returned unemotionally. 'And God knows, you're enough to turn even the most level-headed man's brain into mush. However, I'm not in the least romantic. I've seen enough women who looked like angels and behaved like the scourings of the streets to be able to ignore huge green eyes scattered with gold dust and a mouth that's full and sulkily cushioned with promises of unattainable erotic delights. Even so, I took one look at you and found myself wondering.'

'Wondering what?' The moment the words trembled from her lips she knew she'd made a mistake. 'It doesn't m—'

But he interrupted with blasé precision. 'Wondering whether in bed you live up to the promises you make.'

Aura froze as nausea climbed her throat. Sexy talk, the kind of sensual, seductive words that men used when they wanted to coax a woman into bed, made her shiver with an unremitting fear.

She had been barely fourteen when the husband of one of her mother's friends had told her of his fantasies, all of them starring her, as he drove her home from the house where he lived with his wife and three children. He had seemed to think that her beauty gave him the right to tell her specifically just what he wanted to do to her, in bed and out. His words had been detailed and obscene, summoning scenarios that chilled her right through to her soul.

He had made no attempt to touch her, then or ever, but his perverted pleasure in seeing the shock and fear in her face had destroyed her innocence.

Sickened and disgusted, she had spent the next three years avoiding him, until eventually she had found the courage to threaten him with disclosure of his sexual harassment.

Since then other men had accused her of teasing, of being provocative, believing that her face was the mirror of her character, that the intensity of their desire put her under an obligation to respond.

Oh, she had learned to deal with them; she knew when a light touch was needed, when indignation and threats were necessary. But she had been scarred, her inner soul as much mutilated as whatever had slashed through Flint's skin. And she still felt that sick helplessness when a man looked at her with that knowing speculation, when a certain thickness appeared in his voice. She hated being fodder for fantasy.

Strangely enough, in spite of Flint's words, she didn't feel that sinking nausea now.

One of the things she liked so much about Paul was his

light touch, his wry, self-deprecating amusement. He never made her feel that he wanted too much from her, and when he looked at her it was without greed, with tenderness. She felt safe with Paul.

Since that first experience she had viewed compliments on her looks as preliminaries to demands she had no intention of satisyfing, but listening to Flint Jansen's gravelly voice as he passionlessly catalogued her physical assets brought heat bursting through her in a drenching flood of sensation.

Appalled, mortified, she said huskily, 'Mr—Flint, I know you're Paul's oldest friend, and I know you and he are very fond of each other, but you shouldn't be talking to me like this. I'm going to make Paul very happy. Please take me home.'

'I hope you mean that,' he said, every menacing syllable clear and silky above the pounding of her heart, 'because if you don't, beautiful Aura, if you find a richer man than Paul one day and decide to shuck him off like an old coat, I'll come looking for you. And when I find you, I'll make you sorrier than you've ever thought you could be.'

CHAPTER TWO

WITHOUT waiting for a reply he switched on the engine and backed the car around, then set off down the hill while Aura fought the hardest battle of her life. Never before, not even in childhood when she had been notorious for tantrums, had she been so furiously incandescent with rage, a rage all the more difficult to deal with because it was stretched like a fragile cloak over debilitating fear.

What an arrogant, brutal, cocksure, conceited *bastard*! Oh, she would like to ruin Flint Jansen's life, she'd love to have him come begging to her so she could spurn him with a haughty smile. She'd turn sharply on her heel and walk away, she'd make him *grovel*—

Shaking with frustration and fury, horrified by her thoughts, she dragged air into painful lungs, then set her mind to looking coolly and rationally at the situation.

Eventually, after a huge expenditure of willpower, she succeeded.

In one way Flint's attitude was rather touching. So often the only feelings men allowed themselves to express were connected with anger. Flint's suspicions at least showed he had Paul's interests at heart.

And, viewed objectively, someone who had been engaged twice before had to be a risk in the matrimonial stakes. If you didn't know the circumstances, such a history did seem to show a certain lack of staying power.

Unfortunately, her eminently rational thoughts did nothing to ease the fury that simmered beneath her imposed and artificial restraint. Flint *didn't* know the circumstances; he had just jumped to conclusions, so how dared he accuse her of being a tramp, of not loving Paul, of marrying him for his money?

Nothing would give her greater pleasure than to rub every word in his face, force him to acknowledge that he was wrong...

After another calming breath she tried to convince herself that all she had to do was make Paul happy. If she did that, Flint would be compelled to admit how very wrong he was. Staring blindly through the windscreen, she conjured up a vivid and highly satisfactory scenario of her and Paul's twenty-fifth wedding anniversary, when Flint, proud head lowered, would have to grovel. She could see his face so clearly, see the gracious smile with which she received his abject apology...

Much later, she realised that Paul had not appeared at all in this immensely gratifying dream. The scene that sprang fullblown from the depths of her brain had only two players—her and Flint Jansen.

Neither spoke until they reached the unit. Aura made to open the door, but Flint said crisply as he turned the engine off, 'I'll see you inside.'

'You don't need to,' she said, curt words spilling into the cold silence like little pebbles thrown into sand.

Taking no notice, he got out and came around the front of the car. For those moments, as the street-lights edged his silhouette in gold, he looked like some dark huntsman straight out of myth, lean and lithe and supernaturally big, an ominous, threatening, purposeful presence in the quiet, seedy suburban street.

Holding herself rigidly aloof, Aura slid her long legs out of the car and stood up, then preceded him down the path. A light inside revealed that her mother hadn't gone to bed.

The last thing Aura wanted just then was for them to meet. Her emotions were too raw and antagonistic to be properly controlled, so at the door she turned and said with what she hoped was aplomb, 'Thank you for the ride home. Goodnight.'

Unfortunately, before he had a chance to answer, the door opened.

'Paul,' Natalie cooed in the voice she reserved for him alone, 'dear boy, *do* come in! I want to talk to you about the new flat—I was thinking that what it really needs is a new—'

'Paul didn't bring me home,' Aura interrupted swiftly.

Her mother peered past her, her eyes widening. 'Neither he did,' she said.

Aura watched her regroup as she surveyed Flint. Over her mother's face flashed the famous smile that had reduced so many men to abject submission.

'Darling,' she purred languidly, 'don't just stand there letting me make a fool of myself, introduce us.'

With angry resignation Aura complied, heard her mother invite Flint inside, and his immediate acceptance. It was useless glaring at Natalie, who was invulnerable to suggestion, but Aura sent a contemptuous glance at the man smiling with cynically amused admiration down at her mother.

As though it impacted physically on him he lifted his head, returning Aura's fulminating glower with a long, considering look from narrowed eyes that challenged her to object.

To her fury and despair, Aura couldn't meet his gaze. Turning away, she dumped her bag on the table with a short, abrupt movement.

'How kind of you to bring Aura home, Flint. You must have a nightcap before you go,' Natalie said sweetly, making expert play with her lashes as she ushered him into the cluttered little sitting-room. 'Whisky, surely? You look like a whisky man. I think we've got some somewhere.'

His expression reminded Aura of the smile on the face of the tiger. 'Not for me, thank you.'

Aura bit her lip. She should have been pleased at this unusual interest. Following Lionel's death and the subsequent revelations of his shady, secret life, her mother had sunk into a dangerous apathy that developed into a full-blown nervous breakdown when she'd realised that the only assets she had left were a small annuity Lionel hadn't been able to get his hands on. It provided barely enough money to keep her.

For the first time in her life, Aura had found herself needed by her mother. At first she hadn't understood how ill Natalie was, but when she'd come home from a much-wanted job interview to find her unconscious from an overdose of sleeping pills and tranquillisers, she had realised that for the time being she was going to have to give up her ambitions to make a career in marketing.

Even then, she had hoped that she would have time to finish designing a market research programme she had begun at university. Unfortunately, Natalie had needed her constant attention, and as the tap of the computer's keys seemed to drive her to a frenzy, Aura had given up on it for the time being.

It had been a miserable six months. The only thing that had sustained Aura was meeting Paul. It had helped Natalie, too. She was slowly returning to her normal spirits.

Witness, Aura thought grimly, her swift reaction to Flint Jansen.

It was difficult to see what was going on behind the clear, hard glitter of Flint's eyes, but Aura was prepared to bet that it was appreciation. The clear skin and sultry green eyes Natalie had bequeathed to her daughter were almost unmarred by the years. Tiny lines of petulance and self-indulgence were beginning to etch into the ivory skin, drag the full, lush mouth down at the corners. Even so, Natalie was exquisitely beautiful.

'No?' she said now, with a knowing, flirtatious smile.

'Well, then, a cup of coffee, and while it's being made you must sit down and tell me how you come to be driving Aura home.'

'Paul had to wait for a phone call from Britain,' Aura interposed curtly, not caring whether he thought her rude, 'so Flint very kindly offered to take his place.'

'Only for the drive back,' Flint said in a voice as smooth and bland as cream.

Flakes of colour heated Aura's cheeks. 'Naturally,' she retorted too quickly.

'I'm staying with Paul until the wedding,' Flint told Natalie, 'so if you want me to take a message to him, I'll do it gladly.'

Aura's brows drew together as she stared significantly at her mother, willing her to be silent. But Natalie had learned that the best way to get what she wanted was to use a mixture of cajolery and sexuality on the most powerful man within sight, and it was too late for her to study new tactics.

'No, no,' she said, smiling at Flint as though he was the most fascinating man she had ever met, 'it's just the new flat. I couldn't work out what I didn't like about it, and only a few minutes ago when I was sitting looking at this hideous affair here I realised that it was the carpet. Too middle class and tacky. We'll have to get it changed, but don't you worry about it, I'll discuss it with Paul when I see him next. Now, do sit down and tell me all about yourself. Aura, aren't you going to make us some coffee, darling?'

Sure that Flint was too astute to be taken in by her mother's calculated seductiveness, she watched with astonishment when he gave her mother a slow, tantalising smile and sat down.

Natalie, who adored flirtations and knew just how to conduct one, eyed his hard, unhandsome face with an interest that had something of avidity in it, and proceeded to show how skilled she was in such sport.

Flint responded to her sophisticated coquettishness with a lazy, dangerous charm that had Natalie eating out of his hand in no time. Fuming, Aura had to make coffee and listen to her mother being questioned by an expert. Within five minutes Natalie had artlessly divulged that dear, kind, *thoughtful* Paul had not only bought a flat for his mother-in-law to be, but had also offered a car.

'Only to have Aura throw it back in his face,' Natalie sighed. 'So middle class and boring and prissy of her! It would make life infinitely less stressful, especially now. As it is, unless friends are generous enough to put themselves out for us, we have to use public transport.'

Her voice registered the kind of horror most people reserved for crawling over oyster shells. Flint's brows shot up.

Much encouraged by this, Natalie went on, 'And what difference is there between moving before the wedding and moving after it? I'm not complaining, but it would have made life so much easier for us all if we'd had the new flat, which is four times the size of this dreary little place, to entertain. But no, Aura had some idea that it wasn't the done thing. As though I'm no judge! Not that it really matters, it just means that I'll be stuck here until they come home from their honeymoon. I've been ill, so I can't cope with moving by myself.'

Whenever it seemed she might run down, Flint asked another seemingly innocuous question, and away she went again, spilling out things Aura would much rather he didn't know. Cosseted and adored all her life, Natalie had been valued only for her looks, for her pleasing ways. She naturally gravitated towards men who looked as though they could protect her. Flint filled the bill perfectly.

If you liked that sort of overt, brash male forcefulness.

Aura's fingers trembled as she set the tray. She knew she was being unfair; Flint's air of competence, of authority, that inbuilt assurance that here was a man who was master of himself and his world, was not assumed. It was as natural a part of him as his smile and the complex hints of danger that crackled around him.

Aura knew better than to display her anger and resentment, but when she appeared with the tray she very firmly took command of the conversation, steering it away from personal things to focus on the man who sat opposite, his lean, clever, formidable face hiding every thought but those he wanted them to see.

Fortunately, Natalie knew that men adored talking about themselves. She demanded the details of his life, so they learned that he was some kind of troubleshooter for his firm, that he travelled a lot overseas, that he had been born in the Wairarapa and still went back as often as he could, and that he was thirty-one, a year younger than Paul.

Which, Aura thought as she sipped her coffee, probably explained Paul's protective attitude to him at school. He certainly didn't need protecting now. A more confident, invulnerable man than Flint Jansen it would be hard to imagine. She could see him troubleshooting right across the globe, keen intelligence fortified by disciplined energy and confident control, the hard-edged masculine charisma warning all who came up against him that here was a man who had to be taken very seriously indeed.

He could tell a good story, too. In a very short time he had them both laughing, yet although he seemed perfectly open Aura realised that he was revealing very little of either his work or himself. What they were being treated to was a skilfully edited version of his life, one he'd clearly used before.

A quick, unremarked glance at her watch informed her that he had only been there thirty minutes. It seemed hours.

Restlessly, she thought she'd never be able to look around the small, slightly squalid room, rendered even smaller by the furniture that her mother had managed to salvage from the wreck of her life, without remembering Flint in it. Somehow he had managed to stamp the dark fire of his personality on it as Paul never had.

At least he hadn't paid much attention to her; his whole concentration had been almost entirely on her mother.

Which worried Aura. She knew skilful pumping when she heard it, and thanks to Natalie he now knew that they had no money beyond her pathetic little annuity. Natalie even told him all about Alick's generosity over the years, thereby reinforcing, Aura thought savagely, his estimation of both Forsythe women as greedy and out for what they could get.

Still, it didn't really matter. Paul knew she wasn't like that, and Paul's opinion was the only one she cared about.

Perhaps he had noticed that surreptitious glance at her watch, for almost immediately he rose. Aura overrode her mother's protests by telling her crisply that Flint had been flying most of the day and must be exhausted.

'You don't look tired,' Natalie murmured. 'You look—very vigorous.'

Aura stirred uneasily. She was accustomed to her mother's innuendoes, but her coyness grated unbearably.

Flint's smile hid a taunt as he responded, 'Aura's right, I need some sleep.'

'Ah, well, we'll see you tomorrow,' Natalie said sweetly, looking up at him from beneath her lashes. She held out her hand. It was engulfed by his, but instead of shaking it he kissed her pampered fingers with an air.

Natalie laughed and bridled and, amazingly, blushed.

Austerely, Aura said, 'Goodnight.' She did not hold out her hand.

His smile was measured, more than a little cold-blooded.

'I'll be seeing you,' he said, and somehow the words, spoken softly in that sensuously roughened voice, sent shivers down her spine.

When at last he was gone, and Aura was able to breathe again, she said drily, 'Well, there's no need for him to ask any more questions. You've told him all he ever needs to know about us.'

'Oh, for heaven's sake, Aura, try not to be too drearily bourgeois.' Into the weary flatness of her mother's tone there crept a note that could have been spite as she added, 'You're not the tiniest bit jealous because he wasn't interested in you, are you?'

For some obscure reason that hurt. Aura's lips parted on a swift retort, then closed firmly before the hot words had a chance to burst out. Over the years she had learned how to deal with her mother, and an angry response was the worst way. The nasty incident on One Tree Hill must have shaken her usual restraint.

Smiling wryly she said, 'No, not in the least. You can have the dishy Flint; your friends might laugh at the difference in ages, but they'll probably envy you. However, I wouldn't bore him with any more details of our personal affairs, or you'll see him rush off to more exciting conversation.'

From her mother's expression she saw that her shaft had struck home. If Flint Jansen pumped her mother again he'd probably get what he wanted easily enough—he was that sort of man—but with any luck, from now on Natalie wouldn't spill out unasked-for details.

It had been a strange day. As Aura curled up in her cramped room and closed her eyes against the glare of the streetlight that managed to find her face every night through the gap between the blind and the window-frame, she tried to woo sleep with an incantation that never failed.

In two weeks' time she would be married to Paul, darling, gentle, kind, understanding Paul, and she would be able to relax and live the serene, happy life she had always longed for.

Of course there would be troubles, but they'd be able to overcome them together. Her mother, for one. Natalie would always demand the constant attention she considered her due. But when they were married, Aura's first loyalty would be to Paul. Dearest Paul. She intended to make him so happy, as happy as he would make her.

Two weeks. A fortnight. Only fourteen more days.

Firmly banishing Flint Jansen's fiercely chiselled face from her mind, she turned her head and drifted off to sleep.

She woke the next morning slightly headachey and as edgy as a cat whose fur had been stroked the wrong way. The clear sky of the night before had been transmuted into a dank, overhanging pall of heavy cloud; rain hushed persistently against the window panes.

Listening to the early traffic swish by on the road outside, she wondered why she felt as though she had spent all night in a smoky room. It couldn't be the weather. It had rained for most of the autumn, so she was quite reconciled to a wet wedding day.

And everything was under control. Mentally she went through the list. The caterer knew to ignore any instructions her mother gave; her wedding-dress was made in the simple, flowing lines that suited both her figure and the informal occasion, not the elaborate and unsuitable costume Natalie had suggested. And the florist had no illusions about the sort of flowers she wanted.

A wedding, even one as small as theirs, was like a juggernaut, caught up in its own momentum, rolling serenely on towards an inevitable conclusion. The simile made her smile, and stretch languidly. This wedding was going to be perfect, from the hymns to the best man—

Flint Jansen.

Like the outburst of a nova the memory of the previous evening lit up her mind, and with a shame that sickened her she recalled the dream that had woken her halfway through the night. Explicit, sensual, only too vivid, they had lain tangled together in a bed swathed with white netting. Through the wide windows came the soft sounds of the sea. Scents that hinted at the tropics floated on the heated, drowsy air.

She tried to convince herself that the other man in that wide bed had been Paul, but it was Flint's bronzed, harsh-featured face that had been above hers, Flint's hard mouth that had kissed her with such passion and such bold eroticism, Flint who had touched her in ways Paul never had.

'Oh, God,' she whispered, burying her face into her hot pillow.

Somehow Flint Jansen had slid right through her defences and taken over that most unmanageable part of her mind, the hidden area that manufactured dreams and symbols, the secret source of the imagination. Such a betrayal had never happened to her before.

Perhaps that vengeful little daydream on the way home from One Tree Hill had given her inner self permission to fantasise? Had the strength of her anger carried over into her unconscious and been transmuted for some reason into the passion she hadn't yet known?

In the end, after mulling over the whole wretched business for far too long, she was forced to accept that for some reason she was physically attracted to Flint.

Of course it had nothing to do with love, it was a mere matter of chemicals. Aura might be relatively unsophisticated, but she knew that such an explosion of the senses usually died as quickly as it flamed into being. She had seen what happened to those of her friends who believed it to be love. They had found that within a horrifyingly short time, when desire was sated, they were left with nothing but the dross of a failed affair.

Jessica Stratton, her best friend and bridesmaid, had tripped into such a pit only a year ago. Recalling the subsequent disillusionment, Aura sat up, shivering in the cold dampness of her room, and reached for her dressing-gown.

'I don't even *like* him,' Jessica had wailed. 'I thought it was the greatest romance since Romeo and Juliet, I thought he was wonderful, and then I woke up beside him one morning and saw a boorish, sports-mad yob with hairy toes and a bad case of egotism. He wasn't even a good lover; he did it by numbers! What on earth did I see in him?'

'Chemistry,' Aura had told her pertly, secretly rather proud that she had never fallen prey to it.

Clearly pride went before a fall. Because when she looked at Flint Jansen funny things happened to her legs and her spine, and her insides melted into a strangeness that was shot through with exhilaration and eagerness.

Paul's touch was warmth, and love, and happiness. What she felt when Flint looked at her was a heated sexual excitement, the basic lust of a woman for the most potent man around.

Her soft, full mouth firmed in distaste as she shrugged into her robe and tied it. Appetite, that was all it was, a primeval pull at the senses, a straight biological urge that had nothing to do with love or trust. She-animals felt its force, and mated with the strongest male because of it.

In spite of his striking, unhandsome face and unyielding expression, Flint was a very sexy man, edged with an aura of danger that some women found smoulderingly sensual. However, she was immune to what he offered.

Uncomfortable and disturbing although her reaction to Flint was, she could deal with it. All she had to do was remember that it would pass. She would not exchange the pure gold of her feeling for Paul, the affection and companionship, the fact that she respected and admired and loved him, for all the enticing tinsel and gloss of sexual desire, however it blazed in the moonlight.

Braced by common sense, Aura showered and cleaned her teeth in the tiny, dingy bathroom, then made coffee and took her mother the glass of mineral water and slice of lemon that was her first meal of the day. When that was done she sat down to her toast in the dining end of the sitting-room.

Almost immediately the telephone rang. 'Hello, sweetheart,' Paul said. 'Everything all right for tonight?'

'So far, so good.' Aura smiled at the gloomy day outside. 'I've no doubt there'll be more crises today, but at the moment I'm on top of everything.'

She could hear his smile. 'Good. How did you get on with Flint last night?'

So unnerved was Aura by her dreams that she immediately wondered whether somehow he knew...

No, of course he couldn't!

'Fine,' she said automatically. 'It was rather touching, really. He took me to the top of One Tree Hill and tried to satisfy himself that I have your best interests at heart.'

There was a moment of silence before Paul said in an amused voice, 'Did he, indeed? And do you think you convinced him? Or did you tell him to mind his own business?'

Aura laughed softly. 'You know me too well. To be honest, I don't really care what he thinks. If I convince you, that's all I worry about. And I've got a long time to do that; at least sixty years.'

With immense tenderness he said, 'Darling, I love you.'

'I love you, too.'

'Not as much as you're going to,' he said quietly, almost as though he was making a vow. Before she could answer he said, 'Enough of this! I can't spend all morning dallying with you, I've got work to do. It's this afternoon you're going to do the flowers, isn't it, so you'll be here when the caterers come at three?'

'Yes. It shouldn't take me more than an hour to arrange the flowers, and all I've got to do for the caterers is show them where things are in the kitchen. I'll have plenty of time to come home and get changed before you pick me up.'

'Good. Although it would take a lot less time if you'd just get off your high horse and accept a car. All right, we've been through it all, but you must be the most stubborn, exasperating woman I've ever met. I have to go, darling, I can hear Flint surfacing, and if I'm not to be late I have to leave within three minutes.'

Aura hung up, wondering whether Flint would be in the flat that afternoon.

Of course not, she scoffed as she finished her toast and drank a cup of coffee. He had this important, slightly sinister-sounding job; he'd be at work giving the women there a thrill.

After the final fitting of the wedding-dress, she had lunch with an old friend of her grandmother's before catching the bus to Paul's apartment, walking the last hundred metres through the downpour that had been threatening all day. Her umbrella saved her head and shoulders, but she grimaced at the cold wetness of the rain on her legs and shoes. Much of this, and she'd have to think of getting a coat.

No, she thought as the last of the autumn leaves fluttered like dank brown parachutes to land in a soggy layer on the footpath, after they were married she'd have a car and life would be more convenient. But she still didn't regret not having accepted Paul's offer.

At least Flint couldn't accuse her of unseemly greed.

Even the perfect, radiant flowers of the camellias were turning brown under the rain's relentless attack, while pink and white and yellow daisies were being beaten into the dirt. In one garden dahlia plants in a wide bed were still green and leafy at the base; only the stalks that had held the brilliant flowers towards the sun were blackened and stiff.

Aura was overcome by a sudden, stringent melancholy, a weariness of the spirit that gripped her heart. It was the weather, she thought, shaking off her umbrella before she tapped out the code that opened the street door of the apartment complex. June was often fine, but this year it had decided to go straight into winter.

In two weeks' time she'd be married to the nicest man she had ever met, and they would be flying to a luxurious little island of the coast of Fiji for their honeymoon, where she would have nothing to do but soak up the heat and the soft tropical ambience, and learn how to please Paul.

As though summoned by an evil angel, Flint's voice echoed mockingly through her mind. 'It's about lying in a bed with him, making love, giving yourself to him, accepting his body, his sexuality with complete trust and enthusiasm...'

The door opened to her suddenly unsteady hand. She walked quickly across the foyer, nodding to the porter, her heels tapping coldly on the smooth, shiny marble. In the lift she pressed the button for the third floor.

Oh, she was a fool, letting him get to her like that. Of course she wanted to make love with Paul; she enjoyed his kisses, his caresses, they made her feel warm and loved and secure. That was why she had broken the other two engagements. Although she had liked both men very much, she had been unable to let them touch her beyond the mildest of caresses.

Paul was different. He had understood her wariness, the tentative fear she had never really overcome, and he hadn't tried to rush her into a sexual relationship before they were married.

Of course Flint didn't have the faintest idea that she was still a virgin! Forcing her mind away from his relentless tone as he accused her of being no better than a whore, she opened the door into Paul's apartment.

The flowers had already arrived. Great sheaves of roses and carnations and Peruvian lilies stood in buckets in the kitchen, with sprays of little Singapore orchids and exquisitely bold cymbidiums, all in shades of pink and bronze and creamy-green. After hanging up her coat, Aura tried to banish her odd weariness by walking slowly around the big rooms of the flat, working out where to put vases.

An hour later she was arranging the roses in a huge vase on the hall table when, against the sounds of Kiri Te Kanawa's magnificent voice singing Gershwin, she heard the front door open. A quick glance over her shoulder revealed the lean form of Flint Jansen strolling in through the door, completely at home, a perfectly detestable smile not softening his arrogant face.

Aura's eyes evaded his and flew to the cheek she had slapped. Little sign of the blow remained, except for a slight reddening of the skin about the thin scar. Remorse and self-disgust roiled unpleasantly inside her.

'Hello,' she said, nervously banishing the fragmented images of last night's dream that threatened to surge up from wherever she had marooned them.

The smile widened as he conducted a leisurely survey. Aura had slid her wet shoes off and was standing barefoot in a narrow tan skirt topped by a jersey the exact gold at the heart of the big cream chrysanthemums; her bronze and dark brown scarf was twisted a little sideways. Beneath Flint's narrowed scrutiny she felt like an urchin.

'The spirit of autumm,' he said blandly, closing the door behind him and advancing into the hall. 'Don't let me interrupt you.'

'I won't.' It was a short answer and far too revealing,

but she felt as though someone had tilted the stable world on which she stood. An odd breathlessness made it difficult for her to speak. Turning back to the flowers, she pushed a splendid bronze-pink candelabrum of cymbidiums home.

'I'm sorry I slapped you last night,' she said abruptly.

Silence stretched tautly between them. She kept her eyes on the flowers in the vase.

'Are you? I didn't leave you with much option.' There was no measurable emotion in his tone, nothing to tell her what he was thinking.

Her shoulders moved. 'Nevertheless,' she said gruffly, thrusting another large sprig of black matipo into the back of the arrangement, 'I don't normally go around hitting people.'

'Your apology is accepted.' Clearly he didn't care a bit.

From the corner of her eye she watched him pick up one of the long-stemmed rosebuds. Hastily Aura averted her gaze, strangely affected by the sight of the fragile flower held so carefully in his lean strong hand as he raised it to his face.

'It has no scent,' he said on a detached note.

'No. Most flowers cultivated for the markets have lost their scent. Even the carnations have very little.' She was babbling, so she drew in a deep breath. Much more of his presence, she thought with slight hysteria, and she'd end up hyperventilating.

'A pity. I'd rather have scent and fewer inches in the stem.'

'Not all roses have scent.'

'I prefer the ones that do.'

She nodded. 'So do I.'

He held out the stem. Carefully avoiding his fingers, she took it.

'Will they open?' he asked.

She shrugged, and put the rose into the vase. 'I don't know. Sometimes they do, sometimes they die like that.'

'Poor things. No scent, no blossoming, no seeding. Hardly flowers at all. I wonder what gave anyone the idea that these were preferable to the real thing.' He walked into the sitting-room, saying off-handedly, 'I'll get you a drink.'

'No, thanks, I don't need one.'

But when he reappeared it was with a wine glass in one hand, and a glass of whisky well qualified with water in the other.

'You might not,' he said, 'but I do, and as I never drink alone, you can accompany me. You look as though you could do with something. It's only white wine, dry, with a hint of floral bouquet and a disconcerting note of passion. Heavy day?'

'Not really,' she said, reluctantly accepting the glass. He had made the description of the wine too intimate, too personal, his abrasive voice lingering over the words as though he was applying them to her, not the wine.

'What shall we drink to?' he asked, not trying to hide the note of mockery in his voice.

Eyes the colour and clarity of a topaz searched her face; he seemed to be trying to probe through the skin to the thoughts in her brain, the emotions in her heart.

Determined not to let him see how uncomfortable she was, she said lightly, 'The future is always a good toast. It covers a lot of ground.'

'So it does. Well, Aura Forsythe, here's to the future. May it be all that you need.'

Made gauche by the unexpected wording, she said, 'And yours, too,' and swallowed some of the wine before setting the glass down.

'Do you intend leaving yours to fate?' he asked with apparent disinterest, tilting his glass so that the light refracted in the liquid like a thousand glinting cyrstals, exactly the same shade as his eyes.

'What else can I do?' Picking up a marbled swordleaf of flax, she positioned it carefully, as carefully as she kept her face turned away.

He laughed softly. 'Oh, I believe in making my own future. Somehow I thought you would too.'

'I don't believe one can,' she said, stung by the inference that she was a manipulator.

'Of course you can. There is always the unexpected, but we lay the ground rules.'

'We plan,' she returned crisply. 'But quite often our plans go awry.'

'Not mine,' he said with such assurance that she believed him. 'Not when you know what you're doing. And I make sure I do.'

Aura had always been quick to read signals. The circumstances of her upbringing had honed a natural skill to razor sharpness. His voice was even, without inflection, his eyes hooded in an immobile face, his words laconic, yet the threat was naked and open between them.

'But of course,' he finished almost indifferently, 'you have to understand what you're doing. And gathering information can take a little time.'

Aura moved a chyrsanthemum flower a few centimetres to the right. She had nothing to fear from Flint because there was nothing he could do to hurt her. She loved Paul, and Paul loved her, and because of that, she was safe.

Turning her head, she gave Flint a mocking smile. 'I'm afraid you won't find very much more about me. Apart from my previous two engagements I've lived a fairly dull life. Earnestly middle class, according to my mother.'

His lashes drooped, hiding the dazzling shimmer of his gaze. 'If there's anything to be discovered, I'll find it.'

It was stupid to be so alarmed by a simple statement.

But in spite of her confidence, Aura's skin prickled, its tiny hairs pulled upright by an atavistic fear that had no base in logic.

Carefully not looking his way, holding her shoulders straight and high, she stepped back to survey her work. Perhaps the vase needed another chrysanthemum? She sorted through the flowers.

'Leave it,' Flint commanded smoothly, 'it's perfect. A skilful, disciplined piece of work, with just enough surprises to stop it from being boring.'

Ignoring the insinuation, Aura shrugged. 'Thank you,' she said, infusing the polite words with more than a hint of irony. Quickly gathering up the few flowers remaining, she headed purposefully towards the kitchen.

'You left your wine behind,' Flint told her helpfully, following her to put the glass down on the bench.

'I don't drink in the daytime, anyway.' She began to arrange the blooms in a pottery jug.

'That's a very womanly skill. Did you take lessons?'

'No.'

He was lounging against the bench, one hip supporting his lean body, thighs taut as his flat stomach, turning the glass in tanned, long fingers, watching her as though she was something new and intriguing. The impact of his gaze kept her on edge, tightening nerves she had never suspected she had. Outside the rain, dull herald of winter, beat glumly at the windows, washing away the summer and the warm days and cool nights of autumn.

'You surprise me.' His soft voice sent catspaws of sensation through her. 'You're so glossily self-assured, so polished and perfect and finished that I assumed you must have gone to one of those schools in Switzerland where they teach you how to run a mansion and dazzle dowagers and intrigue every man you meet.'

'My mother was sent to one,' she told him indifferently, 'but I wasn't.'

'Why not?'

'My stepfather thought it would be wasted on me.'

At eighteen she had been locked in open battle with Lionel Helswell, and she would have gone anywhwere that would take her away from him. But he had vetoed the plan, in spite of the fact that the fees would have been taken from her trust fund.

He'd been able to forbid her the money because Natalie had said airily that she never understood figures, so she'd signed over the responsibility for everything, including the trust fund, to Lionel. And that upright, small-minded, petty man, with his rectitude and his authoritative air and his rigid ideas of discipline, had spent it all on a sordid secret life of gambling and bought women.

Aura had made sure *she* understood figures, as well as boring bourgeois things like bank statements and balance sheets.

'Didn't the adoring cousin come to light?'

Aura's shoulders straightened. 'Alick had nothing to do with it,' she said crisply.

'But he paid for you to go to university, didn't he?' Flint's voice was unhurried but relentless.

Aura bit her lip. 'Yes,' she said reluctantly.

As always Lionel had refused any support, so she had let Alick stake her on the understanding that she would pay him back. At a polytechnical college in parklike grounds in the west of Auckland she had begun to study accountancy so she would never be at the financial mercy of any man again. Somewhat to her suprise she had discovered that she liked working with figures and with money; at least it didn't make emotional demands on her.

However, before long she had been lured into tackling a

double major in information systems and marketing, which she had enjoyed immensely.

'So you spent as long as you could there,' he said coolly. 'It took you four years—did you play too much to get your papers in the conventional three?'

Aura stared at him. Didn't he know that she had done a double major? No, clearly he didn't. His vaunted information retrieval system had let him down badly! He probably thought she had frolicked around university looking for a husband. And she certainly wasn't going to tell him that she had spent most of her time with her nose to the grindstone.

'I enjoyed myself,' she admitted.

They had been happy, worthwhile, busy years, full of fun and hard work. She had lived in a succession of small flats with other students close to campus, and during the holidays she had worked long hours to pay Alick back, so she had seen very little of Lionel.

He had hated the fact that she was out of his control. The thought made her mouth tuck up.

'You have a maddening smile,' Flint remarked casually. 'Secretive and dangerous and infinitely alluring. No wonder Paul fell so heavily.'

'We love each other.' Her voice was cool and devoid of any emotion but confidence. Flint Jansen was a bully, and the only way to deal with bullies was to keep calm and detached. 'But I'm sure the dossier you have on me must tell you that.'

'No,' he returned, his eyes narrowed intently beneath the screen of his lashes. 'It tells me that each man you've been engaged to has been richer than the last, and that you dumped each one only after you'd met the next poor fool. Your last ex is still licking his wounds. You and your pretty, conniving, useless mother are on the bones of your backside now, with no money to cushion your fall from grace, so I imagine Paul was a godsend. Rich, adoring, and ready to take on your parasite of a mother, too.'

'I don't have to put up with this kind of thing,' she said icily.

His smile was just as cold. 'Yes, you do,' he said with arrogant confidence, 'because I'm not letting you go until you've listened to everything I have to say.'

Anger bit into her, anger and a deep, clawing fear that shredded the restraint she had worked so hard to build over the years. She said in a voice that trembled slightly, 'I don't know why you took such an instant dislike to me—'

He laughed, a low, harsh sound that ripped at her nerves. 'Don't lie, Aura. You know; you're just not admitting it.'

Her green eyes flew to meet his. Did that mean—yes, he was looking at her with contemptuous understanding, the corners of his hard mouth curling.

'For exactly the same reason that you took such an instant dislike to me,' he went on, holding her gaze effortlessly, drowning her in fire. 'When I looked into those great green eyes with their dancing golden specks and saw the false smile that rested so easily on your delectable mouth, I realised that you're certainly not in love with Paul. Because you want to go to bed with me, Aura.'

CHAPTER THREE

AURA flinched as though she had been slapped in her turn.

'You must be the most conceited man I've ever met,' she said, contempt coating every syllable. 'What the hell makes you think that I'd choose you over Paul?'

She let her eyes strip him down in a slow, scornful survey, so caught up in her need to convince him that she failed to notice the sudden, dangerous tension on the big body she was insolently undressing with her eyes.

'You might be taller than he is,' she said relentlessly, 'but brute force has never interested me much. I look for different things in men.'

'Money, according to your mother.'

Aura froze. 'What—?'

'I had lunch with Natalie today.'

He was speaking softly, consideringly, yet his voice blocked out the sound of the rain outside, the thunder of her heart in her ears. But not the astonishment. Apart from a few select luncheons with close friends Natalie hadn't been out of the unit since they'd moved in. A swift pang of betrayal tore through Aura. Oh, Natalie, she thought wearily.

That piercing shaft of emotion slipped the leash of her temper. 'You seem to have a liking for prying and probing and sticking your nose into other people's business,' she retorted on a rising note of anger, green sparks glittering in her eyes.

At least the subject was no longer her unbidden response to his physical maleness.

His smile was pure mockery. 'I'm a concerned and caring human being.'

'I'm sure it does you credit.' Reining in her emotions, she looked him fair and square in the face. 'What really concerns you? The loss of Paul's friendship? But you must have known that he would marry one day. Unless you hoped that he had other inclinations.'

Apparently not in the least upset by the sneering insinuation, his smile turned masculine and predatory. 'I'm heterosexual, Aura, just as Paul is. As I said last night, if you understand the concept of friendship at all, you should be able to accept that I'd do almost anything in my power to keep him from the clutches of a greedy little tramp who's been brought up to use her sexy body and beautiful face as a commodity, trading exclusive access to it for money and security.'

Of course he'd used the word tramp again deliberately, but this time she refused to react. He was some distance away but it was still too close. She saw him even when she wasn't looking at him, felt his presence at some deep cellular level, and was afraid of her intense awareness. And of the bleak bitterness that submerged her legendary temper.

Shoving the blue pottery jug to the back of the bench, she said curtly, 'If that's what you think of me, it's no use my trying to convince you otherwise. I'm going now.'

It was a retreat. Craven, cowardly, yet she knew that she was doing the right thing. Flint's presence sent every nerve in her body dancing a crazy jig. He had threatened her, and she was going to run away; Aura had never backed down in her life before, but instinct warned her that she was at a disadvantage when it came to dealing with this man.

Half-closed eyes gleaming golden slivers, he said, 'I thought the caterers were coming to prepare for tonight.'

She bit her lip. 'You could let them in.'

His smile was arrogantly outlined. 'I could, but I'm sure they need instructions.'

Of course they did. Aura's mouth tightened as she nodded.

With no more than a hint of cynical amusement in his tone, he said, 'Finish your drink, and after you've told them what to do I'll take you home.'

Fortunately they turned up then, and after ten minutes' consultation Aura was able to leave. To her dismay Flint insisted on driving her back, but at least he didn't initiate any conversation. Not that his silence soothed Aura's stretched nerves or eased the panic that crawled like an obscene beast beneath her brittle composure, but she was grateful for it, nevertheless, and even more grateful to find that Natalie was still out.

He didn't come in and she closed the door with a relief that left her weak and shaking. The shrill jangle of the telephone made her jump; her hand shook as she picked up the receiver and her cousin's deep, pleasant voice almost brought tears to her eyes.

'You sound beleaguered,' he said. 'Is Natalie playing up again?'

'No.' She swallowed the hot words of complaint that came to her lips. She was grown-up now, and Alick had other loyalties. 'I think I must be indulging in that well-known syndrome, bride's nerves,' she said, trying to sound cheerful.

'You're entitled. Would you like Laurel to come over?'

'No, I'm just being silly. Have you arrived, or are you still in Kerikeri?'

'We got to the apartment ten minutes ago. What time do you want us to pick you up?'

Automatically Aura began to refuse, but Alick was accustomed to getting his own way, and when she hung up she had agreed to go the party with them.

Almost immediately afterwards Natalie came in, sleek and laughing. Aura wanted to fly at her and demand that she stop seeing Flint, stop talking so freely to him, but of course she didn't. Natalie had every right to go where she wanted and see who she wanted.

Anyway, the lunch was a milestone. At last Natalie was breaking out of the lassitude that had held her victim for so long.

But Aura wasn't able to banish her uneasy apprehension. She had managed to change the direction of Flint's thoughts this afternoon, but only because he had let her. He was going to spoil these weeks before the wedding with his hateful insinuations and his shrewd, too accurate understanding of how her mind worked.

Still, she had coped with Lionel Helswell; she could cope with Flint Jansen. The thought didn't exactly cheer her, but it did summon a militant sparkle to her great eyes.

All too soon it was time to get ready. Aura chose a black georgette skirt she had had for years and a black silk blouse of about the same vintage. With it she teamed a jacket the green of her eyes, and a pair of Chanel earrings.

'I don't know why you won't buy something new,' Natalie complained. 'Honestly, Aura, you're taking this economy drive too far. It's just ridiculous. When you're married Paul will pay for your clothes—why not now?'

'Humour me,' Aura returned with a tight smile.

'Oh, you're impossible,' her mother wailed. 'At least you could have bought something to wear tonight.'

'I have got new clothes—'

'Nothing really chic!'

'There's not a great call for chic on a tropical beach.'

Natalie sighed ostentatiously. The sound of a car drawing up outside did little to brighten her expression. Natalie didn't like Alick, and had no time at all for Laurel, his wife.

However, she showed no signs of her dislike when they came in, and after the greetings they set off, to all intents a very cheerful party. Except that behind Aura's laughter there was a dark cloud which had settled into place the first time Flint Jansen looked into her eyes.

In spite of her forebodings the party seemed set to go off really well. Paul was his usual charming and hospitable self, everyone was determined to have a good time, and there already existed that indefinable atmosphere which marked off the merely successful party from the one that would be remembered for years.

It should have been a happy occasion for Aura; this was the first time she had ever acted as Paul's hostess and she was determined to get it right. But the strain of keeping her eyes away from Flint as he moved around the room, and the fear that somehow he could sense her almost avid interest in him, kept her on edge. There was a mechanical quality to her smile and her greetings, a hidden, unhappy tension that wouldn't be banished.

However, he stayed well away from her, not even looking her way, and after half an hour or so she almost relaxed. Until her bridesmaid arrived, cast a look around the room and stiffened, for all the world, Aura thought tartly, like a bird-dog sighting game.

Jessica moaned, 'Oh, God, who is the hunk?'

'The best man. Flint Jansen.' The words were clipped and without expression.

'You mean I get to walk down the aisle beside him? Lucky, lucky me.' Jessica turned the three words into a lascivious growl. 'Oh, I love men like that.'

'Like what?'

'Dangerous as hell. The sort of man who makes you think of pirates and reckless adventurers and arrogant, haughty Regency rakes. A man who expects the world to adjust to him, and gets away with it because we just can't resist men with that casual, in-built authority. Oh, wouldn't I enjoy six months on a desert island with him!'

'Nobody,' Aura observed mildly, 'would believe that you're engaged to a man you show every sign of loving. What does Sam say when you drool over men like this?'

Jessica laughed. 'Nothing. He knows I've never gone from looking to touching.' She eyed Flint with appreciation that held more than a hint of speculation.

'Isn't he worried that you might?'

Her best friend snorted. 'When would I get the time? Building up a modelling agency doesn't leave me any time for playing around, believe me. Besides, I love Sam, even if he is always off on business trips. Flint Jansen is not the sort of man it's safe to love, or even play with. He has a distinctly untamed look, and I'll bet he's hell on his women.'

'I bow to your superior knowledge,' Aura snapped.

Jessica looked sagaciously at her. 'Does Paul know you're a virgin?'

'Yes.'

'Good.' Jessica hesitated, then said cautiously, 'You know it doesn't always work out perfectly the first time, don't you?'

Touched, Aura laughed. 'Yes, mother hen. I know quite a lot about it, actually. I haven't exactly had my head stuffed under a pillow since I grew old enough to read novels and magazines.'

'Theoretical knowledge is not the same as the real thing, but you'll be all right. Paul's a dear, and he's not going to rip your clothes off and take you in a storm of uncontrollable passion.' Jessica's eyes moved from Paul's face to that of the man beside him. 'But I'll bet his best man could, if he felt like it.'

Something hungry and feral moved in the pit of Aura's stomach. Appalled by her body's betrayal, she said, 'He looks very self-possessed to me. Not the sort to lose his head.'

'Yep, but imagine if you were able to breach those barriers. Wow!'

Abruptly, Aura said, 'Sometimes you talk an awful lot of rot.'

'True.' As though compelled, Jessica's eyes followed Flint around. 'You know, he's just gorgeous. That scar really does something, doesn't it. I wonder how he got it. Not that it matters—it's terribly evocative and buccaneerish. I wonder if he'd be interested in modelling. He moves like a dream, too. If the camera likes him he'd be perfect.'

For some reason the suggestion irritated Aura. 'He's too busy haring off around the world saving Robertson's from assorted villains who want to snitch some of their profits. Come on, Mrs McAlpine is looking a little lost.'

'Hmm. How are things going there?'

Aura shrugged. 'She still doesn't think I'm good enough for her darling son, but it's not personal; she doesn't think anyone's good enough.'

Even if the older woman had reservations until the day she died, Aura wasn't going to worry about her. She knew she could make Paul happy.

An hour later she was dancing in his arms, waiting for the sense of security, the deep inner contentment that Paul's touch, his presence, his dearness, had always given her.

It didn't come. Oh, she felt safe. She also felt empty, alone.

Her teeth sank a moment into her full bottom lip. Of course she was strung up; all brides were. It went with the territory. It was practically indecent not to wonder whether you were making a mistake.

That was why she wasn't able to respond to Paul as quickly as usual. Forcing her body to relax, she let her eyelids droop until the rest of the room was just a blur of light and colour and movement.

Laughter, low and intimate, grated across her ear. When she lifted her lashes a fraction she saw Jessica's slender form in Flint's embrace. In spite of Sam's absence, Jessica was enjoying herself. Or perhaps she was drumming up business for her agency.

From the predatory glint in Flint's eyes, he didn't find it at all hard to hold Jessica far too closely. Not that many men would. She looked just what she was, a smart, sophisticated businesswoman, but as well as being beautiful, she was intelligent and kind and fun.

Aura was stabbed by an emotion so intense that it felt like a spear ripping through her flesh. To her horror, she realised it was jealousy.

'That was a big sigh.' Paul's voice, with his smile evident in it, caressed her ear.

'Mmm.' She snuggled into him, tilting her chin a little defiantly when she caught his mother's eye.

'You'll be able to sleep in tomorrow. And in a couple of weeks' time, darling, you can spend as much time in bed as you like.' His voice was soft and significant.

Aura suddenly found herself wishing they hadn't decided not to make love until they were married. Not that it had been a joint decision. When he realised just how afraid and wary she was Paul had told her understandingly that he could wait.

Now she wondered whether, if that hurdle had been surmounted, she'd be aching with forbidden desire for another man. Almost certainly the act of loving would have sealed their commitment to each other, and she would be confident and unashamed, not tormented by a shameful need that burrowed secretly beneath the shining surface of her self-esteem.

A poem of Blake's came to her mind; he might have written it for her.

O Rose, thou art sick!
The invisible worm
That flies in the night,
In the howling storm,
Has found out thy bed
Of crimson joy:
And his dark secret love
Does thy life destroy.

The attraction she felt for Flint ate into the fabric of her love like a worm, spoiling it.

'Mmm,' she murmured huskily, knowing it for a lie. 'Sounds good.'

'Darling, it will be more than good, I promise you.'

He kissed her hair, but all Aura could concentrate on was Jessica's laughter, breathy, knowing. Jealousy and a bitter resentment of the woman she had called friend for more than half her life ate into her composure.

Then, thank heaven, the music stopped. Aura pulled away from Paul and, without looking at the other two, began to walk towards the stereo.

'No, your cousin's putting on another tape,' Paul said, sliding an arm around her waist.

Aura stiffened; an instinctive withdrawal darkened her eyes, blocked her throat. Alick had chosen something smooth and slow, a sentimental ballad touched in places with salt, sung by a soprano with a voice like bitter chocolate. Steeling herself to relax, Aura moved back into Paul's embrace.

But, smiling above her head, he said, 'I think we should swap partners, Flint. I want to find out just what Sam's up to.'

He looked down at Aura just too late to catch the feverish dismay that flared in her eyes before being swiftly hidden by long, thick lashes.

She couldn't shake her head, she couldn't shout at him for being so unperceptive, she couldn't stamp and grind her teeth and yell as she used to when she was a child; she had to smile, and smile some more, and let Flint Jansen take her into his arms.

It was a revelation, an explosion of the senses. His smooth animal grace and controlled vitality made him a superb dancer, but that wasn't what set her body springing to life. It seemed to Aura as though light streamed through her, filling her with the sparks that sunlight summoned from her diamond, lifting her into a rarefied region where gravity no longer held its ponderous sway.

Her reactions became keener, more acute. Her nostrils were teased by a faint fragrance of male, infinitely exciting, infinitely tantalising. The material of his jacket beneath her fingers was suddenly *there*; before, she had barely noticed it, but now its smooth matt texture intrigued her fingertips. And Flint's hand around hers was warm and firm and strong, the long fingers holding hers loosely yet with an assurance that sent flutters of sensation along her nerves.

The heat in the pit of her stomach burst into flames, urging her body into instant life, an awareness which was barbaric in its intensity, violent, miraculous.

Her eyes were dazzled by the whiteness of his shirt against the fine black material of his dinner jacket. How well the austere garb suited his big, lean body; it should have clothed his potently male charisma in conventionality, but instead the contrast heightened it.

'You're very quiet.' His voice was low and amused, its sexy roughness abrading every nerve and cell inside her.

'I'm tired.' It was the only excuse she could think of. She would die if he realised the effect he had on her. Her only hope was to stay silent until the dance had finished and she could get away from him and the overwhelming, totally terrifying response he summoned.

'Arranging flowers exhausts you?'

She smiled weakly and didn't answer.

'Or perhaps it's too many late nights?'

The razor slash of sarcasm in his voice startled her. Even as she told herself not to do it, she glanced up.

He was watching her with fire smouldering in the crystalline depths of his eyes, a fire that was immediately extinguished, yet she recognised it, because the same dark fire had burned inside her when she'd heard Jessica laugh in his arms.

It was sexual jealousy, primitive and unrestrained, as harsh as an Antarctic winter, as hot as a solar flare.

A fierce exultation almost loosened her tongue, but she curbed it. Her defences against this destructive, cataclysmic response were few and puny. Silence, passive resistance, was all that she had.

And her honour. She had pledged her love to Paul. She was not going to break that vow, not for the meretricious fool's gold of sexual attraction.

'No,' she said remotely. 'Brides are supposed to exhaust themselves. It's part of the mystique.'

'I don't know much about brides.' His voice was bland, as though he had a secret amusement he wasn't going to share.

Yet her sharpened senses told her that he was not impervious, that he was just as stimulated as she was by their closeness. 'Never been married?' she asked steadily.

'Never.'

'Did you and Paul make some sort of vow of bachelorhood?' She used Paul's name deliberately, trying to dampen down the strain that sizzled between them.

Flint's ironic laughter sent a febrile shiver down her backbone. 'No. I'm away too much to make for a good marriage.'

Some of Natalie's teachings came into her head. Men liked to talk about themselves, about their jobs. It just might save her now. 'What exactly do you do?'

His shoulders moved. 'I mend fences,' he said. 'If they're irrevocably damaged, I stop too many sheep from falling over the cliff.'

'That tells me nothing except that you grew up on a farm, and I already knew that.'

'My job's not for discussion. Besides, I'm thinking of giving it up.'

Her upwards glance caught a strange look on the tough, hard-honed features. She'd swear that Flint was just as surprised at what he'd said as she was. 'Are you going to swallow the anchor?' she asked lightly. 'Take a desk job?'

'No.' His hesitation lasted barely a second. 'I'll make wine.'

Aura missed a step. 'Wine?' It seemed an odd career for a man who earned his living in various hot spots around the globe, some of them very dangerous indeed, if Paul was to be believed.

'My great-grandfather was a vintner,' Flint said. 'He grew grapes and made his own wine. I want to produce a red wine as good as those they make in France.'

He was smiling, she could hear it in his voice, and she was seized by a stupid, unattainable desire to have him smile at her without any agenda, openly, frankly.

'That's every winemaker's ambition, surely,' she said, more to hear what he had to say than to object. If Flint said he was going to give French winegrowers a run for their money, she believed him. He was that sort of man. Success was written in his face, in the way he walked and moved.

'It won't be the same as those they grow in France,' he said, taking her point immediately. 'It will be different, because the climate and the soil are different, but it will be a world-class wine, nevertheless.'

'Why red?' she asked, intrigued. 'We produce some of the best white wines in the world; why not make them?'

The wide shoulders moved a little beneath her hand. 'The challenge is in the reds.'

Yes, he'd want a challenge.

'I know they're growing superb wines in all sorts of places in New Zealand now, even in Otago, where you'd think it would be far too cold. Where will you go?'

'I've got land just north of Auckland,' he said, almost indifferently. 'It's perfect for growing wine with character. A hundred acres on a peninsula with an estuary and a river on three sides, soil that's iron sandstone with clay, an ideal climate, hot days and cool nights and some fairly ferocious frosts in winter, and a range of hills to keep off the worst of the winds.'

'Doesn't it rain too much there?'

'Not according to the climate charts.' The aloofness had vanished from his voice, replaced by an enthusiasm he couldn't conceal.

'And what do you know about making wine?' she asked with interest.

'Quite a lot,' he said, 'but I have a French friend who wants to get away from a tricky family situation, and he's an expert. Between us we'll show the world that it's not only the Australians who can produce good red wine in the South Pacific.'

'It sounds fascinating,' she said.

'Hard work,' he returned dismissively, glancing down at her with a sardonic amusement that raised her hackles. 'And very little money for years, if ever. A life on the land is not at all romantic. It's sheer slog, often expensively frustrating, with the weather and everything else against you. You're a high-flyer, too polished, too finished, to be able to settle down in some small country area.'

His insulting opinion shouldn't hurt, but it did. She had to force herself to smile up at him, watching with a secret, passionate pleasure the slow darkening of his golden gaze, the tiny muscle that flicked a betrayal against the harsh sweep of his jawbone. Yes, he felt it too, the wildfire need that swept like silken doom through her veins. Recognised it, and resented it as much as she did.

And then, thank heavens, the music stopped, and she pulled free of his arms.

'Thank you,' he murmured, smiling dangerously, hooded eyes concealing his emotions.

Ten minutes later, once more safely in Paul's arms, she saw him dancing with a cousin of Paul's whose name she couldn't remember. The tall, lovely blonde was gazing into his eyes with open, acquisitive eagerness.

To hide the obscure pang of pain that sawed through her Aura said on a half laugh, 'It looks as though your best man's made a conquest.'

Paul laughed. 'I'd have been surprised if he hadn't. Ever since he was fourteen Flint's only had to walk into a room to have half the women in it make eyes at him.'

Aura said dismissively, 'It's that macho air. Some women find it impossible to resist.'

'But not you?'

She lifted her brows at him. 'Well, I can see why he attracts interest,' she said, trying to sound objective and sensible. 'Alick's got it too, that inner hardness, a sort of toughness of mind and character. It's exciting, but it takes a rare woman to cope with it. I want other things in my husband.'

His mouth quirked into a smile. Aura sensed that she had disappointed him, but she would not lie to him. 'Some time you must tell me what they are,' he murmured, his eyes on her mouth.

Her smile was demure. Oh, she loved him, loved him for all the things Flint didn't pretend to; she loved him because he was kind, because he was tender and thoughtful and safe, and because he loved her. Set against all that, what did Flint have to offer but a wild thundering in the blood that would inevitably lead to disillusion? Men like Flint were too arrogantly masculine for safe taming.

'Some time in the not too distant future,' she promised, fluttering her lashes upward in a parody of flirtatiousness, 'I will.'

His arms contracted around her. He was aroused, and for one paralysing second Aura wanted to twist away from the telltale hardness of his body. As though he understood, he held her only for a moment before gently releasing her.

'I'll look forward to it,' he said softly, the words a vow.

An hour later she and Jessica were sitting in a corner of the room, discussing a few minor, last minute details about the wedding.

'I really think I've covered everything,' Aura said with a sigh. 'I just hope there aren't too many snags.'

'Oh, it'll be a howling success,' Jessica assured her confidently. 'You've always been efficient and sensible, and you've got the knack for making an occasion fun. Look at tonight. Most pre-wedding parties are horrors, with both sides of the family eyeing each other up in affronted astonishment, and the friends wondering how on earth they're going to see the evening out. But everyone's having a marvellous time, and that's due to you. You make people want to enjoy themselves.'

'I was well taught.' Aura's roving gaze rested on her mother, flirting with one of Paul's widowed uncles.

Mrs McAlpine was watching them too, clearly unhappy with the situation. She needn't get her plaits in a tangle, Aura thought cynically. Natalie liked all the preliminaries to flirting, the sideways glances, the hammering pulses and slow, significant pauses, the magical meeting of eyes. Her great beauty ensured that she indulged frequently in such byplay, but she never followed through. She was essentially a frigid woman. If she married again, it would be to have a man about the house—rich, naturally—not for the pleasure of his lovemaking.

Her maternal grandfather, Aura decided, not for the first time, had a lot to answer for.

For a while Aura had assumed that her mother's deep-seated inner coldness was hereditary. Then she had met Paul, and her worries had almost dissipated. Almost, but not quite.

It was bitterly ironic that it should be the best man who finally routed her fears. She wasn't unresponsive in Flint's arms; she damned near burst into flames.

'Who's the woman dancing with Flint? The tall blonde with the hungry eyes?'

Aura shrugged, keeping her eyes fixed on her mother. 'Paul's cousin, Belinda somebody.'

'She's certainly not trying to hide how she feels, is she? It's a wonder she doesn't just throw him down on the floor and have her way with him here and now.'

'Here?' Aura concealed her raw emotions with a caustic inflection. 'Don't be silly, Mrs McAlpine would disown her.'

'Wouldn't she just! A very proper lady, your mother-in-law.'

'Future mother-in-law.'

Jessica sent a sideways glance towards her. 'OK,' she said amiably. 'Future it is.'

They relapsed into silence. Unwillingly, Aura watched Belinda laugh at Flint, press her long, curvaceous body against him as they turned, and once more had to fight back a tide of corroding jealousy. Jessica's voice was a welcome relief.

'Paul and Flint don't seem to have anything in common, do they? It's odd that they're still such great friends,' Jessica said thoughtfully. 'Even after—'

She stopped, an odd occurrence for Jessica whose tact was notorious.

'Even after what?' Aura stared at her friend.

Jessica shrugged uncomfortably. 'My big mouth! You'd think I'd learn, wouldn't you? Oh, hell, apparently it's common knowledge. Drusilla Evans told me. Yes, I know she gossips, but you must admit her gossip is usually accurate. She said that a couple of years ago Flint more or less walked off with one of Paul's girlfriends. Mind you, it can't have gone deep, because they still remained friends.'

A movement from behind caught the corner of Aura's eye. She recognised Paul, and wondered sickly whether he had heard. Swiftly she said, 'Gossip is gossip, and none of it's worth believing.'

But in her mind she saw Flint as a predator, taking what he wanted without worrying—no, that was silly, it was wrong, because he was very concerned about Paul. Guilty conscience, perhaps? *No!*

Jessica bit her lip and fell silent as Paul came up and slid his arm around Aura's waist. 'Everything's going like a dream,' he said. 'You've done wonders. Hasn't she, Jessica?'

'I was just telling her so.' After a worried glance at Aura, Jessica launched into a very funny story about a party she had attended the week before, and soon the disquiet was dissipated in the nicest manner, by laughter.

But later, when they were dancing again, Paul said abruptly, 'I heard what Jessica was telling you, and it didn't happen quite the way she thinks. I'm not such a wimp that I'd let Flint get away with stealing a girlfriend.'

Aura's brows shot up. 'Did either of you consider,' she asked with tart emphasis, 'that the girlfriend may have felt that she was in control of her actions, not just an object to be stolen or kept?'

Paul grinned unrepentantly. 'My little feminist! All right, but Jessica used the word first. Anyway, Gemma fell out of love with me and into love with Flint, who was not interested in her.'

'An awkward situation.' Aura spoke without expression. Something in Paul's tone, in the way he had brought the matter up, convinced her that Gemma's defection had mattered very much.

'Yes. I was cool to Flint—well, I knew it wasn't his fault, but until I met you she was the one woman I'd thought I loved. And I don't think I could have borne it if Flint had been in love with her. It would have seemed like the rankest betrayal, which is stupid, of course.'

'Well, yes, it is a bit, because none of us is exactly in control of our emotions,' Aura said gently, for the first time in her life understanding with an acid clarity how true this was, 'but it must have hurt. In a funny sort of way I felt the same when Alick and Laurel got married. Alick had been my substitute brother, and I'd got into the habit of relying on him. Then Laurel came along, and although he was still there for me, I knew that nothing was ever going to be quite the same again. I despised myself for being jealous, but it didn't stop it.'

He gave her a quick spontaneous hug. 'I do love you,' he said. 'My sensible angel. Somehow you've robbed the whole thing of its last nasty little sting.'

Hidden beneath the affection and the respect, Paul nurtured a deep envy of his friend, envy of the raw sensuality that emanated from Flint, the stark, uncompromising maleness that was at once a threat and a challenge to every woman who saw him.

Paul's unexpected vulnerability shook her. Aura loved him at that moment more than ever. He must never know of that unwanted, savage tug of attraction, not even after it had been dissipated to nothingness by time and familiarity and the real gold of her love for Paul.

A quick glance across the room revealed Flint still dancing with Belinda, smiling down at her lovely face with lazy approval. As though Aura's gaze was tangible, he looked up, transfixing her with the golden fire of his eyes, then deliberately turned away. Whatever he said into Belinda's ear made her bridle and flush.

Sheer, black rage, the like of which she had never experienced before, fountained through Aura, terrifying her with its strength. She wanted to tear Belinda from Flint's arms and throw her out of the room, out of the apartment into the dark, wet night, and she wanted to slap him senseless. How dared he smile like that at another woman?

She fought a vicious battle for victory over the vulgar, indiscriminate desire that held her prisoner. Slowly, laboriously, she used her considerable willpower to banish the bastard emotion so that common sense could reassert itself.

Although she succeeded, it took even more effort to force herself to smile and talk and behave normally, to pretend that nothing was wrong, that she was the same as she had always been. Inside her psyche some fundamental shift had taken place, some rearrangement of her inner self, and she didn't know how to defend herself against the shaming, painful flaw that marred her self-image as surely as the scar marred Flint's face.

Except, she thought acidly, somehow he managed to turn even that into an asset. The cruel mark that would have disfigured anyone else merely emphasised his elemental attraction.

The evening wore down. By two in the morning everyone had gone, even Alick and Laurel, Paul having announced his intention of taking Aura home. Glowing and sweetly mischievous, Natalie had left an hour before with Paul's uncle, and Mrs McAlpine had been driven home by the extremely reluctant Belinda, who at the last moment had kissed Flint with obvious enjoyment. An enjoyment, Aura realised with sick self-derision, he had reciprocated.

'I shouldn't be long,' Paul said, looking ironically at his friend. 'Don't wait up for me, though.'

Flint's teeth showed briefly in the smile that made Aura think of a hungry tiger, burnished and gleaming in a tropical forest. She almost flinched; only the armour she had spun out of determination kept her outwardly serene, although it didn't protect her from the maelstrom of emotions the evening had unleashed.

Until she had seen Flint smile into Belinda's face she had been more or less in control of her feelings and her life. Her poise had been hard-won, and secretly she was rather proud of it.

But that openly sexual smile had wrenched it all away, torn free the shield of her restraint and revealed in all their wildness and untamed greed the desires that prowled beneath the thin veneer of civilised reserve.

Instinct warned Aura that nothing was ever going to be the same again.

She was caught in a trap from which there was no escape, the trap of her own needs and desires. Oh, she loved Paul, but, set against the primitive sensations Flint roused in her, love didn't seem to be enough.

Rationalise it however she did, she was in trouble. If Flint came back to New Zealand and started up his vineyard just north of Auckland they would see quite a bit of him. Although Paul made friends easily, his loyalty was to the old friends with whom they did most of their socialising. Yes, she would certainly see Flint, and this ache of longing wouldn't die of starvation.

'You're very quiet,' Paul murmured in the car.

She shrugged, staring out through the windscreen. Rain dashed down, was smoothed away by the rhythmic sweep of the wipers. Street-lights danced in the drops. 'I hate winter,' she said dully.

'Waste of emotion. It comes, and eventually it goes. And admit it, darling, it's not always like this. We get glorious weather as often in winter as we do in any other season. It's just cooler.'

She sighed. 'Mmm.'

'What's worrying you?'

'Nothing.' What else could she say?

I want to go to bed with your best man and best friend? No, I don't love him, I don't even like him much, but when he looks at me I get these strange sensations in my body and I don't know what to do.

A sudden shiver shot down her spine. She yawned. 'It went off well, didn't it?'

'Yes, but I knew it would. You're an excellent hostess.' One hand covered hers briefly, squeezed, and was withdrawn.

Nice hands, she thought, looking at them on the wheel with horrifying detachment. He was a nice man, well made, attractive, sexy in a wholesome way.

Her teeth tightened on her lip, cutting through the thin outer layers of skin. What the hell was she going to do?

At the unit he came in, looking about him with concealed distaste. 'I wish you'd let me move you into the new flat,' he said.

Aura smiled. 'So does Mother.'

'I'll bet. Are you going to make me a cup of coffee?'

They talked of the party, of other things, comfortable, relaxed, and when the coffee was drained he turned her into his arms. Aura held her face eagerly for the kiss, and it was nice. He kissed her gently, then a little less gently, but when she pressed herself against him in an agony, trying to summon the quick leap of the flesh she had felt in Flint's arms, nothing happened.

Paul's lips lingered on the smooth curve of her shoulder. There was no covetousness in his kiss, yet Aura's skin crawled. He laughed softly, and she realised that he had mistaken her shiver for one of anticipation.

'No,' he said, straightening up, 'I'm too old for making love on a sofa with your mother in the next room. I can wait.'

Half of her was pleased, as though she had been threatened, then reprieved. The other half was wretched. She needed reassurance. If they had already been lovers this lightning flash of craving, this rage of sensation would have been satisfied, and she wouldn't ache every time she thought of Flint.

But of course Paul was right. Now was not the time, or the place.

She couldn't sleep. Every quarter hour the chimes of the ponderous old clock that took up far too much room in the flat's small sitting-room resounded in her ear. Normally she never heard it.

After dawn came in, grey and wet and intrusive, she managed to drift into an uneasy doze that was interrupted almost immediately by the shrill stridulation of the telephone.

It was Paul. 'Darling, I've just got a rather panic-stricken call from that firm I'm acting for in Samoa. They want me up there for a day or two to clear up a small mess.'

'You're a solicitor! I thought it was Flint who was the troubleshooter,' she muttered, rubbing sleep from the corner of her eyes.

He laughed. 'And so he is, infinitely more glamorous than I am, I can assure you. Respectable partners in respectable law firms act as troubleshooters in an entirely

different way. This is just to tidy up a case I've been working on for some months. There's no derring-do or danger
involved. Flint would find it incredibly boring. It's just that
things have moved a little more quickly than we expected,
and they need help now.'

'But it's the weekend!'

'Which is why I want to get up there today. Tomorrow
is a day of rest, and no one will be talking then. Don't be
cross, sweetheart. I'll be home on Tuesday, Wednesday at
the latest.'

As cheerfully as she could, she said, 'Of course you must
go. Just don't dare be called away when we're on our honeymoon!'

'I'll make sure of that,' he said tenderly. 'In two weeks
and nine hours, darling, we'll be married, and nobody will
be able to tear me from your side.'

Ice coagulated in her stomach. She felt as though he'd
thrown her to the wolves, which was completely ridiculous,
because she didn't need to see anything of Flint Jansen
while Paul was away. Briskly she said, 'Enjoy the sun.'

'Not without you.'

I need you, she screamed silently as she belied her emotions by replacing the receiver very gently. Damn it, how
can you go away when I need you here now?

CHAPTER FOUR

Was Paul blind? If he loved her, surely he could sense the anguish she was enduring?

But of course that was unfair, because she was doing her best to hide her emotions from everyone. Even herself.

Especially herself.

And they weren't emotions, they were a simple matter of hormones. Physical attraction, she thought grimly, was like a cold: inconvenient but not fatal.

On her way to the kitchen she glanced through the window. Judging by the lighter sky in the east, the depression that had kept them drenched these last days might finally be on the move. The possibility should have lifted her spirits.

She made coffee and ate a slice of toast, deliberately keeping her mind off everything but the most mundane thoughts. The newspaper had little of interest in it, but her glance fell on a review that made her bite her lip. An Australian Opera Company had brought *The Pearl Fishers* to Auckland for two weeks, and she and Paul were booked to go and see it that night. Opera was not her favourite form of music, but she had been looking forward to this one.

'Oh, damn,' she mumbled, folding the paper up with quick, savage movements.

Hoping the sun might lift her mood, she went out into the garden and began to weed the front border. It was still too wet; great clumps of earth clung defiantly to each root ball, but valiant green spears of daffodil and jonquil leaves were pushing their way through and she could no longer resist their mute appeal.

At eleven o'clock Natalie came strolling out to collect the mail. 'What are you doing, you stupid girl?' she demanded. 'You'll ruin your nails.'

'I'm wearing gloves.' But Aura got to her feet. The small bed was clean and free of clogging growth. 'Look, there are all sorts of bulbs coming up.'

'We won't be here long enough to see the flowers,' Natalie said, dismissing them without even looking.

She was fond of saying that she liked gardens but not gardening. Aura had long realised that her mother liked gardens as a background to her beauty, and adored flowers as gifts not for their own sakes, but because they were homage.

'Sometimes I think you set out to make things difficult,' Natalie complained over her shoulder as she bent down to collect the mail. 'Your nails can still tear, even through gloves, you know. At least you'll be able to afford a gardener when you and Paul decide to buy a house.'

Possibly, but when that happy day came Aura had every intention of doing as much as she could in her own garden. In the meantime she would enjoy the lovely grounds around the apartment block.

They would move when it was time to have children. In the past she had dreamed of Paul's children, but now, even as she smiled, the children who sprang to her mind bore no imprint of the man she loved; they had tiger eyes glowing golden beneath black lashes, and skin bronzed by the summer sun into an antique patina. Instead of Paul's smooth good looks their features were blunt and strong, with wide mouths and high, stark cheekbones and strong jaws. Too energetic to be the handsome children she had imagined before she'd met Flint, they possessed a natural arrogance that translated into their walk and their movements, even the tilt of heads that gleamed with a distinctive copper sheen in the sunlight.

Pain almost overwhelmed her. She was jerked from it by a sharp little sound from her mother. Natalie was thrusting a piece of paper into her pocket, and although her head was turned away, Aura was sure she had gone pale.

'What is it?' she asked brusquely, remembering other occasions when the mail had brought bad news, when mingled with the letters of condolence there had been more and ever more bills.

'Nothing.' Natalie sighed. 'At least, nothing to do with you. An old friend from schooldays has just lost a—grandchild. Oh God, I hate this place! I don't think I'll ever be able to hear the name of this wretched suburb without remembering how miserable I've been here.'

'Well, it won't be for long now,' Aura said gently. She smiled sympathetically down at her maddening, silly mother, who was relying on her to rescue her from these surroundings. All her life someone had looked after Natalie; it only natural that she expected her daughter to follow suit.

Although, she thought grimly as she followed her mother into the house, the salary she'd get only one year out of university wouldn't go anywhere near satisfying Natalie's needs.

Still, if Aura had been working she wouldn't feel so beholden to Paul, who had waved the magic wand of his love and his wealth and made everything all right.

There were other disadvantages, too. Like the prince in every fairy story, Paul was conventional. He didn't see why his wife should work. Aura had a battle in front of her, but Paul, she thought as she scrubbed her hands, was reasonable. It wouldn't take long for him to understand that she'd go crazy with boredom if she had nothing to do. These last months had been bad enough, but at least she'd had Natalie to look after. Now, with her mother well again, Aura was ready for the challenge of a career.

'Last night was a success,' Natalie said in her most brittle voice. 'A credit to you. Or to me, I suppose, because I taught you.'

Not really. Aunt Helen, who was really a distant cousin, and Alick had been her instructors in social graces and duties, but Aura wasn't unkind enough to point that out. 'I'm glad you enjoyed yourself,' she said instead.

'That brother-in-law of Mary's is rather a dish. He comes from Dunedin. I remember going to his wedding with your father.' Natalie gave a small, sad smile before picking up the latest *Vogue* and riffling through the pages. 'Oh, by the way,' she said after a few minutes, 'Flint rang.'

'Flint?'

'Mm.' Natalie's voice was vague. 'He's going to be out all day, but he said he'd collect you for *The Pearl Fishers* round about six tonight.'

'Flint did?' Aura's voice resounded stupidly in the quiet room.

'Yes. Apparently Paul arranged it.'

Of course. He wouldn't want her to miss a treat. Aura's mouth settled into a hard line. Flint was enough of a hazard to her peace of mind at a distance; spending an evening in his company would be sheer, stupid recklessness.

She waiting a few minutes until her mother went into her bedroom before ringing the apartment. Rather relieved when no one answered, she left a message on the answer-phone refusing Flint's kind invitation to take Paul's place. She hoped he couldn't discern the panicky note in her voice.

The early sun was soon banished by another pall of heavy clouds, followed almost immediately by rain. Natalie spent most of the afternoon on her bed, looking weary and as despairing as she had in the months after her husband's death, but refused to admit to anything other than tiredness. There was no sign of the letter that had startled her. However, when afternoon began to thicken into evening, she dragged herself to her feet and decided to take a bath.

'Aren't you going to have one before you go out?' she asked listlessly.

Aura shook her head. 'No. I cancelled.'

Natalie looked at her for a long moment, then nodded. 'Probably a wise decision,' she said.

Aura sat down with a book. She tried hard to concentrate on the words, but Flint's image danced between her eyes and the page, bringing with it that feverish, unbidden excitement. Exhausted by the pull and tug of her emotions, her mind spinning in ever-decreasing circles, she longed to put her head down and slip gratefully into a coma, one that would last long enough for this whole horrible situation to go away.

Except that it wouldn't solve anything. How was it possible to love one man and want another?

'Darling!' Natalie called from the bathroom.

Pleased to be summoned from the dark wasteland of her thoughts, Aura answered mechanically, 'Yes?'

'Get me the bottle of perfume on my dressing-table, will you?'

It was new, and very expensive. Knowing that it was no use complaining, Aura picked it up. Natalie was incapable of resisting the luxuries she had been brought up to consider necessities.

The slam of a car door outside brought Aura's head up. 'I wonder who that can be?'

'Who knows?' Natalie sounded excited, like a child faced with an unexpected treat.

Accustomed to constant entertaining, she used to adore parties and occasions, but it had been months since she had shown any eagerness for a social life. Her interest now was an indication of her improvement. An improvement, Aura recognised with a growing dread, that started when she began to go out with Paul.

Slivers of ice attaching themselves to her spine, she frowned at the big Jag that had stopped at the kerb. Yes, that was Flint getting out of it—she'd be able, she thought with painful honesty, to recognise him from a mile away.

For a stupid moment she toyed with the idea of refusing to answer the door, but every light in the place was blazing. And a peremptory knock demanded an answer.

'Hello,' she said coolly, trying to preserve some sort of composure.

He loomed, tall and forbidden and infinitely intimidating; every cell in her body acknowledged his presence.

'Are you wearing those clothes tonight?'

She looked down at her trousers and jersey. 'What's wrong with them?' she asked numbly.

'Nothing, I suppose.' His glittering gaze followed the contours of her body with too much interest.

Aura's breath died in her throat. Her body leapt into vivid life, almost shuddering with a singing anticipation.

'But don't you think,' he went on smoothly, 'that opera demands a little more formality? Especially as we're having dinner first?'

'I'm not—'

'Yes, you are. We don't want to disappoint Paul, do we?'

Torn between a desire so strong she could taste it, sweet and wild and heady, and a fear that drained the light from her eyes and the colour from her skin, Aura said huskily, 'I don't think it would be a good idea, Flint.'

Her shamed glance pleaded with him not to press the matter, but he asked, 'Why not?'

Anger at an obtuseness she knew to be deliberate sparked into life. She retorted crisply, 'I don't really want to go with you. I'm not ready—'

'Then get ready,' he commanded.

He was punishing her, she realised. The momentary flashflame of emotion died into listless fatalism. He looked quite capable of picking her up and carrying her off as though she were some mindless, helpless captive.

'Very well,' she said stiffly, despising herself for capitulating. 'You'd better come in. It will take me twenty minutes or so to get ready.'

Any remote hope she might have had that Natalie would object was extinguished when she came back into the sitting-room. Flint was smiling at her mother, his mouth relaxed into amusement, and Natalie looked better than she had for months, a very becoming colour hinting at her pleasure. When Aura appeared wearing black lace and her grandmother's rare green garnets, her hair restrained in an old-fashioned chignon, her mother smiled almost wistfully.

'Run away and enjoy yourselves,' she said.

Natalie's upbringing, perhaps her nature, had insulated her against the violent tumult of uncontrollable emotions. Her affections were directed very firmly at one person— herself. It would never occur to her that her daughter might feel obliged to call her wedding off because of an inconvenient hang-up over the best man. Paul was much the better bet as a husband, so Natalie, in her own inimitable way, would have been faithful to him.

Aura was not finding it so easy to compartmentalise her life and her inclinations.

Once in the car she sat quietly, refusing to fill the silence with pointless chatter. By forcing her to come out with him, Flint had revealed how little he cared for the usual social conventions, so she wasn't going to indulge in them either.

The front that brought the afternoon rain had moved over, and above them a clear sky was spattered with stars, hazy in the city air. No doubt just north of Auckland where Flint had his land the stars would be huge and brilliant, glittering like pale, precious gems in a sky as dark and fathomless as black velvet.

Aura adjusted the Edwardian gold and seed-pearl and green garnet bracelet. Its familiar shape and weight on her slender wrist should have comforted her, as should the heavy warmth of the matching stones in their golden setting around her throat, but she was beyond comfort.

Anticipation, forbidden and headily ungovernable, curled like alcohol through her veins, fuzzing her thoughts and kicking in emotions she had never experienced before.

Flint said, 'Your father didn't have much to do with your looks, did he?'

'No.' She thought of the father she had never really known. 'He was tall and dark and craggy.'

'What happened to him?'

The smile that curved her lips was sad and angry, but her voice was coolly detached. 'He went to Africa.'

'And left you behind? Why?'

Her shoulders lifted. 'He was a doctor, and he wanted to help people who really needed him. I was eight when he went, and I don't really remember much about it, except that I cried for weeks afterwards. And every time—' She stopped.

'And every time—?'

Every time she cried Natalie would stop her own wailing long enough to inform her he had left them and wasn't coming back because she'd been such a naughty girl. But she wasn't going to tell Flint that.

Aloud, she said, 'Oh, nothing. He had a dream, but it wasn't Mother's dream. When she wouldn't go with him he went alone.'

'Leaving you and your mother behind. What sort of man was he, to dump his responsibilities like that?' The scorn in his deep voice revealed exactly what he thought of that sort of man.

Aura smiled ironically. 'He was an old-fashioned man like Dr Livingstone, who thought that wives should follow their husbands even if it meant their early death, or their misery.'

'It was unfortunate that his high ideals didn't encompass his wife and child.'

Although Aura had often thought exactly the same thing, she wasn't going to listen to Flint run her father down. With an undertone of warning she said, 'Who knows why other people behave the way they do? I certainly don't judge him.'

'Didn't his departure affect you? Apart from the weeks of crying?'

The question was delivered in a casual tone that didn't fool Aura at all. She shrugged. 'You get over things.'

'How long did you live with Alick Forsythe?'

To her surprise he and Alick had got on well at the party; both powerful men, confident and arrogant. For some reason she hadn't expected them to so clearly enjoy each other's company.

But there was a flick of emotion in his question that snagged her attention. Her eyes scanned the harsh, blunt profile, returning to her hands when she realised that it revealed nothing but strength and a disciplined authority.

In a reserved voice she said, 'I lived in Kerikeri for a couple of years, from ten until I was twelve.' They had been the happiest years of her life.

'Why?'

'Oh, after my father left I ran wild. Natalie couldn't control me.' Natalie didn't really try. 'When she remarried I didn't approve of her choice,' she went on flippantly. 'I had a nice line of tantrums, specialising in high-decibel hysteria. I behaved so badly they sent me to boarding school, but the third time I ran away the school decided I was in need of specialist care and suggested I stay at home while

I got it. We had a family conference, and it was agreed that I should live with my Kerikeri cousins.'

'And did you run away from there?'

She laughed. 'Oh, no, that was quite a different kettle of fish. I was an uncivilised little savage, but I knew where I wanted to be. I adored Alick, and his parents, and especially his grandparents, who were darlings but very firm. I soon learnt that tantrums weren't going to succeed, and I stayed put, even when Alick lost his temper with me.'

She had tormented him unmercifully until that happened. Alick's anger had frightened her, but he hadn't hit her, and he hadn't used any of the psychological terrorising that her stepfather was so expert in. That episode had marked the turning point; from then on she had trusted her cousin.

'And you didn't want to go back home?'

She laughed harshly. 'No. Never. I loved it at Kerikeri.'

'I see.' He was silent for a moment, before asking, 'You didn't run away when you went back to boarding school?'

'Nope. I was a reformed child.' Amazing what unconditional love and firm discipline could do.

'What became of your father?'

'He died five years ago, still in Africa. I believe he was happy.'

'You don't know?'

Her shoulders moved an inch. Staring straight ahead she said calmly, 'He didn't write, didn't contact us.'

She had written to him for years, but no reply ever came back. When he left he had cut wife and daughter out of his life as though they had no further meaning for him. Perhaps they hadn't.

'Your stepfather died recently, too, didn't he?' His voice revealed nothing more than mild interest, but if he knew about Lionel Helswell he must have heard of the circumstances of his death.

Perhaps he anticipated some kind of pleasure from forcing her to tell him. If that was so, she was prepared to deny it to him.

Lightly, cynically, she replied, 'Yes. He got tied up in a financial scandal, used most of my mother's money and all of mine in an attempt to bail himself out, and when that had all gone put a gun in his mouth. Good job, too. He was a mean-minded martinet, and, like all bullies, fundamentally a coward. I don't miss him in the least.'

'Except that he dumped the responsibility for your mother on you. When did this happen?'

Aura shrugged. 'Six months ago.'

'Three months before you met Paul.'

Refusing to react to the steel in his words, she replied serenely, 'Yes, just before I met Paul.'

And he could make what he liked of that. She had already told him more than she had wanted to about her own life.

'Do *you* have relatives, or were you spat out of the ground, fully carved in stone?' she asked pertly.

He laughed. 'I have parents, and a variety of aunts and uncles and cousins.'

They talked a little about the Wairarapa; several of the girls Aura had been to school with came from there, and he knew their families. It was meaningless, harmless conversation. Keeping her eyes firmly fixed in front, she stared sightlessly as they made their way through suburbia towards the city, finally stopping under the wide *porte-cochère* of a hotel with a well-known and highly recommended restaurant on its top floor.

Flint had booked a table by the window so she was able to look out over the harbour, but Aura saw nothing beyond a blur of lights, the sheen of obsidian water, for her whole attention was taken by the man who walked beside her.

She had never experienced such utter absorption before, as though the only thing of any importance to her in the world was this man. She wanted to stop time, to hold back its inexorable flow and imprison the moment like a fly in amber, or the crystal brilliance at the heart of a diamond.

Yet beneath the mingled delight and pain lurked deep guilt. At last, with anger and despair, she accepted that she could not marry Paul. What had been unimaginable before was now the only honourable way to behave.

With that thought came the horrifyingly daunting prospect of cancelling the wedding.

The cruel, bitter irony of it all was that whatever she did she was doomed to loneliness. There was no future for her with Flint. She didn't trust him, she didn't like him; all she felt for him was a forbidden desire so potent that it overcame even love.

Because she did love Paul. That was what hurt so much.

The lamplight glittered on the diamond on her finger, transforming it to blue fire. Paul, she thought sadly, aware that even now she was thinking of him in the past, oh, Paul, my dearest, forgive me.

She looked up, to catch Flint's gaze, piercing, predatory, on her downcast face. A delicious shudder stabbed her spine, turned her bones to honey.

She began to talk with the sophisticated ease of a woman who knew her way around the world. Her *savoir-faire* was a shield, a thin, barely opaque barrier against those far too perceptive eyes, but it and pride was all she had for shelter.

Halfway through the delicious meal a caustic comment made by Flint about one of the other patrons surprised a catch of laughter from her. He surveyed her with gleaming eyes, his hard mouth curved, and she felt that look right down to her toes, felt it scorch a pattern through her that couldn't be erased.

Her heart leapt into feverish speed. The smile faded on her lips, an unruly hunger sharpened its claws on her body, and she was gripped by a need so acute, so frightening, that she lost colour. She had never known such passion, never understood how powerless reason and logic were against it.

Common sense told her that if she went ahead and married Paul she'd live a happy and fulfilled life. Paul loved her, and Flint manifestly didn't, yet all she wanted to do was follow him through whatever hells he might drag her. This 'dark, secret love' of Blake's poem was terrifying, but if he said *come*, she'd leave without a backward glance everything that had been so important to her and walk barefoot with him across the world.

Only he would never say that word. He saw her as someone with her eye to the main chance. Oh, he wanted her, but he was strong enough to deal with that. His sexuality wouldn't get in the way of his intelligence; that cold, clear incisive brain was completely in control of his hormones.

'What is it?' he asked.

Aura shrugged. 'A goose walked over my grave.' And added rapidly, 'So do you think we're really going to have power cuts until the southern lakes fill in the spring?' referring to the latest political scandal.

'It seems ominously like it,' he said. If he realised she was evading his question he chose not to probe, instead delivering an extremely trenchant criticism of those he considered had brought the country to this pass.

Playing devil's advocate, Aura made him justify every statement, and tried to enjoy the rest of the meal, acutely aware that remorse and apprehension dimmed her usual easy conversation. She was relieved when at last they were sitting in the seats Paul had chosen for her pleasure at the theatre.

Unfortunately, as the story of two friends as close as brothers who loved the same woman unfolded in front of her, she barely heard the ravishing music. At any other time she would have smiled at the weakness of the libretto. Now, it struck too near home.

Yet in spite of the emotions that churned through her, submerging her integrity in a dark tide of desire, she had never felt so vividly, achingly alive; it was as though all these years she had slept in a cocoon, watching the world but not part of it.

From the age of fourteen she had mistrusted men. Her assailant's spoken rape had corrupted her in ways she was only just beginning to understand, so that she had protected herself by freezing off her budding sexuality. That, and the misery of life with a mother too weak to protect her from a stepfather intent on breaking her spirit, had led to the two engagements Flint was so suspicious of. They had been escape bids.

Looking back, she could even work out why she had chosen each man. The first one, when she was barely eighteen, had happened a month after Alick and Laurel's first child was born. Her cousin had always been Aura's refuge, her anchor. The baby boy had signalled irrevocably that Alick's main loyalty now lay with Laurel and his new family. Aura had been once more relegated to the periphery.

And the second engagement had been a vain attempt to refute her first fiancé's accusations of frigidity.

Aura regretted both of them, because she had used both men, and hurt them.

After those fiascos she had refused to become serious with any man until Paul came along, the ideal, chivalrous hero of every virgin's dreams, offering protection and an unthreatening, unselfish love. Paul was safe. And he understood. When she tried to tell him she was frigid he had laughed softly.

'No one with your love of textures and colours and perfumes, no one who uses their senses as you do, is frigid,' he had said. 'You might have had bad experiences in the past, but making love will come naturally with you with the right man, a man you can trust.'

Then he'd kissed her, and she'd liked it, and because he was so patently trustworthy she had learned to love him.

He had been right. But it was Flint who had smashed through her barriers. She didn't trust him as far as she could throw him, but she wanted him with every sense honed to a painful intensity.

He had ripped the shield of ice away, melted it in the heat of his personality and exposed her unprotected, untried self to his potent, explicit masculinity.

By the time interval arrived she was tense and on edge, so she drank the glass of white wine he bought her too fast. Fortunately, friends and acquaintances kept her answering questions about Paul's absence with what she hoped was the correct mix of regret at his absence and pleasure in Flint's company.

But she was almost convinced that everyone who talked to her, looked at her, knew of her hypocrisy.

The second half was sheer hell. Aura tried to concentrate on the stage because it was easier than facing her misery and self-reproach, but she couldn't take in what was happening. Brilliantly clad people passed before her vision, sang and postured, and she saw nothing because her brain was feverishly sorting through alternatives.

She couldn't marry Paul feeling like this.

Yet this would die; something so intense couldn't last for long. Paul was everything she wanted. It was aridly ironic that in spite of the runaway fire Flint roused in her, she didn't want to give up the security of Paul's love for the doubtful bliss of an affair with Flint—even supposing he wanted one. And the incident with Gemma made that highly unlikely. Loyalty, she thought agitatedly, was probably more important to him than satisfying a sexual need.

He wouldn't have any difficulty with that; she had only to glance around the foyer at interval to notice jealously the interested scrutiny he was getting from far too many women. His combination of raw sexuality and worldliness was overwhelming.

Aura's teeth sank into her lower lip, worrying the soft flesh. Exhausted, wracked by bitter pangs of conscience and equally bitter need, she asked herself why this had to happen to her. Just when she was getting her life together, when she could see some sort of peace and tranquillity ahead, she had to be dealt a wild card like Flint Jansen.

But that was self-pity; she had seen it render her mother ineffective too often to surrender to its power.

Like a force of nature, Flint had happened. And somehow she was going to have to deal with him and his effect on her life.

After the final curtain came down she stopped her polite applause and got to her feet, went out with him and into the car park. It was chilly; she shivered and instantly Flint switched on the heater. The motorway was surprisingly full of traffic, some of it erratic. Aura watched a car swerve in front of them without feeling any concern. Insulated from the world by her dilemma, she struggled to stay behind the façade of good manners.

Almost immediately the wayward car swung back into the next lane. Flint muttered something short and crisp, but his hands were steady on the wheel and he didn't show any outward sign of irritation.

'The driver must be drunk,' Aura said remotely.

'It certainly looks like it.' His voice was hard and unhurried.

The errant car wove its dangerous way through the traffic, then without warning shot over into their lane. Aura's hands covered her silent gasp. There was a terrifying squeal of brakes, the seatbelt tightened unbearably across her chest, and she heard her voice cry out Flint's name. Sparks flashed as the two vehicles collided in a nightmare of noise and motion, then the front car pulled away again, tearing off into the darkness.

'Are you all right?' Flint demanded in a voice she didn't recognise.

'Yes.' The whisper of sound alarmed her, so she repeated it more loudly. 'Yes, I'm perfectly all right.'

'I'll pull off and make sure we haven't done any severe damage to the car.'

Gritting her teeth, Aura wondered how on earth he could be so controlled, his hands so steady on the wheel.

'I got his number,' she said numbly, and quoted it before she forgot.

'Good girl.'

Such a tiny compliment, meaning nothing, yet the glow of his words affected every cell in her body.

Once they'd rolled to a stop on the verge he picked up a cell phone and dialled the emergency number, gave the number of the offending vehicle and his own name and address, and suggested crisply they get a traffic officer to intercept it quickly before the idiot killed himself or others.

The person at the other end said something. 'Oh, yes,' Flint replied in a voice as cold as ice, 'I'm more than happy to be a witness.'

Aura's skin prickled into a cold sweat. Putting the phone down, he commanded, 'Stay there,' before opening the door.

In the glare of the motorway lamps and the hard white headlights of the passing cars he looked harsh, like an ancient god of war, of strife and death, his features outlined strongly as he checked beneath the bonnet of the Jag.

When he returned Aura asked quietly, 'Anything wrong?'

'Nothing that I can see, but there's a strong smell of oil. I'm not going to drive the rest of the way to your place in case I've missed something. My flat's only a mile from here, so I'll take you there and ring a taxi to take you home.'

'I thought your flat was being decorated,' she said foolishly.

Sending a swift glance in her direction, he set the Jag in motion again. 'We won't be inside long enough for the smell of paint to worry us.'

He lived in the top floor of a big apartment building on the side of Mount Hobson, another of the small volcanoes that dotted the isthmus of Auckland. This building was not brashly modern like Paul's apartment block, and the security was unobtrusive. The porter looked up as they came in and nodded at them both, but beneath the respectful smile Aura was sure she detected a prurient interest. On the way up in the lift she shivered again, and once she had started she couldn't stop.

'Shock,' Flint said succinctly. 'I'll make some tea. You sit down and try to keep warm.'

Ignoring her protest, he stripped off his coat and dropped it around her shoulders. Warm and a little heavy, it smelt of his particular masculine essence. Rubbing her cheek for a guilty second against the collar, Aura watched as he moved about the luxurious kitchen with self-contained familiarity. He looked bigger in the stark white shirt than he had with the jacket on.

Her eyes lingered on the breadth of shoulder, the long arms, the way the muscles flexed as he leaned over to pour the hot water into the teapot.

Because this would probably be the only time she would ever be in his apartment, she dragged her gaze away and tried to look around, but she was unable to absorb anything beyond a dim impression of size and spartan elegance. After a minute or so she gave up and concentrated on stopping the tremors that racked her body.

Counting as she took in even breaths failed dismally, and

she was beginning to wonder just what she had to do to regain control when Flint emerged from the kitchen with a mug of tea, only half full.

'Try this,' he said.

The hand she held out was shaking so much that she stared at it in dismay.

He said, 'I'll hold it for you.'

She braced herself stiffly as he sat down beside her on the sofa.

'I can't get it to your mouth if you turn your face away,' he said, the amusement in his words making her cringe.

Every instinct shouted at her to grab the mug herself, but his lean fingers held it firmly, and she was not going to indulge in an undignified wrestle for possession which would proably spill the wretched stuff.

With a stubborn effort of will she turned her head and let him hold the mug to her lips. The liquid within was hot and milky and disgustingly sweet.

She must have pulled a face because he said instantly, 'I know it tastes foul but drink the lot, it will stop that trembling.'

Her teeth chattered on the china.

He made an impatient sound, jerked the mug away and put it on the table, then gathered her into his lap like a baby, cradling her in his warm embrace. 'No, don't move,' he said quietly. 'You just need a little reassuring.'

'I f-feel s-stupid,' she managed to say, but that wasn't entirely what she meant. As well as weak and fragile, she felt an overwhelming urge to give in, just lie in his arms and let whatever was going to happen, happen.

'Why? It's a perfectly normal reaction to shock,' he said gravely, picking up the mug. Patiently, he held it to her lips until all the tea had gone.

'I'm s-sorry,' she muttered. 'It's so silly—I don't normally fall to bits like this.'

'You're in the habit of being clipped on the motorway?'

His voice sounded harsher, even a little grating. If she looked up she would see the angular line of his jaw.

Her smile was distorted into a grimace. 'N-no.' She drew a deep, jagged breath, trying to summon the energy to get up, move away.

Now that the sweet, hot tea was working its cure Aura was too aware of other things, the flexed muscles beneath her thighs, hard as a sheet of steel, the rise and fall of his chest against her shoulder, a faint masculine scent more erotic by far than the finest perfume. The steady, solid thud of his heart pulsed through her body, a primitive counterpoint to the skipping, thudding beat of her own. His heat encompassed her, at once comforting and a warning.

Aura was still trembling, but for a different reason. Needles of desire, sharp and pitiless, coalesced in the base of her stomach, were transformed by some mysterious sorcery into a fire that sprang fullblown to raging life. She was assailed by hunger, fierce, basic, not to be gainsaid; the moments when she had seen the other car hit them and wondered whether they were going to live or die had edged every emotion, sharpened sensation to a pitch that wouldn't be denied.

Yet deny it she must.

She said thinly, 'I'm all right, now, thank, you. I think you'd better ring for the taxi.'

'Certainly.'

But when she went to get up her legs didn't want to support her, and she had to clutch his shoulders to get her balance.

Startled, she looked down into eyes that were a continuation of the flames licking through her body, eyes that held a stark, heated promise, eyes that demanded and threatened her with pleasure untold.

She thought she whispered a denial, but if she did it was

far too late and far too quiet, because he kissed her as though she was the gold at the end of his rainbow, the summit of all his ambitions.

His mouth was cruel, taking, not asking, and she could have fainted with the ecstasy of it. Yet the kiss frightened her, too, for it freed the wildness she had spent years trying to conquer and control, the wildness that urged her to yield, to follow where that kiss led, to grasp what it promised.

Temptation consumed her with its beckoning lure, tearing her apart. Aura had to resist it with every small bit of courage left.

She tried to push him away, but when her hands reached the collar of his shirt they curled around it, holding him close. Closing her eyes in surrender, she gave in to the demand that was eroding her will into nothingness.

After a moment his head lifted. Her lips were soft and red and throbbing, and they felt bereft.

Now, she told herself sturdily. Pull away, stand back, lift your head and let him see that you don't want any more...

'You kiss like a dream,' he said softly. 'But then, I knew you would. Your mouth is like a crushed rose, enigmatic yet sensual, hiding secrets and sweetness. I've wanted to kiss you ever since we met, when you looked at me with those hungry eyes, surprised yet expectant, as though you'd been waiting for me all your life.'

Shaking her head, Aura sprang free, backing away with her eyes fixed on his face. The scar stood out in bold prominence, thin and white against his bronzed skin.

'No.' But she stumbled over the word.

'Yes. You want me, Aura. Admit it.'

'No!'

Another step backwards, slow and secret, holding his fierce raptor's gaze with her own so he wouldn't notice her sly progress towards the safety of the door. Faced with such extreme danger she wasn't conscious of thinking; she reacted like a small animal in the presence of its greatest predator, doing what instinct bade her.

In a second she would turn and run for the door and the safety of the lift. He wouldn't chase her across the foyer with a porter on duty. Once outside, once free of the mindless enchantment that was scrambling her brain, she'd be safe.

He said roughly, 'Stop looking so terrified. I'm not going to hurt you.'

It seemed a good idea to acknowledge that. She nodded, and slid her other foot behind her.

Swift as a hawk striking death from the sky, moving with the lethal grace of a hunter, he was on his feet, and before she had time to turn he had caught her by the arm and swung her back, shaking her slightly.

'You're not running away from this,' he said calmly enough, but there was a ring of inexorable determination in his voice.

'Let me go!' she panted, trying to jerk her arm free.

His fingers tightened, and she cried out at the pain.

Swearing, he loosened them, but his free hand came up and caught her other arm so that she was held in a remorseless grip. Aura dragged air into tortured lungs, eyes measuring distances, measuring him.

She would have to knee him in the groin. She had never deliberately hurt anyone in her life, and she didn't think she could do it to him, but panic expanded inside her like a balloon, blocking out logic, blocking out everything but her knowledge that one kiss had changed everything.

Very quietly he warned, 'Try it, Aura, and you'll regret it more than you've ever regretted anything.'

She said desperately, 'Flint, I have to go home.'

'Not until you admit that you want me.'

'Go to hell,' she whispered, letting her lashes fall to hide her frantic gaze.

'Admit it, Aura. You want me to kiss you—that's what frightens you so much. You want to go to bed with me, lie with me in a tangle of sheets while we discover each other's mysteries, and then lose ourselves in them. *You want me*, Aura. Say it.'

Her pulse was rocketing into the stratosphere, his quick words summoning a white-hot response from deep within her, but although she had to dampen dry lips and swallow, she shook her head. If she once acknowledged his power she'd have no control over the rest of her life.

He laughed, and she thought she saw a flash of unwilling respect in the golden gaze. Then he pulled her close against the fierce heat of his body and kissed her again, a deep, deep kiss that probed past more than just the physical barriers of her resistance.

Aura tensed, but for the first time ever there was no faint niggle of disgust, no automatic rejection that had to be controlled before she could relax. Yet she would not give in.

Struggling, she turned her head from side to side, bit at him with small, sharp teeth. He laughed again, and bit her back, her lips and her cheek, under the fine line of her jaw, and down the sweet smoothness of her throat, little nips just short of pain that stimulated her unbearably.

The shock of strong teeth against her skin sapped Aura's resistance. She said something, words she didn't recognise escaped from her astonished mouth, and he lifted his head and kissed her again.

And she was lost.

CHAPTER FIVE

THIS was what she had longed for, this intimate mingling, the knowing, fierce exploration of her mouth, the sudden thrust that gave birth to racking shudders of sensation. Without volition her hands slid up, reached past shoulders as broad as the sky, to finally cling to his neck. He pulled her savagely into a body that was rigid with need.

Never before had Aura experienced such a feeling of rightness. She felt like the first woman, offering everything she was to the only man.

Flint wanted her. He couldn't hide that; he didn't even try. This man who could steal her soul with a kiss was as much at her mercy as she was at his. Stabbed by delight, by burgeoning rapture, she pressed against him, desperately trying to get closer to the male vigour and potency that had called to her from the moment she saw him.

He laughed deep in his throat. 'Yes, you like that, don't you. Do you like this?' as his hand slid around to cup the full curve of her breast.

Aura wavered, but the instantaneous excess of response as his thumb passed across a wildly sensitive nipple stopped the unborn protest.

'I see you do,' he said, and kissed her again, sealing her mouth as he carried her across the room to lower them both on to the long sofa, burying his face in her scented throat, his fingers working in the heavy mass of her hair to free it from confinement. As soon as the shining waves slithered across his wrist he lifted his head and stared intently at the burgundy floss that clung like living silk to his fingers.

Fascinated, Aura watched him spread a wide swathe

across her throat. He looked at her with fierce hunger in the glittering golden depths of his eyes.

'At first I thought you dyed it,' he said, his voice raw. 'It's like wine transformed into silk, fire rendered into solidity...' He teased the tress apart, then kissed her white throat through the licking, curling flames.

His words and the unexpected caress affected her unbearably. Shuddering, she whispered his name on an expelled breath, reacting helplessly when the contours of his face hardened even more, drew into lines of desire that should have terrified her.

But this was what she had been born for: to have Flint manoeuvre the fastening of her dress down and shape with gentle fingers the contours of her breast, the slightly rough tips of his fingers eliciting tremors that stoked up the inner heat at the junction of her body.

Lost in a sensual haze, abandoned by principles, by reason and logic, Aura touched her lips to his throat, licking the spot where his pulse throbbed. Instantly, his slow, seductive exploration stopped.

The harsh noise that erupted from deep in his chest brought her lashes up; she froze, but he said through clenched teeth, 'Go on.'

With wondering fingers she flicked the front of his shirt open and as her breath stopped in her lungs found the hot skin of his chest. Beneath the antique pattern of hair it was smooth and as fine-grained as satin.

Instinctively responding to a great surge of need, she tensed her muscles, arching her back. He cupped her breast, moulding it into the shape of his hand, and bent his head and kissed it, his mouth closing over the pleading peak.

Aura bucked with surprise and a fierce, untamed craving that whipped from the top of long-repressed desire like spindrift in a storm, carrying her with it. She groaned, the little sound guttural and surprising in the quiet room.

Beneath his tongue her nipples clamoured with a ruthless sensitivity that could only be soothed by his ministrations, yet the heat and moisture of his mouth did nothing but intensify it.

Aura didn't know when he slid her dress down so that her breasts were barely covered by the soft lace, she only knew that he was looking at her with such violent hunger that it summoned an answering depth of longing. Now she knew why people died for love, why kingdoms had fallen and governments toppled and lives been ruined by this savage delight.

He lifted his face. Almost all colour had been burned away in his eyes so that surrounding his enlarged pupils there was a rim of pure, blazing gold. Aflame in the dark fire of his gaze, she made no protest when he pulled her dress down to her waist and ripped his shirt open. Instead she went eagerly into an embrace as hard and final as fate, her breasts crushed by the hard wall of his chest. He kissed her, and she responded with the same fierce power, undulating her hips against the betraying rigidity that revealed he wanted her as much as she wanted him.

The pressure at once appeased and exacerbated her need. Winding her arms around him she pushed against him once more, rejoicing in the mounting thunder of his heart, yielding herself in a surrender she barely understood.

He turned, taking her with him, and in the same movement pushed the froth of lace dress all the way down, carrying her slip with it, so that all she had on was the black silk camisole and her garter belt and french knickers, and the black stockings that clad her long slender legs.

Aura's hands fluttered in an instinctive effort to cover herself.

'No,' he said thickly, his hand roving across the slightly curved surface of her stomach. His forefinger made a slow foray into the tight little indentation of her navel, and to her bewilderment that too was a pleasure point; his touch sent ripples of excitement through her.

'Did you think this might happen?' he asked, still in that same impeded voice. 'Did you dress for me tonight, Aura?'

Shivering, she tried to summon indignation as she shook her head, but his smile mocked her, and those tender, probing, inexorable fingers slid beneath the silk material of her knickers and touched her where she was moist and slick and hot, a mute, truthful capitulation, an appeal for something that had never happened before for her.

Aura shuddered, her back arcing helplessly as she closed her eyes, unable to meet the unchecked triumph in his face, the consummately male satisfaction that was echoed in his heavy-lidded gaze.

Rigors of sensation rushed through her; she was helpless before the smooth skill of his fingers, unable to resist, unable to want to. 'Flint,' she said weakly, on a sharply indrawn breath. 'Oh, God, Flint...'

'What do you want?' His voice was a low growl, the words indistinct. 'Tell me what you want, Aura, and I'll give it to you, I'll give you everything—'

The fire of his touch began to build, to drag her down in flame and thunder, to—

'Tell me now that you love Paul,' he said savagely as he got to his feet.

Paul. Oh, God, *Paul*!

Aura's hand flew up to cover her mouth. Huddling deep in the soft cushions of the sofa, she turned her head away from his unrelenting gaze.

Paul. She had forgotten Paul, forgotten everything in the sorcery of Flint's lovemaking. And she had stupidly thought that because she was enchanted, he would be, too.

But that fleeting glimpse of his face, its hard features clamped in contempt, showed her just how wrong she was.

Anger, the bitter inhumanity of betrayal, welled up like black marsh water.

The wild passion of his lovemaking and her response had sliced through the chains forged by the years and her will around the tempestuous core of her personality, so it was the old Aura who retorted on a rising note of fury, 'I do love him, damn you to *hell*, you arrogant swine. This means nothing! *Nothing!*'

There was silence. Then, 'I wish I didn't believe you,' he said silkily.

His eyes were burning trails of ice over her face. Aura dragged a sobbing breath into painful lungs, and found some measure of control. Lethargically, she said, 'I don't expect you to understand.'

She turned her back and began scrambling back into her clothes. His harshly unamused laughter swept her head around.

'Do you understand yourself, Aura, or have you been so brainwashed by your parasite of a mother that you can't see beyond security?'

'I love him!'

His laughter was discordant, filled with a rage she understood because it burned within her, too. Long fingers on her shoulder turned her to face him.

'If you love him, why is your breath coming so quickly between your lips?' His thumb traced the line of her mouth, gentle yet inexorable. Fire seared through her.

'Why do you look at me with a famished desperation?' He kissed her eyelids closed. 'Why does that maddening little pulse beat faster than I can count in the ivory column of your throat? You want me, Aura.'

'It isn't love,' she said angrily, grabbing at her sanity.

'Who said anything about love? But if you feel like this about me, what sort of marriage are you going to have with Paul?'

His words beat at her like stones. If she let him see her defeat she was lost. She said mordantly, 'As good a marriage as I'm likely to have with anyone.'

'Do you really think he'd be satisfied with your sort of love? He's a man, Aura, a man with a man's needs, and the milk-and-water affection you've got to give him won't fulfil them. When he takes you into that bedroom on your honeymoon he won't accept meek resignation; he'll want a woman who meets his every approach with ardour and passion. Lying back on the sheets with resignation is going to infuriate him; he'll want you to touch him and kiss him, to open yourself to him and to explore his body with the same desire you've shown me, the same desire he is going to show.'

He looked down at her, contempt and something else turning his face to stone. 'I've seen him kiss you, remember,' he said uncompromisingly, 'seen you dance together, and it's more than plain that although he's panting with lust, you're not affected at all. You've got him so strung up with your virginal, touch-me-not air that he thinks it's going to be all right on the night, but it won't be, unless you're a far better actress than you've shown any signs of being. Because he'll want a response like the one I got from you. And you won't be able to give it. You'll have to act, and lie to him, just as you've been lying to him all along.'

Covering her face with her hands, Aura fought back nausea, and images that terrified her; images not of Paul, but of herself lying in a bed with the man who spoke so cruelly to her now, of his lean body poised to take and invade, of the contrast between her pale hands and his bronze skin as she discovered with loving subtlety all the manifold differences between man and woman.

Powerful and seductive, the images tugged at her heart, sent heat through her body, yet Flint had offered her nothing, not marriage, not even a love affair.

'Some sort of friend you are,' she said acidly.

His teeth showed in a bitter, unamused smile. 'Yeah. But eventually he'll thank me.'

'My mother used to tell me that, and I didn't believe her, either. You've got a nerve, abrogating his right to decide.'

He laughed and touched her cheek, his long fingers gentle yet commanding. Aura resisted, but without hurting her he turned her face so that she had to meet the blazing golden brilliance of his gaze. Even as she shut her eyes she knew it was too late; he had recognised her submission.

'You know you don't want to marry him,' he said crisply. 'Knights in shining armour are not for you, Aura. You don't need rescuing.'

'You're cruel,' she choked, torn in two by hate and desire.

He laughed again and his finger touched her mouth, sliding between her lips until she opened them. 'It takes a diamond to cut another diamond,' he said, stroking the wildly sensitive flesh of her upper lip in a whisper-soft enticement, then running his finger across the sharp cutting edge of her top teeth. 'You're cruel, too, cruel and imperious and vibrant with life, with your full, sulky red mouth and those witch's eyes, like jade sprinkled with gold. You want so much more than he can give you, you want everything that life offers. You won't get it with Paul.'

He put his finger into his mouth, tasting her, his narrowed gleaming eyes watching the way her breath hissed through her lips, the subtle droop of her lashes in unwilling response to the primitive little action.

'You don't know that,' she retorted, whipping up scorn because she was too close to surrendering.

He shrugged. 'I know Paul far better than you do. He's conventional and rather old-fashioned. Look at his mother; that's the sort of life he sees you leading. He'll keep you chained by love until it turns into dissatisfaction and despair, and then into hatred...'

'Not Paul,' she retorted.

'You're nothing but a leech,' he snarled, suddenly furious. 'At first I thought it was the money, but it's not entirely that, is it, although the money's important.'

White-faced, her eyes gleaming with supressed tears, she spat, 'I am not marrying Paul for his money!'

He surprised her by nodding, his gaze never leaving her face. He was pale too, and the scar stood out lividly on his cheek, ending in a devilish flick along the unyielding line of his jaw.

'Not entirely, perhaps. You want his strength and his stability, you want to use him as a shelter from the world, make him take the place of your father and your cousin. Nice, safe relationships, both of them, except that your father left you, and so did Alick in a different way. He got married. You had no one to rely on then, so you went looking for someone who would take care of you.'

'No!'

'Oh, yes. Your stepfather killed himself—another man who left you, but this time he left you with a silly, flirting, useless mother on your hands.'

'You are foul,' she shouted, losing control entirely. 'I did not "go looking"!' She mimicked his tone, mocking him with angrily sparking eyes and contemptuous mouth.

His smile was cool and aggravating. 'I don't blame you, not entirely. You've been well conditioned. Your mother found men she could lean on, so you followed her footsteps and conveniently fell in love with Paul. Of course, he wants you to depend on him because that way he can pretend to be the stronger. But his sort of strength is not what you need. If you marry him, in five years' time you'll be bored stiff and giving him hell.'

'Whereas you're strong, I suppose,' she jeered.

'I'm strong,' he agreed, a simple statement of fact by a man who knew himself so well he didn't need to boast. 'But don't think you're going to change one support for another. I'm not offering you anything, Aura, not a shoulder, not a shelter in bad weather, not anything. You're not going to be able to say that I seduced you. When you come to me you'll be free, and you'll understand exactly what you're doing.'

He spoke with a callous detachment that shattered the last shreds of her composure. 'I want to go home!' she said raggedly into the aching silence.

'The taxi must be here by now. Just remember one thing.' His voice hardened, became merciless and unsparing. 'Sooner or later, whether you marry Paul or not, you and I are going to make love. Ask yourself which will hurt him most.'

It wasn't a threat, it was a straight promise. With the implacable words ringing in her ears, echoing through her soul, Aura swung on her heel.

'All this,' she said in her haughtiest voice, 'because I refuse to go to bed with you.'

The instant the words left her tongue she saw them strike home. His smile was devilish, his pitiless eyes lit from within by the fires of hell as with calculated slowness he pulled her into him, letting her feel the merciless, naked force of his sensuality, and the aggression bound up with it.

She fought, but he was too strong. Not that he hurt her; with insulting ease he let her tire herself out. He was aroused, but instead of the involuntary withdrawal she felt in Paul's arms she was almost suffocated by a ferocious exultation.

It was this which made her mind up. She lifted her flushed, passionate face and said between her teeth, 'If you do anything more I'll sue you for assault and attempted rape.'

He laughed, his breath soft and heated across her incredibly tender mouth. 'And I'll countersue,' he mocked. 'You can't marry him, Aura.'

She knew that, but if she said so she would have no protection against the desire that beat through her, linking them in a conflagration strong enough to destroy everything she had ever learned in her life and set her adrift on a sea that was unknown and more perilous than any other.

Closing her eyes against the command in his, she fixed her jaw, set her mouth into a mulish line. 'I'll do what is best for me,' she said thinly. 'I'm no foolish girl, to be seduced out of my mind.'

'No, you're not. That ripe beauty hides a tough little adventuress, determined to keep on a course that you must know will short-change Paul, even if he never learns that you don't love him.'

'I do love him!' she swore.

'So you're going to go through with it?'

Jerking herself free, she spoke as calmly, as steadily as she could. 'It isn't anything to do with you, Flint. I'm going home. *Now*.'

His bluntly chiselled face was unmoving, no emotion but residual passion flickering in the depths of his eyes, yet Aura sensed that at that moment she was in greater danger than she had ever been in her life.

Then, to her astonishment, he laughed. 'All right,' he said, and took her down to the foyer and put her in the taxi, saying with sardonic amusement, 'Thank you for a very interesting evening, Aura.'

Fury contested with chagrin and a grief so deep she refused to acknowledge it. Staring straight ahead she said tonelessly, 'Goodnight.'

By the time she reached home, however, the fury had

died and the wilderness of ardour had been swamped by shame; she was left with the bitter taste of gall in her mouth.

All of her rationalisations were revealed for what they were: specious and self-serving. Flint was right. What she felt for Paul had nothing of the fiery inevitability, the rightness she felt in Flint's arms.

And because of that, she couldn't marry Paul, even though she loved him. She walked slowly up the path towards the front door, twisting Paul's diamond on her finger, watching the cold light of the moon sparkle within its heart. The starry pink and white flowers of jasmine glimmered in the darkness, their musky, potent scent floating sweetly on the fresh, crisp air.

She rubbed her cold arms, listening to a siren wobbling along the motorway, spreading fear and desolation. An ambulance; she spared a thought for the person it carried, or was heading towards.

She didn't want to be here. She wanted to be in the country somewhere, where the only night noises were pleasant, unthreatening rural ones, dogs howling a lullaby to the moon, moreporks calling wistfully from the bush, the soft liquid chuckle of a stream running through paddocks.

It was utter cowardice, of course. She just wanted to run away from the mess her life had suddenly become. Only there was no one else to deal with it. It was her mess, and she was going to have to clean it up as best she could.

When Paul came back from Samoa she'd have to tell him that she couldn't marry him. After that, it would be Natalie's turn. All the people they had invited to the wedding, as well as the florist and the caterer and a dozen others, would have to be told. The presents would have to be sent back. And she'd have to do it all, because Natalie wouldn't be able to.

Her heart quailed. It was going to be awful, and the years

that followed would be awful too, with her mother constantly casting it up at her that she had whistled away security for them both on a whim. Natalie would never do such a thing. And Aura wasn't going to be able to tell anyone, much less Paul, why she had changed her mind.

Flint had made it obvious that he didn't see any sort of future for them together. She couldn't hurt Paul even more by telling him that she had fallen in lust with his best friend.

Because that was all it was. She had no illusions about that. Love implied shared interests, shared commitments. She had that with Paul. This overwhelming hunger that had her caught fast in its thrall was superficial, a thing of dazzle and flash with no substance to it. She and Flint shared nothing except a flaming attraction which would peter away in time. That time couldn't come too soon for her.

Aura had always thought that it was mainly men who were able to separate their emotional lives, loving in one compartment, lusting in another, and no communication between the two. Perhaps there was something wrong with her.

Or perhaps, she thought, unlocking the door, it was just bad luck, like being caught in an earthquake or a tidal wave. Flint had had much the same effect on her life as a natural disaster.

When she woke after another almost sleepless night it was to hear Alick's voice outside.

A moment later there was a tap at the window. 'Are you awake?' he asked.

Aura groaned. 'Just. Wait a minute.'

By the time she opened the door Laurel was standing there while Alick appeared to be examining the connection where the power line went into the unit.

'He thinks it looks a bit wonky,' Laurel explained.

Aura liked Alick's wife very much, but at that moment

she didn't want to have to meet her too perceptive, golden-brown eyes.

'We thought you might like to have a quiet day with us,' she went on, eyeing Aura with exactly the shrewd glance she dreaded. 'Actually, it will be with Alick. I'm spending the rest of the day with my mother, but Alick says it's months since he had a cousinly chat with you.' She followed Aura into the room and closed the door behind her, confiding with a twinkle, 'I think he's rather jealous. He's always had a special feeling for you, and now that you're going to get married—what's the matter?'

Aura shook her head, but Laurel's slim figure wavered through the tears in her eyes. Laurel looped her arms around her. 'I don't know anyone I'd rather confide in than Alick,' she said, holding Aura gently.

After an inelegant sniff Aura said on a wobble, 'No, I don't either.'

Laurel squeezed her then let her go with a little push towards the bedroom. 'So put some clothes on.'

Obediently, Aura dressed, went in to tell her mother what she was doing, and left.

Because this was a flying visit, the children, two sons and a charming, self-possessed three-year-old called Miriel who was Aura's goddaughter, had been left at Kerikeri. The apartment seemed empty without their voices, like little birds, in every room. Within a few minutes of their arrival Laurel left them.

It was a superb day, blue and gold and green, so fresh and clear that it tasted like wine on the tongue.

'Let's go out on to the terrace,' Aura said. 'How's the weather at Kerikeri? It's been just awful here, rain and more rain and winds from every point of the compass but mostly from the south and west, and bitterly cold.'

The sun lapped her in a tide of warmth. Still babbling about the weather, she collapsed on to a lounger.

'All right, young Aura,' Alick interrupted calmly, 'what's the matter?'

Her lips trembled. It would have been altogether too easy to fling herself on him as she used to when she was sixteen, but this was something that even the kindest of cousins couldn't help her with. Resolutely keeping her face turned away, she shook her head.

'Sometimes,' he said dispassionately, 'it can help to talk things over with a more or less impartial observer.'

She had taken her woes and fears to him for so long that it had become a habit, one she had tried to break. Was Flint right? Had she become accustomed to looking for support?

'Come on, Aura,' Alick said insistently. 'Spill.'

She surrendered. 'I can't marry Paul,' she said baldly.

He nodded. 'Flint, is it?'

'Is it so obvious?' she blurted. Would Paul realise who it was?

'Not to anyone else, I imagine, but I've known you far longer than most people.'

She bit her lip against an onslaught of tears. He waited silently until she regained enough composure to speak. 'The awful thing is that I don't love Flint. I mean—I don't know him. I do love Paul, so much, he's everything I want in a man, and I can't bear to hurt him, but—' she clenched her hands, forcing the words out for the first time '—I don't want to go to bed with him.'

'And you do want to go to bed with Flint.'

Alick's voice was without censure, but Aura nodded in shame. 'Yes,' she whispered.

'Do you remember Jenna? I was engaged to her when I met Laurel.'

Aura had forgotten. Alick and his wife were so ideal a couple, so much in love, that the girl he had chosen first had faded into the past. 'Jenna,' she said after a moment. 'Yes, I remember her. She was nice, but very young.'

'At the time she was exactly what I thought I wanted. But I knew the minute I met Laurel that it wasn't going to work.'

'Yes, but Laurel was in love with you,' she said wearily. 'I remember; it was obvious right from the start. Flint is not in the least in love with me. He's made that quite plain.'

'Has he? That doesn't really matter. What does matter is that you can't marry Paul McAlpine feeling the way you do about Jansen.'

It seemed so easy, stated in Alick's calm voice. Aura gulped and nodded. 'I know.'

'So what are you going to do about it?'

Wretchedly, Aura sighed. 'I'll have to tell Paul. He's in Samoa, and won't be back until Tuesday. Then it will be Natalie.'

'You can leave her to me,' he said cynically.

She sat with her head bent, pleating the folds of her skirt between fingers that trembled. 'It's not so simple,' she muttered. 'Paul's buying a flat for Mother—she'll be so angry, so upset.'

'Come on now, Aura, you know better than that! Your mother made a mess of her life. There's no need to make a mess of yours as well just to keep her in clover.'

'Paul will be hurt.'

He said remorselessly, 'Jenna was hurt when I broke it off with her. I don't know what's going to happen between you and Flint, whether he's just an excuse because in your inner heart you know that marrying Paul is wrong, but the point is that you don't want to marry Paul.'

Her teeth clamped down on her lips so hard she could taste the blood. 'But I do,' she wailed.

'Really? Then what's all this about?'

'Oh, *hell*.'

'Face facts, Aura.'

'I hate people who tell me to face facts,' she shouted, thumping her clenched fist on the arm of the lounger.

'That's Natalie speaking, not you. It's not going to be fun,' he admitted with wry humour, 'but Laurel and I will help as much as we can.'

For a moment she was tempted. 'No, I got myself into this,' she said huskily, 'I'll deal with it.'

The sun was setting smokily and dramatically behind a bank of clouds when she arrived back home in a far more stable frame of mind. Unfortunately, it was short-lived.

When she walked through the door her mother leapt to her feet, and in her surprise dropped a piece of paper.

'I'll get it,' Aura said, automatically reaching down to pick it up.

'No, no, it's all right.' Natalie's voice was even more betraying than the speed with which she snatched the paper away.

But Aura had recognised the heading. She asked in a ghost voice, 'How much do you owe on your credit card?'

Natalie's hand shook. 'Only a few thousand,' she said unsteadily.

'A few thousand?' Aura took advantage of her mother's shock to wrest the account from her. She looked down, and felt the colour run from her skin, leaving her cold and disorientated. 'That's more than a few thousand dollars.'

'Yes, well, how do you think I've been able to keep going?' Her mother was angry now, her usual tactic when confronted with money.

Tears next, Aura thought, fighting a bewildering sense of disconnectedness.

Sure enough, Natalie's eyes misted delicately. 'It's all right,' she said placatingly. 'I'll be able to pay for it as soon as you get married.'

'What do you mean?' Aura's voice was constricted, the emotion so tightly restrained it sounded harsh.

'Well, when I move into the new apartment I can sell this one, and pay the bill.'

Aura sat down, holding herself very stiff while she strove to assimilate this new blow.

If she didn't marry Paul there was no way she or her mother could pay the bill.

She said dully, 'What on earth did you spend it on?'

'I had debts when Lionel died—he wouldn't give me any money for a year or so. I had to pay for the funeral, and then—I had to get a dress made for the wedding. Well, I can't wear just any old rag, can I...' Natalie gestured vaguely, before beginning to weep in real earnest.

'It's all right,' Aura said tonelessly. 'Don't cry. We'll manage.'

'Of course we'll manage,' Natalie said, patting her eyes with a tiny, lacy handkerchief. She held out her hand for the bill, and spent the rest of the evening resolutely ignoring it and her daughter.

Who was racked by an inner torment she couldn't let her mother see. Inactivity fretted her nerves to shreds, for of course she couldn't do anything until she had told Paul. Unable to sleep again that night, she greeted the new week with resignation. She had clung to her great-grandmother's garnets through everything else, but now they would have to go. And even though they were the much rarer and more valuable green stones, they were not going to sell for anything like the amount Natalie owed.

A visit to the firm of jewellers who had sold her great-grandfather the garnets so many years before confirmed her fears. Dry-eyed, she handed them over, got the cheque, and paid it into Natalie's credit card account.

On her way back home, she sat slumped in the bus, trying to work out ways of getting the rest of the money. Her computer set-up wouldn't bring much in, but it might buy time. They would have to mortgage the flat. I had better, she thought grimly, make sure Mother hasn't already done that.

She came home to find Natalie staring at a heap of presents that had arrived by courier. She looked sideways at Aura, then said quickly, 'Oh, good, you're back in time.'

'In time for what?'

Her mother laughed. 'Oh, in time for you to take these over to Paul's.'

'I'll take them over later,' Aura said vaguely. 'Tomorrow.'

'Oh, take them now. You know they clutter up this place far too much. Get a taxi, there's a good girl, and drop that pile off. Didn't I see another registered parcel card in the mail?'

'Yes.'

'Then you'd better collect it, too, hadn't you?'

There was no way Aura was going to be able to carry the boxes to the nearest bus stop. What the hell, she thought numbly. She had just enough money to pay for a taxi. So she rang one, and when it arrived piled the gifts into it and directed him to the post office. She collected the registered one and put it into the cab, when a sudden idea came to her.

'Wait a moment,' she said, and dashed across the pavement to the phone box. She dialled Paul's number, then stood with white knuckles waiting for someone to answer the call.

No one did, so Flint wasn't there. No, of course he wouldn't be, he'd be at work. If he had any decency at all, she thought savagely as she got back into the cab and gave Paul's address, he'd have moved back to his own apartment.

But his presence was stamped all over the flat. The morning's newspaper lay folded on a table, a rinsed coffee-mug sat upturned on the bench, and a silk tie that didn't belong to Paul had been slung across the back of the sofa.

Her stomach lurched. Setting her mouth into a thin line, she took the parcels into the spare room they had set aside for gifts.

Once they were safely stowed she stood for a moment staring around at the array. There were some lovely things there, chosen with love and care, objects she had looked forward to seeing in her home. Sudden tears stung her eyes unbearably.

She had almost reached the door when it was pushed open. The blood drained from her skin as Flint's tall, lithe form strode through, blocking the light from the landing.

Unable to speak, she stopped abruptly. His eyes raked her pale face, came to rest for a wildly unsettling moment on her mouth, then moved to hold her appalled gaze.

'You look like death,' he said.

'Thanks. What are you doing here?'

Almost absently he said, 'Organising myself out of here and into my own place.'

Aura bit her lip. The silence was so oppressive that she gabbled, 'I've just put some wedding-gifts in—in the room.'

His mouth hardened. There was a moment of taut silence before he said levelly, 'I see. So greed overcame integrity. But perhaps you didn't have much integrity to begin with.'

Anger burned deep and revivifying beneath the shock and the pain. He jumped to conclusions far too fast. 'Whatever I do, it's none of your concern,' she snapped back. 'Mind your own business, will you?'

'Just tell me,' he commented. 'Are you planning to go ahead with it?'

She lifted her head arrogantly. 'I've already told you what I'll do. I'll do what's right for me.'

He said something between his teeth, something she was

rather glad she didn't hear, then snarled, 'Like hell you will! What got to you? Has Natalie sung a sad story about how awful it is to be poor, perhaps? Or did you decide that so many women down the centuries have gritted their teeth and counted their bank balances whenever their husbands touched them that it must be easy to do?'

'You make me sick,' she said frigidly, turning to walk past him and out of the door.

He grabbed her arm. 'That's nothing to what you do to me, Aura—'

'Let me go!'

He exerted some of his strength. Not enough to hurt her, but more than enough to pull her inexorably close to him.

She said icily, 'Take your hands off me, you coward.'

His eyes had narrowed into golden slits, but at that they opened, and it was like looking into the pits of hell. 'That's a funny word for you to use,' he said offensively, his breath stirring the strands of hair across her forehead. 'You're a lying, betraying bitch, a cold little whore with her eyes firmly fixed on the main chance, yet you call me a—'

Stung, as angry as he was, she spat, 'Yet in spite of all that you want me! So what does that make you, Flint?'

'A fool,' he said, his lips barely moving. He lifted his free hand and ran a long finger from one side of her jaw-bone to the other, tilting her face to meet his merciless scrutiny.

It was like being hit with a cattle prod; a violent shock of electricity sizzled through her, arching her body into the warmth and heat of his. Aura tried to wrench herself away, but his hand on her arm kept her close. Something ugly and violent moved in the glittering depths behind his thick, straight lashes.

'Yes,' he said, cupping her jaw, stroking up towards her ear, toying with the small sensitive lobe.

The breath stopped in Aura's throat. She had never

thought of her ear as an erogenous zone, never realised that it could send such intensely erotic messages to the rest of her body. She stood with wide, dazed eyes while the small caress seared through her inhibitions and the fragile bonds of her honour.

'You have an amazing air of innocence, as though everything we do is fresh and new to you,' he said softly, watching her with a cold smile barely curving his hard mouth. 'Does it surprise you when you enjoy a man's touch, Aura? Hasn't any other man made you burn like this?'

Her throat was dry; she couldn't have spoken even if she had found words to say. His finger moved, slid into the sensitive inner reaches of her ear, and she shivered, mutely begging him to stop, to let her go.

'I wonder why?' he said in that gravelly voice. 'Was it because you chose them for their money?'

Trying to hide from the mesmerising spell of his gaze, to free herself of the boneless lethargy that had swept over her at his touch, she closed her heavy lids.

Abruptly he let her go. 'Do you want me to tell him?'

For a moment she was tempted, but almost immediately shook her head. She couldn't take the coward's way out.

'Tell him as soon as he gets home,' he ordered, looking at his watch. 'Or I'll do it for you.'

Aura looked at him with astonishment and anger in her heart. He had manipulated her, once more. Thank God, she thought defiantly, she didn't love him. But oh, when he touched her, her body knew its master.

Then Paul said from the doorway, 'What the hell is going on here?'

Shame flooded Aura in chilling waves, cutting the ground from beneath her feet. The face she turned to the door was slack-jawed in shock, her crimson cheeks and drowsy eyes giving her away completely.

She couldn't think of anything to say, anything to do, except stare at a man she had never known existed. Her gentle Paul was gone and in his place there was a hard-faced stranger.

He knew, she thought, panic-stricken as she realised that he had seen her in Flint's arms.

'What do you think?' Flint asked harshly, looking at his friend with cold speculation.

'It looks as though I should have been protecting my interests.' Paul's pleasant voice was icy. 'How long has this been going on?'

'Nothing's been going on,' Aura said quickly, but her face and tone gave her away.

'Don't lie to me,' he said wearily. 'For God's sake, Aura, don't lie! What I saw a moment ago wasn't—' He closed his eyes a second, then forced them open. He looked only at her, not at the man who stood beside her with the watchful, alert patience of a tiger ready to make a kill. 'It wasn't what Flint said, or even the way he touched you, it was the—how long has it been going on?'

Aura took a deep breath, her eyes filling with useless tears as they searched his beloved face.

'Since I saw her,' Flint told him, his face implacable.

'No,' Aura whispered hopelessly.

He looked at her with something like contempt. 'Yes.'

'Have you slept together?'

The question came toneless and fast. Aura looked at the man she was still engaged to and saw fists clench. 'No!' The word burst from her lips, but Flint's abrasive voice overrode hers.

'What do you think?' he asked again. This time there was a note of insolence in the question, as though he wanted to provoke Paul.

Anger and a corroding bitterness darkened Paul's face. 'You've never let friendship stand in the way of a woman you wanted, have you, Flint?' he said, the white line around his lips belying his calmness. 'Get out, both of you.'

'Paul—'

The imperative summons of a beeper interrupted, but Aura scarcely heard it. When she said his name again, he didn't even look at her, merely repeated indifferently, 'Get out.'

Amazingly, Flint reached over and grabbed a telephone, beginning to punch in numbers. Equally amazingly, Paul didn't try to stop him.

Aura turned away, her dreams shattering on the floor behind her. The sound of Flint's voice barking orders into the telephone was the last thing she heard as she closed the door behind her and walked out, away from the happy life she had so longed for, out into a darkness and cold nowhere as extreme as the desolation in her heart.

It was raining, but she didn't notice, bent only on reaching the sanctuary of home. She didn't think about the scene she had just endured; once she began she wouldn't be able to control herself, and it would be too humiliating to walk the three miles home weeping.

In the end that was what she did, rain mingling with the tears and washing them away in a chilly flood. Fortunately Natalie wasn't there. Still offended, she had decided to dine with friends a little out of town; if the weather worsened she intended to stay the night. Aura prayed that she would.

After she had showered and changed into old jeans and a jersey, she sat down with her notebook in front of her and began methodically to call every guest, every firm, to tell them that the wedding was cancelled.

Two hours later she put the receiver down, exhausted, feeling as though she had been beaten with a stick. Tears trickled down her cheeks; she bent her head and wept for everything she had thrown away because of bondage to a man who didn't love her, a man she didn't love.

The knock on the door made her freeze with sheer terror; she couldn't let anyone see her like this. As she tried to stop the sobs that forced themselves upwards, she crouched like a threatened wild animal into the chair.

'I know you're there.' Flint's voice, commanding and abrupt. 'Let me in, Aura.'

A tiny flame of hope, wavering in the winds of uncertainty, sprang to life inside her. Wiping her eyes, she walked across to open the door.

He looked big and vital and braced against some undefined tension, his harshly-contoured face and dark hair sprinkled with raindrops. The hand over her heart clenched tightly as she let herself recall the honeyed tide of desire his touch aroused.

'Crying?' His gaze travelled from her red eyes to her quivering lips. Some swiftly hidden emotion darkened the pure golden depths beneath his lashes. 'It's a waste of time. You certainly don't look as though it's doing you any good.'

'You're so kind,' she said, swallowing so that her voice was firmer. 'What do you want?'

'I want you to promise that even if he wants you to, you won't see Paul alone.'

CHAPTER SIX

AURA stared silently at him as the fragile flicker of hope died.

Impatiently he said, 'He's not reacting well to this.'

'Did you expect him to?' she asked in a voice whose bitterness was at her own folly.

'That doesn't matter. You are not to see him unless Natalie or someone else is with you, understand?'

Her mouth opened to tell him to go to hell when the beeper burst into life once more. He muttered a curse, then demanded, 'May I use your telephone?'

'Yes, of course.' Not that her permission was necessary; he was already halfway across the room.

It was a short conversation. He said, 'Yes, yes, yes. All right, just make sure that no one goes anywhere near the place or I'll deal with them myself. How the hell do I know, you're the man on the spot! Fob them off as best you can until I get there,' and hung up. 'I have to go,' he said, turning to meet her bewildered eyes. 'I'm due at the airport now, Aura, just promise me, please.'

'All right, I promise. Where are you going?' A confusion of emotions drained Aura's voice of all expression. Overriding her bleak acceptance of his departure was a sudden foreboding.

His features tightened. 'It doesn't matter.'

The foreboding became fear. She looked at him with eyes that took in everything, the striking features, the arrogantly outlined mouth, the scar, mute witness to some situation he hadn't been able to handle. Although the fact

that he had survived presumably meant that he had dealt
with it successfully.

'Take care,' she said, hardly able to articulate the words.

He hesitated, then swung towards her and kissed her as
though she was all that he had ever wanted, as though he
was famished for her and would never kiss her again.

Aura gave herself wholly to him, moulding herself to the
lean strength of his big body.

'Goodbye,' he said huskily, and was gone, striding
through the rain to where a long, blue car waited. As soon
as its door swung closed behind him the vehicle purred off
into the rapidly thickening afternoon.

Aura walked across to the kitchen and automatically put
the kettle on. When she had made tea she had sat down
and attempted to formulate a plan of action.

But her mind kept slipping back to the scene in Paul's
apartment. How strange that he had turned up at that particular moment, when he wasn't due back until tomorrow.
Her mind worried at the strangeness, until a faint niggling
suspicion, a hint of unease, shreds and patches of information fed into her brain by barely understood mechanisms,
consolidated into the conviction that Flint had known Paul
was arriving home early. That was why he'd turned up. Not
to collect his gear and go back to his own flat; no, he'd
come for the express purpose of forcing the issue.

How had he known she would be there?

That was easy. Natalie, of course. She had almost pushed
Aura out of the door with those parcels. What story had
Flint spun to persuade her to make sure Aura was there at
a certain time?

Flint had looked at his watch in the apartment as though
wondering how much longer Paul was going to be.

Yes, that was typical of Flint. He was accustomed to
being the man in charge, the man who took control and

fixed things. It would be like him to engineer a confrontation.

With conviction came a cold, hard anger, sweeping away the dull lethargy that had pitched her into despair. Drinking her tea, she began to make lists. Being busy would keep the pain and the remorse at bay for a few days, although eventually she would have to deal with them.

But her hands shook slightly, and the skin was clammy. 'It's because I'm cold,' she said aloud, and got up.

The power shortage had persuaded her to use the heater as little as possible, and most days she didn't put it on until after dark, but the black clouds were being chased across the sky by a brisk sou'-westerly, and the temperature had dropped.

God, she thought wearily, will this winter never end?

The days that followed were sheer hell.

First of all she had to cope with Natalie, who ranted and wept and accused her furiously of ruining her life. Questioning that rapidly degenerated into a shouting match elicited, just as Aura dreaded, that her mother had mortgaged the unit to buy back some of her old furniture for the new apartment. With splendid disregard for actual value, she had contacted the new owners and offered them whatever was needed to persuade them to sell.

The furniture was being held in store; the business of organising its sale took up time and effort that Aura could ill afford, and because it had to be auctioned, no money came in to help pay back the mortgage.

As it was, the agent she dealt with told her that she wasn't likely to get much more than half of the amount her mother had paid for it. Natalie was no help; once more she retired to her bed, refusing to eat or get up.

The sheer logistics of cancelling the wedding exhausted

Aura. Alick and Laurel helped, but she insisted on doing the brunt of the work.

'You're punishing yourself,' Laurel said astutely.

Aura shrugged. 'It stops me thinking.'

She heard nothing from Paul apart from an impersonal note informing her that the engagement ring had arrived safely. There was one very sticky telephone call from his mother. Laurel, bless her, had met Mrs McAlpine and they had agreed that she should deal with the presents from their side of the family.

'How is Paul?' Aura asked his mother tentatively.

'Broken-hearted. How did you expect him to be?'

Aura had always known that his mother didn't like her, but she was shocked by the venom that showed through the crisp tones. 'I'm sorry,' she said.

'I'm sure you will be, when you realise what you've done. Just as I'm sure Paul will come to his senses and see how disastrous a marriage between you would have been.'

'No doubt he will,' Aura said quietly, 'in which case both of you will perhaps feel some sort of gratitude to me. After all, a broken engagement is bad enough, but a broken marriage is much worse. Goodbye, Mrs McAlpine. Thank you for all you've done for me.'

Jessica, too, was a great help whenever she could get time away from the agency. It was she who told Aura that Paul had gone abroad.

'Big-game hunting in Africa, I suppose,' Aura said acidly. Trust a man to run away and leave the women to deal with everything.

Jessica didn't catch the allusion. 'No, he's gone climbing mountains in Nepal, so Mrs McAlpine told Mother. I can just see Paul up a mountain, somehow, can't you? He should be at home among the glaciers. How are you?'

Like everyone else, Jessica was dying to know who had

broken the engagement and why, but, also like everyone else, she didn't ask.

'I'm fine,' Aura lied, collapsing bonelessly on to the sofa.

The days had dragged by without a word from Flint. Not that she'd expected him to contact her, but this casual underlining of how little she meant to him hurt.

She straightened up. 'I've done everything that needs to be done. I hope. Now I just want to crawl away and die somewhere.'

'Not you, you've got too much spirit for that. How's your mother?'

Aura cast a harried look towards the bedroom door. 'Not well,' she admitted.

Jessica grimaced, then asked, 'What are you going to do?'

'I'm going to find a job,' Aura told her.

'Doing what?'

Aura shrugged. 'Doing anything that gets me a hell of a lot of money.'

To her horror the tears she had been able to hold back until then flooded her eyes. She sniffed, but they continued to fall.

'What's she done now?' Jessica asked in an outraged voice, hugging her close as she stuffed a wad of tissues into her hand.

In as few words as possible, Aura told her

Jessica said on an appalled note, 'Your great-grandmother's garnets? Oh, Aura—'

'Yes, but they weren't enough. Not nearly enough.'

'So you need money, and you need it fast. Can't you borrow it against the value of this unit? Just temporarily? Because that software thingy you've been working on is going to sell for megabucks when you finish it.'

'If I ever do. I had to sell the computer, too. And the unit's no good. It's mortgaged.'

Jessica looked her horror. 'How's she going to make the payments?'

'She can't.' Aura drew in a shaking breath and firmed her voice. 'Neither can I. If I could get an uninterrupted three months I could finish the marketing research programme. I'd have to hire a computer, of course.'

'And of course you can't get an uninterrupted three months, either.'

'No, and even if I do, it's not going to mean instant money, and that, Jess, is what I need. Because if I don't get it, I can't pay the interest, let alone any principal, on the loan. And you know what that means. This place will be sold over our heads.'

Jessica snorted. 'Even if you do get some money or a job, what about your mother then? Is she going to be able to cope, or are you going to be mortgaging your life to bale her out, time and time again?'

Aura's mouth tightened. 'She'll just have to learn to live within her income. Damn it, Jess, it's not as though she's poverty-stricken. She has a small income—bloody Lionel couldn't dip his sticky fingers into her trust. My grandfather set it up too tightly. The only reason he got into mine was because she and my father were trustees, and she signed everything over to Lionel when she married him. She should be able to manage!'

'Yes, but she's never had to watch her spending.'

'Oh, damn my grandfather.'

'You can't blame him entirely,' Jessica pointed out, exasperation vying with a need to be fair. 'He may have started her off wrong, but she's had a good few years to grow up. She didn't *have* to let Lionel run through everything you both had. She could have taken some interest in her own affairs.'

Aura sighed and frowned and rubbed her forehead. 'I know. She's just going to have to learn how to deal with life.'

Jessica looked at her keenly. 'It's about time. You've played nursemaid for long enough. Look, I might be able to do something about this. I can't promise anything—'

'I'm too short to be a model,' Aura said, blowing her nose with vigour and feeling oddly better.

'Yes, but you've got fabulous legs and hands and face, and wonderful skin and hair, so you should be able to do well with those, and God knows, the camera adores you. Remember, in our school photos the rest of us invariably looked like gargoyles, but there you were, always exquisite. It used to make us all sick. As it happens, there's a big cosmetics firm that's going to make a push for the Pacific market, and they want a local model, somebody from here or Australia, but a woman with exotic looks who'll be suitable for the Asian market too.'

'I can't model.'

'Oh, of course you can. All you have to do is swan around looking glamorous, and you do that instinctively. You'd wing it, no problem, if they decided you were the one. They're being rather fussy, but you're interesting, and you're new, which they're rather keen on, and you'd certainly show off their stuff. You've got those wonderful eyes, and perfect cheekbones, and a mouth that might have been made to show off lipstick.'

'Jess, I know you mean well, but I've—'

'Don't say no yet. Look, it's not going to take much time. You'll be working like hell for six months or so all around the Pacific, but then it will be finished. You could send your CV around and apply for a proper job next year. It would get you out of New Zealand until the heat dies off, and it would certainly tip your bank balance the right way.'

It sounded seductive, but Aura couldn't make a decision yet. Vaguely she said, 'I'll see.'

'What you need,' Jessica said firmly, 'is time out.'

Aura smiled sardonically. 'Not a chance of it, I'm afraid.'

But that evening Laurel and Alick came along, offering her just that: as long as she liked at Kerikeri, or anywhere else for that matter.

Aura smiled. She had become very good at hiding her emotions behind a mask. 'You're so kind,' she said, 'but would you mind very much if I said no? Honestly, I'm not feeling madly social at the moment.'

Alick began to say something but Laurel broke in firmly. 'Of course we understand,' she said, 'but Natalie, you'll come up, won't you? It's been a while since we've had you there, and you really do need a change of scenery.'

Natalie sighed, and wept a little, and without looking at Aura agreed that a small holiday might be just what she needed, although of course she really adored the tropics at this time of year, and the fares to Fiji were so low right now...

When neither Laurel nor Alick reacted to this blatant attempt at manipulation she gave in with a good grace.

Aura felt as though a load had rolled from her mind. As Laurel and Alick left she gave them both a fierce hug and whispered her thanks.

'It's not too late to change your mind,' Alick said, returning the embrace. 'We'd love to have you, and the kids adore their cousin Aura.'

Aura shook her head. 'I adore them, too, but—not just now.'

Ten o'clock the next morning saw her waving them away in Alick's big car. On her way up the path her nose traced a faint, sweet smell. It was a tiny gold narcissus shaped just like a miniature hoop petticoat, blooming in the border she had weeded only a fortnight before. A fortnight before, when she had been going to become Paul's wife.

Perhaps it was a little omen, a promise that however bleak her days, hope was never lost.

Hope seemed to have become very much mislaid, however, in the days that followed. Aura missed Paul. She missed him alarmingly, missed his pleasant temperament, his humour, his never-failing thoughtfulness. But she missed Flint with a hunger that ate deep into her bones, a desire almost physical in its intensity that coloured her days and darkened her nights with an ever-present ache of loneliness.

She didn't love him, not as she loved Paul, but some part of her was bereft.

Lust. An ugly word for an ugly emotion, if emotion it was. She wanted Flint, longed for the sensual pleasures he could give her, and despised herself for this obsession, because she didn't like him. She could respect his strength, admit his good qualities, appreciate his cold, hard intellect, but the man himself meant nothing to her.

On the day that was to have been her wedding she stayed at home. Jessica tried to persuade her to spend the weekend with her and Sam, but Aura refused, just as she refused Laurel's telephoned plea to go up to Kerikeri. Deliberately emptying her mind, she went about her chores racked with regret, with remorse and self-disgust.

During that weekend she made the decision to give Jessica's plan a try. Delighted, Jessica was immediately all business; she gave her the address of a photographer and introduced her to her partner, an alarmingly beautiful woman in her mid-thirties who Aura had met a couple of times before.

Apparently she approved. Eight days after she had handed in her portfolio Aura found herself ringing Alick for the name of his lawyer.

'What do you want a lawyer for?' he asked after he'd given it.

'Mind your own business,' she said automatically.

'I made you my business twenty years ago.'

She was already regretting her curtness. 'Sorry.'

When she had finished telling him he said, 'Hm. Are you sure you want to do it? I can lend you any money you need, you know.'

'I know, but it's time I stopped relying on you.'

'Well, don't let your pride stand in the way of common sense. By the way, Natalie's been prospecting up here, and unless I'm reading things wrong, she's getting her own future sorted out.'

'A man, I gather.' Aura hid the note of hope in her voice with dryness.

He laughed. 'Yes, a nice rich Canadian who thinks she's wonderful.'

Oh, if only it happened! Aura said guiltily, 'I hope he knows what he's doing.'

'I think he does. Don't worry about him, Aura, and don't worry about your mother, either. She'll fall on her feet.'

Life suddenly became at once simpler, and infinitely more complicated. The company and the agency took over her life. She met executives, got used to being looked at and discussed as though she were a piece of merchandise, attended a modelling course, and discovered that photographic sessions involved a lot of hard work and boredom.

At least she no longer had to worry about Natalie's debts. The money she received as an advance paid them off, and, following Alick's advice not to let pride stand in her way, she borrowed enough from him to keep herself going until the next payment was due.

Two months later she was in Cairns, posing against a swimming-pool in sunlight so bright she was glad it was just her legs they were photographing and not her face. This session was for sunscreens and moisturising lotions, and it was going well, as was the campaign.

It still surprised her that she, ordinary Aura Forsythe, photographed like a houri. Originally the job had been a means to an end, but now she was determined to give her employers value for the indecent amount of money they were paying her. At first she had worried about whether she could actually do the work, and been heartily relieved when word came back that they were delighted with the shots so far.

The actual work she still found dull, but fortunately the camera lens transformed her boredom into a profoundly seductive glower. She enjoyed the travel, and she liked the crew she was working with.

She should have been happy. Especially here, in Australia's tropical north, a place she'd always wanted to visit.

When the first day's work was finished she relaxed for a moment in the coolness of the hotel foyer. She had just tilted her head against the white cane back of the chair when she heard his voice.

'Thank you, that's all.'

Of course she was hallucinating, if you could do that with voices. It wasn't the first time this had happened; she had quite often 'seen' Flint, only to discover that the man bore no real resemblance beyond the most obvious aspects of height and build and colouring.

Fortunately for her sanity few men were as tall as Flint, or possessed his breadth of shoulder. Few had hair that exact shade of brown bordering on auburn; few moved with his lean ranginess and lethal power-packed grace, and even fewer had his unpressured, commanding air.

So she opened her eyes to prove herself wrong, and there he was, checking in at Reception. No other man had such a forceful profile, or a scar curling sinisterly down his tanned cheek. He towered over everyone else in the foyer, reducing them to nothingness, his hard-honed masculinity barely trammelled by the lightweight tropical suit he wore.

Aura's heart stopped. She didn't breathe, couldn't move; he had come, he had found her!

When he turned and casually scanned the foyer Aura almost sagged with pain, because clearly he hadn't known she was there. For a moment astonishment flared in the golden eyes, until he reimposed control and they turned to quartz, clear and depthless.

She was not going to fall apart, she was not going to make a fool of herself. It took all of her willpower, every tiny spark of it, to force herself to nod as he walked towards her, to stretch her lips in a smile.

'Aura,' he said with as little emotion in his tone as in his eyes.

The sound of her name on his lips gave her more pleasure than a hundred of the photographer's easy compliments. She inclined a serene, composed face towards him. A couple of months assuming expressions in front of the camera had given her much more confidence in her ability to hide her thoughts.

'Hello, Flint. What are you doing in Cairns?'

'Business,' he said briefly. He stood looking down at her with hooded eyes.

Several women passed in a laughing, chattering group, their glances flashing from one to the other, lingering on his impassive features. Aura had to fight the desire to send them on their way with a few scathing words.

'Has something gone wrong in Robertsons' operation here?' she asked lightly, wondering whether he could hear the intensity behind her words.

'Something did, but it's all right now.' He sat down opposite her. 'What are you doing?'

She shrugged, and told him.

'Modelling?' He didn't try to hide his surprise. 'You have the face for it, but I thought you had to be six feet tall and built like a greyhound.'

'I'm modelling for a range of cosmetics. All they need is a face and legs and skin,' she told him casually.

His brows lifted. 'Are you enjoying it?'

'It's a living.'

'I imagine you'd be very good at it,' he said, and it wasn't a compliment.

Her answering smile was ironic. 'Thank you,' she said sweetly.

Nothing had changed. He still thought she was nothing but a money-grubbing little opportunist, out for what she could get. No doubt he considerd modelling to be another way of selling herself.

'How long are you here for?'

She said, 'Another day. You?'

'I'm leaving tomorrow morning.' He smiled, and his eyes glinted as they slowly searched her face. 'Have dinner with me tonight,' he said.

Of course she should refuse, and of course she didn't. She might not love him, not as she loved Paul, but instead of being weakened by absence the strange, physical enchantment that imprisoned them both in its unseen snare had strengthened into an unholy sorcery. She could taste her need on her tongue, feel it throb through every cell in her body.

'I'll meet you in the bar at seven,' he said, getting to his feet in one smooth motion.

Although convinced that she might just have made the greatest mistake in her life, Aura nodded.

Back in her room she looked at herself, and sighed. Her eyes were brilliant and huge in her face, the pupils dilated into wildness. Even her lips seemed to have altered, grown soft and hungrily sultry.

She had learned ways of putting on cosmetics that dramatised her physical assets, and after she showered she used them, outlining her eyes with subtle precision, colouring her mouth carefully. Her hair she swept up to give her a bit more height; she picked a frangipani flower from the floating bowl in her bathroom and tucked it into the swirl on top of her head, pleased that the satiny petals with their golden throat contrasted effectively with its burgundy lights.

She chose a plain dress the exact colour of her eyes, letting its soft draping do all the emphasising necessary. When she was ready she surveyed her reflection in the mirror. She looked a different woman from the one who had been engaged to Paul; she looked—glamorous, she thought with a faint smile. Almost decadent.

The hotel was small, elegantly making the most of its location on a tropical lagoon, much of the public area open to the warm, fragrant air. Before she reached the lifts she stopped and looked out across the fairy lights in the exquisite, palm-haunted garden. Unknown, sensual perfumes floated on the sultry air. Excitement bubbled within her, keen and poignant.

She was not naïve enough to believe in any future for them. He didn't love her, just as she didn't love him. But they were both free agents.

He was waiting for her in the bar, but so, unfortunately, were the rest of the photographic crew. They waved; Aura smiled and waved back, but headed steadily towards Flint.

Getting to his feet, he gave her a narrowed, unsmiling look. 'Do you want to join your friends?' he asked.

'If you want to meet them it's all right by me.'

'Not particularly.' His voice was indifferent to the point of rudeness. He waited until she had sat down before saying, 'What would you like to drink?'

'Dry white wine, please.'

'You won't get New Zealand whites here, but if you'll trust me I should be able to find you one you'll like.'

'Yes, of course I trust you.'

It sounded oddly like a vow, a promise. He gave the order to the waiter who had appeared the instant Flint looked up—he had that effect on waiters—then sat back and looked her over.

'You look different,' he said, the rasp in his voice more blatant. 'It's amazing, but you're even more beautiful than you were when I saw you last.'

The beginnings of a blush stained Aura's cheeks. 'Tricks of the trade,' she said dismissively. 'It's amazing what you can do with cosmetics.'

'Then I suppose I should be flattered that you took the time to use them, but I can remember seeing you with no make-up on at all, and you were just as stunningly beautiful.'

The blush heated into a fullblown wave of colour. He laughed quietly, and as the drinks arrived changed the subject, slipping with polished ease into an approximation of the pleasant chit-chat of old friends. Picking up her glass, Aura noted that he had ordered the same wine for himself, and sipped the delicately flavoured liquid with interest.

'How long have you been here?' she asked. He had been right about the wine—it was delicious; but then wine was clearly his hobby as well as his future.

'I got here at the crack of dawn this morning.'

Aura lifted her lashes. 'You keep long hours.' Not a hint of desolation, of anger because he hadn't contacted her, of the pain his defection had caused, disturbed the calmness of her voice.

Something of the forceful assurance of the man showed through for a moment. 'It's part of the job. In this case somebody panicked over nothing so I had very little to do. How long have you been here?'

'A day.'

'Where do you go when you've finished with Cairns? Back to Auckland?'

'Bali,' she said. 'I believe I have to pose draped over a water buffalo, and then wade through a rice paddy or two.'

'Be careful of water buffaloes, they don't like Westerners' smell.' He gave a white, ironic smile. 'There are some truly impressive rice paddies there. Whole hills, mountains almost, terraced by heaven knows how many people over the centuries.'

Aura, who had travelled very little, envied him his experience, although, she thought fleetingly, she didn't envy the cynicism that hardened his eyes, or the lines it had bracketed on either side of his mouth. Not that they detracted from his appeal; in a strange way they added to it.

He didn't talk about his job at all, but they drifted from scenery into politics, and she realised that he had a grasp of the inner workings of many other countries that could only come from an insider's understanding.

They had never sat like this, just talking, ignoring the blazing pull of the senses. She enjoyed it very much. Paul rarely discussed politics with her; he said that he spent all day thinking, he wanted to relax his brain when he came home. Aura had thought this entirely natural. Until that moment she hadn't realised how much she had missed the ebb and flow of conversation, the exhilaration of sharpening her wits against others equally keen.

When at last the wine was finished, he said, 'I thought you might like to go to a restaurant a few miles away in the rainforest. The food is superb, and the place itself is interesting.'

'It sounds lovely.'

They went by taxi, drawing up outside a two storeyed building, the upper floor supported by massive wooden columns. Beside the steps great pots stood, some with plants burgeoning in them, most empty, their superb shapes and glazes harmonising with the building and the setting. Creepers festooned down, flaunting brilliant flowers in a variety of forms and hues. Plants with monstrous foliage, huge leaves cut and slashed into a myriad shapes, added to the tropical ambience, the air of other-wordliness. Around them the trees of the rainforest pressed closely.

'It's like a jungle hideaway,' Aura exclaimed in delight.

'I think that's the impression the owners wanted to achieve.'

Until that moment Flint hadn't touched her, but he took her elbow as they climbed the steps, and the touch of those lean fingers sent a feverish tremor up her arm and straight to her heart.

She sent him a swift sideways look. What would it be like to live with him, to share the mundane things of life, a bathroom, breakfast, weeding the garden, washing the dishes? Heaven, she thought hollowly. It would be heaven.

The restaurant was small, the tables rough-hewn wood; the chairs, however, were extremely comfortable, and the food, a marvellous combination of South-East Asian flavours with European, wonderful.

Over dinner they talked of everything, of books, of films, their likings in art. Yet although she was singingly happy, almost exalted, Aura hungered for more personal subjects; she wanted to know so much about him, things he had no intention of revealing.

Crushing the useless, wishful need, she set out to enjoy this evening, because this was all she would ever have of him: dinner in this restaurant, his conversation, and the hidden yet compelling tug of attraction that seemed to be binding her ever tighter, ever more helplessly, in its coils.

'How *did* you get that scar?' she asked over coffee, spinning out the time.

He gave her a sardonic look. 'When I was fifteen I was

carrying a coil of number eight fencing wire across a paddock. A hen pheasant flew up from under my feet. I tripped, and the wire-end caught my cheek.'

Aura grinned, her eyes glinting mischievously. He laughed, wryly amused.

'It looks very piratical,' she said. Perhaps it was the wine, or perhaps just the magic of the evening, but now she was bold enough to follow with her forefinger the thin line from his cheekbone to the sharper angle of his jaw. As her finger quested down it tingled at the slight abrasion of his beard and the heat of his skin.

Eyes gleaming, he waited until she had reached the end, then pressed his hand over hers and kissed her palm, his tongue tracing the slight indentation of her life line.

Silently he asked a question. Colour heated her cheeks. Silently she answered it. He put her hand down and looked across the room, summoning the waiter.

Without speaking she sat beside him as the taxi drove through the sweet darkness to the hotel. She waited while he paid the taxi off, went with him into the foyer of the hotel and across to the lifts. There were a couple of other people in their car, so they didn't speak until they were in the corridor.

'I have a suite. I think we'll be more comfortable there,' he said.

Aura froze. For a moment her brain balked, scraps of thoughts floating through it.

Oh, I want to—he'll think me a slut—he already thinks I wanted to marry Paul for his money...

'Yes, all right,' she said composedly.

Nothing, she thought with a bleak humour that surprised her, could be as wonderful as she imagined making love with Flint to be, so it was bound to disappoint her. And then, perhaps, she'd be able to get on with her life and find a man she both loved and wanted.

His face impassive, Flint unlocked his door, then stood back to let her go through.

Already Aura was regretting her decision, but the reasons for making it still held. She was tired of being bound on the rack of her own desires. She wanted to sate them, and by exhausting them be free once more.

His room was bigger than hers. Neater, too. Apart from a briefcase set beside the desk there was no sign of his presence. A half open door on the far wall revealed a huge bed.

'Would you like something to drink?' he asked.

She shook her head. The frangipani blossom in her hair fell to the floor, and she stooped to pick it up, holding the warm thing in the palm of her hand. 'I don't really want a drink,' she said under her breath.

'What do you want?' His voice was just as quiet.

Aura's fingers contracted and the flower was crushed, although its fragrance lingered on her skin. Turning, she dropped it into a wastepaper basket.

'Must I spell it out?' she asked in a low voice.

'No.' He came up behind her, and took her shoulders in his hands, drawing her back against his chest. The curtains weren't drawn so she could see their reflections in the glass, she small and pale in contrast to the wide shoulders of the man who held her, his darkly intent face turned, as was hers, to the window.

The slow movement of his thumbs over the slender bones of her shoulder, the soft warmth of his breath stirring the tendrils of hair, the heat and promise of strength that emanated from the lean graceful body behind her—all joined to set strange tides pulsing through her.

'Why?' he asked levelly.

Her shoulders lifted in the smallest of shrugs. 'Why did you ask me? Does it matter?'

'No, I suppose not. We both knew we had unfinished

business together.' He turned her and looked down into her face with unveiled appreciation, his eyes pure flame.

Aura felt that look burn through her, so that the old Aura, the woman who hadn't understood that passion could be a living force, sloughed away like a paper skin, curling and twisting into the unquiet past. She had never before felt so much part of a moment, so vividly, hectically aware of this moment, this man, this room.

'You are so beautiful,' he said levelly. 'You tear my heart out, do you know that? I look at you, and I'm unmanned, a supplicant at the gate of your beauty. Are you going to let me in, Aura?'

His words affected her so powerfully that she couldn't speak. There was nothing personal in his desire, merely a detached male hunger for beauty, the need to make it his, to assume command over it and by doing so lessen its impact.

But that was what she wanted, too. That was why she was there. His simple, stark statement of passion shook her as florid protestations could never do. Appalled and excited in equal parts by his honesty, she nodded. By satisfying his desire and hers she could at least give him something, although it wouldn't be the one thing she wanted to give him. He wouldn't take her love.

For of course this passionate attraction she had so despised was not just lust. It was love. She loved this man as she had never loved Paul. Paul had been the answer the lonely, forsaken child in her had sought, the man who would be loyal and never leave her, never let her be lonely and unsure again.

What she felt for Flint so far surpassed that need to be protected that the two desires had nothing in common.

'Yes,' she said, and reached up her arms and brought his face down to meet hers, his mouth to touch hers.

For a moment he stood still, long enough for her to wonder whether he was so dominant that he needed to take the lead at all times. Then his arms tightened around her and she knew that she had been wrong. He kissed her with elemental, white-hot hunger, immediately taking advantage of her silent gasp to thrust deep and sensually into the sweet depths he found.

Her knees gave way, and still with his mouth on hers he picked her up and carried her through to the bed, tearing his mouth free only to bury his face in her throat for a moment. His eyes caught and held hers as he slid her down his body, revealing as nothing else could his state of arousal.

Aura gasped again, and his hard mouth tilted crookedly. 'You drive me insane,' he said roughly. 'No other woman has ever been able to make me hard just by looking at me. Do I do that to you, Aura, with your hair like a burgundy flame and your green, green eyes set like jewels in your black lashes?' His fingers found the hidden zip of her dress and worked it down. 'Does your body tighten, and your breath hurt your lungs, and your heart beat like a kettledrum in your ears?'

The dress came loose; he flipped it over her head and looked at the rich treasure revealed to him, smooth ivory curves of breast and waist and hips, the plane of her stomach with its seductive dimple, the narrow silk briefs that hindered further exploration.

Those intense, half-closed eyes surveyed her with intimate thoroughness, lingering on the rosy-apricot aureoles of her breasts until they hardened into tiny nubs, tiptilted, provocative. Wildfire zigzagged through her, uniting between the fork of her legs into a conflagration. She had never felt so exposed, so vulnerable, and she had never realised that she could enjoy such an experience.

'Undress me,' he said harshly.

No doubt it would have been more suitable to a virgin

if her fingers had trembled and been unable to undo the little buttons of his shirt, but they didn't. Swiftly, competently, they moved down crisp white material that was warm from his body heat, then pushed the sleeves back over his shoulders, pulling them down until the shirt dropped on to the floor.

Dry-mouthed, she stared at him. For the first time a hint of panic darkened her eyes. He was overwhelming, the male predator incarnate, with his wide bronze shoulders and chest where the hair curled in evocative patterns over smooth muscles, hinting at the disturbing, elemental power concealed there. Yet there was something intensely tantalising about him too. Aura touched the bold parabola of a muscle with her finger, then spread her hand to catch the heavy thud of his heart in her palm.

His skin was like oiled silk, warm and slightly clinging to her sensitive fingertips, smooth and sleek and potent. Aura leaned forward and applied the tip of her tongue to the spot she had touched. Beneath her hand she felt his pulse speed up; his chest lifted as he dragged air into his lungs. An oblique smile tilted her lips. Like a small cat she licked along the line of a muscle, tasting the musky, salty tang of aroused male, of Flint.

She half expected him to say something, to stop her, but he didn't move, held still by an effort she barely recognised.

'You taste—of heaven,' she said.

He laughed deep in his throat and said, 'And what do you taste of, I wonder?'

He lifted her, and stripped off the sleek silk briefs, then pushed his own clothes free. Aura's eyes dilated. She swallowed and stopped an involuntary gasp by sheer force of will. He was so big, and so—

She knew it was possible, but she didn't see how it could happen.

He must have realised the source of her sudden dismayed silence, for as he came down beside her he said quietly, 'We'll take it easy,' and before she could answer he lowered his head and kissed the tender upper curve of her breast. His mouth lingered, as though the taste of her skin excited him as much as his did her.

'Yes, you taste like the essence of woman,' he said against her skin. 'Sweeter than violets and more potent than brandy. You make me drunk.'

Aura's breath came hard and fast through lips already reddened by his kisses. More than anything she wanted to experience again the ecstasy of the moments in his apartment when he had touched her, and kissed her, and her whole being had risen to meet his.

CHAPTER SEVEN

BUT he was in no hurry. He held back, reimposing a fierce control over his emotions and actions, his hands moving slowly and tormentingly across her skin.

Outside a bird called from the lagoon, unknown, alien. Aura shivered as much with a sense of doom, of no going back, as with the wild pleasure that was coursing through her.

'You have a mouth made to kiss, made to crush, made for me,' he said softly, holding the weight of one breast in the palm of his hand. He looked at it with the awe and possessiveness of a man who holds infinite value in his grasp. 'And skin like ivory satin.'

Transfixed by the smouldering light in his eyes, she held her breath. He spoke a lover's words, yet they were not delivered in a lover's voice, and the look in his eyes was not tender.

Unease widened her eyes; then she gasped as he kissed a hard, tight little nipple, and taking it into the warm cavity of his mouth suckled strongly.

Sensation, swift and heated as fire, smooth and sweet as honey, shot through her. She closed her eyes, unable to cope with the feelings he aroused, unable to watch his mouth work its primal magic, unable to bear the contrast between the blunt angles of his dark face and the smooth pale curves of her body.

Utterly ravished by need, she sighed his name.

'Touch me,' he said against the curve of her breast, taking her hand and holding it over his heart.

She explored him as he explored her, amazed afresh at

the polished swell of muscles that flexed in response to her tentative hands. Each touch, each caress, each new step on the voyage of discovery added to the last, extended the next, until in the end his fingers slid carefully down and discovered her secret core, eager and hot, awaiting him.

Aura's lashes flew up. His heavy-lidded gaze was fixed on her face in a scrutiny that held all the old watchfulness. If she winced, or tensed, he would wonder why, and perhaps guess.

And that would be the finish. He didn't want a virgin in his bed, he wanted a woman with experience, a woman who could match his expertise. She couldn't give him that, but she would give him something she could only surrender once.

She turned her head into his chest, and delicately bit at the tight nubbin she found there. A deep breath expanded his chest, then his hand slipped a little further, sending shivers of delight through her. His thumb moved, found the centre of pleasure, and she shuddered.

'Yes, you want me,' he said softly. 'How much do you want me, Aura?'

She lifted weighted lashes and said on a sigh, 'More than anything.'

'More than anything?' He laughed and turned away.

For a horrified moment she assumed he was rejecting her as he had before. Even as she formulated the thought she realised what he was doing. There would be no unwanted child from this mating.

Seconds later, one sure movement brought him over her completely, the powerful body, beautiful in its uncompromising masculinity poised, gathering strength, until he said harshly, 'Now,' and took her in a single powerful thrust that pressed smoothly home.

Later she would think that the first moment of possession changed her fundamentally; at the time, she was so anxious in case he found some evidence of her virginity that she didn't really appreciate what had happened. But after that moment of union he stopped, almost as though he waited for her to do something.

As Aura's wondering eyes, dilated and languorous, almost afraid, took in his clenched jaw and stark bone-structure, she realised two things: he was fighting for control, and in the silken sheath that surrounded him there was no betraying impediment. She was able to relax, and the responses her anxiety had blocked out roared back into her consciousness,.

A feeling of fullness, of completeness, was strengthened by a return of the overpowering excitement he had coaxed from her with his expert manipulation of her body. She stretched languidly, acutely conscious of his immediate, quickly leashed reaction. A desire to show him that he couldn't control everything led her to move her hips experimentally.

'No,' he said harshly.

'Why?' Her voice was quiet in the quiet room, slow and deep and husky. 'Don't you like it?'

He gave an odd groan. 'I like it too much. No, damn you, don't! If you want me to be any good for you, just lie still.'

She tried, but as he moved, establishing a leisurely rhythm of advance and withdrawal as the scent of their lovemaking and the tactile delight of skin against skin, as his skill and strength fanned the flames of passion, a disturbance rioted through her, carrying her into an unknown region where all that mattered was reaching some unattainable objective.

Racked by a feverish need to know, a consuming hunger, taken over by something greater than anything she had ever experienced before, Aura was heedless of everything but the mindless, sugar-sweet tide of delight that raced through her and the beloved weight pressing her loins into the bed, the slow penetration of her innermost secrets.

Until that moment she had never thought of herself as passionate; she had believed her sultry face and slender body were at bewildering variance with her nature. But now, locked in the most primal embrace of all, giving with all her heart and body, taking just as eagerly, she was forced to accept that these frenzied moments when the dark fire built higher and higher, when every sense was sharpened to an acuity almost painful, were what she had been born for.

She looked up at the man above her and inside her, crying out with pleasure because she was not the only one in thrall to this consuming, primal heat.

Flint's skin was drawn tight over the fierce bone structure of his face, beads of sweat stood out across his brow; his mouth was hard, almost snarling as he muttered, 'Aura, I can't—dear God—'

The slow, almost teasing movements of his body were suddenly transmuted into fierce thrusts. His head jerked back, and as she watched, her pleasure immeasurably heightened by his, tension snapped inside her, flinging her through waves of ecstasy into a rapturous present that had no beginning and no end, into a place where she was stripped to her barest essentials, where this violent and elemental sensation was all that mattered.

He groaned her name, and his body tightened and she was pierced by wonder and awe when the ripples of her own climax swept back up into waves to meet his and match it.

She heard her voice, shook to the beat of her heart, and thought she might die of pleasure. And then he collapsed, the tension in the long muscles slackened, the proud body at last brought low by satiation.

Aura lay in his arms, holding him in her turn like a

precious burden. Very slowly, so slowly that there was never a moment when she first realised it, she discovered that it didn't really matter that this man who lay breathing deeply in her arms, his heart thundering against hers, who had possessed her in a way transcending the physical...that this man was more dangerous to her than the tiger she saw in him could ever be. She could never trust his loyalty, nor that he would always be around for her. But she loved him.

She had fought a valiant action against that love, clinging to her childhood need for stability, longing to be protected and cared for, longing for a father. It was strange how the wildness inside her had known better than she did what she needed. Something in Flint's lawless character had chimed with hers.

A small, replete smile touched a mouth softly swollen by his kisses. Aura was overwhelmed by an ecstasy that had little to do with the physical satisfaction enfolding her body in such lethargic pleasure. So this, she thought wonderingly, was what it felt like to love, to be helpless before its power.

It was as far removed from the affection she had felt for Paul as an eagle was from a sparrow. It was magnificent, and yet it was mundane too; she wanted to live with Flint, to see him in the morning when he was unshaven and the sexy roughness of his voice was transformed by the night's disuse to a rasp, to laugh with him over something small and insignificant, but important because it was part of their shared life. She wanted to argue with him and love him and look after him, and be looked after in her turn.

It didn't even seem to matter that he felt nothing like this for her.

She turned her head, her heart melting at his closed eyes, the relaxed contours of his face. She had done this for him. The long lashes quivered, and slowly lifted to reveal golden eyes as cool and enigmatic as the transparent heart of a crystal.

'I must weigh a ton,' he said, and eased himself over on to his back.

She wanted to cry out, but a strong arm swept her close and held her with her arm across his lean waist, her cheek on his chest.

The lights glimmered against the perfumed darkness outside. Wrapped in a contentment so profound it seemed like Nirvana, Aura lay against the man she had learned too late she would give her life for, and let her mind drift.

Before long she was asleep.

She woke some time before dawn, but it wasn't the lightening sky that woke her, or the songs of birds she had never heard before. It was the gentle touch of Flint's hand on her breast, and the sound of his quickening breath in the quiet room.

She said drowsily, 'Flint?'

'Who did you think it might be? No, don't tell me.' His voice was husky, and his caress became a statement of possession. Almost before she had time to react he bent his head and kissed her answer from her mouth. 'You look so rare and precious and exquisite in my bed,' he said against her lips.

Fighting the instant leap in her blood, Aura levered her eyelids upwards. He was an outline in the dim room, the sloping line of his shoulders blocking out most of the faint light that filtered through the pavilion of mosquito net shutting them off from the world. Again she was awed by his size, and then heartened by memories, for last night they had fitted perfectly, her smallness taking him and enveloping him as if it had been meant.

It was going to happen again; she could sense his determination with her skin, with the infinitesimal receptors that had once been of use in the days when humans had no language.

'Aura?' he murmured.

She drew a shallow breath and said, 'Yes.'

It was answer enough.

There was no repeat of the passionate, almost frenzied haste of the night before. This time he touched her confidently, and the slow progress of his hands over her skin sent imperative messages to the melting centre of her passion. It was different because she knew what he could do to her, she knew what was to come, and instead of dulling her expectation the knowledge increased it.

This time, made bold by recollection, she was more forward, discovering with lazy, sleepy excitement that his skin pulled taut beneath her questing strokes, that when she bit gently at his shoulders he shivered.

Natalie believed that men were far more interested in sex than women; she said it was one of the things women had to put up with in exchange for security and companionship. A child of her time, Aura had read magazines and books and knew with the logical part of her mind that this was not so, that making love should be equally pleasurable for both sexes.

But it had taken Flint's passionate overwhelming of her defences last night to convince her emotionally. Now that she knew it was true, she prepared to abandon herself to her senses, to explore and enjoy his body as he so clearly did hers. Investigating him with a cold candour, she ranged over his sleek hide with a murmurous delight in all the things that were different.

She sensed that he wasn't accustomed to being touched quite so familiarly, and her fingers stilled.

But he said, 'No, don't stop.'

'You are so beautiful,' she said, turning her face into his flat stomach.

It expanded as he laughed. 'That's the first time anyone's used that term for me.'

She tasted the skin there, nibbling along a rib until he pushed her mouth away and pulled her up to kiss it.

'Now you,' he said quietly against her lips, '*you're* beautiful, but you know that, don't you. Other men have told you often enough. Have they told you that when you smile your eyes gleam, and you have a maddening way of lowering your lashes?'

'No,' she said, as his mouth roved the smooth length of her throat.

'Nobody? What a hopeless set. You were made for love, Aura. Your breasts fit into a man's hands as though they had been made for him, and whenever I look at those amazing legs I imagine them wrapped around me, holding me tightly, and my whole body clenches. But the reality is so much more spectacular than all my imaginings.'

For the first time since she was fourteen she didn't shrink with a cold nausea at the thought of being part of a man's fantasies. The sound of Flint's gravelly voice sent her pulses careering, banished forever the taint that one man's perversion had imprinted on her memory.

'Your palms have an innocent, unprotected look,' he murmured, 'just like the insides of your elbows. As for that tormenting place where your neck meets your shoulders, and the little hollow in your throat, and...'

He kissed each place he mentioned, stroked across heated skin with slow fingers, tantalising her with the contrast between his rough voice and his gentle touch, his blazing sexuality and the intense restraint that fettered it.

Desire burned with metallic lustre in his eyes, captured his mouth and forced it into a straight line. Although he continued to drug her with dark words of passion his lips hardly moved, yet his hands shook.

And when she kissed him, when she touched him in her

turn, she could see the involuntary secret imprint of her fingers, her mouth, on his skin, in the building heat that scorched through them both.

When at last he groaned, 'I want you—Aura, I want you *now*,' she was eagerly compliant—no, there was nothing of compliance in the way she moved, inciting him, tormenting in her turn, moving over him so that he lay beneath her like a sacrificial victim, bronzed skin gleaming with a faint dew of sweat that would mingle with hers.

'Now?' she said, and before he had time to answer, she slid over him, taking him into her.

It didn't hurt, but for a second she froze, her eyes dilated, her body thrumming like a guitar-string with sensations so acute she thought she might faint.

'Aura—'

She couldn't stay still. The fire in her blood hurtled her along a path of unhindered eroticism; she lowered her face to kiss his hard mouth, burgundy hair falling like a warm curtain of silk around his face, and with a skill that was new and untried gave herself up to an innocent, sweet carnality.

When it was over she thought dazedly that she had never expected it to be like that. People tried to describe it, but there were no words, no ways...

She yawned, and he laughed. 'Got to sleep,' he said deeply.

Aura didn't think she could ever sleep again, but she did, while outside the dawn sky lightened into the warmth of a tropical winter, and the man beneath her lay with his arms around her slender form and his eyes wide open, staring at the ceiling.

The dream started innocuously. She was laughing up at Paul, her ring winking on her finger, while they were dancing to a Strauss waltz. 'The Blue Danube'.

'It isn't blue, of course,' Paul told her, smiling. 'The

Danube is really a muddy brown,' and then he tripped, and she realised that there was a hole in the floor, a hole that got bigger, with Paul teetering on the edge of it, a hole that ate through the floorboards and became a black pit where things gibbered and waited.

Paul's face was distorted with terror; he called her name, and she clung, trying to hold him back from the pit. In the background the band continued to play, and everyone else danced sedately around the edges, ignoring the pit and the dreadful things waiting there and Paul's struggles, even though he was trembling on the brink.

Aura couldn't scream; whimpering, she tried to drag him free, but he slid through her fingers and inexorably into the darkness, and she called desperately, 'Paul, don't go—Paul, hang on—Paul Paul Paul Paul...'

But someone was shaking her, someone was hauling her away, and as she struggled, Paul disappeared into the darkness, his eyes fixed despairingly on her, and she burst into harsh sobs that tore her to pieces.

'Wake up! Aura, stop it, you're having a nightmare!'

She opened desperate eyes. After a horrified moment they focused on Flint's face. She heard Paul's name dying on her lips, echoing in the quiet room.

'It's all right,' Flint said, and tried to pull her into his arms, but she huddled away against the pillow, holding herself rigid.

Something bleak moved in the depths of his eyes, but he said evenly, 'It was just a dream, Aura. A nightmare. I'll get you a drink.'

Shuddering, she tried to dispel the lingering miasma of the nightmare. By the time he came back from the bathroom with a glass of water she had almost succeeded. With one hand she pushed tangled hair back from her face, with the other she clutched the glass. Her teeth chattered, but she managed to drink the water down without spilling it.

He took the glass from her, flicked away the cloud of netting and sat down on the side of the bed. Now, when it was too late, she wanted him to hold her, to convince her that she had nothing to fear, but she couldn't make the first move. He was distant, wrapped in a remoteness she couldn't penetrate.

'All right now?' he asked her.

Not trusting her voice, she nodded.

'Do you get them often?'

'No.' It came out creaky, but at least it was usable. She hesitated, then said, 'It's the first time it's ever happened to me.'

'And no prizes for telling what caused it.'

She bit her lip, because of course she knew what had brought it on. Her unconscious mind was accusing her of the betrayal she had committed. Making love with Paul's best friend had been the final straw.

'I'm all right,' she said, staring down at the sheet, keeping her gaze there by sheer force of will because she couldn't bear to look at his calm, reasonable expression.

'I didn't realise you were so badly affected by—the break-up.' His voice was steady, uninflected.

She shook her head. 'It doesn't matter now. It's over.'

'It's clearly not over for you,' he said, still in that same impersonal tone.

She sat mutely as he got to his feet and went across to the window. A swift, angry movement of one strong brown hand looped back the thin curtains. That hand, and her memories of what it had done to her during the night, made Aura flush, warmed her a little against the misery of the dream. But their lovemaking now seemed just as unreal as the images her mind had called up from the pit of her secret fears.

It meant nothing to Flint but the appeasing of an appetite; he had told her that she was beautiful, told her what her beauty did to him, but he hadn't spoken a word that could be construed to be loving.

Aura looked away. Outside the world was flooded with heat and light, but there was grey desolation in her heart, a disillusion as heavy and foreboding as the bleakest thundercloud.

'I'd better get back to my room,' she said drearily, struggling to her feet and looking about for her clothes.

He said, 'What are you going to do?' There was nothing but an impersonal concern in his voice.

Aura couldn't wait to get away. As she climbed into her clothes she said, very fast, 'Go on to Bali, and then back home.'

'Will you be seeing Paul?'

Her fingers stilled on the catch of her bra. She looked over to where he stood looking out the window. The bluntly arrogant outline of his profile was etched against the soft blue wall; the sun summoned copper lights from his hair. He was a glowing statue in the tropical light, with all a statue's warmth.

'No,' she said, shivering.

'It's probably just as well.'

Desperate to get away, she pulled her dress over her head and stuffed her stockings into her handbag, sliding arched bare feet into high-heeled sandals.

'Goodbye,' she said bleakly, heading for the door.

He looked at her then. For a hopeful moment Aura searched his unyielding features, then turned away, welcoming the numb acceptance that replaced the aching loneliness. In his face, in his eyes, there was nothing but guarded detachment, as though he expected her to make a fuss.

Pride stiffened her back, brought a smile to her pale lips. 'Aura—'

The smile solidified, but was maintained. 'It was good.

Let's leave it like that,' she said, opening the door and closing it behind her with a sharp, final click.

Fortunately there was no one else in the corridor. Back in her room she showered, but even as the water washed away his scent from her body, and toothpaste banished his taste from her mouth, she knew that what had happened the night before had been irrevocable. For him it might only be a one-night stand, but for her it had been commitment. In the most basic way of all, she felt that he belonged to her just as she now belonged to him.

The white towel clung not unpleasantly to her body. At least, she thought wearily, I don't have to worry much about being pregnant.

He had taken care of that both times.

Bali was hot, and the water buffalo didn't want anything to do with her, only reluctantly yielding to its master's determinaton. The emerald paddy fields were truly monuments to the skill of generations of men.

At any other time Aura would have enjoyed it. As it was, she went through the motions wrapped in a grey fog of despair that fortunately translated on film to a look of exotic sensuality.

When she got back to Auckland it was still raining, and there had clearly been no one in the unit for some time. Sighing, because Natalie had been in Kerikeri too often these last months, she rang Alick's phone number.

Laurel answered, her cool voice warming when she heard Aura's greeting. 'How was Cairns?' she asked.

'It didn't rain once while I was there.'

'And Bali?'

'One or two showers. Nothing like this.'

Alick's wife laughed. 'Come on, it doesn't rain all the time here.'

'No, it just seems like it. Is Natalie still with you?'

Laurel's voice altered subtly, although it was still warm. 'Yes. She has some news for you. I'll get her.'

Natalie's voice was velvet with satisfaction. 'Darling, I'm getting married,' she said brightly.

'Oh.' The Canadian?

'He's a darling, you'll love him. He's over here organising a farm he's bought halfway between Whangarei and the coast.'

'Natalie, are you sure?'

'Yes, I am sure. Very sure. We're having a quiet little wedding up here in Kerikeri—Lauren's dealing with everything, bless her—' and Alick's paying for it, Aura thought cynically '—and then we're going on a trip around the world. You'll be able to come and see us, darling. Joe lives quite close to Calgary.'

Aura was willing to bet that her mother had never heard of Calgary until she met Joe, but she spoke of it now as though it was the hub of the universe.

Hoping fervently that both Natalie and Joe knew what they were doing, she went up to Kerikeri two days before the wedding, and soon realised that Joe Donaldson knew exactly what he was in for. She also discovered, to her astonishment, that Natalie was in love.

'Amazing, isn't it?' her mother confided, looking younger and even more extravagantly beautiful. 'I thought that after your father—'

'Did you love him?' Aura had often wondered.

'Oh, yes.' Natalie smoothed down a lock of hair, gazing at her reflection with eyes that saw into the past. 'And we were happy, until he decided that Africa was more important than his family. I knew that I'd never cope with Africa, but he insisted we go with him. Sometimes there are situations where no amount of compromising will work. He had a vocation. I didn't go with him, but I loved him, and he loved me.'

'So why on earth did you marry Lionel Helswell?'

Natalie shrugged. 'He—oh, he promised to look after me, and although I know it's not what women of your generation are supposed to want, that's what I was brought up to expect in a marriage. That's the way I am. It's too late for me to change now, Aura.'

'Yes, I suppose it is.' Aura smiled.

'Joe's not like Lionel, Aura.'

No, the thin, shrewd, cheerful cattle rancher and oilman was nothing like her other stepfather. His good heart was patently revealed whenever he spoke. Aura thought that this time her mother had chosen well. 'I hope you'll be happy,' she said.

'I will be. What about you?'

Aura smiled steadily. 'I'm fine.'

Natalie was Natalie. Because she was happy, she assumed everyone else would be. 'Well, all's well that ends well. Promise me you'll keep in touch.'

'Of course I will.'

'You'll be able to come and see us whenever you like. And you have Laurel and Alick if things go wrong. Laurel is very fond of you.'

Aura smiled painfully. 'I'm a big girl now.'

Her mother laughed, and sprayed the air with perfume, walking through it so that it clung to her in a faint, subtle mist of fragrance. 'Oh, life is wonderful,' she said happily.

Back in Auckland Aura organised the sale of the unit, then moved into a big old Kauri villa in Mt Eden with five other women, and for the first time since boarding school found herself coping with communal living. She enjoyed the company and the casual camaraderie, and the conversation and activity kept her from feeling too lonely.

The advertising campaign hit the magazines and newspapers and to her surprise she became a minor celebrity, interviewed by journalists and offered work she didn't want, and couldn't take anyway because her contract was exclusive.

'It's those eyes,' Jessica told her cheerfully as she riffled through pages of proofs. 'They photograph wonderfully, all sultry allure and mischief. The coloured contact lenses were a brilliant idea. I don't know how you manage to look innocent in brown and earnest in blue, but it works.'

'The camera lies,' Aura said shortly. She wandered across Jessica's office and stared out of the window. Sunlight danced on the Waitemata Harbour, lovingly delineated the curves of island and peninsula and bay, picked out the corrugated iron roofs of the houses on the North Shore. A frigate was in dock at the naval base, and the two little green volcanoes in Devonport rose like exotic Christmas puddings above the sleek grey ship.

'It doesn't lie, it just loves your face, and your hands, and your legs. Actually, it loves you. If you were four inches taller and half a stone lighter you'd make a fortune.'

'I don't want a fortune. And I don't want any work when this runs out. I want to work at the job I've been trained for.' Aura knew she sounded abrupt, but she was becoming desperate. An aching grief was eating away at her heart.

More than anything she wanted to be able to get her teeth into some hard work, the sort of mental exercise that would force her to snap out of this slough of self-pity she seemed permanently immured in. She had bought another computer and spent as much time as she could working at it, but the interest and excitement seemed to have faded into the same dull greyness that tainted all of her life now.

'I think you're mad,' Jessica said comfortably. 'Although I'm not surprised. You were always as stubborn as a pig. How are things going?'

Aura knew what she meant. 'I'm surviving,' she said lightly.

'I saw Paul at a book launch the other night.'

'How did he look?'

'Grim. About as grim as you do when you think no one's looking.'

Aura's brows knotted together.

'Don't frown,' Jessica said automatically. 'It helps to talk, you know.'

'I've already bored you once.'

'Don't be an idiot. Just remember, I'm always here. Oh, there's an article about Flint Jansen in the latest *Wine and Food*. It seems he's going to stick his neck out and make wine on the coast out from Warkworth. Opinion seems equally divided as to whether he's going to succeed.'

Aura felt the blood drain from her skin to her heart. Fortunately she had her back to Jessica. It took her a moment to say calmly, 'Oh?'

'Yep. The man photographs like a dream. You know, I wonder if I could coax him on to our books. We need good older men, ones who aren't pretty, sweet and cuddly, or mock sullen, or husbandly. He's the real thing, you can tell. I wonder if I'd ever have the courage to ask him.'

Aura managed to laugh and change the subject, but on the way home she stopped at a bookshop and bought the magazine. She forced herself to wait until she was in bed before she opened it.

Flint's face made her stomach flip. He was smiling, not for the camera but at a shorter, clearly French man beside him. Behind them were rows of vines, dressed in their spring green. More rows of vines formed a formal pattern across the slope in the background. At the end of each row a rose bush put forward its first red blooms. Blue hills reared up in the distant background; not very far away water glittered.

He was smiling. But then, why shouldn't he? He didn't have a broken heart that kept him on the winter side of the sun. Aura's gaze travelled greedily over his face, recalling how it felt when he kissed her, how hot his mouth had been against her breasts, how much she loved him...

Oh, God, she was being aroused by a photograph! She made herself read the article, and as she read she was overcome by longing to see this place he had chosen to settle down in. Warkworth was an hour's drive from Auckland, a pretty town on a tidal river, and Flint's Shangri-La was less than fifteen minutes from Warkworth. She could hire a car for the day and go. Perhaps tomorrow...?

As though the weather approved of her decision it was sunny the next day, one of those delicious spring days when the sky is a blue so vivid it hurts the eyes. The crisp, fresh air, with enough of a hint of summer's languor to take the edge off it, was clear enough for her to be able to pick out individual trees on top of the range of hills that marked the western and northern horizon.

Insensibly Aura's spirits began to lift. Just after Matakana, so small it could barely be called a village, she turned east and followed the road towards the coast, driving between green paddocks where little black and white calves ran and butted each other and played in the sun. She would drive past the gateway, that was all.

At the end of the road there was a gate, and behind it a building with a Mediterranean air that was obviously the winery. Aura turned around in the gateway and drove back up the road a little before stopping the car and getting out. A warm little breeze flirted with a few tendrils of hair that escaped from beneath her scarf. Settling her sunglasses more firmly on her nose, she looked around.

No sound but the call of an over-excited lamb broke the silence. It was just as Flint had described it. A tidal river ran around three sides of the neatly planted vineyard. The tide was out, so muddy banks made sinuous pathways on each side of the river channel. Birds waded across the sleek mud, and above them a skylark's pure song was interrupted by the lazy, laughing caw of a gull.

The river seemed to wind up to the blue hills a few miles away; on its way to the sea it separated the vineyard from a long sandspit with a jetty and car parks. Years before she had caught a fussy little ferry to Kawau Island from that jetty. It was too early in the season for holiday traffic, so the car parks were almost empty.

Aura breathed in peace, and looked across the river and the sandspit, up a bushclad hill where expensive houses had been built, far enough away not to be obtrusive, and somehow not spoiling the view of the tranquillity.

It was a perfect place, an ideal home for a warrior who'd given up fighting the quiet battles of his profession. Aura stood for long moments, until the sound of a car coming down the road froze her into place.

Please don't let it be Flint, she prayed.

She stood with her face turned away and unease crystallising into panic in her stomach as the car slowed, then stopped.

A voice with a distinct French intonation said, 'You are lost, *m'selle*?'

Slowly, reluctantly, Aura turned. There was only one person in the car. Relief sent colour licking through her cheeks. 'No, I'm just admiring the view.'

It was the Frenchman Flint was in partnership with. Although he was eyeing her with typical Gallic appreciation, she found nothing offensive in his candid admiration.

'Me, also, I am admiring the view,' he said with a twinkle, and she laughed.

The breeze caught her scarf. She managed to catch it before it tore free from her hair, but he said nevertheless, 'It is a crime to hide such hair.'

She smiled, and said, 'The wind's a little busy. Goodbye, *monsieur*.'

She liked him, she thought as she drove home. She could be very happy there, beside the river, with the vines growing about her. She liked Warkworth, too.

Oh, who was she fooling? If Flint asked her she would live with him on the top of Mt Cook, the highest mountain in New Zealand, called by the Maori people Aoraki, the cloud piercer.

That night she cried a little before she went to sleep, but somehow the visit had eased a sore patch in her heart. The next day she caught a plane to Fala'isi for another shoot.

Fala'isi was an island in the Pacific, set like a green jewel in a sea so blue it hurt the eyes. The crew was booked in for the usual hectic week, and on the last evening just before dinner Aura was disturbed by a telephone call from New Zealand.

'Aura?' It was Jessica, her voice tinny and far away.

'Jess? What's the matter?' The telephone seemed to have waves on the line, a positive sea of them, and behind the crackle and hiss Jessica's voice ebbed and flowed, so that all she could hear were disconnected words.

'—asked where—didn't, of course—but—so I wanted to make sure—'

'Jess, I can't hear more than a word you're saying! There must be sunspots, or something. Look, fax would be better.'

'What?'

'Fax it. F-A-X.'

'Oh, all right. No, wait—' Inexorably her voice faded into static.

Aura sighed, fossicked through the information the hotel had packaged for visitors, found the fax number and read it out, slowly and clearly, three times.

'OK,' Jessica said clearly before another wave of electronic interference broke over the line.

Aura put the telephone down and rubbed gently between her brows, telling herself very firmly not to frown. It hadn't worried her before, she had felt free to do what she wanted with her face, but modelling tended to make you conscious of such things. In many ways it was a narcissistic way to earn a living. She admired the creativity that went into it and the models for their sheer stamina, and she would always be grateful for the money she earned, but she would be glad to give it up.

Picking up a towel, she went off down to the beach.

She expected to find a fax waiting for her when she came back, but enquiries revealed that nothing had arrived. Probably Jessica had decided it wasn't worth worrying about, she thought with resignation. After all, she'd be in Auckland in thirty-six hours.

She ate dinner with the rest of the crew, turned down an invitation to an island night, and went up to bed. It had been three months now, and she shouldn't still be missing Flint with every breath of her body, every heart beat, as though someone had torn a necessary part of her away.

Perhaps it was just because she was back in the tropics. Not that Fala'isi was much like Australia, beyond the superficial resemblance of heat and palms and a warm sea. The sound of this sea resounded in her ears, its great smooth rollers crashing on to the reef that protected the white beaches, and the air smelt faintly of the tang of the tropics, coconut and sweetly scented flowers and salt, the rich, moist scent of fertility and life.

She switched off her light and lay on her side, looking at the window. If only Flint hadn't been so remote that last morning. She had known then that it was over. If they had quarrelled she could have used the emotion to connect with him, but she had no weapons against that calm, impersonal kindness, that armour of self-possession.

A tear gathered in the corner of her eye, trickled on to her pillow. But she would not cry. There must be an end to this pain sooner or later.

The rest of the crew left on the early morning plane, but, as she'd decided to stay on a day, she planned to lie late in bed. However, dawn found her awake, so she got up and put on shorts and a top and went down through the quiet hotel, exchanging greetings with the few people who were about, then walked along the gleaming sand, looking at the small island on the reef where she had been photographed the day before.

A tall figure at the far end of the beach made her grimace; she didn't want to have to smile at anyone else. She would turn before he did, and head off along the other way. In the meantime she ordered herself to enjoy the freshness of the air, already warm, yet tangy with the scent of the forest on the high inland mountains, and the soft sound of the waves as they touched languidly on to the coarse white coral sand. The sun caught spray as a particularly large comber hit the reef, and for a second rainbows hung suspended in the crystal air.

Sudden tears prolonged the rainbow. Aura sniffed. Here it was always summer. At home, in spite of the show of freesias with their exquisite lemon scent, and daphne, spicy and pink, it was still spring, and the year was just gearing up for the magical slow slide into summer.

Homesickness washed over her. It had been a mistake to stay the extra day. If she had left with the crew she would have been in Auckland by now. She turned abruptly and walked as quickly as she could down the beach and into the hotel.

A touch on her shoulder made her jump and whirl around.

'Why are you crying?' Flint asked curtly as she stared at him in something very close to horror.

'Was that you on the beach?' she said stupidly.

He nodded. He looked the same, impregnable as ever, and she hated him for it. She'd been slowly dying inside,

and he'd just gone on his way without feeling anything.
No doubt when he thought of her it was with a faint contempt. Or did he think she was a good one-night stand?

Because whatever other opinion he had of her, he
couldn't deny that. It had been as good for him as it was
for her.

It was ironically amusing, when you thought of it. She
had given her virginity to a man who thought she was little
better than a whore.

And she had the feeling that she was never going to be
able to find another man to live up to him.

CHAPTER EIGHT

'WHAT are you doing here?' Aura asked jerkily, averting her face. 'Or is this just a coincidence, like the last time you found me in a hotel?'

'No.' Flint spoke with a clipped intonation that made her withdraw even further. 'This time I came looking for you.'

'How did you know where I was?' she croaked, voicing the first foolish question that came to mind because she couldn't ask the more important ones.

'I rang Jessica. She told me.'

'No. She wouldn't tell anyone where I was.' Of course, that's what last night's call had been about. Jessica had been trying to warn her.

He smiled unpleasantly. 'Oh, when I told her why I wanted to see you she gave me your address.'

'Why?' she asked warily.

'Why did I hunt you down?' He put his hand into the pocket of his trousers and pulled out a river of green fire. 'To return these.'

Aura's eyes widened, but she made no attempt to take them from him. 'Where did you find those?' she demanded. The day after she had signed the contract she had gone to the jeweller's to buy them back, but they had already been resold.

'I bought them.'

She swallowed. 'Why?'

His smile was self-derisory. 'Oh, put it down to senti-mentality.'

Frowning, she asked, 'How did you know I'd sold them?'

166

'I met your cousin Alick one day in Auckland. He'd just come empty-handed out of the jeweller's. Apparently Natalie had gone weeping to him to ask him if he could buy them back.'

Her face lit up. 'Dear Alick,' she said tenderly.

He slid the chain of green fire through his fingers, watching them with narrowed eyes. 'Unfortunately, dear Alick was unsuccessful, and he had to leave for Frankfurt the next day. The jeweller couldn't tell him who had bought them— they'd been through a couple of hands since he sold them, gaining value as they went—but he did say he'd heard a rumour that they were going to America.'

'So how did they get here?' Aura asked tentatively.

He looked into her face. 'I offered to track them down, which I did. Then I made the buyer an offer he couldn't refuse.'

'For Alick?'

'No,' he said, smiling unpleasantly, 'for me.'

'But why?' she asked numbly.

He laughed softly. 'I said it was for sentimental reasons. You wore them the night I first kissed you, remember? The night at the opera. I've always hoped that one night I'll make love to you when you're wearing nothing but your lovely skin and these.'

He tossed the necklace towards her. It sparkled and flashed in the drowsy air. Aura caught it, feeling the weight and the interplay of colours, the cool smoothness of the gold warmed by his body heat.

'Why did you bring them here?' she whispered.

He hesitated, then said, 'Because you came up to Matakana.'

She closed her eyes. Had he been there, watching her? Humiliation clogged her throat, cast a clammy pall over her skin. 'How do you know?'

'Jean-Pierre told me.'

'He doesn't know me.'

Flint's mouth moved in a cold smile. 'No, but when he raved about a woman with hair the colour of the best burgundy, and great green eyes that were sad enough to kill oneself for, and a mouth that was made to speak French, not clumsy English, I knew who he'd seen.'

Aura said nothing; she was too busy cursing herself for giving in to that compelling need to see the vineyard.

Flint said, 'We can't talk here. Come up to my suite.'

He spoke so matter-of-factly that she couldn't find the words to object, and within minutes she found herself in an opulent sitting-room, so many questions fighting for supremacy that she couldn't ask any of them.

She stood irresolutely, watching his reflection in the mirror as he picked up a telephone and ordered breakfast from room-service. Broad shoulders and lean hips, an effortless animal grace that sent shivers of response down her body; the arrogant epitome of force and power.

When he had replaced the receiver he turned to where she hovered beside a leather sofa and commanded, 'Sit down. I'm not going to eat you.'

Not yet, anyway, his smile and glance, swift and predatory, promised.

Aura sat down, and this time she was able to ask, 'Why did you go to so much trouble?'

'Can't you guess, Aura?'

Slowly she shook her head. 'No.'

'What have you been doing since I saw you last?'

'Working.'

'Still modelling?'

Her hackles rose at the distaste in his voice, but she said firmly and without emotion, 'Yes.'

'Why did you take it up?' He spoke idly, but she knew him too well. There was nothing idle in his interest.

She shrugged. 'You know why. For the same reason I sold the garnets. I needed the money.'

'Your mother's just married an extremely rich man. By all accounts he's as generous as he is rich, and he's certainly besotted by Natalie. You don't have to work. You could have an idyllic life with them.'

Still not looking at him she said coolly, 'No.' She would never take money from a man.

His dark brows lifted, but he pursued, 'You're doing fairly well, I gather. Do you plan to make it your career?'

'No. At the beginning of next year I'm looking for a job.'

For some reason this amused him. 'Really? What?'

'I did a double major in information systems and marketing,' she said acidly. 'I don't expect to have much difficulty finding work.'

This time she surprised him. His brows shot up further and he looked more than a little taken aback. 'I see.'

Something compelled her to add, 'Didn't Paul tell you?'

'Paul and I didn't discuss you at all,' he said shortly.

She raised delicately mocking brows. 'How about this dossier you had compiled?'

His smile was ironic. 'It was sketchy, little more than gossip. I told you about it to gauge your reaction. I'm afraid I imagined your degree to be the usual fashionable BA. Paul may have tried to tell me, but I cut him off whenever he started to talk about you. Where did you do this degree?'

It couldn't do any harm to tell him. 'At a polytech in West Auckland.'

'What decided you to graduate in those subjects?' he asked absently.

She shot him a suspicious look, but there was nothing to be discerned in the harsh features but mild interest. 'Originally I decided to be an accountant.' Her mouth twisted wryly. 'It seemed a good idea, and maths and accounting were two of my best subjects at school.'

A quiet knock on the door heralded a waiter with a breakfast trolley. When he had finished setting the table and was gone, Flint said, 'Would you like to pour the coffee?'

He didn't tell her how he had it and she didn't ask. She had forgotten nothing about him. Although the food smelt divine as only coffee and bacon could, he didn't sit down. Nor did he ask her more about her education.

Instead he said distantly, 'Have you seen Paul lately?'

Aura flinched. 'No.'

'Neither have I, but I hear he's recovering.'

'Good. I'm glad.'

He walked across to a window, stopping to stare moodily out at the sunny beach. Someone was sweeping the sand, singing in a deep bass one of the cheerful songs that seemed to grow in the very air here.

Aura sipped a little coffee, then put the cup back. She looked at the food, but her hunger had died.

'That's not why I wanted to see you,' he said at last. 'Why did you go up to Matakana?'

Aura's heart began to beat heavily in her breast, in the hollow at the base of her throat, echoing in her ears. She looked down at her coffee, noting the way the steam wisped across the rich liquid in the bone-china cup.

'I read an article in a magazine,' she admitted reluctantly. 'I just wanted to see the place.'

'Did you like it?'

'Oh, yes. It was beautiful.'

Another silence.

Then, 'I tracked you down,' he said deliberately, 'because I've discovered that I can't live without you.'

Coffee cascaded into her saucer. Aura managed to straighten it before any overflowed further, but her hands were trembling too much to hold it safely, so she had to set cup and saucer down on the table with a little chink that sounded far too loud in the quiet room. She sat with her head bowed, unable to look away, her whole attention bent on the words that had just rasped past her ear.

'Did you hear me?' he demanded.

'Yes, I heard you.' Her voice was cool and steady.

'And,' he said deliberately, 'because it seemed that if you'd taken the trouble to come up to Matakana you were at least getting over Paul.'

'It's a matter of having to,' she said stonily.

'Do you still dream about him?'

She shook her head. Still not looking at him she said, 'It was only that once. Flint, it won't work.'

'Why not?'

'Because I don't—'

'I know that I've done everything possible to make you hate me, but there were times when you liked me, Aura. When we aren't fighting we get on well. And now there's no reason to fight.' His urgent interruption caught her attention as nothing else could.

She looked up. He had turned his head and was watching her. The autocratic pirate's face was set in lines of rigid control.

'Flint…' she began, exhausted.

With the speed of a cornered animal, he came away from the window. Before Aura had a chance to continue he pulled her up from the sofa and into his arms, holding her tightly against the disciplined male hardness of his body.

'If there's no other way,' he said in a voice that ached through her, a voice where cynicism and a black desire were blended, 'I can reach you like this.'

His mouth crushed her protests, reduced them to cyphers in her brain, to shadows, and then to oblivion. The kiss had something of desperation in it, as though he had been starved for this, had lain awake for long nights eaten by need for her.

For a second Aura resisted, until a reciprocal fire and passion overwhelmed her self-control. Her endless yearning and the sudden masculine assault swept away her defences. She sank into mindlessness, glorying in capitulation, dimly aware in some distant region of her brain that her surrender was composed of intricate strands of conquest and yielding woven together to form a pattern of equality.

Eventually he lifted his mouth to mutter, 'If this is all there is for you, it will do for the time being. You drive me mad, you've taken up residence in my heart, in my mind, in my soul, and nothing I can do will get rid of you. I've never needed a woman before, never wanted one that I couldn't do without, but you stormed into my heart, demolished all the walls and took it over, and since the first time I saw you I've been only half a person.'

Aura said with difficulty, 'It's not—'

'No,' he said. 'Don't say no, not yet. Let me dream a little longer.'

'Flint—' The rest of the sentence was obliterated by another kiss. Sighing, Aura gave herself up to rapture, returning it with all the passion that was in her.

'You do want me,' he said at last when she was breathless and trembling, looking at her with such naked passion blazing in his golden eyes that her resistance leached away.

She smiled sadly. 'Of course I want you.'

His smile was a mixture of triumph and pain. 'I don't know how to deal with this. I thought it would be easy, that I'd use this violent attraction between us to get you into my bed, and then infiltrate your defences so cunningly that before you knew it you'd love me. But I'm greedy; I want it all, and I want it now.'

'What do you want?' He didn't answer, merely watched

her with intent, half-closed eyes. 'What do you want?' she insisted.

He looked away, his face hard and taut and hungry. 'I suppose you deserve your pound of flesh.'

Releasing her, he stepped back. After a momentary hesitation he said through his teeth, 'I want you to love me as much as I love you.'

Aura's heart went into overdrive. '*Do* you love me?' she asked, dry-mouthed.

'Of course I bloody well love you!' He stared furiously at her, and then laughed, a harsh, mirthless sound. 'If you knew how many times I've tried to work out how I'd approach you. I thought, she deserves tenderness, she's had precious little of it, so I'll be tender. But I can't do it, not without knowing how you feel.'

'All you had to say,' she said quietly, 'was that you loved me. Because I've loved you since the second time we met.'

He went white, then as the dark colour flooded back into his skin he grabbed her in a swift, clumsily desperate movement that was a far cry from his usual grace. He didn't kiss her again; for long seconds he stood staring over her head, with his arms so tight around her that she could barely breathe, his heart beating like a trip-hammer against her.

He swore, muttering something short and succinct and vicious. And then at last his arms loosened, and he pushed her chin up, gazing into her eyes. Aura looked back, her mouth curving.

'That bloody smile,' he said quietly. 'You looked at me like that that first night, and I thought—oh, God, I thought, what the hell am I going to do about this? All right, you little witch. When are you going to marry me?'

Her heart leapt into her throat, and then the light died in her eyes and he demanded, 'What is it?'

'We can't get married,' she said miserably.

'Why not?'

'Paul—'

His arms slackened a moment, and she tried to step away, but he said angrily, 'No. He's not going to stand between us like an angel with a flaming sword, I'm damned if he is.'

'But he's your friend.'

'And you,' he said smoothly, 'are going to be my wife.'

'He'll hate it,' she said, giving in, not realising it.

Her words fell like heavy stones into mud, flat, no reverberation, no echo.

'Yes,' he replied uncompromisingly, 'I'm afraid he will. But there is nothing we can do about that. We are not responsible for Paul's happiness.'

She bit her lip. 'I didn't want to come between you.'

'There's nothing for you to come between. He doesn't consider me a friend any longer. And even if he did, I'm not going to wait for years until he's got over you. These last few months have been hell, waiting for you to get him out of your system. Aura, I love you, and I'm damned sure you love me. Our commitment has to be to each other. I want us to marry.'

Against that simple statement of need she had no defences. 'Yes,' she said simply. 'All right.'

He stood very still. 'Just like that?' he asked incredulously.

Her smile quivered on her lips. 'What do you expect me to do? Object for the sake of objection? You know I love you.'

'I thought you might have some mistaken loyalty that would keep you away from me.' He laughed softly, exultantly, and kissed her forehead. 'I thought I might have to take you to bed again and again until I got you pregnant, and then persuade you into marrying me. Actually, I was rather looking forward to that.'

She laughed too, her green eyes tender and soft and

amused. 'I'll bet,' she said. 'I can see I'm going to have a hell of a life.'

His arms were warm and strong about her, offering not safety but risk, not tranquillity but excitement, nothing of the kind tenderness she had thought she wanted. Flint was fire and danger and exhilarating turbulence; life with him would be far removed from the haven of serene calm she had longed for. And she wouldn't have it any other way.

Smiling, she lifted her face in mute invitation.

Hours later, when the swift tropical darkness had enveloped the island in its purple embrace, she stirred. Instantly Flint's arms tightened around her.

'No,' he said into her ear.

Smiling, she rubbed her cheek against the swell of his chest. 'I'm not going anywhere.'

'Good.' He yawned, then kissed the tangle of hair that swirled across his shoulder. 'Each time we make love I think nothing could be better, nothing could ever match it again, and each time it's more exciting, more unbearably electrifying. I suppose one day I'll get so excited I'll die.'

'Not while we're making love, I hope,' she said, laughing.

He grinned, the lazy, eminently satisfied smile of a man who has the world in his grasp. There was something very tigerish in that smile. 'Why not? It would be a wonderful way to go.'

'For you, perhaps. I wouldn't like it at all.'

'OK, I won't.' His arms contracted about her. 'When are you going to marry me?'

'I've got a photo shoot in Thailand in a fortnight's time, and a trip to Japan in January. I can't get out of them, Flint.'

For some reason she expected him to object, but he said calmly, 'No, there's no reason why you should even try. Shall we get married before you go to Thailand?'

'So soon?'

He laughed at her scandalised tone, his golden eyes gleaming with tender mockery. 'Why not? Do you want a big wedding?'

'No!'

His shoulders moved in a shrug. 'So why wait? I have to work for Robertson's until the end of the year, and then we can move to the vineyard. We'll need to build a couple of houses; I'd contracted the same architect who designed the winery, but as soon as I realised I was in love with you I put him off; you're going to have to approve his plans. Jean-Pierre is very magnanimous; he says he'll stay in his caravan until our house is finished, provided you cook him a couple of dinners a week. You'll like him.'

Aura looked down into his confident, hard-hewn face. People didn't change just because they were in love. Natalie was still Natalie, and Flint would always try to bulldoze her into doing what he wanted.

'What if I can't cook?' she asked demurely.

'He'll teach you,' he said, laughter tilting the corners of his mouth.

'As it happens, I'm not a bad cook, but I'm always ready to take lessons. If you put the architect on hold you must have been pretty confident I'd marry you.' Her voice was very wry.

He grinned. 'It was the only way I could stop myself from slitting my wrists.' The humour leached from his face. 'I had to believe you'd get over Paul and turn to me, otherwise I think I'd have gone mad. For the first time in my life I was desperate.'

'I'll bet you were hell to live with.'

He flushed slightly, and laughed again. 'You know me too well,' he said drily. 'Well, will you be happy living on a vineyard?'

'It sounds wonderful.'

He kissed her soft mouth. 'Of course. Everything's wonderful. In fact, if I'd tried we couldn't have worked things better. The business is going to need a good accountant and money manager, and you are clearly sent by providence to be that.'

She pulled a face. 'You don't even know yet whether I can do it.'

'Am I taking too much for granted? Would you rather work in town?'

For the first time Aura allowed herself to hope that this time everything would work out, that the future would be as bright and shining as it seemed to promise. She said, 'What would you do if I said I would?'

His hand in her hair contracted, but he said evenly, 'I'll try to persuade you that you'd be happier working with me, but I'm not an ogre, my heart, my darling. You will make your own life.'

'I can't think of anything I'd like more than working with you.'

He kissed her, and kissed her again, and after a highly satisfactory interval she sighed, and asked the question that had been nagging at her ever since the last time they'd been together.

'Why did you make love to me that first time? Not that first time we—' beneath his amused glance colour heated her skin, but she kept on doggedly '—we—ah—slept together, but in Auckland. After *The Pearl Fishers*.'

He was silent for a moment. Then he said heavily, 'I was desperate to stop you from marrying Paul, driven by a compulsion stronger than honour or friendship. At the time it seemed all I could do was bypass your better self and home in on the sexual attraction, because I knew you felt that just as strongly as I did. It was the only way to break the ties of loyalty that bound you to him. But as well, I couldn't resist. You had me so tied up in knots that I had to kiss you. Perhaps I even thought that it might do nothing for me, that it was only because you were forbidden that I wanted you.'

She flinched, and he said harshly, 'Yes,' and in the monosyllable was all his pain and self-disgust, and beneath it, like true metal under corrosion, the shining edifice of his love. 'But if I did,' he went on, 'that first kiss showed me just how wrong I was. I knew then that I had to have you. Yet although your response nearly blew my mind, you were still determined to marry him.'

She said, 'I loved him. But after that night I knew I couldn't marry him.'

'You knew?' Lifting her chin, he stared down into her face with quick antagonism. 'Then why the hell didn't you tell me?'

'How could I? Not before I told him—I owed him that, at least. I had to wait until he came back from Samoa. And I didn't know how you felt. You told me you weren't offering anything but an affair. I was utterly wretched.'

'You and me both.' The anger died as fast as it came; he kissed her gently, stroking her hair away from her cheek. 'I needed you to want me because you loved me, not for security, not for any other reason but that you couldn't live without me. When you still wouldn't give in, I realised I'd have to force the issue. I know Paul. Under that surface placidness there's a very possessive man. He'd have tried to keep you any way he could.'

'He didn't,' she said.

'Because I told him we were already lovers.'

She sat up and stared at him. 'You *what*?'

In spite of her indignant struggles he tucked her back against him. 'Calm down. It was the only thing I could think of to keep him away from you, and even then I didn't know whether it would work.'

'You lied,' she said dangerously.

'Yes. Don't worry, it's not a habit. I won't lie to you ever, I swear. I was damned near in despair. You see, I always knew you loved him. That's why I asked you not to see him by yourself, when I got called away. I thought he might be able to persuade you to go ahead with the wedding. If you had, you'd have torn yourself and him to pieces. Because I would have taken you away from him. You and I were meant to be, my darling.'

He had understood much more than she gave him credit for. She lay for a long time with her cheek against the steady throb of his heart.

At last he said unevenly, 'God, I could have ripped up the whole world when that bloody beeper sounded, but there was nothing I could do, nothing I could think of in the way of damage control except to ask you to stay away from him.'

'And you left me in Cairns because you thought I was still in love with him?'

He kissed the top of her head, his arms tightening around her. 'You were still bound to him, emotionally if not legally. You needed time.'

She nodded. Flint had the clearer vision. She had been anchored to the past by chains of memory, and they had been flawed and false. She didn't want peace and tranquillity, a husband who worshipped her as though she was something rare and fragile to be kept safe, locked away from harm. She needed a challenge, just as he did; Flint understood her better than she did herself.

Soberly she said, 'Yes. I did love him. But I love you far more, and I'm in love with you as well. I know the difference now. I think perhaps I always did; I just wasn't ready to admit it.' She told him about the dream she had had the night she had met him. 'I should have listened to what it was trying to tell me,' she finished.

'You wouldn't be the woman I love if you'd just dumped

him. I knew you had to have time to get over him,' he said sombrely. 'At Cairns I was starving and afraid. I used the attraction between us to get you into bed—and found to my delight that it was the first time for you—but I couldn't go on doing that. You had to put him into the past where he belonged, and learn to love me, and to do that you had to have time, without pressure, time to discover the truth for yourself.'

She turned her hot face into his neck. 'How did you know that it was the first time?'

'Oh, it was all very new to you.' His smile was wickedly satisfied. 'It wasn't difficult to realise why. I know it's not modern to say that I'm glad you were a virgin, but I felt like the ruler of the universe when I realised.'

'Chauvinist,' she accused.

'In this, I'm afraid so. Unrepentant, too. Saying goodbye to you that morning was the hardest thing I've ever done, but too much had happened too fast. I told myself I'd wait patiently for some sign from you.' He laughed. 'Although I must admit I was getting damned restless when Jean-Pierre told me you'd come up to the vineyard.'

'Mm.' She kissed his jaw, and along the scar, her eyes dreamy. 'I do love you,' she said.

'And I love you. With all my heart.'

EPILOGUE

'AURA, what the hell are you doing in there?' Beneath the exasperation in Flint's tone was the ever-present note of tenderness, discernible even through the dressing-room door.

Aura grinned. 'I'm getting dressed.'

'It had better be worth this wait.'

'Trust me,' she growled seductively.

'I don't trust you an inch, but I'll wait another five minutes.'

Pulling a face at the door, she slid pearls into her ears, one creamy white, one black, two teardrops that must have cost Flint a fortune three years ago when their son was born.

'There,' she told her reflection, 'you're ready. And though I say so myself, you look stunning.'

The freshly floral scent of Joy floated up to her nostrils as she opened the door and walked into the bedroom, sleek and sophisticated in a wool georgette dress the exact colour of her skin. Its narrow skirt revealed legs in the sheerest of stockings and high plain, ivory shoes. Seen from the front the dress was demure, with loose long sleeves and soft folds, but at the back the material was draped in a deep cowl that showed her spine almost to her waist. A wide satin band hugged her hips, finishing with a bow at one side.

She had put her hair up and clipped a matching satin bow at the back of her head. It was definitely dressing to kill, and from the look on Flint's face when he saw her she had succeeded.

181

'There,' she said, twirling so that he could see the back. Smiling, she looked over her shoulder. 'Was it worth waiting for?'

'You're always worth waiting for,' he said, examining her with the bold eye of possession. 'But this time you've outdone yourself. How long do we have to stay at this thing?'

Laughing, she finished her twirl, stopping just in front of him so that she could look up into his fierce face. 'Until, my darling, everyone at this presentation has decided that Southern Red is the most exciting development in winemaking that's hit the world since the Californian experience.'

He sighed elaborately, spanning her waist with hands that were strong and lean and tanned with years of working in the vineyard. 'It is,' he said, his voice ringing with confidence. 'It's going to be right up there with the best in ten years' time.'

'I know.'

He laughed under his breath. 'You never doubted, did you? Not even when people told us we were crazy.'

She shook her head. 'No. You once told me that you were not in the habit of making mistakes. I believe you.'

'I was damned arrogant.' His hands tightened for a moment and the golden glitter of his glance sharpened. 'It's a wonder you let me anywhere near you.'

Aura reached up and cupped his cheek. 'You're still arrogant,' she said pertly. 'But I love you.'

His grin was part teasing, part amusement, all pure male satisfaction. 'You know, I must have had all the gods on my side when I fell in love with you. You've worked wonders. Thanks to you we've come in well under budget, and the publicity has been tremendous. Who but you would have decided to launch our first vintage with a reception in a marquee? Silk-lined, at that? And managed to whip up such a storm of publicity that we've even had British wine buyers asking for invitations?'

She hugged him. 'They wanted to come because the wine is magnificent,' she said. 'And that, my dear heart, is because you and Jean-Pierre are brilliant. Everyone senses history in the making. And it's going to get better. Darling, this is the start of a dynasty! Now, we'd better go. I'm sure your mother thinks no one can cook crayfish as well as she does. I've already had to haul her out of the kitchen twice. She just doesn't seem to understand that she's here to be fussed over and waited on.'

'Not my mother,' Flint said cheerfully.

Aura laughed. The house was full, with Natalie and Joe occupying one bedroom, and Flint's parents in another. They had very little in common, yet they seemed to get on like a house on fire.

Life, she thought, as she turned down the stairs, had very little more it could offer her.

'Hello, Aura.'

For a painful second she froze, before slowly turning. Yes, it was Paul, five years older, his blue eyes watchful beneath hooded lids.

'Paul,' she said, and her smile broke through. 'Paul, how wonderful to see you!'

'Ah, it's great to see you, too. Marriage and motherhood and growing wine obviously agrees with you.'

'It does, indeed. You look good, too. Have you talked to Flint?'

'I've seen him. I haven't spoken to him. I'm a bit embarrassed—the last time we met I said some totally unforgivable things to him.'

Flint had never spoken of that final interview, but since then neither man had seen the other, and she knew that the loss of Paul's friendship still hurt her husband.

'He forgives a lot more easily than he used to,' she said drily.

'There were things I had no right to say,' Paul said, looking at her intently. 'I'm afraid I blamed him for—'

'It doesn't matter.'

'I've missed you both.'

'Then why don't you go and say something to him, Paul?'

He nodded. 'Yes, I think I will. You're even more beautiful than I remember. I hear you have children.'

'A son, Andrew Paul,' she said deliberately, 'and a daughter, Sophie. Andrew's three now, and Sophie is eighteen months. How about you, Paul? Are you married?'

'No,' he said, smiling faintly. 'Perhaps I had to exorcise you.'

Aura laughed. 'And now you have.'

'And now I have,' he said slowly, and laughed too. 'I think I knew even when we got engaged that you weren't in love with me, although you loved me. It was pride and bloody-mindedness that made me so obstinate.'

'You're too hard on yourself.'

'I'm not a fast learner, but eventually I get there,' he said, but absently, and with his eyes fixed above Aura's head on someone approaching.

The familiar sizzle in her nerves warned Aura of Flint's arrival. She turned her head and smiled, letting him see that she wasn't in the least worried by the encounter. Something dangerous in the golden eyes faded.

He looked across at the man who had once been his best friend. 'Paul,' he said, his voice giving nothing away.

Paul's smile was twisted but he held out his hand. 'It's good to see you, Flint,' he said, and there was no mistaking the sincerity in his voice.

They shook hands, and Aura relaxed. It was going to be all right.

Much later that night, when everyone had gone and they were back in their bedroom overlooking the silent river and the Sandspit and their glimpse of Kawau Island across the bay, she said demurely, 'Well, I think that was a success, don't you?'

He laughed, and kissed the back of her neck. 'Don't fish. It was a magnificent success, and you were perfect. Darling, you tied my life up with a big ribbon when you married me.'

'Well, at least no one is going to forget Southern Red in a hurry,' she said, smiling at their reflections in the mirror.

'Oh, we're properly on the map. And next year the vintage is going to be even better. I like your idea of founding a dynasty. How many children does it take to found one?'

'Well, Andy tells me he's going to be a grader driver, so we'll have to do without him. I think we should budget for a couple of extras,' she said soberly, 'just in case Sophie decides not to become a winegrower.'

He flung his head back and laughed, his strong arms hugging her against him. Aura's eyes glimmered greenly beneath half-closed lids. They had such a good life, she and her love; she had never known that happiness could swell up inside you and colour the world.

She turned and kissed him, then slid free. 'Do you think you and Paul will ever be real friends again?'

'I hope so.' He dropped cufflinks on to the dressing-table.

'I'm glad he came,' she said, sliding the pearls from her ears and putting them carefully away in their box. 'He's been on my conscience.'

'Mine, too.' His eyes gleamed, little flames licking up through their translucence, setting fire to every cell in her body. 'Did I tell you that wherever you walked tonight people stopped talking and watched you? And every man's face had the same look—awe and envy.'

'You might have muttered something like that,' she said, smiling, 'but you can always tell me again. Not that I care about any other man but you.'

'I know. And I can't tell you how that makes me feel,' he said. 'Like the luckiest man in the world.'

Her eyes misted. 'You got more than your share of looks,' she said. 'Women go all wobbly and weak-kneed when you smile that tiger's smile at them. And I distinctly heard Jess groan when you kissed her.'

'Sam should take her in hand,' he said, but absently. 'You know, I've spent all evening wondering about that dress. Hold out your hand.'

She did so, and he slowly began to undo the little buttons at her wrist. While his deft fingers moved across the pale material he told her what he planned to do when he had taken the exquisite thing from her, his words explicit yet tender, so that when at last he pulled it over her head and she was standing there in silk briefs and stockings and her shoes, she was blushing all over.

'If Paul had never spoken to me for the rest of my life,' he said, eyes glittering like jewels, 'it would be worth it. You are my world now, you and the children. You're all that's worthwhile to me, all that I need, all that I hope for. I go to bed at night with you in my mind, and when I wake I think of you. I've never regretted what happened.'

She slid into his arms, hugging him fiercely, feeling the increasing speed of his heart, the little signs that revealed to her just how she was affecting him.

'Neither have I,' she said quietly. 'It took me a long time to accept that if we hadn't met before I married Paul it would have made no difference. Married or not, I love you, and I would have followed you without a backward glance. That's what made me feel so guilty.'

'Yes.' He looked down at her face, his own hard and predatory. 'Me, too. I'd have broken Paul's marriage as easily as I broke his engagement. Without a qualm, throwing away a lifetime's friendship, because you were *my* woman, not his.' His voice roughened into a harsh purr. He bent and kissed the pulse that throbbed in the base of her throat. 'Because I love you,' he said against her skin. 'Because you are my other half.'

'Because we were meant for each other.'

He lifted her and carried her across to the bed, his face intent and purposeful, the dark fires of his love no longer threatening. As Aura drew him down to her, scanning his beloved face with slumbrous eyes, she smiled.

MILLS & BOON®

WEB/RS1 V2

LOOK OUT...

...for this month's special product offer.
It can be found in the envelope containing
your invoice.

**Special offers are exclusively for
Reader Service™ members.**

You will benefit from:

- Free books & discounts
- Free gifts
- Free delivery to your door
- No purchase obligation – 14 day trial
- Free prize draws

THE LIST IS ENDLESS!!

*So what are you waiting for —
take a look* **NOW!**

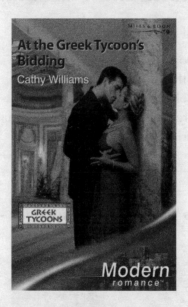

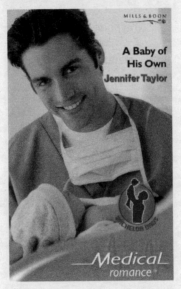